CLAIMED by BLOOD

DAUGHTER OF CAIN

MARIE MISTRY

2

AUTHOR'S NOTE

Claimed by Blood is a Paranormal Reverse Harem novel containing sexual scenes featuring multiple consenting partners over the age of 18. This series is written in British English and contains foul language, dark themes, descriptions of **torture, suicide, alcohol, sexual abuse, rough sex, knotting, BDSM, violence, and death.** There is also reference to **infertility** and the past suicide of a background character, and the story will explore characters' ongoing grief relating to that. **The prologue also contains a scene of child-on-child violence and child murder, which can be skipped without consequence to the story,** but is referenced in dialogue later on.

Self-care is important, and I love my readers, so if such subject matter upsets you, please don't read this book.

This book has been professionally edited, but we're all human. So, if you spot a typo, please contact Marie directly using the form on her website or any of her social media links. Please don't report it to Amazon, as this feature can lead to books being taken down. Likewise, if you find a major trigger which isn't listed, please let Marie know and the list will be updated.

This book is dedicated to those who waited so patiently for its release.

And to me, because this one was damned hard to write.

CONTENTS

Prologue	1
Chapter 1	9
Chapter 2	17
Chapter 3	23
Chapter 4	37
Chapter 5	43
Chapter 6	55
Chapter 7	64
Chapter 8	71
Chapter 9	81
Chapter 10	94
Chapter 11	105
Chapter 12	113
Chapter 13	125
Chapter 14	136
Chapter 15	143
Chapter 16	155
Chapter 17	163
Chapter 18	171
Chapter 19	183
Chapter 20	196
Chapter 21	205
Chapter 22	220
Chapter 23	232
Chapter 24	246
Chapter 25	256
Chapter 26	268
Chapter 27	275
Chapter 28	281
Chapter 29	291
Chapter 30	309
Chapter 31	323
Chapter 32	329

Chapter 33   342
Chapter 34   350
Chapter 35   358
Chapter 36   369

Acknowledgments   379
Books By Marie Mistry   381
About the Author   383

PROLOGUE

Warning: This prologue contains child murder and child-on-child violence. If such material is triggering for you, it can be skipped without consequence.

SAMUEL — CENTURIES AGO...

THE GIRL STANDS OUT AMONG THE ONE HUNDRED OR SO OTHER children my brothers and I have collected. It isn't her dark hair or fair complexion; those aren't uncommon in the mass of shaking, huddled babes below us. It isn't the piercing, ice shade of her eyes, either. There are at least a dozen with colours more exotic.

No. All of the assembled girls hold the promise of beauty. Most of them have features which—once they've sprung into womanhood—might turn into something extraordinary. Being pretty isn't enough to stand out here.

The few who might seem plain are mostly my choices. I chose girls with brains, or even those who showed a hint of wit.

As usual, my brothers have gone for looks in the hope of

impressing our sire. Their sword-measuring contests know no end. It doesn't matter whether it's who can conquer the most land or who can bring the shiniest toys to impress Cain's Court.

Fools. They don't realise we've been asked to bring him our replacements. Possibly even our executioners.

In this room, among these screaming, angry, terrified girls, is the hand that will take our lives.

I'm willing to bet it will be *her* hand.

She's barely eight years old, but that doesn't make her the youngest here—none of the gathered girls can have seen more than ten short years on this earth and a few are barely older than five. That was one of Cain's requirements. The girls had to be young enough to be… malleable.

Unlike the others, she's completely still. Watching things unfold as she examines the competition.

She's too young to wear that silent, observant expression.

Her mother possessed the same habit, and I pray it doesn't give her away.

Cain bursts through the main doors in a flurry of dark, lush velvet. His flair for the dramatic never ceases to amaze me. Most who've lived half as long as he has have become tired of showmanship.

"Darling girls," he purrs. "Why are you so upset?"

Every eye turns to him. He doesn't even have to raise his voice. The human children recognise the danger in their midst and react instinctively, just like prey.

One of them—a young one perhaps only six or seven winters old—wobbles up to him and mumbles, "I want my mama."

Cain shakes his head, smiling fondly. "Don't be foolish, child. Your mother is dead. Gaius killed her for me before he brought you here. Can't have any pesky parents muddling your loyalties, can we?"

The babe stumbles back as if struck, before dissolving into tears.

The vampire lord rolls his eyes. In a blur of motion so fast I barely catch it, the child drops down to the ground.

Dead.

My gut churns, and vomit scalds the back of my throat. By now, I shouldn't be shocked by how many boundaries my sire is willing to cross. That I still am disgusted after so many centuries in his court… well, perhaps it means there's some hope left for my soul.

Who am I kidding? My soul is as damned as his.

The other girls, on seeing the young one fall, start backing away. A few of them scream and bolt for the other doors, or even the other vampires. Hoping for escape or someone who will save them from the monster who's been revealed in their midst.

Only a few stand their ground.

She is one of them.

I shouldn't be surprised.

"Silence."

Cain says the word quietly, but it travels. In moments, the older girls—the ones who have figured out their only route to safety lies in pleasing this man—shush the younger ones.

He nods to a footman by the door, who brings forward a pewter tray covered with a wrinkled piece of dark silk and sets it on a small table in the centre of the room. The servant bows deeply to his lord before making a hasty retreat back to his post.

Cain strides through the girls towards the table and rips the cover away, displaying five long daggers, polished to a blinding sheen.

What is he up to?

"I had these commissioned especially for this evening," he begins, holding one up to the light. "The workmanship is exquisite; I think you'll all agree." He hands it to a girl with bright blonde hair, letting her test the weight of it. "Now, you'll be locked in this room until dawn. When I return, I will take the five girls holding these knives as my daughters. You'll be raised and educated and given the best life money can buy. When you're old enough, I'll even pass on my gifts. The rest of you—the ones who don't manage to get one of these pretty little blades—will be killed."

I barely have time to process what he said before an older, dark-skinned girl with corkscrew curls lets out a war cry that would make the women of Sigurd's country proud. She rushes towards the table, pushing aside the handful of girls between her and the blades to grab one, before leaping over the top, aiming for Cain's heart.

Our sire catches her with both of her wrists in one hand and holds her out at arm's length, smirking.

Foolish child, but her bravery is commendable. I wonder which of my brothers brought her in.

"Nice try." He slings her to one side without care.

She collides with two other girls, taking them both down to the floor.

Without speaking another word, Cain turns on his heel and strides from the room, letting the heavy lock snick shut behind him.

There's a clatter as the blonde drops the knife she was handed. The sound echoes louder than a thunderclap in the otherwise silent hall.

Then the furore begins.

I turn away as blood starts to flow. Sweet Christ. I brought some of those girls here.

I brought *her* here. Now her life is in greater peril than it would've been had I just left her alone. I'm as culpable as Cain is. Someone has to stop this...

4

My thoughts must show on my face, because the others notice.

"What's wrong, little brother?" Sigurd asks, lounging on the edge of the balcony with a grin. "Lost your stomach for blood this eve?"

His fangs are out, the bastard. He's actually salivating over the thought of being amongst the bloodshed below. Probably getting off on their screams.

Sick swiving whoreson. I hope whichever of those girls kills us makes his death hurt.

"Trouble, my sons?"

I should've expected he'd come up here to watch. I'm not sure if Cain is more interested in watching the seeds of discord he's been sewing between us sprout, or the girls below battle for the chance to live past morning. Perhaps he's come to witness both.

Whatever his reasons, I no longer have any way of rescuing the girl without drawing his attention to her. If I do that and he finds out who she is…

"Sire." I drop a hasty bow. "Is this truly necessary? Surely interviewing them would suffice? Killing babes…"

"The strong will survive, and only the strong deserve what I have to offer them." Cain brushes off my concern with a knowing twinkle in his eye.

Shite, I didn't mean to draw his attention to me. Now that he knows he's drawn a reaction, he'll watch me more closely.

"As you say," I grind out, cursing myself silently as another scream echoes from below.

"Watch, Samuel. You'll see how only cunning and strength will win this test."

With my sire's orders hanging over me, I can do little else but turn back to the massacre and watch the horror he's unleashed.

The instant I look over the railing my eyes are drawn

5

straight to *her*. She's covered in blood, holding one of the knives in both hands like it's a sword—and to one of her size, I suppose it could be. She's kneeling on top of the corpse of a bigger, burlier girl, staring down the rest of the room like she's challenging them to come and take the blade from her.

None of them dare.

Did she attack first, or was she merely defending herself?

I can't leave my eyes on her for too long, or Cain will suspect something, so I search the room for the other four knives.

Against all odds the corkscrew-haired girl has kept hold of her knife, and is currently brandishing it threateningly at a group of girls trying to corner her. Her rage is palpable, even from here, and I find myself wishing her luck. Another blade is in the hand of a huge, angry-looking brunette. She appears to be protecting a smaller ginger girl, who cowers behind her back.

The fourth blade is switching hands so fast I can barely trace it. Caught in a huddle of grasping palms and anguished screams as a few girls watch on like hungry lions.

But where is the fifth?

The glint of metal draws my gaze towards a large plinth displaying one of Cain's many treasures. The rake-thin blonde who dropped her knife at the start is cowering behind it. Yet, her hands are empty.

It isn't until she shifts that I catch sight of the steel nestled down the front of her shift.

She's hiding with it.

The whole ordeal barely takes an hour. Fear drives the girls into a frenzy, and soon there's only a handful left. Of course, *she* is still crouched on the top of her first kill, and the remains of the handful of others who were desperate enough to approach are scattered around her. Her fair skin is painted in blood and her green dress is stained black with it.

The blonde has somehow still managed to evade detection, partly by convincing everyone who approaches her that she doesn't have the blade. Her strategy seems to rely on staying very still and looking decidedly unthreatening.

The raging corkscrew-haired girl is almost as bloody as *she* is, and appears to have driven most of her attackers away, towards the struggle for the fourth blade.

The larger brunette girl is still defending the small redhead, but she's tiring. The second she finishes off their final attacker, she sighs in relief.

Her respite only lasts a moment. The second defender's grip loosens on the blade, the redhead snatches it out of the larger girl's hand and drives it straight into her back.

Beside me, Cain purses his lips in displeasure. I wonder if he considers the redhead's actions cowardly. Yet, how can he disapprove when he just admitted hoping for cunning daughters?

Only three girls remain around the fourth blade. Their hands are bloody, and it keeps slipping between them as they fumble for it.

Until, out of nowhere, a girl with straight dark hair and chestnut skin dives between them. She's been smart and waited until they're all tired for her time to strike. It works. Within seconds, she's the only one still holding the knife.

It's over.

The five have been chosen. The blonde who hid, upon realising the danger has passed, sneaks out of her place and stands, dragging the knife out of her shift as she does so.

I wish it was silent. But it's not. Weeping, gasping, and the gurgling sounds of tiny lungs taking their last breaths fill the air.

Those sounds will haunt me for the rest of my unnatural life.

I should never have brought those girls here. God in heaven, forgive me, for I can never forgive myself.

Every cell in my body wants to take the sword at my side and run Cain through with it.

It won't work.

In the centuries of my long, long life, I have seen Cain survive everything which would kill any other vampire. White Oak. Silver. Beheading. Burning. Nothing works.

I have one last distant hope, and it requires me to play the long game.

The world passes in a kind of slow daze as Cain lifts his hands and begins to clap. My brothers, beside us, do the same, applauding until the five girls look up at us. *Her* eyes meet mine.

Perhaps her survival is God granting me a chance to make everything which happened here right. If she hadn't lived, there would've been no one left with the power to end the unnaturally long life of the monster beside me.

"Congratulations," Cain says, as the double doors sweep open and vampire guards enter the room, disarming the children and restraining them as a precaution. "You are my five chosen daughters. Forget your old life. Your families, your homes. Even your names. Today you are reborn as daughters of Cain."

CHAPTER ONE

EVELYN — 2082 PRESENT DAY

The blood drips from my sword onto the marble. Human this time.

There's plenty of it. Cain wanted a message sent and I, his puppet, complied. They'll have to use a bag to gather up all the chunks of his body so they can remove it from the throne room.

What was this one's crime? I can barely remember.

I've blurred most of the last month from my mind. Buried it under layer after layer of numbness until I can't feel my own hand grasping the steel of the handle.

This must be the tenth victim, maybe the eleventh? My skin is stained with the red of their blood, but I don't allow myself to focus on that.

"Thank you, my daughter." Cain's lips whisper across my cheek as he passes me to examine the mess at our feet. "Perhaps the others who feel they can refuse to donate blood to my Court will recognise the error of their ways now."

I doubt it. Cain picks the subtlest of rebellions as excuses to make me prove myself now. Ever since Frost escaped —*again*—a week ago, he's been poking at my loyalty in subtler ways. Analysing my every expression.

Immy is always at his side, scanning my emotions, just like she has been for the last week. Her eyes are always wide and watery, and she still shakes slightly whenever he turns his focus onto her. For Cain's part, he doesn't treat her any better than he did before I went into the ground. He barely lets her speak, and when she does, he snaps at her for it.

But still, her situation has markedly improved. Gone are the drab and hideous clothes he once forced her into, and she walks slightly more confidently—especially on the rare times I've seen her alone.

We haven't talked.

No. Ever since the gala, she's been holed up in his office with him night and day. No one else goes in.

Why her? What are they discussing? Not knowing has me on edge.

Callie hasn't stopped whining about the unfairness of it. As Cain returns to his throne, our blonde sister leans into him and is instantly rebuffed. The panic on her face would be funny if it weren't so tragic.

Callie wants his attention, needs it to feel secure and safe. Me? I'd give anything to escape it.

She and Immy are the only two of my sisters here today. Bella has somehow escaped this execution, and Morwen has been hunting for Frost and his pack since the Gala. Cain made no secret of his displeasure when the pack managed to rescue Vane from right under her nose while she was distracted by my 'betrayal' of Frost. She's been trying to hunt them down and atone for her mistake ever since.

"That will be all, Evelyn." Cain waves his hand, dismissing me. "I'll call for you when we unearth the next."

Dismissed. But I can't even let myself feel the relief. Not with Immy right there.

"Sire," Callie pipes up. "There's one left."

"Ah, yes. How remiss of me. Evelyn, I have someone here for you."

I catch the scent of his blood before I see him. All of my thralls are mouthwatering, and I've not had any of them since the Gala. Now, Draven's blood calls to me like a siren's song, making my fangs ache. The sensation is like a bomb-blast, breaking apart my carefully constructed numbness with a sledgehammer.

No. The numbness is my only armour against Immy. I grasp at it, tugging it back around my mind as I turn on my heel and stride back to my spot before Cain's throne.

The body of my last victim has already been swept away, and Draven has been dropped face-down in his place. My thrall's hands are missing, his clothes are ragged and soaked in blood, and his hair is a greasy mess. He's a far cry from the immaculately dressed vampire I met when I was first freed.

Now he's a bloody worm writhing on the floor. His eyes are blank and crazed, and every move seems to send more blood streaming from his wounds.

"One last one." Cain beams like it's the best idea he's ever had. His expression quickly sours and he grinds the heel of one of his Oxfords into the centre of Draven's back. "He deserves it for allowing that wretched ghoul to escape on his watch."

So that's where he's been all this time? Guarding Frost? I shut down all thoughts of him instantly. I can't allow Immy to see even a hint of relief that fills me at the reminder of his escape.

I raise my sword, barely glancing down at my traitorous thrall. I can't look around the room at my audience either. Fixing my gaze on the throne at the head of the room has become self-preservation at this point, and it allows me to see the exact moment that Immy bites her lip and taps her fingers on the side of her chair. Cain smiles in response.

Another test.

Did I pass this one?

It's incredible how things have changed. I was once the favourite, and Immy a barely tolerated pest. Now she's everywhere Cain is. His distaste for her may not have changed, but she's useful to him now in a way she wasn't before.

She's become our sire's living emotional thermometer, and with her at his side, his tests have gotten more and more demanding. Instead of just acting the part, I now have to feel the part as well. The level of mental discipline it requires is exhausting, and sooner or later, I'm going to slip up.

I bring the blade down in a sweeping arc, putting all my force behind it because holding back will be seen as treachery.

Cain's hand—warm and sure—grips mine. His strength easily stops my arm mid-swing before I can take my thrall's traitorous head.

"I've changed my mind," he announces, to the Court. "I'll allow you to keep this one."

I stare at him, confused. *What's his angle?*

All around him, the other vampires are hanging on his every word, waiting to see what their king will do.

"I did once promise you a pet if you wanted one," he remembers, turning his attention back to me as he releases my hand. My sword clinks against the marble, the sound shocking in the silent room. "I'm afraid Callista might have broken him a bit, but I'm sure he'll regrow his hands with time. Just make sure you keep him on a short leash when that happens."

Callie's anger is a palpable force. She expected me to

finally kill the vampire she sired, not for him to be so publicly transferred into my ownership.

She can have him for all I care.

No. Now Draven's being used as an extension of my punishment, and no doubt he has orders to spy on me. The thrall bond makes him an ideal candidate to root out any hint of disloyalty I still possess.

I finally allow myself to stare down at him. He's passed out, probably from blood loss. Clearly his week has been hell.

Good. He deserves it.

Cain is waiting for my answer, I realise. "A generous gift, sire. Thank you."

How the hell am I supposed to get him out of here? His legs are broken.

As if reading my mind, Cain waves forward a pair of lycan guards. "Escort Evelyn's new pet to her room."

They jump into action, grabbing Draven under his arms and hauling him away again. The blood makes it difficult for them to grip him properly, but they manage. They drag him along the floor, leaving a trail of blood in their wake.

I follow them with my eyes as I wait to be dismissed again.

Only it doesn't happen.

Cain moves closer, embracing me with one hand on the back of my head in a paternal gesture that doesn't fool me. He only uses physical affection as a tool, and this time is no different. His mouth moves closer to my ear, shielding his next words from the others.

"You can fuck him and feed from him, but remember, you both belong to me. If Imogen detects even the faintest trace of an emotional bond between the two of you, I'll kill you both."

"I have no interest in forming an attachment to him, Sire."

It's true. Draven betrayed me at the gala. I don't trust him, and I'm even less inclined to drink from him. Pity my body doesn't agree. The scent of his blood lingers in the room, even in his absence, and breathing through my mouth hasn't stopped the still-present ache in my fangs.

"I'm glad to hear it. You're also forbidden from killing him. His life—like your own—ends at *my* whim. As long as you follow these rules, I've decided to allow you to sleep outside of your coffin..." He pauses, as if waiting to deliver the death blow. "But *only* when you sleep with him. If you want to sleep alone, you sleep in silver."

"I understand, sire." I curtsy low, taking the dismissal for what it is.

The walk back to my room is hell. I know the limits of Immy's power: she struggles to feel someone if she can't see them. So from the second I cross into the hall, I'm safe. It doesn't mean that I can let the mask drop from my face. There are still too many eyes here.

Even in sleep, I'm watched by the cameras I know are hidden in my room.

I have no privacy. There hasn't been one second where I can just sit and process everything that's happened.

For the last month, I've been operating purely on survival mode. Barely sleeping because I can't afford the mind-fog from the silver messing with my senses while I'm under such scrutiny.

In some ways, Draven's arrival is a blessing. Not that I plan to sleep in the same bed with him in the way Cain's suggesting. The *last* thing I want to do is fuck him.

However, tying him up, gagging him, and dumping his ass at the bottom of the bed so I can finally sleep? That's definitely on the table.

The guards went ahead of me, so Draven is already on the floor in front of my door when I arrive. I swipe my access card across the reader on my handle and kick his unconscious body into the room. He groans under his breath, but doesn't wake, even when I slam the door closed behind me. Ignoring the grand bed which has been installed on the far side of the room I stalk into the bathroom like it's my salvation. Which it is.

I've got to get this blood off me.

The water is scalding when I step under it, and I tip my face up into it, letting it wash the silent tears down my face.

Even if Cain has cameras in here—which I wouldn't put past him—the water will hide the evidence. I can't sob, or scream, or rage at the world like I want to. I can't even curl into a ball on the floor for fear of him knowing.

But, for the few minutes I spend in the shower, I can cry.

When I finally leave, Draven is just where I left him. Still passed out and making a mess of the carpet. Briefly, I debate giving him some of my blood to heal him, only to dismiss the notion almost immediately.

That's the kind of thing which will put Cain into a killing rage.

Instead, I grab a bag of blood from the fridge and sink my fangs into it, drawing deeply despite the way it tastes—like dirt and plastic. Then, with a sigh, I grab a second bag and slice it open, tipping the contents into Draven's mouth. The bleeding stops, the stumps of his hands closing up with the promise of nourishment.

Wounds dealt with, I drag him into the shower and hose him down so he won't mess up my new sheets, before dropping him at the bottom of the bed. It's almost dawn, and I have plans to get more than two hours of sleep for the first time in weeks. If he dares to wake me up, I'll drain him unconscious.

His hands will regenerate, with time. It would be faster with my blood, but I selfishly want him to suffer.

If he hadn't turned on us at Cain's gala, Frost and I

could've escaped alongside Vane and the rest of the pack. Now Frost is out there, free, and I'm stuck here.

The tiny taste of freedom I had for those few weeks I spent with the pack has made me bitter. I've tried over and over again to remind myself that this was inevitable. Tried to force myself back into believing my sire is correct and righteous in his pursuit of a society where vampires are at the top and everyone else is a second-class citizen. It doesn't work.

I almost hate my thralls for giving me that small glimpse of a life beyond this.

I'm still mostly naked except for my underwear, but that's because Cain still hasn't seen fit to provide me with any clothes beyond a few variations of that stupid dress and a single robe. The silk sheets slip over my skin, and I sigh as my head hits the pillow.

Cain didn't scrimp on this. The bed is like a cloud.

When I wake up, I'll remember it's just another tactic to manipulate me. A narcissistic system of reward and punishment designed to keep me eager to please him. Right now, I don't care.

Sleep has never felt so good.

CHAPTER TWO

FINLEY

The pack is breaking.

Gideon refuses to see it—probably because he has no idea how to fix it—but I'm no stranger to how tension undercuts life in a fractured pack. The stress seeps into everything, even more so now that Frost is free. The two alphas are butting heads constantly, and even Silas and Vane can't keep me distracted from the arctic atmosphere in the safe house.

My eyes are fixed on my screen. Ten smudged glittery nails glint in the light as my fingers hover over the keys, waiting for my brain to tell them what to do. But I can't seem to focus on work, and whenever I do, the lines of code just don't make sense. The bad manicure was a failed attempt to distract myself from everything, but it didn't work.

The thrall bond to Evie pulses with pain, and I grimace even though it's a daily occurrence now. At least it's not physical pain. Instead, it's mostly emotional—the kind omegas like me are naturally driven to fix. Even when I close my eyes, I can't get away from her exhaustion and fear, but when I mention it to Gideon, he brushes it off.

My hands curl into fists.

He thinks I should ignore it.

Easy for him to say. He's a master at sticking his head in the sand when it comes to relationships. With his thrall bond walled off, he can't feel her like I can. None of them can. I was the only one she let in.

"We need to extract our people," Frost growls for the hundredth time. "Not make plans to hide for the next century."

"Cain found us once," Gideon objects. "You escaped by sheer luck. Cain won't let you slip from his grasp a third time."

"No. I escaped because the guards were drugged," Frost objects. "Who would've done that if not Eve or Draven, huh?"

"You don't know that they were."

"My fucking hybrid nose is somehow powerful enough to scent ghouls miles away, and yet you're doubting my ability to scent drugs in a coffee cup from across the room?"

They're down the hallway, but I can hear them from my desk. I let my head thump forward onto the keyboard, ignoring the sharp dig of plastic on my forehead as I try to force myself to focus on just breathing.

Silas rubs at my shoulders in an effort to soothe me.

Damn, I didn't even hear him come in.

"It'll be okay," he promises. "Vane will sort both of them out in a second."

I know he will. The beta has been ending their arguments daily since his rescue. But, despite that, my omega instincts have been going haywire for the last week. I thought I was bad before, but now I'm *this* close to snapping.

Vane's quiet voice rumbles through the space, cutting off Gideon's next retort. He speaks too softly for me to hear, and normally, that would be the end of it. He's older than all of us, and the alphas usually respect his opinions.

Not today.

"I'm not leaving her in that hellhole for one more fucking day!" Frost roars.

Gideon growls, and the sound reverberates through the floor. "You go in there and you're putting the whole pack at—"

I shove out of my chair, shrugging off Silas's hand in my haste to get through the door.

Our latest safe house is a cramped apartment in Boston, so it's only a short walk from the bedroom I've taken over as my office to the living area where the other three are arguing.

Gideon is still raging, but he cuts off as I burst into the cosy room. The two of them must have been sitting opposite one another to start with, but now they're nose to nose over the steaming mugs of blood and coffee on the table.

"I can't take this anymore!" I snarl, pinning them to the spot with my glare. "Evie is fucking traumatised by what she's going through. I feel it every single day. But instead of giving a damn, all you two do is stand here and argue. If you won't save her, I swear to God I'll go out there and do it myself."

The stunned silence which fills the room on the heels of my statement is priceless. I don't think anyone in my pack has ever heard me yell or raise my voice in anger before. It's not something omegas typically do. Confrontation is anathema to us. We're usually happy to let the alphas and betas battle it out and then soothe their hurt feelings later.

We *definitely* don't stare down alphas and make threats.

My gut churns as what I've done starts to sink in. Instinct takes over and I drop to my knees, baring my neck in a sign of submission. Everything in my stupid lycan brain is on hyper-alert, waiting for our alphas to decide whether to kill me for challenging them.

Two sets of footsteps head in my direction, but I keep my gaze fixed on the floor even as they pull me up by my arms.

"Finn," Frost says, keeping his tone deliberately calm and coaxing. "Finn, look at us. You're safe. You're with us."

The whine which issues from the back of my throat is embarrassing, but I can't hold it back. The pleading sound makes Gid sigh.

"Omega," he murmurs, the gentle intimacy in his tone sending a shockwave of reassurance through me. "Relax."

His permission is all my body needs. I slump between them, sucking in a lungful of air.

I didn't even notice I was holding my breath.

"You two get your shit together and make a plan to extract Evie," Vane growls. His hands are on his hips and his big brother attitude is in full swing. "If your bullshit sends Finn back to the state he was in when he joined the pack, I'll gut you both."

"No more," I whisper, clinging to Gid's arm like a lifeline in the storm. "Please. No more threats. No more arguments. I can't… You have *no idea* what it's like."

Gideon sighs again and tugs me to the sofa. I'm as limp as a noodle as he positions me between him and Frost, knowing that my instincts will need the reassurance of being surrounded by pack. Silas claims the spot on the floor between my legs and stares up into my eyes as Vane takes the spot behind me, guarding my back.

For the first time in a week, I feel settled.

Almost.

"We need to find a way to communicate with Eve," Frost starts.

"There isn't one." Silas groans. "We've been over this. Her camera and mic were taken and destroyed. Her tablet probably hasn't been replaced, but it's connected to one of the most secure network—"

"I have a back door."

They all turn to look at me.

"What?" Frost's tone has changed. Now it's a complex mix of disbelief and indignation, sprinkled with an angry undertone I don't want to think too much into.

"Well, when you gave it to me to unblock it—"

"And you decided to put Biteme on it," Gideon grumbles, earning me another glare from nearly everyone in the room.

Except Silas. He just chuckles.

At least someone finds me funny.

"Yes, and that." I shrug it off. "I made sure there were plenty of back doors and trackers in it, just in case. I didn't know if Cain would change his mind and decide to split you up or…" I trail off, because listing every paranoid thought I had while they were undercover will probably get me written off as insane. "But I might be able to reactivate them. Even if they've done a software reset."

Frost is on board, he rocks forward onto the balls of his feet, forehead creasing in excitement. "Once we can reach her, we can ask her about Draven."

"Son of a bitch sold us out," Vane growls. "That's the only explanation. He was summoned early when we busted Evie out of the Court the first time, and then he disappeared for the majority of the gala."

"Draven's always been a loner," Frost argues. "But the two of us have a history."

"And history is exactly that," Gideon protests. "History. Cain and Callista have had decades to mould him into their perfect weapon, setting him up to betray us."

I flinch as his voice rises towards the end, and everyone notices.

Vane's warning growl echoes across the space. Gideon makes a face in response and rubs the back of his neck.

The irony of it is that normally I like our alpha best when he's growling and snappy. When he brings that attitude to the bedroom it makes me pant for him in all the right ways. Even outside of the sheets it's one of the things I love about him. I have no idea why, but something about watching Gid being his normal grumpy self is endearing.

Maybe it's because he's at his worst when he's worried about the pack. It's his way of showing he cares.

"Fine," Gid concedes.

God, it would be funny seeing how much giving up control is killing him if not for the urgency filling my chest.

"We'll take Evelyn's opinion of the situation into account before we make any further decisions," he decides, but when I try to stand up to grab my tablet, he and Silas keep me pinned in place. "But we'll sort it out tomorrow. Right now, you need time with the pack."

Silas must sense I'm about to argue because he rubs my calf. "You're no use to Evie if you're exhausted and strung out like you are now."

How many times have I used a similar argument against them? It sucks being on the receiving end.

CHAPTER THREE

EVELYN

When I wake again, it's dark. I've slept for the whole day, and for the first time since I returned to Court I'm not tired or groggy from silver. I turn over and discover Draven exactly how I left him.

Good.

Vampires may sleep soundly, but if I'd woken up to him cuddling me I might've ripped his throat out myself.

His hands are regenerating, but it's a slow process. The bones will regrow first, and then his vampirism will finish the job by working outwards to restore muscle and tendons and finally the skin tissue. It's a gruesome thing to witness, but I've seen it dozens of times before.

I shrug on the black silk robe which is my only other garment besides *that dress* and grab my tablet from the table to scroll through the news feeds of the day. Cain still hasn't announced Frost's escape, so the general news is *still* constantly replaying my 'victory' over his nemesis. One month on, you would think they'd have given up.

No such luck. It's featured daily. The latest headline focuses on the traitors I killed yesterday, praising my continued dedication to protecting my sire. Every single journalist lauds me as the favourite once more.

They couldn't be more wrong.

I flick the news feeds away and pull up my list of subjects. When I'm not in the throne room, cutting Cain's enemies into pieces, I have very little to do. I've been forbidden from training—I suspect because Cain wants to keep me weak—and I can't leave the tower which houses the Court.

To allay my boredom, I've begun busying myself by using a virtual encyclopaedia to bring myself up to speed. Technology, weapons, science. Everything has changed. I have a note on the tablet which holds all the topics I'm aware I'm behind in, and it grows longer every day. Still, I scroll to the top and—

I blink once. Twice.

There, at the top of my reading list, the cursor is dancing, typing its own message across the screen.

Are you safe?

I pause, staring at the words. How on earth?
Is this a trick?

My eyes dart around the room, waiting for Cain's men to come rushing in, accusations of treason on their lips. When nothing happens, I glance down at the tablet, to find a new line scrolling across the page.

Evie its me F

Finn. The omega with a talent for computers. My thrall. I don't trust it. This could so easily be another of Cain's tests.

It's exactly the sort of thing he would do. I put the tablet down, determined to ignore it.

Only to stare at it as a new sentence appears

V says he played the guitar and you spied on him

That one gives me pause. No one else knew that. Or did they? Vane was briefly Morwen's captive, before he was rescued on the night of the Gala. But it's not something that would've come up in an interrogation. Glancing at the door once more, I reach furtively along our bond. His hope and trepidation smack into me straight away.

It *is* him.

I sit back down and pick up the tablet. Slowly I start to type my response, glancing at the door between every word.

Electric devices are monitoring me.

I pause, then type the words I know I will later regret.

Is Frost alive?

The pause before he replies seems to stretch for hours, and I barely breathe until the cursor starts to move again.

I'm downloading new software onto your tablet. Open it.

The note erases itself, destroying my reading list in the process, but I don't care. I close the app and watch as a small, blank icon begins installing itself onto my tablet. As soon as the loading wheel fills up and disappears, I tap on it.

At first, I'm disappointed. It's just a blank window.

Then words start scrolling across the screen.

Finn: I'm in. Tell me everything.
Evie:

The keyboard pops up. A single, blinking line beside my name invites me to type. But I can't.

Finn: Evie??? still there???

My hands hover over the keyboard, and terror fills my gut as I check the room again, before I start to type once more.

Evie: This is dangerous. I can't be caught. He already suspects me.
Finn: I promise this is safe. The app will wipe itself from your hard drive when we finish

I stop responding, staring at Draven's sleeping form. Did he just move?

Finn: give me an update, are you unharmed???
Evie: He cut off Draven's hands.
Finn: do u trust D?

I frown, wondering why he's shortening his words. Come to think of it, he's not even using punctuation correctly. Is this another thing to add to my—oh, wait, I don't have a list anymore.

Damn.

Evie: I don't trust anyone anymore.

It's true. I have no idea whose side Draven is on. My gut says he's a plant, tortured to pull on the strings of my pity so that he can get under my guard.

Finn: hold tight we've got a plan to get u out
Evie: It won't work.

I have no idea how Frost got out—*if* he got out—but security is now airtight. The pack can't have anyone left on the inside.

No one is coming to rescue me. The only way I'll continue to survive is by playing Cain's games.

A knock at the door catapults my heart into my throat. I swipe the app away and click the tablet off before heading over to it.

Draven still hasn't moved, I note, as I cross to the door and take a deep breath, trying to scent whoever is behind it.

Muted, but floral. A natural scent that's close to fresh laundry.

Immy.

Everything in me shuts down as I turn the handle. The process of wiping away my emotions is automatic now after a month of practice. But as it's just the two of us, with no background noise to muddy the waters, I'll have to be extra vigilant. I've barely opened the door half-way when a second smaller body rushes through and collides with my own.

Immy hugs me like she's drowning and I'm the only thing that will keep her afloat. The suddenness of the contact shocks me enough that it shatters my emotional block and my surprise and confusion leak out before I can get it under control.

"I missed you so much!" she whispers, and I'm caught off guard again by the slight hitch in her voice. "Quick. Find your coat. We're going out."

She finally releases me and gives me a tiny shove into the room.

"I don't have a coat," I object, tugging my robe tighter around my body.

27

It takes a lot of effort not to let the bitterness in my statement show. A month of wearing the same dress has been taxing and has sent rumours flying. Some vampires must suspect it's a punishment, I'm sure, though they'll never openly admit it.

Immy shakes her head, smiling softly. "I convinced him out of that at the same time I convinced him out of the coffin. There should be a few different outfits in your wardrobe now. You still have to wear the dress to Court, but that's it. And you can leave the tower now. I argued that it made no sense to keep you locked up when he has cameras all over Manhattan."

My hackles rise in disbelief. There's no way Cain would give in that easily, and I'm equally unconvinced that Immy actually has the spine to argue with him over anything. Is this some trick? Is she angling to get me punished?

"It's true," Immy insists. "I told him the mortals would sense something was amiss if you were the only one who refused to wear modern clothes."

Cain *is* big on appearances, so it *could* be true. But I still don't trust her. She grabs my hand and pulls me through my own room to the walk-in wardrobe. At first, I can't see any difference. The rows of unbroken red dresses are just the same. There are a few different length versions, and a couple with hoods sewn on, but that's as much variation as I've been allowed. The other side of my closet has been filled with Draven's clothes—something I didn't notice yesterday. Immy stalks past everything and pulls open the dresser at the back.

The cloth within is still a mixture of red and black—I suspect that Cain intends to keep me dressed in the colours of blood and death until the end of time—but the pieces are different. Denim, cotton, and a hundred other beautiful fabrics which aren't lace and velvet.

I almost want to cry, but I recognise it for what it is.

Setting Immy up as my saviour. Convincing me she has my best interests at heart.

Not. Falling. For. It.

"Get dressed," Immy says, grinning as she heads for the door. "And don't forget your coat. I'll be out here."

I stare at the clothes as she leaves, trying to figure out her angle. This has got to be a ploy. We both know she was the one who betrayed Frost and me two centuries ago. She has to be delusional if she thinks I'll ever put my trust in her again.

For almost a month, I agonised over the thought of her stuck in a coffin because of my actions. Frost was captured, and the rest of the pack put in danger because I begged them to attend the gala and rescue her as well as Vane. All because I was convinced there was no *way* my soft-hearted sister would *ever* have betrayed me.

She won't fool me a second time.

I dress slowly, rebuilding my emotional blocks and checking them over and over again as I slip into the jeans and soft red blouse. I take Immy's advice and shrug a cosy parka over the top of my ensemble. When I emerge, she's leaning against the wall, staring at Draven's sleeping body with an unreadable expression on her face.

"You look great," she says.

So does she.

I'm not used to this new version of my youngest sister. Before I was locked in the coffin, Cain gave her outfits tailored to make her frumpy and childlike, but that's changed. She's doesn't dress like a femme fatale as Callie does, nor in Morwen's black leather or even Bella's practical business wear.

Instead, she looks sweet—innocent even—in an oversized beige turtleneck and washed-out jeans. It's such a relaxed look, almost mortal in its simplicity, that I almost miss the fact that the jumper is made of cashmere and her jeans are tailored perfectly to her curves.

It's not the sort of thing Cain would choose, which means she must have chosen it herself. Our sire always picked colours that clashed with her bright red curls, but the neutral colours she now favours show them off to their best advantage.

She shrugs the large, black cocoon coat over her shoulders and leads the way to the lift at the end of our hall. Just when I think she's going to press the button and call it, she turns left, pushing through the discrete doors to the stairs beside it.

Immy turns her head back towards me with a sheepish smile. "Sorry, I don't like elevators. Not after the coffin."

Her words take me aback, and all I can do is nod.

"Race you to the bottom," she calls.

What is she playing at?

I don't have time to figure it out because she's already gone, zipping down the steps with a quiet giggle. I'm not in the mood for games, not today, so I jump over the rail and free fall straight down the centre of the staircase. I land in a crouch just as she reaches the final step.

"That," she pants. "Is cheating."

A ghost of a smile tugs at the corners of my lips before I realise what's happening and put a stop to it. I will *not* fall for this again. She's using my memories of the time when she was my best friend and playing them to her advantage. I have to be smarter than this.

Her lips thin, and she shrugs my indifference off, heading for the door. "Come on, I want to show you some of the best places in the city. Callie and Bella probably took you on a blood tour, am I right?"

"Pretty much," I reply, trying to keep my voice even as we cross the foyer.

Fresh air. It's foggy and rainy, but I don't care. This is the first time I've been outside in weeks and I gulp it down with gusto, ignoring the humans as they stare and gawk.

"This way." Immy hooks her arm in mine, and I tug my hood up before allowing her to lead me away into the brightly lit streets. We end up outside a quaint little row of shops with brightly coloured awnings, and she stops beneath the last one.

"This place is one of the best cafes in the city," she begins, pulling me inside. "Quiet too, which is nice."

She gets our blood to go, handing me one of the two disposable cups before dragging me back into the rain. We walk farther and farther from the bustling high-class shops. For almost half an hour we don't even speak, passing bars and restaurants in silence. It doesn't take long before the awkwardness shifts to become fraught with underlying tension.

Eventually, we reach a pedestrianised area which over-looks the river. It's a sort of urban garden, which stretches on as far as I can see in each direction. Above us, a curling metal sign pronounces the space 'Eden Community Gardens' in yet another barely veiled Cain reference that makes me roll my eyes.

Humans love to imagine that our sire is the very same figure mentioned in their holy texts, and I understand Cain's reluctance to challenge the notion. Why would he, when Abrahamic religions cover most of the world, and the church has been perfectly under his control for centuries?

As far as Cain's concerned, it's just another way for his existence to pervade their lives—no different from the portraits of him hanging in every home and business.

I'm certain, in reality, Cain pre-dates the first-born son of Adam by thousands of years.

"Cain ordered all major cities to build communal food gardens," Immy explains, striding between the open areas of land. "Keeping humans healthy with access to free vegetables has dropped morbidity rates and prevents them from getting serious anaemia. This one surrounds the whole of Manhattan Island. It was one of his more popular policies."

It's also almost completely deserted. Most humans are tucked away in bed at this hour.

"Vampires don't come here." Immy releases my arm and tugs her coat around herself, crossing her arms over her chest as she puts distance between the two of us. "I guess there's no point. But it makes it the perfect place to go when you just want to be alone."

"You say that like it's something you experience often." I peer over the rail into the water below before following Immy who's begun a slow stroll along the water's edge.

"You have no idea," she mutters.

I bite the inside of my cheek. Time to cut the bullshit. "Why are we here, Immy?"

Her breath catches, and she seems to shrink slightly before she answers: "Because I missed you and I wanted to talk to you before that snake Draven wakes up and starts following our sire's orders."

I frown at her, but deliberately take the bait. "What orders? I already guessed he was a plant—although what further surveillance Cain needs when my room is already full of those stupid cameras is beyond me."

Immy's eyes are watering, I realise, and it's not just the sharp wind coming off the river.

"They're going to blame me," she whispers. "Cain wants you to trust Draven so he can use him to control you, so he's going to lie to you and tell you I ratted you and Frost out. When I didn't. *I wouldn't.* You *know* I wouldn't."

I frown at her. "Immy, you can't expect me to believe that. You're completely sane, without even a hint of blood lust. If you were stuck in a coffin like I was, that should be impossible."

"I wasn't in it as long as you were," she insists. "Cain left me in there for a couple of decades, but he didn't want to waste blood keeping me alive, so he released me and set me loose on the villagers." Her tears start flowing down her freckled cheeks, thick and fast. "I slaughtered all of them before I got control of myself."

Plausible, but I still don't believe her. It must show on my face, because she swipes away her tears and keeps walking. Her breathing hitches oddly and she takes several deep breaths before she can continue.

"Draven was Frost's second in command," she says. "He ratted you out to Cain in exchange for immortality. As a reward, Cain spared him from meeting the same fate as the rest of the rebels and let Callie turn him. But you know our sire hates traitors, so he let Callie play with him until he was certain Draven would obey him without question."

Again, still plausible. It even fits with what my thralls said about how Draven joined them.

"So where have you been for the last nineteen decades? Not at Court, or the Gala wouldn't have been such a big event."

She shrugs. "Cain sent me everywhere. At first it was punishment, letting me rage on whichever city or town had upset him. Then, when I finally clawed my way back to sanity, he used me to turn more of the politicians he needed on his side for the Triumph."

"And none of our sisters knew?"

I can understand Callie or Morwen not caring about the

identity of a vampire running riot amongst dissenting humans, but Bella was just as shocked as I was by Immy's reappearance, and she makes it her business to know everything.

Immy shakes her head. "At first he took my name away," she whispers. "No one was allowed to call me by name. I was just 'it' or 'the vampire.' Just like when we were kids."

I wince at the memory of the days before Cain named us. Stripping us down to nothing more than nameless children with no identity beyond 'daughter' was a crude but effective method of indoctrination.

Any adult who endured what we did would've struggled to retain their sense of self. Children had no chance.

Immy nods and brushes away the moisture gathering in her eyes with a shaking hand. "Cain has no shortage of blood-frenzy-ridden vampires at his command. Even when I 'earned' my name and my sanity back and was sent out to deal with other vampires, I was forced to use aliases and dye my hair." She winds an escaped auburn curl around her finger. "No one had any reason to believe I was Imogen, Daughter of Cain. Most people forgot I even existed..."

She trails off, and I know what she's thinking. Even before the coffin, most people tended not to notice or care about Immy.

"And now you're betraying him by telling me about his plan for Draven?" I have to work hard to keep my scepticism out of my voice, and I don't fully succeed.

She turns her wide, beseeching eyes on me again. "I thought maybe, with you out of the way, I could make him love me," she admits. "I tried so hard. Did everything perfectly. Even started pushing back in little rebellions like you and Morwen do."

"He doesn't love." How could she be that stupid?

Another soft hiccough-sob. "He loved *you*. I felt it every

time you walked into the room with him. I wanted that. All I ever got when he was alone with me was hatred and contempt. Even Morwen doesn't elicit that response from him."

Why does she sound surprised by that? It's not like he ever bothered to conceal those feelings from her.

"I was desperate," she says. "But it didn't work. And it took decades of being alone to realise I lost the one person who ever did love me. You."

A tiny part of me which I thought I sealed away the night of the Gala cracks open. The hurt and sadness rushes past my emotional block, and I curse myself under my breath.

I've been doing so well at keeping my feelings locked down. Now I might as well shout them aloud to the world. Imogen's words make sense, but I won't be fooled a second time. I don't trust her, and I don't trust Draven.

"So, from now on," she continues after a few deep breaths. "I'm on your side, Evie. No matter what. I'll earn your love back. I promise."

Her declaration falls onto an awkward silence, broken only by the rhythmic lapping noise of the waves.

"You're welcome to try," I whisper. "But your loyalty should remain to our sire, for your own self-preservation, if nothing else."

Because if Cain ever hears her say something like that, he'll kill her. If—by some miracle—she's being sincere, I don't want that to happen.

And if she's lying, my response will go back to Cain, who will approve of it more than some emotional display of sibling forgiveness. I'm not even sure I have the acting skills to pull off such a performance.

Because taking her at her word would be stupid. She's been locked inside Cain's office for the last month, and she's had too long to perfect this story.

Immy wipes her eyes again and offers me her arm. "Come, let's stop talking about such heavy things. I missed you. Let me tell you about what you've missed. Did you know they renamed the Old Country twice while you were gone?"

CHAPTER FOUR

DRAVEN

I WAKE UP WITH HALF-REGENERATED HANDS IN A STRANGE BED that smells of Evie, but the vampire herself is nowhere to be seen. The room is silent and I stiffen as I realise I'm alone, and out of a cell, for the first time in a week.

Curious. This isn't the kind of oversight I'd expect from Cain.

I'm also... a lot less messy than I would've anticipated. Someone has washed the worst of last week's dried blood from my body—though they haven't been thorough in it. Now all that remains is the fresh stuff from the half-regenerated hands.

Ah, there's a shower. I can see the tiles glistening from here.

I stumble towards it and hiss as I trip, stumble forwards, and land against the wall. My oversensitive hands make contact with it and the already stinging flesh turns into an inferno.

I sigh in disappointment. Regrowing limbs is such an inconvenience.

Working the dial with no hands is interesting, to say the least, but I manage. Freezing cold water pummels me. Eventually, it gets to work, and numbness sets in. I can't really wash myself with stumpy, barely there fingers, so I settle for just sitting under the spray until I can bring myself to move again.

It gets the worst of the remaining blood and gore off, but I can't wait to be properly clean once more.

There's a glass of half-finished blood on the table, and I down it before going on the hunt for more. The more I can feed, the faster my hands will return to normal. I need them back if I'm going to have any hope of defending myself.

Just because I'm no longer in a cell, doesn't mean my punishment for letting Frost escape is over.

I'm willing to bet it's just begun.

Blood. Finally. Why do modern decorators insist on hiding the fridge inside false cabinets? I sink my fangs into one and almost immediately the stinging starts to worsen.

My new nerves are functional. Good.

I snatch a second bag and close the fridge in favour of investigating Evie's space. Red furniture, black walls, little luxuries like inbuilt speakers and a top-of-the-line television. She's got it all.

An outsider might believe she's been welcomed back into the fold. But the coffin neatly made up in the corner, the bugs and cameras hidden in every lamp and socket, and the wardrobe full of dresses tell a different story.

There are no personal touches here. Even her desk is bare except for the tablet. That's telling. She's not made herself at home, which tells me more about where her loyalties lie than anything else.

My poor doll has been just as much a prisoner as I have.

I cross to the window and look out. It's a miserable night, and rain pelts against the glass. Cain has given her a room which overlooks Eden Park, although the view is mostly hidden by thick fog.

Where is she? Back at Court?

The other guards gossiped that she was there almost every night, slaughtering Cain's unlucky chosen one after the other. Once again, he's building her reputation among his people as a heartless executioner. Isolating her.

Behind me, the handle turns. I spin on my heel, chastising myself for putting my back to the door. I'm normally more careful than this, and I blame blood loss for the lapse.

Whoever is on the other side opens it the slightest crack and keeps it there. I hear Imogen's voice on the other side, but I can't make out her words.

Then Evie herself slips through the opening and shuts the door between her and her sister.

I soak in the sight of her, cataloguing the changes in my pretty little doll. She's wearing modern clothes, and her coat is dripping with water as she hangs it neatly on a peg by the door.

She was outside… with Imogen? Or is she allowed to leave the skyscraper which houses the Court unsupervised? I can't imagine Cain being so callous with her security, so I'm guessing it's the former.

Her clothes may be shiny and new, but Evie is decidedly the opposite. Her mouth and eyes are lined with strain, and her expression is stony as she discovers me missing from the bed.

"Miss me, doll?"

Her head whips around, and her eyes pin me to the spot.

"Not in the slightest." Could her voice be any more arctic?

Grinning, because that's a challenge if ever I heard one, I savour the sound of her voice. In the month since I last saw her, she's lost most of what remains of the slight Eastern European accent she had before. Her vampire instincts to adapt and survive have all-but erased it.

I don't miss it. The tiny inflection reminded me too much of the place where this whole shit-show started.

I raise a single, questioning brow. "You were quick to put me in your bed for someone who claims they didn't."

There's a knife at my throat before I can take my next breath.

Ah, a threat. How novel. Despite myself, excitement trickles down my spine, breaking free of the ice I prefer to surround myself with.

Only Evie can draw these novel little emotions out of me, and damn if I didn't I miss that about her while Cain had me stuck on guard duty.

"Let's get one thing clear," she growls, all traces of the vulnerable woman from before buried deep. "Cain may have forbidden me from killing you, but he said nothing about maiming. Touch me, and I'll slice your hands off, followed by your cock."

I grin, raising one, still-regenerating finger to her blade to push it away. She lets me, but the wariness doesn't leave her.

"Knife play, doll? Now you're just trying to turn me on."

I wondered when the legendary warrioress of old would come through. Up until now, she's been recovering, but that intriguing core of steel is peeking out. Finally. Perhaps being forced to survive alone, without the pack to mollycoddle her, has done her some good.

She scoffs in annoyance and stomps over to her desk, collecting her tablet and heading to the armchair in the corner.

I follow her with my eyes, curious to see what she'll do next. After over a month without her, I soak in her presence like a sponge, amused once more by the unpredictability of her reactions. I've given up trying to restrain my impulse to study her. This new obsession I've developed is satisfying in a way few things other than bloodshed ever are. It would be foolish not to make the most of the break from my usual boredom.

She does her best to ignore me, she really does. But every so often her eyes flick across to where I'm standing.

"So, what are the rules of this little arrangement Cain's cooked up?" I ask, needling her just because I can. "Will you be taking over from Callista when it comes to my torture, because I've got to say, you're woefully under equipped for that."

Cain's dungeons are by far the best interrogation facility I've ever had the privilege of being in. He makes torture into an art form, and I learned a few new tricks during my most recent stay.

Evie doesn't seem to notice my question, and for a long minute, I think she's tuned me out entirely, before she answers.

"As long as you sleep in that bed with me, I don't have to sleep in the coffin."

"That's the only rule? I don't believe Cain was so generous as to release me from captivity just to be your teddy bear."

Evie shakes her head, sliding her finger across the screen. "I'm to keep you on a short leash—his words not mine. And the *second* one of us develops any kind of tender feelings for the other, both our lives are forfeit."

I purse my lips. That won't do. That won't do at all.

I'm well acquainted with my own personal brand of sociopathy, I know I'm at no risk of feeling anything which could be described as 'tender.' But I'm quickly learning that I'm a possessive, selfish bastard when it comes to her. Evie is mine, and that includes her emotions. I want every one of them. Love. Hate. Lust. Pain. All of them are just different facets of the same woman, and I want them all.

"So, he said nothing about fucking?"

Her scowl does little to deter my grin.

"If you think, for one second, I'm going to let my guard down around you enough to fuck you in front of a room filled with cameras and bugs, you've got another think coming."

Hmm… when she puts it like that, it does sound kinky. Cameras won't stop me, though. If someone else sees me fucking her, hears her screaming my name… well, they'll know who she belongs to.

Evie has no idea the possessive tangent my thoughts have taken. No, she's gone back to staring at the screen, ignoring me once again. That simply won't do.

"What are you doing?"

She rolls her eyes, hugging her tablet closer. "Educating myself. Now be silent or go away. You were never this verbose before."

I snort. "So, you're already disobeying? I thought I was supposed to be on a short leash?"

She doesn't dignify that with a response. If her plan is to follow Cain's orders by ignoring me, it won't work. I can be patient when I want something—it's why I haven't rushed the throne room and tried to put a silver stake into Callista's heart—and I definitely want Evie.

CHAPTER FIVE

EVELYN

Draven is driving me *insane*.

It's been exactly four hours and twenty-six minutes since I returned from my stroll with Immy. He's spent all of them staring at me.

It's the most infuriating thing. He doesn't move. It's like having an undead statue in the corner of the room.

The second the sun begins to rise, that stare turns molten.

He's still young—in vampire terms—and I can see the instant his biology starts to make itself known. What surprises me is that it takes so long. It's almost an hour after dawn when his laser-like stare loses a fraction of its intensity and his shoulders start to slump.

I'm older. The sun can't force me to sleep.

But when he starts taking his clothes off, I quickly lose my feeling of smug superiority.

"You can't tell me you make a habit of sleeping naked," I hiss, as he removes the last pieces of his underwear and strolls, shameless, towards the bathroom.

"Why not?" he calls. "Surely you don't have any objections. It's just skin after all."

I hiss under my breath and slam my tablet down. I've spent the last few hours trying to figure out a way to contact Finn, but it looks like whatever software he's put on my tablet only works when *he* activates it.

It's probably for the best. Draven could easily have caught me out if he'd seen.

I stride into the walk-in closet and pick the most concealing nightwear I can find. A fluffy, fleecy set of stripy pyjamas which cover me from my neck to my ankles.

It takes all of my willpower to ignore him, spread out across the entire bed, as I head for the fridge.

Only to find it empty.

Damn him. He drank all of our blood?

Before I can close the door, he's behind me, mouth at my throat. "If you want to drink, you drink from me. I'm your thrall, remember?"

Each word is accompanied by his warm breath whispering over my skin. I automatically tilt my head to one side, giving him better access, before I realise what I've done and step away.

If I drink from him, I'll end up fucking him. The venom will slip into his body, I'll lose control of the situation, and it will happen. Our thrall bond is so close to being complete, that sex might just drive us over the edge, and that would give Cain another spy on my emotions—one I'd have no defence against.

"Fine." I shove past him and head for my side of the bed. "I'll starve."

"So much hatred when I've done absolutely nothing to earn it."

I glance back, but the cold dare in his eyes makes me

stumble. He catches me before I can right myself and pulls me so I'm pressed against his bare chest.

"Tell me, doll. What's going on in that pretty little head of yours?"

With his arms around me, his scent enveloping me with every breath, it's hard to think of my reasons to remain calm and unaffected. I'm thirsty—something I've been carefully avoiding since I returned to Court—and he's right *there*. His blood tempts me in a way none of the bagged stuff ever could.

He's my thrall. My body wants me to take advantage of that. He's also very male and very, very nude. My thick pyjamas are doing *nothing* to disguise the hardness of him pressing into my ass.

"This is toxic," I whisper. "This mess of lust and hunger and hatred I have for you and you feel *nothing* for me in return. You're a void on the other end of our bond."

Draven strokes a piece of my hair away from my throat.

"So you want me to feel? Do you wish I could give you sweet little words like your omega and your beta?"

"It would be fake."

His lips trace my pulse, followed by the barest caress of his fangs.

"You know what amuses me?" he asks, trailing those feather-light kisses up to my jaw. "You think what we have is toxic, when in reality it's the simplest relationship you'll ever have."

"How so?"

I feel his grin against my neck. "You *own* me. Period."

Maybe he's right. Maybe I do own him. But owning Draven is a bit like owning a rabid dog.

Every now and again, you expect to get bitten.

His fangs sink into me on the heels of his statement. I can't hold back the strangled, surprised moan which escapes my throat. His venom is a subtle, dangerous thing. Sliding through my veins like bubbles in my blood. Igniting a fire that sparks across my nerves until my nipples pebble against the soft fabric of my top.

In revenge, I yank his arm up to my own mouth and bite down on his wrist.

Thanks to just one mouthful of my powerful blood, his hands have completely regenerated. I take my first sip as he withdraws his fangs from my neck and licks the wound shut.

I'm surprised he stopped so quickly. He barely used enough venom to give me more than a light buzz.

I'm aroused, but a far cry away from sobbing and being mindless with need. I could easily shove him away and tell him to stop.

It would be the smart thing to do.

Apparently, I'm not that smart.

I cradle his wrist against my own face, as he moves us the last few paces until we're on the bed. I don't even fight him as he manipulates me until I'm bent backwards over the mattress, still sucking greedily on his arm. That smoky note to his blood is still there, exactly as I remember it.

His free hand finds the waistband of my trousers and a single finger hooks beneath it, tugging experimentally.

"If you don't want this, now's the time to tell me to fuck off," he murmurs.

My traitorous fangs just dig in harder, delivering a fresh shot of my own, more powerful, venom to his bloodstream.

"Good."

In one swipe of his claws, my pyjama bottoms fall away, shredded. He kicks my legs open and delves between them with his free hand, groaning when he discovers the damning evidence of just how much I want this.

"Poor doll, you're soaked."

The fake pity in his voice does something to me, and I

clench on nothingness as his fingers play in the dripping folds of my sex, spreading fire and moisture everywhere he touches.

I withdraw my fangs and don't bother licking the wound to close it. Snapping my legs around his waist, I flip us until he's on his back beneath me.

"I still hate you," I growl, sinking my fangs into his jugular.

"Good," he retorts, bucking up against me so his erect dick rubs across my sopping pussy.

The heat of him is like a brand, and I moan.

He needs to do that again.

Instead, the bastard takes the head of his cock in one hand and rubs it over my clit in a rapturously slow back and forth that quickly has me trying to move forward and put him where every single cell of me needs him most.

Draven doesn't give in to my unvoiced demand. No. He just taps my clit with the head in reprimand. My spine bows at the sudden contact, and I stop drinking long enough to hiss.

"Fuck me."

"All you had to do was ask."

Our coupling is hard and violent. His hands grab my hips with bruising strength and he slams me down onto his length with no warning. I cry out at the sudden stretch and the force of my invasion, but he stays still, letting me adjust.

I almost thank him for it, before I remember why I hate him. My hands find his chest, and I forget all about drinking from him as I steal back control. Rotating my hips once in a figure eight motion before rising up and dropping down once more.

Beneath us, the bed creaks, but I ignore it. My hips snap back and forth over him as he watches with hooded eyes from beneath me.

One of his hands leaves my hip and finds the collar of my shirt. *Rippp*. The fleece gives way like tissue beneath his claws, floating away from my body to reveal my naked torso.

"Beautiful," he whispers, watching my breasts rise and fall with each thrust like he's hypnotised by the motion.

"Shut up," I growl, rocking onto him faster.

He does as I ask, but his silence can't be mistaken for meek compliance, because the thumb of his free hand quickly finds my clit. My head falls back and my eyes drift shut as I lose my rhythm under the rising wave of my own climax.

"Look at me."

I almost disobey out of spite, but I want to see him come undone. My eyes snap to his, and that's all it takes.

I fall apart with a scream. Pleasure overwhelms my senses, and Draven takes over as my legs give out completely. His hands are bruising against my hips as he lifts my body up and slams me down onto his cock over and over. No mercy. No gentleness. Just unrestrained male power drawing out my climax. Prolonging the pleasure.

All I can do is quiver and shake above him until the sensation of my own orgasm triggers his and his dick pulses inside of me, filling me with a groan. He jerks me onto him one last time, then his hands finally release my hips. Those calloused fingers aren't done with me yet though. They wind into my hair and drag my face down to his for a brutal kiss that steals what little breath I have left.

When I collapse against his chest, I'm trembling and sweaty.

I'm too spent to regret anything right now, but in the evening, I'll have plenty of time to reflect on why having sex with this man was a bad idea.

It may be weak of me, but right now, I just want to lie

squeak, he drags me upstream, forcing me to tap into my supernatural speed to keep up.

The banks on either side of us grow steeper and steeper, until we're walking along a small ravine. *Did he know this was here the whole time?* He must have, because he stops abruptly, grabs my waist, and jumps over the bank, revealing a quiet wooded glade surrounded by ancient trees.

"What's this all about?" I demand, the moment we stop moving.

He offers me a sardonic raised brow. "I'm not sure what you mean, doll."

"Nice try." I stand my ground as he prowls closer, staring into his eyes without flinching. "I want to know what's going on."

"Will you believe me if I tell you?" he asks, instead of answering me.

Shrugging, I glance away, because in truth, I probably won't. "That depends on what you tell me."

"Before I spill my soul"—his eyes darken as his tone loses its mocking undertone for the first time this evening—"I want to know what you want."

The impossible. "I want to serve my sire and uphold his law in his glorious new world." *I yearn to escape him.* "I want to hunt down Frost and the other traitors and serve him their heads." *I would kill to be held by Finn and Silas and the rest of the pack again.* "Anything else is immaterial."

"Au contraire, doll. Your wants are the only thing I care about, although the fact you just lied out of your ass to me does sting a bit." He prowls closer, and I finally give ground, taking a step back.

Only to come up against a tree.

Draven's smirk grows as he rests an arm on the bark above my head. "Shall I tell you what your little bond just told me?"

I shake my head, mute.

"You hate your sire. You hate him so much that you'd do just about anything to be free of him. What you want, more than anything, is to be back in the arms of your pack where you feel safe."

Everything in me shuts down and a fine tremor spreads from my spine to my limbs. God. He could get me killed.

"Like I said, you own me. Your wish is my command."

"You work for him. *You* betrayed us at the gala."

His head lowers, until his breath fans against the sensitive shell of my ear. "Cain has believed I am his sleeper agent for the last century. He and Callista"—he says her name like a curse—"believe they broke me and have since remade me into their puppet."

Between us, the thrall bond cracks, the ice giving way to a searing, burning hatred that steals my breath.

"Until you stepped between your sister and me, the only thing I cared about was vengeance. Frost was the best way to get it."

I shudder. "And now?"

His tongue traces the spot his breath has made unbearably sensitive. "Now, I want to give you yours instead." He pauses. "On the night of the gala, Cain was counting on your betrayal. He had hundreds of his best men stationed covertly among the guests. The second you tried to leave, you would've been killed. My attacking Frost—and your decision to act along—is the only reason you both lived."

The implications hit me like a tonne of bricks. "You freed Frost."

Draven shrugs as if that kind of treason isn't jaw-droppingly dangerous and stupid. "I drugged his guards' coffee. He did the rest."

"How do I know you're telling the truth?"

He pulls away, taking his smoky scent with him. I suck in

a lungful of air, trying to dispel whatever remains of the bubble of intimacy he just created.

"You don't. But I don't think you have it in you to continue living like you have been for the last month. How long do you think you can play the good little executioner for a man who can and will lock you back in that coffin the second you don't jump fast enough at his command?"

He's right.

I'm not living. Not like this. I might no longer be shut in a coffin, but I'm slowly killing myself anyway.

The only difference between my situation now and two months ago is that I have a chance to change it. I can't waste that.

I could be wrong. This could be the perfect trap. There's every reason to believe Draven is Cain's spy, and has been all along. So, perhaps I'm stupid for wanting this.

But keeping my thralls and I divided serves Cain just as well as having a spy in our ranks. And with a completed thrall bond, I'll *know* where Draven's loyalties lie. There won't be any hiding it.

Oddly enough, I believe Draven. It's not just because his version of events makes sense—any fool with enough time can craft a decent alibi. No, it's the rage along the thrall bond.

That kind of anger can't be faked.

Something inside of me shifts. The thrall bond between us slams into place with a resounding finality that echoes soundlessly across the space between us. Like Finn, I can feel him perfectly. Draven's metallic ice is the perfect counterpoint to the omega's softness and if I dig deeper, really searching for it, that fury is still there.

Alongside a healthy dose of satisfaction.

And loyalty.

So much damn loyalty. All of it directed at me.

There's no way this man works for Cain. Relief swamps me so fast my head actually swims a little.

Draven has no such issue. He simply nods, like the emotional connection between us is a job well done. "Good. This will make keeping an eye on you much more efficient."

A snort of disbelief works its way free before I can stop it. "Romantic."

Yet, for him, it is. Draven was never going to be the kind of man to declare his undying love for me on the spot. He exists on the outskirts of the pack—of life—looking in. Where most people have positive emotions, or a softer side, there is only ice.

Time will tell if he'll let me thaw it. For now, I'm happy with the deadly protectiveness he surrounds me with and the sense of safety that comes with that.

His knowing look sends a pulse of wetness straight to the spot between my thighs.

"I suppose we should make sure those guards think we were just fucking like bunnies." He prowls close to me once again. "Sink those fangs in me, doll. We want to be convincing."

CHAPTER SIX

EVELYN

I'VE BEEN WAITING FOR MORWEN TO RETURN FOR WEEKS. CAIN has had her out hunting for the rest of the pack from the second the Gala ended. Knowing her, she's pissed that Vane —who she considered her trophy—got away as well.

Considering Frost's recent escape, she's the last person I expect to see kneeling before my sire's throne when I walk into Court later that evening. On either side of our sire, Immy and Callie stare down dispassionately. Somehow, Bella has gotten out of being here *again*.

Immy's eyes flick to mine, lighting briefly, and I give her a tiny nod.

I've spent the entire morning preparing myself, making sure I'm a blank, unfeeling slate. I can't give Immy any cause to suspect that Draven and I have completed the thrall bond.

She lied about betraying me. I know I can't trust her. But, still, I find myself praying that her motivations were selfish, rather than some plot devised by Cain. I want to believe that she was being genuine about wanting to rekindle our relationship, because despite it all, I *miss* my sister.

Perhaps it's naïve of me to hope that I'll get my best friend back again. Time will tell.

"You. Lost. Them?" Cain's hiss is deadly, and it snaps me right back to what's transpiring with Morwen. "They were right *here* in the middle of court. Inside our *home* and you somehow *lost* that trail?"

His eyes find me, still lingering by the door. Aside from my sisters, the throne room is otherwise empty, making me an easy target.

I shore up my defences even more. If he suspects about the thrall bond…

But he doesn't call me out on it. "Evelyn, take your sister's tongue. Then cut off her feet. She can crawl in the dirt until they return."

If Draven is shocked by my drawing a blade and moving forwards without questioning, he doesn't show it. Between us, the thrall bond remains steady and calm.

But Morwen shocks us all by drawing her own sword. Her eyes narrow as she stares me down.

"You want my tongue?" she spits. "Come and fucking get it."

Morwen's refusal to just sit back and take her punishment shocks me right out of my own false sense of calm, but I can't hesitate. That will just end with me crawling on the ground beside her.

My middle sister hasn't changed. She still goes straight for me with the force of a freight train without giving a thought to strategy. She's brute strength and speed, getting in hits where she can.

Normally, I can match that strength and figure out a way around her unrelenting attacks.

I block the first strike, then the second. Dodge the third.

But not the fourth.

Morwen's sword hacks into my side. For a second, I feel the savage impact and nothing more.

Then the burn sets in.

It starts as a sting that quickly blooms into agony. Like mine, Morwen's sword has a blade edged with silver, so I don't start healing immediately. Every inhale becomes a special kind of torture, and I'm forced to keep my breaths shallow as I struggle desperately not to pass out.

"Callista."

Cain says one word and Callie leaps down from her throne, tackling Morwen from the side. Unlike me, she's at full strength. Taking down our other sister is nothing for her. Callie pins Morwen to the tiled floor with one arm, and rakes her claws across her cheek with the other.

Blood spurts out of me at an alarming rate, but no one dares move a muscle without Cain's say so. Callie forces our other sister's jaw open and snatches out her tongue with a victory hiss.

When she tosses it at our sire's feet, Cain just yawns.

"Leave her feet, Callista. I've had enough disappointment in the last five minutes to last me for the next century."

Callie steps back, leaving Morwen to spit her own blood on the floor. The two of us must make a pathetic sight, but there's satisfaction in Cain's gaze as Callie returns to her seat. He offers her his pocket square to wipe her hands with, and I swear her smile lights up the room.

She's a fool. He's not happy with her performance. He's approving because it proved that neither Morwen nor I am any true threat to him.

The fact that he sees Morwen *as* a potential threat is a useful piece of information, and I file it away for safekeeping.

"Evelyn, you're an embarrassment." He spits the word like a verbal slap. "Drink from your thrall before you pass out, then report to the lycan compound with Morwenna. She can make use of the feet I've allowed her to keep by sparring with you until you remember how to use that sword I gave you."

The gurgle that echoes from Morwen's mouth is obviously one of complaint. Seconds later, one of her eyes is gouged out. Cain flicks his wrist, and the blood-splattered orb flies across the room like a gory ping-pong ball with the attached nerve flying behind it like a tail. It bounces from the wall with a wet sound and rolls across the floor until it comes to a stop in a pool of blood.

"If I hear one more noise from you"—Cain's tone is deceptively pleasant as he sits on his throne, licking Morwen's blood from his fingers—"I'll lock you in your sister's coffin."

My crazy sister just smiles, bowing to him.

How she manages to make the gesture of obeisance look sarcastic is beyond me.

A wrist presses against my mouth, distracting me. The first lungful of Draven's scent makes my fangs drop, and I sink them into his vein without waiting. I'm still in pain, but I make a point to meet Callie's eyes as I drink and smirk.

She might've turned him, but I plan to make it very clear that Draven is mine now. Between us, the thrall bond vibrates with possessiveness, shaking free of the emotionless barrier I erected to conceal it.

Then I remember what's at stake and dart a glance at Immy.

Shit. That one impulsive move has given us away.

Her eyes are wrinkled with concern, but she doesn't seem suspicious.

I wait a heartbeat without breathing for her to speak up. To out me.

"Every time Evelyn loses," Cain adds, eyes narrowing on me now. "You may take one of her thrall's fingers. When he

58

runs out of those, move onto his toes. After that… get creative. Neither of you are to return to Court until she's no longer an embarrassment."

I frown at him as I take another mouthful of Draven's blood.

What is he doing?

He doesn't trust me, so why work to make me stronger? Why try to play on feelings he doesn't want me to have for my thrall to ensure I comply?

And why hasn't Immy said anything? I look back at my sister, searching for her motivations. It's useless. The old Immy wore her emotions on her sleeve. This new one may as well be a statue.

None of this makes sense, and I swallow my unease.

Morwen releases an affirmative gurgle, as I withdraw my fangs from Draven's skin, sealing the wound. I meet my sire's stare, searching his eyes for the answer.

Nothing.

I push to my feet and bow, refusing to wince as the healing skin on my side protests being folded in half. "As you wish, sire."

I turn on my heel and follow Morwen from the room, silently sighing in relief the moment the doors swing shut behind us.

Perhaps Immy will break the news to Cain when they're alone. Either way, it's out of my hands.

At least, no matter what hell my sister puts me through, I won't have to kill anyone today. As long as I remain weak, I won't have to. And, I now have plenty of one-on-one time with the sister who's been elusive since the Gala.

Which means I can dig for answers.

I want to know why she didn't kill Samuel. I want to know where he is. And, most importantly, I want to know if he really does have a way to kill Cain.

Morwen rips into the throat of the first vampire she comes across, sinking her face into the wound and drinking until they pass out. The poor man doesn't know what hit him. One second he's strolling along a corridor, the next he's flat on his back with a gaping neck wound.

The next person receives similar treatment, except this time she steals the sunglasses he's stashed in his shirt pocket and slides them onto her face, disguising her regenerating eye.

But when we finally leave the skyscraper and exit onto the road, she hops into the first taxi she sees and slams the door on me.

The message is clear: I'm not welcome.

A cough from behind me draws my attention to Draven, already holding the door of the next waiting car open for me. "Come on, doll, I'd hate to be late for a date with dismemberment."

The ride isn't long, and soon we're standing in front of our destination. I'm not sure what I was expecting from the Lycan Compound, but this... isn't it. The rest of New York is a tribute to glass and steel, reflecting sunlight onto the strange gardens built onto the sides of the skyscrapers.

I researched the city extensively during the long periods of isolation in my room. The vertical gardens are a relatively recent feature, something implemented by Cain when he discovered the negative effects of air pollution on the human circulatory system. Overnight, the world's most polluted cities were required to increase the amount of vegetation they had, everywhere.

The media framed it as an act of philanthropy, which made me snort.

Is it really generous to ensure your food supply doesn't die prematurely?

Regardless, because of that edict, what was once a

polluted metropolis now *looks* like a scene from a science fiction utopia.

The Compound is the one, glaring exception.

It's the only brick building I've seen since I arrived. The architecture is brutal, and the security…

I've never seen so many lycans in uniform in one place. There are more bars inside the building than there are in most high-security prisons.

Morwen doesn't hesitate, she just strides on through. Not a single lycan challenges her or meets her eyes.

Odd.

They're almost… respectful of my sister.

The same courtesy isn't extended to me. I have to meet every stare until they look away. Proving myself in a hundred silent battles between predators. Walking through the halls, acting as though my side isn't still injured and I don't reek of blood in the presence of so many of them is unnerving. Draven sticks close to my back, no doubt feeling my tension along the thrall bond.

Now that we're away from Immy, I lean shamelessly on his ice for support, using it to keep myself focused.

Morwen doesn't stop until we're out of the building and standing in a similarly sparse internal courtyard. The floor is bare concrete, with a couple of markings for some kind of ballgame scratched into it. She turns around in the centre and draws her sword.

"That's it?" I grind out. "No conversation, just get straight to it? You've never been one to follow orders so literally, sister."

She shrugs, looking around at the few lycans who were playing basketball, but have now stopped in favour of watching us.

"I don't have anything better to do than butcher you two. Might as well get this over with." Her voice is back to normal, the vampires she drank from and her age having allowed her to fully regenerate her tongue in record time. She points at Draven with the blade. "Get out of the way, bloodsucker, so she doesn't get too distracted. This is going to take long enough as it is."

Great. She's come to the same conclusion that I have.

I'm pathetically weak. Pretty much defenceless.

But for some reason, Cain wants me to return to full strength. That alone is suspicious. He doesn't trust me, so why give me the order to train after specifically forbidding it since the gala? And with Morwen, no less. The daughter who so openly defies him at every turn.

"This makes no sense," I mutter.

"Less thinking." Morwen grunts, shoulder-slamming into me. "More fighting."

I land on the floor with a hiss, springing back to my feet in a move that was once natural, but now makes the muscles of my back ache.

My body is mostly recovered from my stint in the coffin, but I've lost my edge. Somehow I have to survive Morwen for long enough to ask her about Samuel, and I have no idea how I'm going to manage it.

Parrying her next blow requires all of my concentration, and I'm forced to stop trying to out-think our sire in order to survive my sister.

When her sword almost severs my arm with the next hit, she grins.

"Which finger do you like the most?" she purrs, approaching Draven with a sashay in her step.

Damn her. She's having far too much fun with this.

She may not like Cain, but she does love violence. This assignment would be her idea of heaven if it wasn't so boring.

As for me... I grind my teeth together, forcing myself to

watch as she pulls out a knife and rips his ring finger from his hand. It lands at my feet, and I have to force myself not to dive on it and lick up the traces of Draven's blood.

He's my only immortal blood source, and he's going to be drained by the end of this. This isn't good.

CHAPTER SEVEN

EVELYN

It takes another week of constant training before I get my opening. A week of giving Draven my blood so he can regrow his fingers and toes every night. Of sustaining wound after wound while Morwen rains down the full force of her immortal strength on my battered body. She ignores my subtle attempts to converse completely, becoming a silent machine intent on one thing.

And I am improving—as much as I hate to admit it.

I can hold my own for a few minutes now. Slowly but surely, I'm returning to the point where the motions are automatic, freeing up my mind for strategy.

Still, I want to learn more about Samuel, and Morwen's involvement with him. My determination is why we arrive almost half an hour early on the eighth day.

I have a list of questions a mile long, and I'm not leaving until my sister answers at least *some* of them. Reaching the entrance to the courtyard, I open my mouth to give Morwen a piece of my mind. Only to stop.

Shock roots me to my spot in the doorway.

Morwen is here, but she has her arms wrapped around the waist of a petite woman, drinking from her neck in the middle of the space where we're scheduled to train.

Her fingers are clenched on the lycan female's ass, dangerously close to the hem of her incredibly short skirt. One of the other woman's hands is tangled in Morwen's curls, holding her in place as she drinks. The other is clenched possessively on Morwen's breast.

None of this should have caught me off guard. Morwen having a lover isn't too surprising, given the casual attitude immortals have to sex. But the tender look she gives the lycan after she pulls away and licks the wound sealed could get her killed.

The instant I meet her gaze, her entire body stiffens until she might as well be made of living stone. Her lover cocks her head to one side and then follows her line of sight until she, too, catches sight of me.

They spring apart just as I move out of the doorway and I look back, wondering if Draven saw.

His face is just as blank as always, giving nothing away as he moves aside to take his normal place, waiting against the wall to be butchered.

Shit.

I know without a doubt that I've just walked in on something I wasn't supposed to see, and Morwen is glaring at me with the heat of a thousand suns in her eyes. In witnessing that moment of softness—toward a *lycan* no less—I've backed her into a corner.

It wouldn't take much to let her secret slip to Cain. Our sire would rip apart this wolf-infested building to discover every little hidden truth she's kept here.

I'll bet he doesn't know about the way the lycans call her 'alpha,' and defer to her when they think I'm too far away to hear. A lover will get her tortured and probably killed. Thanks to my fiasco with Frost, Cain ordered my sisters to abandon any meaningful relationships they had. The barest whiff of this kind of treachery, or the lycans considering Morwen their alpha over Cain, may well get every lycan on the planet wiped out.

Morwen knows all of this, so I don't understand why she doesn't just strike me down right here. It would probably be easier to blame it on a training accident and take that punishment rather than risk me spilling her secrets later.

I'm better than I was, but she's still got the advantage when it comes to strength and stamina. Violence has always been the answer as far as she's concerned.

So when she doesn't, and instead just gives her lover a little shove towards the door, my hackles rise.

Too many surprises in a short period of time. My hand falls to the pommel of my sword, resting there in readiness.

"All right, you'll get that talk you're burning for," she growls. "But *only* you. Your thrall waits here." A wicked grin dances on her face for a second. "In fact, let's make it interesting. *He* can do your training on your behalf."

She snaps her fingers and the lycans who were simply lounging around the edge of the courtyard, waiting for the entertainment to begin snap to attention. Some of them prowl forward, while others hang back.

I glance back at Draven, eyes wide with questions. The insane vampire simply grins, giving me a nod.

On any other man, the look would be cocky, but on him, it's darker, more like a threat.

He drank from me last night, I remind myself, *he should be fine.*

The door Morwen leads me through opens onto another spartan corridor, which bends and turns into stairs. I don't think there are any elevators in the Compound, and I wish that was the case everywhere. It's a relief not to have to battle with my own claustrophobia as I follow her up to the roof.

Cool night air blasts me as soon as I step outside, and it takes a long moment of squinting before I see Morwen, already sitting on the edge, overlooking the river beyond.

"You are an idiot," she says as I join her. "Honestly, I have no idea how you're still alive."

I snort, lowering myself until I mirror her posture. "Thanks."

"There aren't any cameras up here," she continues. "And the scans my men did as you passed the front door proved you don't have any bugs on you."

So we won't be overheard or observed.

My teeth sink into my lower lip as I consider what that means. Either Morwen is lying, and this is a trap Cain's ordered her to set up for me. Or, she's telling me that she's powerful enough to create an oasis away from his influence.

If it's the former, I need to be careful. If it's the latter, my sister could be my greatest ally.

"The question is, *sister*, whose side are you really on?" I retort.

Morwen just grins. "Oh, come on, Evie. You already know the answer to that."

The chill is starting to seep into my bones, and I rub my arms to try and dispel it. "I think you're on your own side. Just like everyone else in this fucked up little world we live in."

Morwen grins, letting her body fall back until she's lying on the roof with her legs dangling down to the city below. "You've only just worked that out? Idiot."

"Did you come up here to insult me, or are you finally going to answer my questions about Samuel?" I demand. "You know something about him. Don't deny it. It was written all over your face at the gala."

My crazed sister simply sighs and stares up at the stars. "I could tell you, but if you're going to run back to our sire and get Mia and me beheaded, then what's the point?"

"He doesn't know about her." I guessed as much. "Why would you even risk that kind of relationship with someone if you cared about them?"

"I could ask you the same question about a certain human."

"I was in love."

"You were stupid."

"Yes. Okay. I was. *Happy?* Now tell me why you're recreating my mistakes."

The wind lifts Morwen's hair, and she shoves it out of her face before replying. "Love doesn't ever feel like a mistake until it's too late, does it?"

So she genuinely loves this Mia? *Oh, Morwen, what have you done?*

My own sadness seeps through the thrall bonds I've been trying to ignore, and despite the distance between us, Finn instantly sends a wave of love and comfort straight back.

Damn. We're both screwed.

"Samuel," I press. "I swear… I swear on our mothers, I won't tell our sire anything you tell me."

Morwen's big brown eyes are piercing and full of suspicion as she regards me. "You'll tell him anything if it prevents him from shoving you back in that coffin," she retorts.

"Maybe. I guess you'll just have to trust me to keep my idiot ass out of that situation."

Snorting, she rolls onto her side until she's facing me. "You know I didn't kill him."

"So the hand you presented to Cain?"

"Samuel's idea."

"Does he really know—"

"I don't have a clue, and I didn't really care. He was just…

the only one of them who wasn't a shit to us, remember? So when he suggested letting him run, I didn't have to think about it too hard."

I grimace as I remember the way our 'brothers' treated us. Sure, as children, they didn't mind us. Even bragged about selecting us for Cain. Then, when it became clear *we* were the favoured ones, Sigurd, Gaius, Alexander, and Attila all turned on us.

Of course, that was just another of Cain's tests, to see if we could survive being hated by vampires vastly older and more powerful than ourselves.

"So where is he?"

Morwen shrugs. "If he mentioned anything, I forgot it. Side effect of his gift of being so bland he was basically invisible. If I were him, though, I'd go somewhere sunny."

Makes sense. Because of the low chances of our kind surviving beyond the few centuries needed for them to become immune to sunlight, cities around the equator have always had a smaller vampire presence. Although older vampires don't suffer from sunlight as younger ones do, they still tend to steer clear of those locations by force of habit.

If I were Samuel, that would be the perfect place to hide.

"Could you track him?" I demand, the wheels in my brain working overtime. "If I found a way for our sire to approve the mission, could you find him?"

"Great plan. Let's announce to our sire that I deliberately failed a mission and then expect him to allow the two of us to just wander on down to Mexico, or Somalia, or wherever the fuck he's settled for a second attempt." She rolls her eyes, flopping back onto her back. "I could probably find him again. I did it the first time. But there's no way you're going to get that past Cain."

"Let *me* worry about that."

I can think of something.

Morwen sits up. "You don't actually want to kill Samuel, do you?"

I frown. "I have nothing against him. I just want to know if it's true. If he *did* know of a way to…" I trail off, unable to even say it.

"To kill our sire?" Morwen finishes for me. "Look, hundreds of people have tried and failed. If you ask me, it's a fairy tale. One that you're blindly hoping will allow you to live happily ever after with that pack of yours."

"Is it better to live and die for a cause you believe in, or live in despair for eternity?"

Morwen shrugs. "Life *is* despair." She rubs at her temples for a second. "You realise if you want to keep your thrall, you'll have to deal with Callie. She still wants him."

"Callie can't have him." Morwen grins at my grumpy—and decidedly not jealous—statement.

A plan starts forming in the back of my mind, but it's risky. It requires a lot of parts to line up. Even then, Cain could easily throw it all off by sending others in our place.

"I need you to help me get back to full strength," I mutter. "By the end of the week."

"How do you plan to do that?"

"We both know I'm almost fully recovered. I'm just rusty."

"And then what?"

I hold her stare with my own. "Then you have to decide how far you're prepared to go." I glance back at the stairs. "Or how much you're prepared to risk."

CHAPTER EIGHT

EVELYN

The next time I stride into Court, I'm prepared. Determination lends power to my steps, as I stride past the rows of vampires and bow before my sire's throne. I've chosen a hooded version of the dress, and I wear the fabric over my face, shielding me from the onlookers.

I'm alone, and it feels safer this way. Draven's displeasure at being left behind rankles at the back of my mind, but I managed to convince him it was more important for him to get in touch with the others so they can be prepared to meet us.

Because this is it. I finally have a plan, and I'm going to make it work.

"I didn't summon you, Evelyn." Cain's voice is soft, but there's a hint of displeasure underlying it.

He's not pleased that I'm no longer suffering at Morwen's hands.

"Sire," I bow my head further in apology, then push back the hood to meet his frowning stare. "I brought you a gift."

Reaching into my pocket, I draw out the slimy, still-warm tongue. Morwen clawed it out of her mouth by herself, but Cain doesn't need to know that. I throw it on the floor at his feet, maintaining eye contact the whole time. "If you still require her feet, I can provide those as well."

A bluff, but one he won't call me on because I plan to distract him well before then.

"I have another matter to bring before you. It's of a more... sensitive nature."

The gleam in his eyes is predatory, and he doesn't spare a glance at the rest of the room before he says, "Leave us."

The vampires of the Court, who were practically licking their lips with anticipation at the scent of Morwen's blood, scatter. They head for doors with a grumbling reticence. They all want to know what I have to say. They'd kill to be trusted. A few even linger, practically begging Cain to invite them to remain. He doesn't.

When the double doors slam closed and only Bella, Callie, and Immy remain, I give them pointed looks.

"Now, now, Evelyn, we're a family." Cain steeples his fingers beneath his chin. "Your sisters would never betray me."

But *I* would. The dig he's making isn't even subtle.

"Sire, I have reason to believe there is a credible threat to your life."

His dark brows rise into his hairline at that. "Evelyn, perhaps you forgot during your imprisonment. I am immortal. I *cannot* die."

I bow my head. "I know, sire. But I felt it prudent to make you aware that the resistance is looking for Samuel. They're under the mistaken belief that he has some knowledge which will help them destroy you. I dismissed it when I first learned, because Samuel is dead, but during our time together Morwenna revealed he sired a vampire before his death. A son who may be the source of these rumours."

Cain stiffens, shrugging away Callie's affectionate hand on his arm as he leans toward me. "And how did Morwenna reveal such information, without her tongue?"

I shrug my hair back over my shoulder, revealing the twin puncture wounds. "She fed from me afterwards. I felt it was necessary."

Cain pushes out of his chair and begins to pace.

"Sire," Callie begins. "Surely there's no truth to this, is there?"

The backhand he deals to her face is hard enough that both Callie and her chair go flying backwards, leaving her sprawled on the floor.

"Of course not." Cain is seething. His mask cracking.

Dear God. Frost might actually have been on to something.

"I cannot be killed," he growls. "And I've told you too many times, Callista, not to question me. Don't make me ask Evelyn to bring me *your* tongue next."

He straightens the lapels of his jacket and turns back to me. "You're certain this information is accurate?"

"Yes, sire." I keep my face blank. "Morwen confirmed she didn't see any point in killing a vampire who was so young and not a target. Please, allow me to rectify her mistake."

He's in my face in the next second. "This vampire 'son' of Samuel's is no threat to me, but we can use him as bait. Since it appears *you* are not sufficient enough to draw Frost out of hiding once more, Morwenna will be able to track Samuel's progeny. Imogen, you'll accompany her. The two of you should be sufficient to bring Frost and his merry band of lycans to their knees when they show themselves."

Damn. This wasn't the plan. I'd hoped Cain would send me—given that I was the one who brought him the information—but apparently not. Shit. I need to get on that plane.

I open my mouth, ready to give him the excuse I prepared earlier—that Morwen is unreliable and needs me to keep her on track—but Immy interrupts before I can say anything.

"Sire." Immy hesitates. "I believe we should take Evelyn."

My head snaps up, pinning her to the spot. Her pale, freckled face gives nothing away as she meets my stare.

"I never asked for your opinion, Imogen," Cain snaps, turning to her. "What reasoning could possibly have led you to come up with such an asinine idea?"

Immy flinches, but powers on. "She'll be able to use her thrall bonds to narrow down Frost's location. We'll be able to follow them, even if they flee."

The look of indecision which passes over his face is almost too quick for me to read. I've caught him off guard with this information, and for the first time, I catch a glimpse of what Cain looks like when his feathers are ruffled.

I don't make the mistake of thinking this will make him easier to deal with.

No one has *ever* managed to back him into a corner before and lived.

"Fine," he eventually snaps. "Evelyn, you will go. But you'll take Draven with you."

I nod, clenching my jaw for effect. "As you wish."

I start to turn, but his voice stops me.

"Evelyn." My eyes snap back to him, cursing as I realise he hasn't dismissed me. "Take this. And bring me back his head."

He holds out a familiar ancient blade, sheathed in modern leather, and I nod as I take it from him. The slight dent in the pommel is still there, confirming the weapon's identity, and the familiar grooves worn into the handle still fit my hand perfectly.

Dramatic, as always. Any silver weapon would've done the job, but Cain is making me use this—the dagger that sealed my fate as a child—as a reminder.

I may be older now, and going on a mission half-way across the world, but I am no less under his thumb than I was as a girl locked in a ballroom with no way out except death.

"It will be the last thing he sees, sire." I reply, bowing.

He doesn't smile. "Make certain of it." Reminder delivered, he turns his attention to my sisters. "Bellatrix, you'll ensure no word of this leaves this room. Callista, I want you to investigate these rumours about Samuel. I want to know exactly who's been spreading the idea that I might have such a ludicrous vulnerability. Then I want them dead—including Samuel's progeny. I will *not* have my empire undermined by hearsay."

"With pleasure," Callie purrs, strutting towards the doors.

Bella is already tapping on her tablet. "Sire, what reason would you like to spread to explain Morwenna, Evelyn, and Imogen's absence from Court?"

Cain waves a hand at her as if to give her free reign, and Callie pauses on her way out to shoot a venomous glare at Bella. God, when will she figure out that Cain doesn't allow her to question him because it never serves him for her to do so? Surely she should have figured that out by now?

"Wait."

Callie freezes in place, and Bella stops typing.

My stomach drops when he says, "Come here, Callista."

Callie's footsteps echo, slower than before, and she stops as soon as she's within arm's reach. There's a fine quiver in her frame, as if she expects him to hit her again.

When Cain reaches out to her neck, she doesn't flinch, but her body is still tense as a board.

He rips away her scarf, then using both hands, tears the necklace around her throat in two. The silver coffin shaped locket drops to the ground with a clatter, landing in the pool of Morwen's blood.

"I'm glad that I am able to count on the loyalty of my

beautiful daughters," Cain murmurs, tracing a finger along the burn mark on Callie's throat while meeting my eyes. "Bellatrix, come."

Bella's locket joins Callie's in the pooling blood seconds later.

"Thank you, sire," she breathes.

Callie jerks like she's just realised she never thanked him, then bows. "Thank you, sire."

Cain doesn't acknowledge them. "Evelyn, remove Morwenna's when you see her," he orders. "But make sure you remind her of the consequences of disappointing me."

I bow and turn on my heel, dimly aware of Immy following me as we leave our sire in the empty throne room.

My youngest sister's presence is something I wasn't anticipating; a mistake I made purely because I was relying on the old way of doing things where Immy was invisible to Cain. I still don't know if I can trust her, but at least this way I can keep her under close observation while I find out.

He also insisted Draven accompany me. Which means Cain believes that my thrall is still loyal to him. That makes sense. In Cain's world, a broken man is a loyal man, and Draven is definitely both.

Unfortunately for my sire, my thrall's loyalty is to me.

Only when we're back on our private floor does Immy turn me around. "Where are we going?" she asks.

"We need to pack," I reply rather than answering directly. "Prep for warm weather. Bring weapons."

Shoving open my own door, I tug absently at the fabric of my dress and head straight to the wardrobe. I wore it because I was visiting Court, but I desperately want to change. Tempting as it is, that's going to have to wait. I don't want any delays in getting out of here.

Packing is mostly for show. I'm hoping Finn will have plenty of clothes waiting for me. Even now, I can feel his eagerness down the bond, and I know Draven must have let him in on the plan. My skin feels too tight at the idea of seeing the rest of my thralls again. I barely let myself hope that this would happen, but now anticipation is pouring out of me.

Along with nerves.

The last time the pack saw me, they thought I was betraying Frost. Will they welcome me back? Finn definitely will, if the bond is anything to go by, but what about Silas? or Vane? Even more importantly, what about the alphas?

Reigning in my emotions before leaving my room is one of the most difficult things I've ever done. With any luck, Immy will just think I'm eager for the hunt.

She's almost bouncing on the balls of her feet. "Back on missions together again!" She sighs wistfully as we leave the tower of steel and glass and step out onto the pavement. "God, it's been too long. Finally, something that feels normal."

"I know what you mean," I lie, searching for Morwen's car.

It stands out like a raven in a flock of sleek doves. The thing is bulky, wide, and obviously favours function over form. Like a tank without a gun, only it hovers like everything else in the modern age.

"Well, this isn't conspicuous at all," Immy remarks dryly. "Morwen doesn't change, does she?"

"Nope."

The door flies open as we get close, revealing a scowling Draven already inside. Our sister's grinning face stares out of the driver's side window. "Get in. We've got places to be." Then she frowns as she spots Immy. "Let me guess, she's coming too?"

My answering nod is curt, cutting off all debate on the subject before it can begin.

Both Morwen and Immy could betray me, but at least by having them close, I'll be able to keep an eye on the situation. Not to mention, once I'm reunited with my thralls, there will be enough of us to deal with them should they turn on us.

All I have to worry about is making sure that neither of them can kill Samuel before I have a chance to talk with him. Because Cain was *scared,* and that, more than anything, has me convinced that whatever Samuel knows is worth risking everything for.

Inside the car lacks the luxuries I've grown used to in the city. From what I've seen from my window, most of Cain's vehicles are roomy, with leather seats and darkened windows. This one is nothing like that. There are tinted windows, and it's certainly large, but the fabric of the seats is tough and utilitarian. There's no carpet or other upholstery, just bare, matte black painted metal as far as the eye can see.

Mia is in the passenger seat, so Immy and I file in beside Draven on the bench in the back. My thrall and the lycan are both clinging to handles set into the roof, and when Morwen kicks the vehicle into gear and tears away from the Court, I see why.

She's just as reckless now as she was when she was driving chariots. Some things just don't change.

"I thought we'd take my car," Morwen deadpans, spinning the wheel like she's trying to unscrew it and sending me slamming into Draven's side. Only my thrall's iron grip stops me sliding the opposite direction when she turns the other way a second later. "This thing can withstand a direct hit from a missile and keep driving."

"She tested it," Mia says, with a grin. "It was epic."

Of course she did. I exchange a *look* with Immy, and for a second, it feels so normal that I want to grin. Morwen turns another corner, and the entire car lurches. If we had wheels, only two of them would be on the floor.

I swallow and look at my youngest sister. I hadn't counted on her being here, but now that she is, she needs to be brought up to speed. She didn't out Draven and me, even though she must have felt our thrall bond by now, and I have no plans on giving her a chance to betray us to Cain. Still, my hand goes to the knife hidden in my sleeve as I debate where to start.

"In the interest of honesty," I begin, letting my thigh graze Draven's in a silent search for courage. "We are not going to kill Samuel's son."

Immy's head snaps around. "We're not?"

Morwen shoots me a look in the mirror, and I nod. Better to do this now, with all of us here and armed in case she tries anything.

"I need to know, Immy. Are you with me?" I ask, searching her face for any hint of betrayal.

"Always." No hesitation, and she keeps her eyes locked with mine.

"Samuel has a way to kill our sire." I watch the information sink in. "He was afraid in that meeting, wasn't he?"

Her fangs worry her lip, her already pale skin going ghostly. "Yes," she whispers. "He was."

"We're going to find out what it is. Then we're going to use it."

Morwen scoffs. "What she's saying is; we'll either die a painful death, or finally earn our freedom from the dickhead."

Immy's hands fly to her cheeks, a grin spreading over them. "This is all for Frost, isn't it? You still love him?" Her squeal is so loud it actually hurts my ears. "Ohmygoodness, Evie, that's adorable! Two lovebirds, caught in a quest to vanquish anything which might keep them apart!"

Draven looks at her like she's gone insane, but I'm actually relieved. Immy's reaction couldn't have been any more *Immy* if she'd tried.

She's wrong, of course. I can't allow myself to love Frost again. Not after what happened the last time. Part of me worries that Cain has so thoroughly destroyed any hope I might have of feeling the emotion for anyone—even Finn and Silas. The pack deserves someone who isn't afraid to confess their feelings.

"My point is, if you want out, this is the time to say so." I aim the statement at the other three women, knowing without a doubt that Draven is on board. "I won't take it personally."

"No way," Immy replies. "I told you. You're my sister. Nothing trumps that, not anymore."

"We're doing this," Mia adds, giving Morwen a slow smile. "I won't say I want that bastard dead more than all of you do, but I think I'm pretty close."

The sigh of relief which works its way free of my chest is long and audible. Part of me was convinced that Immy was going to object then and there—and in many ways that would've been simpler. At least then her true motives would've been out there.

For now, all I can do is keep moving forward, and hope. With that decided, I leave my glum thoughts for another day, and allow myself to finally feel the anticipation that's been building since I realised tonight is the night that I'll finally see the rest of my thralls again.

CHAPTER NINE

FROST

WE'VE SECURED THE PLANE AND SETTLED IN BY THE TIME
Morwen's black military hover tank slides to a stop beside it.
It's a small luxury jet with only a dozen seats and a tiny
bedroom at the back. It belongs to Cain, so it's probably
loaded with trackers, but that doesn't matter. We've filled the
thing with enough signal jammers to take out a satellite. So
what if it makes him suspicious? We're going to dump it at
the nearest airfield and take our own craft anyway.

By the time he realises what we've done, he'll be too late.

Currently, Silas, Finn, and I are pressed up against the
windows, not even trying to pretend we aren't ridiculously
eager for our first glimpse of her. Finn could've flown this
thing, but Gideon needs to feel in control right now, so he's
the one in the cockpit, doing… whatever needs to be done to
get this thing in the air. I bet he's watching too. Vane is the
only one of us not openly gawking. He's sitting beside his
brother in front of me, but his body is still subtly angled

towards the window, and I bet he's aware of everything going on outside.

Eve would laugh if she could see us right now.

Morwenna climbs out of the car first, followed by Immy. I didn't expect both of them, but I trust Eve knows what she's doing.

There she is. So much of the tension I didn't even realise I've been holding evaporates as she climbs out of the car behind Immy. She looks good. Better than good. She looks beautiful. Her dress is the same as it was before, but she's pulled the hood up to hide her face.

Look at me, I silently urge her.

As if she can hear my thoughts, she looks up and catches my gaze through the window. Her icy eyes soften slightly, and I wink at her, letting her know that our part of the plan is done.

The pilot has been knocked out, and the crew has been reassigned. We're the only ones on board.

"Could you be any more obvious?" Vane hisses. "We don't know if they're all up to speed with the plan yet."

True, but as I watch, Evie nods.

Then two people I didn't expect exit the military hover vehicle after her. One is a female lycan I would *never* have expected to see anywhere near the daughters of Cain, and the other is Draven.

"Why the *fuck* is Mia here?" Silas's growl is so deep it vibrates in the air around us. "She's supposed to be safe with that pack in Paris!"

"Mia's here?" Vane shoves his brother out of the way so he can look for himself. "Fuck."

The older brother looks about three seconds away from ripping the plane apart and setting the whole thing on fire.

If there's one thing neither of the betas can handle, it's the idea of their baby sister anywhere near Cain. Does letting the omega break the news to them make me a coward? Probably. But I want to live long enough to experience a completed thrall bond with Eve.

"About that…" Finn coughs. "She'sourbestundercoveroperative."

Both men round on the omega, wearing matching glares. "Say that again," Vane growls. "And pray to God you didn't say what I thought you just said."

But Gideon is there, standing between them and the omega without flinching. "She's been working undercover in the Lycan Compound for years. She proved her worth. It would have been a waste of a good operative if I left her in that pack." He stares both betas down. "We can have this conversation later, but if you break her cover, I swear to God, I will leave both of you in New York."

"What has she done to her hair?" Silas mutters, turning back to the window. "Black? Really?"

"Are those tattoos? On her *face?*" Vane is beyond seething. He's furious. "And how many piercings…"

Finn suppresses a small smile, and I roll my eyes. Like *Vane* can talk about piercings when his own ears are decorated with studs and chains.

The brothers have always had one, Mia-sized, blind spot in their lives. Their youngest sister has always been a troublemaker with a heart gilded in leather and studs. If anything, I'm glad Gideon assigned her something to do. It probably saved the Paris pack from being burnt to the ground.

But after what happened to the rest of their family, I can understand why Vane and Silas wanted an easier life for her.

The group outside exchanges long looks, until eventually Morwen, Immy, and Mia all nod. As soon as that happens, Eve leads them to the plane.

The second our girl makes it through the door, Finn is on

her. The omega's arms wrap around her, engulfing her in his taller frame until he gets fed up with their height difference and just lifts her into his arms.

"God, I missed you," he groans.

Damn him, that's *my* line.

When he eventually lets her go, it's Silas's turn. The beta scoops her up and drags in a lungful of her scent. Like Finn, Eve hugs him back.

She's trembling, I realise with a start. Why the fuck is she trembling?

Evidently Vane is having the same thoughts I am.

"Why are you shaking, Princess?" he demands.

Her fangs sink into her lower lip as she replies. "Because this is the only time I've ever actively plotted against my sire. It's different than planning to run away. If he catches us now…"

Silas takes her face into his hands and forces her to look at him. "We have decades of experience of keeping out of Cain's reach," he reminds her. "Even when we've been caught, we've managed to get away. We've got this."

"You'd better," Morwen says as she struts onto the plane, Mia close behind her. "Otherwise, we're all going to die an incredibly painful death."

"Your optimism is inspiring," Finn quips. "Please, do go on."

Morwen hisses at him, which makes all of us stiffen. Fortunately, Mia grabs the vampire's arm and shakes her head.

"That's their omega," she mutters, pulling Morwen farther down the plane and studiously ignoring the glares both of her brothers are giving her.

Evidently the middle sister knows what that means to lycans, because she inclines her head slightly in apology.

Immy finally makes it into the plane with Draven hot on

her heels. I have no idea what took the two of them so long, but I nod to him, and he raises a brow back. He tilts his head incrementally in the direction of the red-haired vampire before shaking his head.

The meaning is clear. He doesn't trust her.

He's not the only one. Then again, I don't exactly trust him or Morwen either.

Cain sent all of them on this mission. Odds are, at least one of them will betray us.

I want to know Eve's opinion. What does she make of her sisters? What about Draven? Fuck, at this point, I don't think I'd blame her if she didn't trust any of us.

"If we get found out, you can just sire a whole army of ghoul-vampire hybrids to get us out of trouble," Silas quips, pressing a soft kiss to Eve's lips. "Don't panic."

I raise a brow at him, and Gideon does the same. Both of us silently scolding him for letting slip pack secrets in front of people whose allegiances remain suspect. To his credit, the younger beta blushes and bites his lip, baring his neck in quiet apology.

Immy and Morwen don't notice the exchange. They're too busy whirling to face their sister, and I see the moment the truth dawns on them both.

"Frost was never special," Immy breathes. "It was your blood all along."

Morwen barks out a laugh. "God, that's ironic as fuck. Do you know how many ghouls he's had me capture trying to create more of Frost? All along he had the answer to the problem buried under lock and key? Typical."

Eve shrugs off the topic and is saved from confirming anything by Vane pulling the door shut, sealing us in with a loud bang that echoes through the cabin. Gideon gives the lot of them one last evaluating look before disappearing back into the cockpit, seconds later, the engines whirr to life beneath us before I clear my throat.

"We're swapping planes in about an hour," I mutter. "Don't get too comfortable. Eve, there's a change of clothes for you in the bedroom at the back."

"I can show you," Finn says, tugging her from Silas's arms and pulling her towards the door.

"Clothes only," I grumble. "One hour, remember?"

Finn's smirk is unrepentant. "Two people can do a lot in one hour. Or maybe it's been so long that you've forgotten?"

The door shuts behind them with a quiet snick, and I grind my teeth, counting the seconds that she's out of my sight. Part of me is waiting for the scent of her arousal to drift under the door, but Finn must sense today isn't the day to test my patience, because it doesn't happen.

Gideon tosses Draven a familiar set of keys. "Your bike is in storage," he mutters.

Draven's hands fist on the keys, going white-knuckled, and I brace myself for violence.

No one touches his bike except him... and apparently Eve.

"Not a scratch?" he checks, stiffly.

"I checked myself," Gideon confirms.

Draven visibly collects himself, and nods. "Thank you."

I blink in surprise... Not that Gideon took care of his bike —the other alpha is always making sure that none of us lose the few possessions we care about—but that Draven is just going to let this go.

Evidently, none of the others can believe it either. Silas is too shocked to come up with a way to tease the vampire, which must be a new record.

Fortunately, Eve and Finn choose that moment to return, practically cuddling as they walk like they can't bear to be apart.

She used to hug me like that.

Fuck.

Mia seizes on the opportunity.

"You know, your profile picture makes you look a lot more muscular," she says to the omega.

It takes me a second to realise what the fuck she's going on about, and then it clicks. Finn joined the pack after Mia was sent to 'safety' by her brothers. The two of them have been working together online for decades with a kind of quiet rivalry, but they've never met in real life.

Eve looks ready to defend Finn, but he's got this. "Can you really talk?" he asks, smirking. "Yours has cat ears."

"Now that we're all here," Gideon begins, cutting off their banter.

His bored monotone shocks the shit out of me. I've been so focused on Eve that I didn't even see him open the cockpit door.

Eve's eyes widen. "Shouldn't you be... flying the plane?"

The other alpha doesn't even blink. "Pilots aren't even necessary for takeoff and landing these days. More importantly, I need our heading."

He turns to Morwen who in turn swivels to look at Eve.

"Egypt," they say in unison.

Draven's jaw clenches, and I grimace.

Yeah, one of the sunniest countries in the world would be a bit of a problem for him, given his relative youth. That could work out in our favour if he turns out to be working against us.

Fortunately, I don't have the same problem, and neither does Vane. The two of us are lucky enough to be part of the fifty percent of hybrid immortals who gained the strengths of both races, rather than their weaknesses, so the sun doesn't affect us.

"Your reasoning?" Gideon demands.

"It has the lowest vampire population in the world," Eve begins. "And I have the vaguest memory of him liking the country—but I might be imagining that…"

"You don't think that would be a bit obvious?" Silas asks the question we're all thinking. "Surely that's the first place Cain would look?"

This time Morwen answers. "You have no idea what the man was like. You'd meet him and then ten minutes later forget everything you'd talked about. If a month or two passed without him being mentioned, you'd forget he even visited. He was just that… forgettable."

"Not to mention we all thought he was dead," Immy adds.

Eve sighs, rubbing her temples in frustration. "It took me days to remember just that much of the conversation."

"Surely Cain wouldn't have—"

"Do you honestly think our sire cares that much about any of his children?" Immy raises a single, haughty brow. "He didn't even bother choosing us himself. He made his sons go out and find the girls they thought were special enough to warrant his attention."

"His one condition was that we weren't old enough to remember too much of our lives before." Eve's hand tightens on Finn's as he leads her into a seat beside me and takes the spot on her other side.

I could kiss the omega right now.

Having her within arm's reach is just too much temptation. I can't help the way my hand sneaks out to stroke the side of her thigh.

Contact. Connection. Rightness.

Something has changed. Can she feel the way the thrall bond shifts slightly? I study her face, inhaling, searching for some clue that she feels it too.

Her hand comes up to rub at her breastbone, and I can barely contain the grin which threatens to surface.

Whatever happened when she was separated from us, the thrall bond is finally growing. Settling back into that space in my soul that belongs to her.

Thank God.

Gideon, apparently oblivious to the monumental change between us, carries on planning like the sensible alpha that he is. "When we land in Cairo, will you be able to—"

"Not Cairo," Eve interrupts. "Too public. Cain's allies will be concentrated there and we'll be noticed. We need to land in a smaller city. One that's out of the way."

Gideon nods. "I can do that."

"By the sea," Eve adds. "That's where I would go. It has the best options for escape."

The alpha runs an exasperated hand through his hair. "You realise Egypt is a massive country which borders two seas and two gulfs?"

Morwen levels an unimpressed look at him, taking her own seat at the back of the plane. "Just get us within a few hundred miles and my gift will kick in. Don't wake me up until we're over the border."

My co-alpha gives me an unimpressed look. Discontent rolls off him in waves, and I imagine this must be his own special version of Hell.

Gideon likes a well-structured, entirely thought-out plan. Flying to somewhere 'near the sea' and waiting for a supernatural gift to 'kick in' is completely the opposite of how this would be going if he had his way.

Lifting one shoulder in a shrug that translates roughly to 'what can we do?' doesn't seem to be the kind of support he was looking for.

Ah well, he needs to loosen up. Maybe this will be good for him.

"I'd prefer a more concrete plan than flying around until your gift kicks in," he grinds out.

Morwen just grins, pulling Mia against her side. "Tough shit."

It might be a side effect of living with lycans for too long, but I could swear she's holding eye contact deliberately, like she's *trying* to incite an alpha challenge.

It's Mia who surprises us all when she presses a kiss to the vampire's jaw. "Try not to piss off my old alpha too much, babe."

Morwen doesn't look surprised at all.

"Wait." Silas looks between the two of them. "You *told* her?"

Oh, he's in for it. I can see his sister working herself up to unleash the full force of a Mia Meltdown. I settle back in my chair, content to watch this one play out. Without thinking, my arm falls around Eve's shoulders, pulling her back against me.

I freeze when I realise what I've done, only to relax as she sinks into my embrace.

God, I might be dreaming, but don't let me wake up.

"I don't hide shit from my girlfriend," Mia retorts. "I suppose honesty might be a bit difficult for you two to understand, seeing as you abandoned your youngest sister in Europe without giving her the slightest idea of what you were doing beyond 'it's dangerous.'"

Neither brother looks guilty. If anything, they look more incensed than they did before.

"Hang on," Eve murmurs quietly. "They're related?"

"That's Mia," I whisper back. "Silas and Vane's younger sister."

We're quiet, but not quiet enough, because Mia rounds on me next. "You forgot to add best hacker in the entire rebellion and all around badass."

I hold a hand up in surrender. "I apologise. This is Mia,

the best"—Finn shoots me a raised eyebrow, and I groan—"Joint best," I amend. "Hacker in the rebellion."

"I'm better," Finn whispers to Eve.

"I got under your firewall!"

"That was one time!"

"It was lazy coding."

"Is she related to Finn as well?" Eve asks, confused.

"No. But she's fulfilling the role of the annoying younger sibling I never had quite spectacularly," Finn grouses.

The bickering might have continued, if not for Vane finally taking the time to say something. "We left you in Paris. Where it was *safe*. Why did you think that joining the rebellion and taking an undercover mission in the heart of the Court was a good idea?"

"Because you weren't the only ones who lost a sister—"

Vane's calm tone doesn't change as he cuts her off. "No. I want to hear the logical path your mind took when you decided to disregard our plans for you to live a safe and happy life with the Paris Pack. A plan which took a lot of sacrifices on our part."

Mia doesn't miss a beat. She's accustomed to dealing with her older brother, even though it's been decades since they last saw one another. "I had skills, which I knew would help."

"Finn has the same skills. So do plenty of others."

"You want me to say it was a revenge-motivated decision. Or one aimed at hurting you because I felt like you abandoned me," Mia observes.

God, it's freaky when they argue like this. I'd forgotten…

Silas and Mia can go toe to toe with their fiery tempers, but Vane was a teacher with a degree in psychology before their pack was torn apart by Gideon's father. He dealt with teenagers all the time. One of his superpowers is arguing so calmly and reasonably that by the end of the discussion you've agreed to your punishment without ever knowing why you were arguing with him in the first place.

"I want to know if you agree with that assessment of the situation."

"I don't."

"Then give me your justification."

"Because I wanted to help. If I just lived a happy life in Paris, while you died, I would've hated myself. And I *wasn't* happy there. You can't just bribe a pack and expect them to like your sister! It doesn't work like that. Once it was clear I wasn't going to be an omega, they didn't give three shits about me."

Vane leans back in his seat, raising a single brow. "So your motivation was purely to leave that pack and help? Why not join another pack and help by maintaining safe houses, or another support role? Why undercover?"

"That was my idea," Gideon admits, drawing the ire of both brothers onto himself without flinching. "There was a limited opening where I thought we could get someone in the Compound. Your sister was the perfect operative."

"How many years?" Silas growls. "How many years have you been chained up for the full moon without a pack, Mia? You should've been running free in a forest." He tugs at a handful of his hair. "Jesus, I thought you might have settled down."

"Oh, I have." Mia grins back at Morwen. "We're quite happy, thank you."

"I'm afraid you really don't make the best spy," Morwen mutters. "You're lucky you're cute or I might've turned you over."

Mia snorts. "Then who would have solved all your technical hitches?"

"You were *causing* my technical hitches, brat. Remember

that time you programmed my tablet to blast sex moans every time I tried to call anyone?"

I don't think Silas or Vane know what to make of that. The idea of Mia being an operative is beyond them, but the thought of her having a blatantly sexual relationship with one of the most infamously crazed vampires in the world might just have broken their minds.

"And you're welcome, by the way," their sister continues. "I single-handedly convinced the world's greatest tracker to continuously 'lose' the most infamous ghoul multiple times over."

"Whatever happened, Mia is here now," Eve interrupts the conversation before it can get any further derailed. "And we're going to need all the help we can get if we're going to kill Cain."

"And Samuel magically has a way to do that?" Immy asks, speaking for the first time. "Are you sure?"

The youngest sister has taken the seat behind us at the back of the plane. Her hands are worrying the fabric of the dress she's wearing as she squirms under all of our attention.

"It's the only lead we have," Silas admits. "If he doesn't, then you're all welcome to join us on the run for the rest of our lives, however short that may be."

CHAPTER TEN

EVELYN

EVEN WITH ALL OF THE WONDERS OF MODERN TECHNOLOGY, the flight from New York to Egypt is long. We're only two hours in and I'm already fed up with sitting around. I have too much energy and I have to *do* something. So, to occupy myself, I start investigating the cabins of our latest jet.

After abandoning Cain's plane in an airfield in Maine, Frost led us onto this opulent aircraft. He did it with such a cocky grin on his face, that I have to wonder if he owns it or if he stole it.

Given the coolers of champagne-flavoured synth blood and the four lavishly decorated double bedrooms, I suspect it's the latter.

All of my snooping can't stop the thoughts going round in a loop in my head.

We're actively rebelling. Going against my sire. As much as *I* orchestrated this, it doesn't stop my gut from churning or my chest from going tight every time I imagine him finding us.

Finn reassured me that this plane isn't bugged, and I have things to discuss with him and the rest of my thralls, but none of us want to do that with my sisters in earshot. To be honest, I'm not sure the pack wants to confide in me. The level of trust between us is ambiguous at best, and I broke whatever fragile faith we had in each other when I decided to save Frost's life by betraying them.

God, I am not looking forward to the tough talks we're going to have in the next few days.

Do they even still want me? I spent all of our time apart just trying to survive, and there's no guarantee that their feelings haven't changed.

Finn was happy enough to see me, and his thrall bond proves that he at least still wants me around. None of the others have outright said anything, but—

The door snicks open behind me, and I whirl on the spot. The rest of the pack files into the bedroom, crowding the small cabin with their large bodies. My dread ratchets up a level as Gideon shuts the door behind them and locks it before leaning back against it.

No escape.

Apparently, those conversations are happening now, whether I want them to or not.

"Is this room secure?" I ask, tilting my head in the direction of the front of the plane, where my sisters are still sitting.

"I have signal jammers all over this jet and the walls are scream-proof," Finley quips, moving past Silas—who's settled on the corner of the bed—to drag me in for a hug. "Want to test it out?"

"Finn," Vane scolds. The largest member of the pack is leaning against the cabinet and Draven has taken the corner beside him, which is the spot with the best view of the door.

My vampire's eyes meet mine for a second. The ice in his

expression should put my guard up, but I'm getting better at reading him now. The quirk of his left brow is a question—a silent demand after my welfare, which I acknowledge with a nod—and the stern cast of his lips is tipped slightly up, letting me know this isn't something to worry about.

I take in all of that just as Gideon says, "We're here to get everyone on the same page. Not seduce her."

Frost looks almost apologetic as he shrugs. "He's right. All we got from you and D was that we had to have the planes ready."

"How do we know we can trust you?" Gideon demands of my vampire thrall. "Finley can vouch for Evie because he can feel her…"

"And I can vouch for him because I can feel him," I interrupt. "While we were stuck in Court, I formed the thrall bond. Draven wants Cain dead as much as I do."

There. I've admitted I want my sire dead.

A tremor runs through my frame, and Finn strokes my back to soothe it away.

"You're safe. You're with us," he whispers.

Nodding, I take a deep breath before I continue, stepping back so I can judge all of their expressions. "I trust Draven." I pause, then add, "I trust all of you. If I'm going to die, I want to die free."

"What about your sisters?" Vane asks. "Morwenna is cosying up to Mia…"

Ah, so that's what's nettling him.

Finn rolls his eyes. "Ignore him. It was always going to be this way as soon as Mia started dating. She has the big beta brothers from hell. It's why she acts out so much."

Understandable. Given the way Silas and Vane were both eyeing Morwen, I'd probably find them overbearing too. My sister is not an easy person to love, but Mia is a grown adult and able to make her own choices.

"Morwen didn't kill Samuel when she was ordered to. Her neck is on the line if she betrays us—although that's no guarantee. Immy…"

"Immy what?" Frost coaxes. "You two used to be close, but she's not acting anything like you were when you came out of a coffin. No bloodlust, no struggle for control."

"She said that Cain released her early and unleashed her on the villagers, to punish them. Her excuse for not coming to save me herself was that she thought she could make our sire love her."

Conveniently, no one can confirm her story, because Cain kept her return a secret from everyone—even my sisters.

"And you believe her?" Gideon drawls.

He thinks I'm an idiot.

"She also blamed Draven for ratting us out all those years ago." I turn to him, reaching for our bond to confirm what I already know.

His outrage hits hard and fast, followed by icy cold determination. "She threw me under the bus to gain your trust."

"It was a plausible story."

"You know I didn't," he growls, pushing away from the corner and pacing towards me. "I was loyal to Frost."

I nod. "I know that now—thanks to the bond—but at the time, it was a toss up."

"So she's lying," Silas growls. "Why haven't you killed her?"

"Have you ever heard of keeping your enemies close?" I smirk. "Immy can go one of three ways: either she lied to try to earn my forgiveness, because she truly does miss our friendship and she'll be as loyal as the rest of us. Or she'll report everything back to Cain like a faithful servant the second she has a chance. If that happens, we can use her to make sure he only hears what we want him to hear before despatching her. She's never been a gifted warrior. Any of us could take her out."

"And the third option?" Frost demands.

"We may be able to sway her to our side." It will take work, but they'd won me over. My softhearted sister shouldn't be too much trouble. "Until I know which way she's going to go, I want to keep her close."

The room lapses into silence, and I can practically feel their unease at the idea of letting Immy—who is most likely a spy—stay so close to us. No doubt, if it was up to them, they'd burst into the next room and rip her head from her shoulders.

Perhaps it's foolish, but I'm not ready to give up on her just yet.

There's a chance I might still come out of this with my sister by my side. I'm going to take it, *but* I plan to be cautious about it.

"What on earth did you say to Cain to get him to let you go?" Silas asks, breaking the silence. "We were sure we were going to have to break you both out. And why is our sister mixed up in this?"

Both he and Vane are tense. How much of that is because of me, and how much of it is due to Mia?

"Mia came because she's with Morwen and she's not a child to be left behind. As for what I said to Cain… I told him the truth." I grimace at their matching expressions of disbelief. "Not all of it, obviously. Just enough. He already suspected you were searching for a way to kill him. I simply laid the bait, by telling him that Samuel sired a vampire."

"Shit." Gideon's head falls back against the door. "So you gave away our *one* lead."

"I gave him a modified version of the truth. Besides, his reaction told me what I wanted to know."

Frost at least, seems willing to hear me out. "Which was?"

"He was afraid." I stare each of them in the eye. "Whatever Samuel knows, it's enough to scare my sire. Fear isn't something Cain is used to feeling, and that will only make him more dangerous."

Finn pulls me back to his arms and squeezes me in a reassuringly tight hug. I find myself leaning into his touch without meaning to.

"I really did miss you," I whisper against his chest.

A feather-light kiss brushes over the top of my head. "We missed you too, sweetheart."

"All of us," Silas butts in, before quirking a brow at Draven, who scoffs. "Eh, kinda missed your silent brooding too, I guess."

"Fuck off."

"So eloquent. Isn't it nearly your bedtime?"

Draven's brows crease into a dark frown. "Mess with my sleep again, lycan. I dare you. I learned a few more tricks in Cain's dungeon. Have you ever been cut open, had your organs doused in gasoline and set alight while they're still inside of you?"

In my chest, his thrall bond is just as icy as before. Completely unaffected in a way that no one should ever be when they're talking about such trauma. The robotic-ness of it disturbs me enough that my hand clenches on Finn's arm for a second.

"We're not there anymore," I say, firmly, leaving Finn's embrace to cross to Draven instead. "It will never happen again."

As I face him, he doesn't reach out to hug me like any of my other men would. The distance between us is only inches, but it might as well be miles.

What happened to make him like this? I could pry using our bond, but I'm not about to do that without his permission.

The emotional connection required to complete a thrall bond is different for each vampire, but it isn't difficult to figure out that for me, it's linked to trust. I refuse to violate Draven's... especially since I suspect he doesn't give it lightly.

"The instant Cain gets anywhere near this, we leave," Vane insists. "I don't care if it means giving up Samuel. Finn and Mia are involved now." His eyes linger on me like he thought about saying my name, but then thought better of it. "The safety of the pack is more important than anything else."

"Both Mia and I will gut you if you give up on this and use us as an excuse," Finn argues. "We're adults. We chose to be here, and we'll deal with whatever if it means taking down that asshole. If you send either one of us away, we'll just give your equipment so many viruses you have to bring us back."

"No one is sending anyone away." Frost runs his hand through his hair and shrugs at Gideon's sharp look. "We'd be lost without Finn, and he's been training with me for years. He's not as defenceless as you think."

Finn glows under the praise, but Gideon's frown only grows deeper. "We'll discuss that later," he mutters, causing Finn's smile to sink.

Asshole.

"We're pack," Silas agrees, and Gideon shoots him a quelling glare.

But eventually, even the alpha has to sigh in defeat. "Of course we are. I just hate the idea of Finn getting hurt." He glances away as he says it, so he misses the way his omega's face softens in response.

I back away, unsure where I'm going but unwilling to interrupt such a private moment. Vane surprises me by reaching across the space between us and freeing my lower lip from where I've begun worrying beneath my fangs without even realising.

"You're one of us too," he murmurs to me. "So wipe that doubt off your face."

I glance at Gideon, but the beta turns my face away from the alpha using his gentle grip on my chin.

"Who do you think decides on pack membership, princess?"

I shrug, looking back at Gideon.

Vane snorts. "It's not the alpha—"

"Because they'd do an awful job," Finn finishes, and I turn towards him, incredulous. "Gid would never let any outsiders in if it was up to him."

"It's you?" My brows disappear into my hairline.

"The omega is the heart of the pack," Silas explains. "They get the final say, because their nature won't abandon those they've formed a connection with."

"We get clingier than a bad ex," Finn jokes, but there's an undercurrent of vulnerability there. One I sense he's trying desperately to hide.

"You've bonded Finn." Vane ignores both of them. "That means you're here to stay. No alpha would get in the way of that."

"Although the betas certainly plan to take advantage," Silas pipes up.

I glance at him, and then at Vane, expecting the older brother to say something.

Only when I meet his gaze again, his eyes are *smouldering*. There's a scorching heat lurking beneath those hazel brown eyes that makes my pussy clench and my chest tighten in anticipation.

For a second, I feel more like prey than I ever have.

Whatever questions I had about Vane's interest are answered by that one look.

He wants me.

"But I betrayed the pack," I whisper. "At the gala."

"You didn't betray them any more than I did," Draven grumbles. "We just went off script a bit."

"Yes, care to explain *that*?" Gideon asks. "We had a plan, and not once do I recall us discussing Frost being handed over."

There's a subtle menace in his voice, and I can practically hear Draven's teeth grinding together in answer.

"Tell them what you told me," I whisper. "Please?"

Draven's shoulders inch down slightly, just enough to let me know the danger has passed.

"He thought I was still his sleeper agent, so I was briefed on the soldiers who were hidden amongst the guests," he mutters. "Cain was planning on Evie betraying him. She would've died, along with Frost, and the rest of you probably would've followed soon after."

Apparently that's enough for the alpha who leans back against the door once more, mollified.

"No hard feelings," Frost replies. "Although, you could've broken me out *before* they started on the torture."

"I'll take that into account next time," Draven says, dryly.

"There won't be a next time, because next time the whole team is going to know what's going on," Gideon growls, looking between Draven and me. "The two of you have spent a large part of your lives operating alone, I get that. But if we're doing this, there are no more lone wolf moments. You're committed to the pack, and that means making decisions as a pack."

Frost rolls his eyes and nods. "He's right. No more solo missions. I know vampires prefer working alone, but it's too dangerous."

"Consider me reformed," Draven drawls. "As it is, I don't think Cain trusts me enough to confide in me like that again. I triggered his suspicions when I drugged your guards' coffee."

They all turn to me, and I want to wilt under the laser-like focus of their attention. Instead, I draw myself up to my full height and take a deep, steadying breath.

"I'm all in." They all let out a collective sigh, but I'm not done yet. "For everything. I want my sire dead, and I want to be a part of the pack. I'm exhausted, and I can't continue living in a world where I can't trust anyone." My breath hitches in my throat as I wonder how much to say. *Fuck it. I did say I was all in.* "I want the full thrall bonds with all of you."

My attention falls to the two alphas. Gideon's expression has closed down, becoming an impassive mask, while Frost is staring at me with such heartbreaking hope that I have to look away.

"If… if you don't want that," I continue. "Then let me just break them. It'll hurt, but… I don't want to live with the uncertainty anymore."

There. I've said it. My cards are all out in the open. I stare at Gideon, waiting for him to take that final step.

At the very beginning, he said he wasn't going to complete our bond. There's no way the small amount of time we've spent together has been enough to change his mind.

Around me, the rest of the pack hisses their denial. Finn hugs me even tighter, and Draven's chill damn near locks down our bond, daring me to try and sever it.

Vane and Silas both growl, "Fuck no."

At the same time Frost vows, "Never again."

But for all their reassurance, my muscles wind tighter and tighter with each passing sentence as I brace for the words I know are coming and the pain which will follow.

Just say it. Get it over with.

Why is he dragging this out?

My eyelids have scrunched shut, and my ears are filled with white noise, so I barely hear the snap of the lock disengaging followed by the hiss of the door whirring open.

When I dare to look again, he's gone.

My mouth falls open, and Finn laughs as he extracts himself from our hug at last.

"He might act like a bastard, but there's a lot more to Gid underneath his skin," the omega whispers in my ear. "Give him time, and he might surprise you. He shoulders a lot of things he shouldn't and takes failure hard, but he's a good alpha. He just... has a lot on his plate right now."

There's a wistful note to his voice, one that nags at my intuition. I know Finn said Gideon was one of his lovers, but I've rarely seen the alpha act affectionately towards the omega.

No more so than any of the rest of the pack, at least.

Inside me, our Finn feels almost... sad?

What's going on there? Is it even any of my business?

I look at Finn, catching my own reflection in his round glasses for a second before he lowers his head and touches his forehead to mine in a gesture of reassurance.

Yes, I decide. *If something or someone is hurting this wonderful man—especially if it's one of my other thralls—then it's definitely my business.*

CHAPTER ELEVEN

EVELYN

"Evie," Finn calls, distracting me from the shower I've been frowning at in confusion for the last five minutes —*where does the water go? Does it just fall on the heads of some unfortunate soul below?* "Come and sit down before we hit some turbulence."

Abandoning the confusing issue of plumbing at thirty-one-thousand feet for another day, I abandon the bedroom and work my way back through the elaborate dining room and into the spacious seating area. Finn and Silas are next to one another, snuggling on one of the two love seats while Mia and Morwen have claimed the other, and are ignoring the narrow glances the two brothers are shooting at them.

Immy and Gideon are taking up the two armchairs in opposite corners, which would've been my first choice for where to sit. Gideon has his head bowed over his tablet, hard at work as normal. Immy is fast asleep with her head tilted back and a tiny dribble of drool running down the side of her face.

Draven is the only one missing, thanks to the sun blinking through the tiny windows on either side of us.

Vane and Frost are on either side of the only free spot, and the larger beta tilts his head to indicate I should sit there. But Finn beckons me over before I make it to them. He's holding my tablet, with a grin on his face.

"Here, I've got something to distract you," he promises, a secret smile playing at the corner of his lips. "Ever listened to an audiobook before?"

I frown at him, and evidently that gives him his answer because he shoves the glass rectangle at me along with my own headphones.

"Just press play," he instructs.

I don't trust the look he's giving me, but I accept both things from him and make my way over to the free space. Vane snorts as I perch on the edge of the seat, unsure of my welcome, and drags me against his side, earning him a grumpy look from Frost.

My legs curl up automatically, and the ghoul makes up for the lack of contact by dragging my feet into his lap and starting the task of unlacing my boots.

"Missed you, Princess," Vane mutters, stealing my attention back.

The murmur is quiet, near whisper-soft, but it draws a snort from Mia.

He tosses a glare back at her. "Shut it, squirt."

"Bossy. Have you told her your plan to take over her life yet? When are you going to drop her off in a random capital with a fake ID in the name of safety?"

Vane growls something under his breath which sounds disconcertingly like 'as soon as possible', but Mia isn't done.

"Just so you know, Evie, Gideon might be the most openly control-freak of the pack, but Vane is the same. He's just sneakier at it."

I lift my head and look back over my shoulder at her. "I'll keep that in mind."

"Mia, stop winding her up," Vane grunts, tugging me back until I'm lying on his lap. "And you, try to get some rest."

He may be just as bossy as Mia accuses him of being, but oddly I don't mind. It's nice to have someone who's genuinely concerned for my well being. In a way, his gruffness is almost charming.

Frost finally removes both of my boots and tugs away my socks as I slip the earbuds into my ears. Who knows, perhaps this audiobook—whatever it is—will help me relax enough to actually sleep.

Hitting the play button, I shimmy into a more comfortable position against Vane's chest and my eyes just happen to meet Finn's across the walkway.

The omega is grinning like the cat who got the cream.

When the first notes of his voice, husky and deep with intimacy, fills my ears, I realise why.

"Don't move." The order which echoes from the earbuds is soft but sharp, and I stiffen without meaning to. *"This is our little secret, okay?"* I meet Finn's stare again, just as his voice says, *"Good girl. Now, Silas and I came up with something to get revenge on you for making us worry so much."*

In the background, the unmistakably sexual sound of flesh stroking flesh greets my ears. Trying to keep a straight face as I glance around wildly is impossible. Immy is still asleep, Morwen and Mia are behind me, and none of my other men seem to know what's going on.

"Now, when Gideon asks why I requisitioned such a sensitive microphone." I can hear the grin in Finn's voice. *"I'm going to tell him, and if I'm lucky, he'll spank me for it. Until then, you can hear every"*—groan—*"slurping second, as Silas sucks me off."*

My cheeks must be burning. Is my breathing going to give me away?

"Our beta has graciously allowed me to be in charge—"

The stroking sound stops, and Silas growls. *"This one time only."*

Finn ignores him. *"Because we both know I have the best voice."*

"Don't push it, pretty omega."

Frost's thumbs sink into my insole, and I jump a mile into the air.

A foot rub? *Now?* With the constant, rhythmic sound of Silas pleasuring the pack omega ringing in my ears?

I squeeze my thighs together, caught between the urge to keep listening, and the urge to throw the earbuds across the room to prevent getting caught.

"You're so tense," Frost murmurs.

Vane makes a noise of agreement. His hands find my shoulders and his thumbs start rubbing soothing lines down both sides of my neck.

At the same time, the Finn in my ears growls. *"Get on the fucking floor, right now. On your knees for me, by my chair. That's it."* The pair of them are grinning at me, but I can barely make eye contact. *"If you were here, Evie, would you let me control things? I don't think you would, but a man can dream. Good boy, lick it. Fuck."* His words cut off as he grunts. *"Lick the slit, that's it. You remember what my cock looks like, don't you, Evie?"* He pants, breath coming harder and faster in response to whatever Silas is doing. *"You remember what it was like when you sucked me off? Remember how long it is? How you screamed when you took me all the way. I'm going to dream of that night forever. Ugnh, fuck!"*

A wet, slurping noise adds to the constant stroking of flesh on flesh, and Finn lets out a moan. *"Silas is so good at sucking me, but even he can't get to the base. Remember how it felt when I fucked up into your wet little cunt? How you fucking squeezed me? All I wanted was to hit that perfect little g-spot, and the moans you made when I did?"*

He cuts off as Silas gags in the background, then whines as the rhythm is broken. Beneath my jumper, my nipples harden, and Frost hits a spot on my sole that makes me jerk. A silent second passes, before the sound resumes.

"You were dripping for us," the omega continues raggedly. *"So fucking wet, and your taste—God, your taste. Just thinking about it."* He curses, and I realise Silas's pace has increased. *"Ever since then I've been thinking about how I could make you come over and over again, just keep eating you out until you flip us, force me down—"*

Frost's hands on my feet freeze, and I look up, cheeks burning as he stares at me, cocking his head.

"—and sink down on my cock. Fuck." He groans. *"Silas, ease off, we don't want this to finish too soon, and your goddamn mouth..."*

Frost's nostrils flare, his eyes fixating on the spot where my thighs are clenched together. Silas shifts on the seat opposite, and the ghoul's eyes flick to him before tracing over my breasts and back to my face in silent question.

In the recording, Finn lets out a strangled curse, followed by a low moan and a whimpered. *"No, don't you* dare *stop."*

"Leave her to enjoy her book," The Silas across from me suggests, his voice muted by the slapping, slurping noises still coming through my earbuds. "Finn went to great lengths to find one long enough to last the entire trip."

The entire trip? Oh Lord, I won't survive.

Vane's thumbs stop moving, and I wonder if he's caught something in Silas's tone that has given the game away. They're brothers, after all.

"You should see this," Finn moans, stealing my attention back to the recording. *"Silas looks so hot trying to take me all the way down his throat. One day, I want both of you on the ground,*

on your fucking knees sucking me. Oh God, just like that. A boy can dream. It's been a long month, and I've come up with some good fantasies. Maybe you and I can get together and use Silas's rope skills against him. Oh, fuck. No, I didn't mean it. I swear."

Frost's hands move from my feet to my lower calves, massaging my ankles, moving unmistakably north. He's going slow, giving me time to pull away, but I'm too wound up to object. My panties are soaked through just from the mental stimulation alone.

"That's it," Silas growls, and the sound of fabric ripping and tearing fills my ears. *"You're not tying me up. Bad omega. I give you the reins one time, and you start getting silly ideas."* A sharp smack echoes through my ears, and my pussy clenches. Hard. *"You've had your fun. So now you can use that sexy voice of yours to describe to Evie exactly what I'm doing to you."*

Finn moans as another sharp slap rings in my ears. I almost jump out of the seat, and I glance around guiltily to see if anyone noticed.

I've been so distracted that I didn't even notice my sisters and Mia turning in for the night. Now, the only people in the cabin are my thralls.

"Tell her," Silas growls, as another slap echoes in my ears.

There's another rip, and the wet sound of lube being squeezed from a bottle drowns out their panting for a second.

"He's got a thumb playing with my ass," Finn gasps. *"God, he won't put it in. Fuck. Now he's grabbed my dick with the other hand and he's squeezing, damnnnn."*

"Tell her how much you wish it was her cunt you were fucking, rather than my hand."

"God, I want that so much." Finn is panting heavily now, the noise only interspersed with another slap.

"Keep talking," Silas orders.

"He's got a finger in my ass. Fuck, he's playing with my prostate."

Frost's hands are almost at my crotch now, his long fingers stroking my inner thighs. My eyes drop closed just as Finn whimpers in my ears.

"Two fingers. God it burns."

"You love it," Silas purrs. *"You're making a mess of my hand. Don't you dare come before I'm inside you."*

The noises that fill my ears are so intensely erotic. Words are lost in favour of harsh, heavy breathing and husky moans that caress my eardrums. My core aches with every single one of Finn whimpers.

"You should see him taking my cock," Silas groans, like he's just remembered he's being recorded. *"He's writhing on it. I bet he's imagining you're beneath him so I can fuck both of you at once. Shit. That's hot. Would you want that, Evie? Finn does. He's leaking so much precum that my hand is drenched. I'm going to make him lick it clean when we're done here."* He lets out a soft growl. *"I'm not going to last. Damn. Just thinking of how your tits will bounce underneath us is so good."*

My breasts are already tight, nerves primed from so much dirty talk. So when an arm brushes over them, I arch on the seat, biting hard at my lip to restrain the tiny mewl which threatens to escape.

God. I need something. Some real contact. Even Frost has stopped at the top of my thighs, just rubbing them softly.

Vane looks down at me with an innocent expression, but there's wickedness dancing in his eyes as that arm bands around my chest, pinning my body to his. Now that he's stolen my focus from the slapping and grunting in my ears, I can feel his hardness pressed up against my back.

They all know.

Finn and Silas's matching groans of completion ring

through my ears just as a hand grabs my waistband and tugs, pulling the seam of my jeans hard against my clit.

Detonation.

Stars fly behind my eyes, and I tumble over the edge of rapture. Pleasure makes my toes curl, my muscles clenching and then releasing as my pussy clenches on nothingness. When my eyes fly open, snapping straight to Finn and Silas on the opposite sofa, I can't even say anything.

Parting my lips doesn't work, and all I end up doing is licking them to moisten them, drawing matching masculine groans from all around me.

Frost's touches retreat back to my calves, massaging out the tension, as my body shivers on Vane's lap.

It's only when my head lolls back that I catch sight of Gideon.

The alpha is looking at me over the top of his tablet. Branding me with his stare alone. For one second before he blinks it away, I see the vast hunger of the beast beneath the man's skin, and it almost tips me over again.

When he breaks that connection, it's like my senses all return in a rush. I almost fall from the sofa in my haste to put distance between myself and what's just happened. Chucking the ear buds at Finn, I glower at both of them.

"Nice book?" Finn asks, smirking.

"Looks like she definitely enjoyed it… for the plot," Silas adds.

CHAPTER TWELVE

GIDEON

THE SOUK IS JUST AS LIVELY AT NIGHT AS IT IS DURING THE DAY, and dodging the dozens of humans trying to sell me something is becoming almost as aggravating as our lack of progress. We've been here for three days, trusting in Morwenna's magical ability to track down Samuel. She got us to this tourist trap on the edge of the Red Sea, and beyond that... nowhere.

If anything, she and Mia are treating this more like a honeymoon than a serious mission. The two females are almost as vexing as Evelyn, and *that* should be illegal.

I curse them both for the hundredth time as Vane and I canvas the tight alleys crammed with street sellers *again*. Searching for anything which might give away the location of an ancient first-generation vampire who apparently has a talent for being invisible.

"You're in a worse mood than usual," Vane comments.

Grunting in return—because he isn't helping matters—I turn yet another corner and head into the souk, ignoring the beautiful geometric architecture and arching corridors in my increasingly futile patrol.

"Tonight is going to be another bust." Why is my beta suddenly so chatty? And on the day when I'm in the worst mood for it. "Why not go back to the resort with the others? Relax with the pack. Finn misses you, you know."

Playing the omega card? Low blow, Vane. Low, fucking blow.

"Finley is…"

Complicated.

Our relationship was already strained, but adding Evelyn to the mix has made everything infinitely more difficult.

Vane knows. He's a quiet bastard, but an observant one. "Want to talk about it?"

"What is there to talk about?"

Yes, I'm being obtuse, but I don't care.

We probably have more to discuss now than we have in years. For the first time in decades, our entire pack is together and free of Cain's surveillance. We're half a world away from his Court. In theory, I should be able to relax at least a little.

But alphas have one fatal flaw. Hyperfocus.

The innate need to keep going without ceasing until their pack is safe and provided for.

Instinct will keep driving me until we have Cain's head on a platter. Given half a chance, I'll forget about food and rest. Normally, I keep a strict schedule to ensure this doesn't happen. Routine and time spent with my omega are the keys to keeping myself functioning.

Unfortunately, I've spent the last few decades limiting contact with Finley. Partly for his own safety, but mostly because he deserves better than to be used as a coping mechanism. Now he's spending every second of his free time around Evelyn—like the rest of the pack—and with jet lag playing havoc on my routine, my carefully constructed world is starting to fall apart at the seams.

Vane knows. So he's just doing what he should, trying to remind me of the million and one other things that exist outside of our plan to kill Cain. The easiest way to do that is by forcing me to talk about them. I should really listen to him. Having betas—good betas—is the key to being a good alpha. Even my *father* understood that.

"You're not going to find anyone if you continue like this," he persists. "Frost and Evie are out searching, so are Draven and Silas. Finn's alone in the hotel with Imogen. We should go back."

Oh, he's good.

Playing the vulnerable omega is alone with the unknown vampire card.

I can't resist the snarl that breaks free of my throat.

"Fine," I grumble. "We'll head back."

This feels too much like giving up. We've only been out for three hours and my scathing inner voice is already on my case, criticising my lack of perseverance. It's a struggle not to just send Vane to check on Finley and continue on alone. Logically, I know that going lone wolf while Cain's forces could begin hunting for us at any moment isn't an option, but damn if it isn't tempting.

Spinning on my heel—and almost crashing into yet *another* human in the progress—I stalk back the way we came.

The resort we're staying at is a fairly nondescript, old-fashioned building. Definitely nothing like the sleek, greenery-covered glass and steel of Manhattan. The dodgy sand-coloured brickwork and loose shutters concerned me when Evie first insisted on this place—the last thing we need is Draven catching light because the sun-shutters don't work—but actually, her suggestion makes sense.

This is perhaps the least modern establishment I've visited in the last decade. There are no holographic displays, just hand painted signage, and no automatic blinds for vampiric guests. In fact, I'm pretty sure the receptionist hadn't seen an immortal in his life, given how long he stared at us. The best part—no surveillance in any of the rooms. Even the hallways lack cameras.

It's as close to invisible as we'll ever be. Fortunately, Mia and Finley are both happily hooked up to an old satellite our pack hijacked a long time ago, so the lack of connectivity isn't a problem.

I scale the stairs—which are on the outside of the building—until we reach the top-floor rooms we've rented for our purposes. They're small enough that we've had to pair up and rent out five, which means we essentially have the whole floor to ourselves. Finley is sharing with Silas at the far end of the corridor, and I frown as my eyes land on the room Evelyn insisted on sharing with Imogen.

I don't trust the youngest daughter of Cain.

Evelyn seems to have completely forgiven her. They've been practically glued together since we landed.

It's creepy, and if I weren't so preoccupied with Samuel, I would've confronted her about it. Her insistence that Draven is on her side, I can understand—I can practically see the thrall bond between them. Frost—who drew the short straw to become my roommate—promised he'd try to warn Evelyn about her while they were partnered up tonight.

It's the only reason I considered him being alone with her a good idea.

My co-alpha can't think logically around her. He's never been level-headed, but his impulsive tendencies get notably worse when she's near. He'll jump to do the slightest thing if he thinks it will endear him to her. I understand it, but still...

Love really does make fools out of the best of men.

I pass Imogen's closed door without pausing because the strength of her scent confirms she's still inside.

Without knocking, I barge through Finley's door, scanning the space for any hint that he's been distressed in the time we've been gone. Nothing. His room is just as messy as I've come to expect from him, and the man himself is sitting at his desk. He looks up from his desk as the caustic scent of nail polish assaults my nostrils.

"Can I help you?" he asks, quirking a brow.

"He's obsessing," Vane cuts in, before I can say anything. "He needs to rest."

I roll my eyes at my beta, because I knew what he was doing all along. "Honestly, are you my beta or my nanny?"

We have bigger things to deal with. Samuel needs to be found, and we aren't going to do that from bed.

Finley cuts off whatever acerbic retort is lingering on the tip of Vane's tongue as he carefully replaces the brush into the bright yellow he's been applying to his nails and wafts his hands in the air to dry them.

"I'm glad you're back," he admits. "I've missed you, Gid."

Biting the inside of my cheek—because he's tugging on my instincts in just the right way—I move closer to him. I'm dimly aware of Vane—the meddlesome git—creeping out of the door in the background.

Because I'm an idiot who can't think of anything better to say, I switch the subject.

"What are you painting this week," I ask, swallowing.

He brandishes his hand in front of me with a soft smile. "Emojis. So if I punch anyone I can do it with feeling."

A startled snort escapes as I shake my head. "If you're punching someone, I've fucked up."

"So I've been training with Frost for the last few decades to sit back and look pretty in front of a monitor? Good to know, but next time can you make it a bit clearer

117

when I'm wasting my time so I can skip leg day without guilt?"

God, his sarcasm is as adorable as ever. Before I even realise how close I've gotten, I'm directly behind him, lowering my face into his neck to scent him. Damn, I missed how he smells, there's an addictive sweetness to him that I've never found in any other man.

Damn Vane for setting me up like this.

The whine which escapes his throat is catnip to my instincts, and I almost purr.

"I shouldn't do this," I mutter, more to myself.

Finley's hands reach back and dig into my scalp, holding me there without care for the still drying polish. "You absolutely should."

"You're not safe." There are a thousand threats nipping at our heels.

"Samuel isn't going anywhere, and Vane's keeping watch. Let go. For me?"

Damn them, this shouldn't be working, but it is. I drag another lungful of his scent in and lick the place at the junction of his throat. This omega deserves better than a fractured pack. Better than me. Better than being dragged into conflict after conflict and used purely to manage his alpha's hyper-fixation.

He should be cosseted and protected by a healthy pack with an alpha who can guarantee his safety.

God knows, I never wanted to lead my own pack anyway. I disbanded my father's as soon as I was sworn in and thought I was done with the title. But Silas and Vane wouldn't let me go lone-wolf, and then Frost came, and Draven, and finally Finn.

Breathing him in, tasting the sweet salt of him under my tongue, I remember exactly why I can't give him up. By some miracle, he's mine. Selfish bastard that I am, I won't send him away.

"Please, Alpha. I need you." Finn's nails dig deeper into my scalp, and I nip lightly at him in response. "Fuck."

"This is going to be rough," I warn. "If that's not okay, now's the time—"

"I know. I want it." Finn is whining and panting beneath me. "Please."

"Take off your clothes and get on the bed." I'm growling, and somewhere inside me, I feel something loosen.

Our situation might be tense and out of control and infuriating. But in this room, with him scrambling to obey my every order, that doesn't matter. I have the control I crave because this selfless man gives it to me.

In my chest, my heart clenches with gratitude all over again, because I'm not worthy, and by some miracle, he doesn't care.

Then, as I prowl towards the bed, admiring the way he looks on all fours, presenting his lithe form to me, an unwelcome thought slams into my head.

What would it look like if Evelyn was underneath him with her pale thighs open beneath his dark ones? Both of them waiting for my orders?

The memory of how she looked when she came apart between Vane and Frost on the plane is seared into my mind, so I shouldn't be surprised when it surfaces. For a second, the image is so strong that I have to scrub a hand over my face to clear it. I won't think of her. Not here. She's taking over every inch of my pack, but this time belongs to me and my omega.

Without another second of hesitation, I dive on him. Our teeth clash as I claim his mouth first, nipping at those beautiful full lips of his before dipping my tongue in to taste him.

I'm not gentle, and he goes wild beneath me as I break the

kiss and snatch up the lube which was already waiting on the nightstand.

My finger slips into his ass easily, and he whines again, thrusting his ass back against me.

"I'm ready, alpha. I promise. Please."

How can I resist when he begs like that? I practically rip apart my trousers in my quest to coat my cock with more lube.

A nice alpha would stretch him properly. A good alpha would go slow so he could get used to my size.

Apparently, I am neither right now.

My hands grip his hips, claws peaking out as I shove into his body like a man possessed. I take him without mercy. He's tight—too damned tight—and I hiss, fighting the urge to come as he strangles my cock. Beneath my skin, my instincts are roiling. My frustration leaks out of me as I finally bottom out. My hips slap against the perfect, hard muscles of his ass.

Shit.

The pressure is overwhelming, and his sphincter is clenching *right* over my knot. Forcing me deeper.

Finley curses and yells out, his hands coming back as if to ward me off. But rather than doing that—or telling me to get the fuck out and not come back like a sane person—he clutches at my hips, trying to force me closer.

"Everything," he whispers. "I want all of you, Gid."

I'm way beyond speech. My voice is forgotten and buried under the savage need that's gripped me. When I try to speak, to tell him to get away from me, all I can produce is a bestial growl.

I'm barely coherent. Every part of me is focused on one thing—him. Every tremor of his body, every arch of his spine as he rams back against my thrusts. One of my hands grabs both of his wrists, folding his arms behind his back and gripping them tight. The move shoves his face into the pillow, muffling his gasps and moans.

Like this, he's pinned and at my mercy, and when he arches his head to one side, offering me his neck, I almost explode. My thrusts stutter, the rhythm collapsing as he purposefully clenches around my dick.

My orgasm hits fast and hard. I erupt into his ass with a groan, filling him with my cum. My mouth moves to his neck, my teeth sinking into the corded muscle, holding him in place.

A second later, my alpha physiology reacts to him, and the knot flares to life at my base, locking us together.

I collapse on top of him, pressing my nose against his skin to bathe in his unique omega scent. We're both breathing heavily, and when I release his arms, he crawls forward and flops down, reaching back to drag me in for a hug.

It's damn tempting, but I pull away, rolling us both onto our sides so I'm spooning him instead. I scan his body on horrified autopilot as the extent of my actions sinks in. The panic hits fast, shrinking my knot in record time, and I withdraw as soon as I'm certain doing so won't hurt him any farther.

He rolls onto his back as I start cataloguing the claw marks on his hips and arms, and there's no blood on my cock —thank God. Getting scratched up isn't such a bad thing to most lycans, but I marked him hard.

Would he hate me if I asked him to turn over so I can check for tearing?

Not that I need evidence to know I was too rough. Just like last time, I lost control, and I hurt him. I fucking hate myself for it.

Shit. He's still hard.

I didn't even make him come. That's supposed to be impossible. Knot plus omega equals orgasms.

This might be *worse* than last time.

My eyes zoom back to his face, and I open my mouth to apologise, only to freeze as I notice the glint of moisture at the corner of his eyes.

Everything in me shuts down. Finn must see the shift in my emotions because he shoves to his elbows, trying to put himself at eye level with me and winces as the movement inadvertently forces him to move his lower half.

"You should've said something," I growl, pulling back. "Are you hurt? Let me see—"

"Gid, I wanted it."

"Wanted to be rutted without proper preparation just because I'm a fucking needy alpha?" I scoff.

He did it to distract me. For me. Because I was weak enough to fall into hyper-fixation *again*.

Fucking threw his body at me because he thought it would help soothe *me*. Damn, omegas and their self-sacrificing—

"I'll admit, it'd be better if you helped me come now, just to even the score..." His suggestive tone falls flat and awkward in the space between us. Glancing down at his cock reveals he's already gone soft, and I grimace.

Great. I can't even reciprocate to try to salvage this.

I shove out of the bed and head for the adjoining bathroom to run him a bath, hoping that the space will clear my head.

"Gid."

He's followed me.

"I'm going back out to hunt." My words are clipped, and I hate myself a little more when he shrinks. "Make sure you relax in this for a bit and add some of those bubbles you like."

Thank God for immortal healing.

He touches my arm, and I almost jump out of my skin.

"Stay. Please."

The lump in my throat is so large I can barely breathe, let alone speak. It takes several swallows to clear it. "You got hurt."

"I had good sex with a man I—"

I cut him off, unable to hear him say it. "You got used. *I* used you, and I'm fucking sorry. I won't… I won't do it again. Now… get in the bath, please. I'll make you something to eat while you soak."

It's not like snacks can fix this, but it's the least I can do.

Finley sighs, but does as I ask. I turn to leave, so he aims his next words at my retreating back.

"You know, you'd have more control if you didn't bottle everything up. How long was it since you and I fucked when we weren't under the influence of the full moon? A year? Longer? It's not healthy, Alpha."

I close the door with a soft snick and pretend I don't hear his sigh of disappointment as I cross the room, silently berating myself with every breath of the sex-permeated air.

I respect my omega's instincts, but whatever Finley believes about me, he's wrong. Control isn't something I can miraculously conjure by letting myself drown in his body every night—if I even deserved to do so.

Ever since the omega joined our pack, and I realised what he meant to me—to all of us—I've felt the pressure to keep him safe. Add in the danger of our work, and it's a miracle I haven't snapped.

So no, sex won't magically hand me back my control.

Cain's death will. Which means I need to get back out there, and focus on finding Samuel.

And if I see Silas on the way, I'll beg the beta to come back here and try to soothe what I've just broken.

I'm halfway through fixing a bowl with nachos when I scent him hovering in the kitchen doorway.

"Go back to the bath," I mutter. "I'm almost done."

"I hate to break it to you, but we have bigger problems than your self-loathing to deal with right now."

His cutting sarcasm is cold and bitter. That tone is a defensive measure he developed in his shithole of a birth-pack, and one he should *never* feel he needs to use around me.

Fuck. I *knew* I hurt him.

Everything in me wants to hug him, to tug him close and reassure him with touch.

But when my touch is what did this, how is it supposed to make it right?

So I keep my distance. "What's happened?"

"Samuel's made contact with Evie."

There's a crash, and it takes me a second to realise that I've dropped the bowl.

I'm halfway towards the door when Finn says. "Vane's already gone. Morwen too—though Mia's heading back here to work on tech support with me."

Meaning it's just me, Mia, and Immy here with him. I'm not about to leave his safety to Mia when the vampire is here —even if Evelyn insists she's harmless.

So my omega and my beta have effectively worked together to bench me. No doubt believing they're doing it for my own good.

"Let's get to work then," I mutter, abandoning the pile of nachos and fractured pottery on the floor as I stalk behind him towards his office.

CHAPTER THIRTEEN

EVELYN

I͟T͟ ͟T͟O͟O͟K͟ ͟A͟ ͟L͟O͟T͟ ͟O͟F͟ ͟W͟O͟R͟K͟ ͟T͟O͟ ͟C͟O͟N͟V͟I͟N͟C͟E͟ F͟R͟O͟S͟T͟ ͟T͟O͟ ͟L͟E͟A͟V͟E͟ ͟M͟E͟
alone, and leaving Immy back at the hotel by herself is not
something I do lightly. But Gideon's idea of having us search
in pairs isn't working. Facing us in groups is too intimidating
a gamble for Samuel to take.

He's far more likely to go to ground if he feels outnumbered.

Better to give him the false belief that he can pick us off
one by one.

Even then, there's no guarantee he won't just hide.
Samuel was never one for outright conflict. It was how he
survived so long when Cain started ordering the deaths of
our other brothers.

I've concealed all my weapons and made myself as
tempting and vulnerable a target as possible. Now, as I stroll
along the lamp-lit streets of the most deserted part of this
town—a place I know Frost sent me because it was the place

I was least likely to be in danger—I pray that I've done the right thing.

Still, it's beginning to feel like a bust, and the waves of pleasure coming from Finn's bond are quickly becoming distracting. As I turn the corner, I'm seriously considering returning to our makeshift base and seeing if he wants another partner.

Only I'm jarred out of my fantasy as I turn the corner and immediately notice the figure standing in the middle of the road.

With his hood up, there's no way I can see his face or make out his features, but it's unmistakably *him*.

"Samuel."

He gives me a small bow, and my hand drops to where the pommel of my sword is hidden beneath the folds of my long coat.

"I just want to talk," I begin, not releasing my grip on the weapon.

Samuel is older than me. He might even be older than any vampire who still lives—except Cain, of course—and to vampires, age equals power.

A sudden burst of sadness and frustration from Finn distracts me, and I automatically glance in the omega's direction, despite the distance between us.

One blink is all it takes. When I look back, Samuel's gone.

"Shit."

I hasten towards the spot where he was standing, only to grimace as I see the open manhole cover.

He's living in the sewers? *Really?*

No wonder we couldn't find him. The smell alone would've overpowered immortal senses.

I eye the hole in the ground suspiciously. Urgency says I should follow and try to pick up any trail I can. That would be foolish. I'm outmatched, and I know it. So instead, I take my phone out and shoot a message to the pack, watching as their replies trickle in one by one.

All of them tell me to stay put.

Ugh, men. As if I was going to do anything else.

They're lucky Finn tucked the device into my pocket before I left this evening. I still haven't gotten the hang of taking it everywhere like they do. It's just one more of the modern habits I have yet to learn.

Frost arrives first, only to stare at the open drain in horror, pinching his nostrils shut with his fingers.

"God, that's foul. Please tell me he's not down there." He sees my guilty look and grimaces. "Great. I should've brought nose plugs."

Oh, right. Being half ghoul—with their sensitive sense of smell—must have its downsides.

Silas arrives after Frost, his face twisted in a similar expression of distaste, and Morwen follows soon after him.

"Is this all of us?" I ask, staring into the darkness.

"Gideon is keeping an eye on Finn and Mia," Silas confirms after checking his phone. "Vane will catch up. He was farther away."

Ah, that explains why Finn felt like he was having the sex of his life earlier, but not the sadness that came afterwards. "What about Draven?"

"He was with me, but he disappeared..." Silas shrugs. "He's not answering my messages, but he does that sometimes. Nothing to worry about."

I grimace, because this just confirms what I already know. Draven is so used to being on the outside of the pack that getting him to communicate and work as part of a team isn't going to come naturally. He's not in trouble—at least, our bond doesn't give me the impression that he is—so Silas is right. Now's not the time to worry about him. Nodding, I step forward and, holding my breath, allow my body to drop into the stinking drain.

I splash down into the tunnel with a hiss of disgust. There's nowhere to walk except directly in the dirty, stinking water. Morwen's landing makes more of it slosh over the edge of my boots, and it takes everything I have not to snarl at her as cold, wet sludge meets my toes.

And the area is tight. Enclosed.

Wide enough that I can reach out and touch the ceiling and the walls on either side of me with my hands. That, combined with the darkness, makes it hard to breathe. My chest starts to feel too tight, and I try to drag in a deep breath to counter the feeling.

I can move my arms. I'm not in the coffin. I can move my arms. I'm free.

"Well, this is homey," Silas mutters, interrupting my silent, internal mantra.

I was so entangled in my own thoughts that I didn't even notice him drop down beside me. With a start, I move farther down the tunnel, making space for the rest of our party.

Only Frost doesn't drop down like the rest of us. He crawls in, using his fingers and toes to cling to the brick walls. I've seen ghouls do it before—scaling buildings like spiders—but I had no idea he had the same ability.

I shouldn't be surprised given that he has all of the other ghoul strengths.

"Neat trick," Morwen grouses.

"It's not like the walls are much better than the water," I mutter.

But I'm just as envious as she is. Even the weeping slime-covered brickwork seems like a better option than the grey, stinking water we're wading through.

"Can you scent which way he went?" Silas asks, craning his head to speak to Frost.

"No need," I say, pointing to the crude arrow scraped into the dripping wall "Apparently he wants us to follow him."

"Could be a trap." Morwen draws a long, wicked-looking knife with an eager grin.

"Probably," Silas agrees.

Another splash from behind us makes us all jump, but it's only Vane. "You forgot your comms," he scolds, holding a box out to all of us. "Gid, Finn, and Mia are all on the other end."

I didn't forget. I just left mine behind because, despite my plan, I never expected to actually find Samuel so quickly, but I flash him a sheepish smile just the same.

"And Immy?" I check.

He freezes as the others start plucking earpieces from the box and hooking them over their ears. "She was in her room."

I take my own earpiece from the box and link it to my ear just as Gideon's voice echoes from it. *"Mia's gone to stand in the hallway. She confirmed your sister hasn't left."*

"She also hasn't triggered any of my virtual alarms or attempted to bypass our firewalls," Finn adds, and I'm glad to hear that—despite the lingering sadness and irritation down our bond—he sounds okay. *"As far as I can tell, she hasn't made a single attempt to contact anyone using her phone or tablet since we left New York.*

"Good." If Immy isn't sneaking out, or obviously reporting to Cain, perhaps she meant what she said.

Sloshing down the tunnel, I do my best to restrain my own runaway hopefulness. Cain might be wrong about many things, but his absolute refusal to trust someone before they've proven their loyalty is the reason he's probably survived this long.

In this case, I might benefit from exercising a similar level of paranoia.

Of course, my sire would never have brought her along with us in the first place.

Now isn't the time to start doubting myself. Shutting down those thoughts, I tune my focus into following Samuel's trail. We're all staying quiet, but the sloshing of our footsteps echoes off the walls. Slowly but surely, the darkness and the sound of my own harsh breathing start to bring back memories of another damp, cold, underground tomb. No matter how many times I try to shrug the memories off, they just keep coming back. Eventually, I just can't take the silence anymore.

"Are we heading away from the town?" I ask, after almost half an hour of walking.

Mercifully, we've left the stinking water of the sewers behind and this latest tunnel is dry and slopes upward. The foul smell remains, but it's less severe than it was. I'm certain we're going the right way—or at least, the way Samuel wants us to go—because every time we've reached a fork, or junction, there's been another small arrow etched into the stone to guide us.

"Your trackers are showing a position outside the town limits, and you're headed towards the desert," Finn confirms, and I sigh in relief at the sound of his voice. I'm not alone, and that more than anything proves to my subconscious that this is nothing like the coffin. *"According to the official government sewer plans, the tunnel you're in doesn't exist."*

How much work would it take to create a tunnel system like this, without anyone knowing? Surely that's beyond the purview of any single immortal.

Unless Samuel wasn't alone.

What if we were wrong? What if our brother wasn't out here just surviving and hiding? What if... what if he was thriving?

"We haven't considered something," I whisper, almost to myself. "What if Samuel *has* sired other vampires?"

It was just an excuse I made up to pacify Cain without him inflicting any punishment on Morwen and delaying our trip, but it's a real possibility. Several centuries alone and on the run would make anyone lonely.

Heck, he might even have a family. One we've accidentally put on Cain's radar.

Why did I not consider that before I opened my big mouth?

"Out here? In the sunniest place on earth?" Morwen scoffs. "It would be difficult to keep newborn vampires alive."

Silas isn't as dismissive. "What better place to do that than in a tunnel system no one knows about?"

"If this is an ambush, we won't know it until they're on top of us," Frost complains. "My nose is useless down here."

"Everyone keep your guard up," Gideon orders.

Great.

Frost moves, righting himself so he's walking protectively in front of me, rather than crawling on the walls. I want to bristle at the move, but I can't. Because although I'm close to full strength, I'm not quite there yet. Plus, with his wall climbing, he has a unique advantage in these close quarters.

It only takes a few more minutes for him to come to a stop, putting my already frayed nerves further on edge.

"Dead end," he says.

I lean around him, trying to confirm it for myself by peering into the darkness.

"Did we miss a turn?" Silas asks.

"No." Vane's denial is absolute.

"Turn back," Morwen says. "If Samuel comes for us now, he has the advantage. We're like fish in a barrel."

I shake my head, pushing past Frost to run my fingers along the tan bricks. "This can't be it."

Somehow, the extra wall is only adding to the sense of claustrophobia which has been plaguing me since I first set foot in this sewer. My hands tremble as I run my fingers between the bricks, searching for a trigger. A loose stone. Anything.

Samuel excelled at hiding in plain sight, perhaps it's a secret door of some kind?

"Eve, we should go," Frost suggests. He's trying to keep his tone gentle, but it's obvious that he's just as on-edge as everyone else.

"Wait, just give me a few seconds." I press at random bricks, hoping to feel one give way, or something.

Frost rests his hand on the brickwork above us, sighing like he's about to give me an ultimatum.

Only to fall forward as the circular wall in front of us spins on its end like a coin, revealing only pitch blackness beyond. Even my eyesight can't pierce it. Whatever the chamber is, it must be immense.

I take a step forward, only to pinwheel back as the floor disappears.

"That's a steep drop," Frost mutters, his hands falling to my waist, holding me in place as he shuffles around me. "I'll check it out. Wait here."

Without waiting for us to discuss it, he sticks one hand onto the wall and crawls out into the blackness.

"If he breaks his fool neck..." I mutter.

Silas coughs. "Don't worry. He scaled the Bloody Tower like this just for a chance to see you, I'm sure he can manage a little spelunking."

Frost... did that? Our bond tightens a fraction before I even realise what's happened.

"Ugh, I hate that word," Mia complains, her voice echoing from my earpiece for the first time.

"What about moist?" Finn teases.

I can almost hear Silas's grin. "No word is worse than smegma."

"What even is—" Mia echoes my thoughts before she cuts off. *"You know what? If it sounds that bad, I don't even want to know."*

She's probably being wise, but I make a mental note to add whatever smegma is to my list of things to research. Hopefully, I don't regret it later...

"How long does he expect us to wait while he shows off for Evie?" Morwen demands, ignoring their banter as she pushes her way to my side. "I'm going down."

Her hair streams behind her as she drops down, following Frost.

"According to Frost, it's a cistern," Finn relays. *"No word from Morwen, though..."*

"Shit." Vane scrubs a hand through his hair. "Trap. I knew it. Tell Frost to get his ass back up here."

"You are not abandoning my girlfriend down there." Mia's screech is so shrill I have to fight the urge to snatch the earpiece from my head. *"If it's a trap, you damn well better go down there and back her up."*

Vane and Silas share a look that tells me they're debating whether or not to actually do as she says. I'm not sure what silent big brother communication passes between them, but they sigh in unison.

"Can we convince you to stay up here?" Silas asks, hopefully.

Alone in the small, stinky tunnel? "No chance."

"I'll go first," Vane says, shoving to the front with an exasperated eye roll. "Evie, follow me. Silas, you protect our backs."

Unlike Frost and Morwen, he waits for both of us to nod before stepping off the edge. Without letting myself think too much about it, I suck in a breath and follow after him.

The fall seems to take forever. I manage to land on my feet, thanks to centuries of practice, but my landing sends shockwaves through my legs.

The cistern is vast. A rounded underground cavern supported and broken up by hundreds of stone arches travelling in every direction. It seems older than the sewers above, and I wonder *when* this was built and by whom.

How long has Samuel been here?

Thankfully, the ground down here is dry. The scent of sewage hasn't permeated this far down, and as I inhale a lungful of surprisingly fresh air, I realise the space is lit as well. An old electric lamp is buzzing on the pillar to my left, and in front of me Vane is looking around at the half a dozen tunnels which seem to lead away from the round chamber we've landed in.

Thud.

That must be Silas, landing at our backs.

The younger brother comes to stand at my side just as Vane says. "We're not alone."

Silas tries to move in front of me, but he's gone before he can take a step. My squeak of surprise isn't fast enough to warn Vane, who turns to see what's happening, and is grabbed just as suddenly from behind. A black sack covers his head a second before he's dragged away into one of the tunnels.

So that's where the others went.

"Evelyn, what's happening?" Gideon demands, but his voice is distorted by static until it's almost inaudible.

Finn is talking too, but I can't make out much. *"...their trackers are offline.... They're too far—"*

I spin on my heel, trying to keep an eye on all the entrances at once as my mind works furiously. We must be deep underground, too far for whatever signal the tech uses to penetrate.

Did they get all of us?

Even Frost?

Perhaps not, since he crawled rather than dropping down as the rest of us did. Although there's a chance that Samuel might have people who saw us come in and realise he's missing, I'm going to assume he saw Morwen get captured and stayed hidden. Which gives us one person who can call the others for reinforcements if needs be.

I attempt to check on my three missing thralls using their bonds, but all I can feel is Silas's tiredness. The other two aren't mature enough for such a deep connection.

Biting my lip, I search the shadows for any hint of our attackers. *Why can't I see them?*

Samuel wanted me to come down here. He led us all this way through the tunnels with those arrows, practically sign-posting his front door.

Vane wasn't stabbed or killed, just restrained and hauled off.

Kidnapping rather than death suggests that Samuel—and whoever his accomplices are—have cause to keep us alive. I just have to hope it's because they want to talk, and not because they'd prefer to torture us before killing us.

"I'm taking a leap of faith," I whisper, raising my hands up above my head in a universal gesture of surrender.

The sack covers my face and pulls tight around my neck. It smells sweet—herbal, almost. A fist collides with my gut, forcing me to suck in the sickly, disinfectant type air until my head goes woozy and I can't think clearly. Another breath and I'm done for.

Everything goes black.

CHAPTER FOURTEEN

FROST

WHEN I WAKE UP, MY HEAD IS POUNDING LIKE I'VE BEEN ON A week-long bender. My face is smooshed into Silas's stinky armpit and there's a knee pressed uncomfortably into my spine. A second later, the scents of rotting rubbish, alcohol, and piss filter past my beta's body odour, along with other unwelcome—yet familiar—notes of death and decay.

Looking over the contorted pile of limbs, it doesn't take me long to find them. They've lined up along the entrance to the alley like silent sentinels.

Damn.

It never takes a ghoul pack long to find me. They always gravitate towards my pheromones, no matter what I do. And this group is looking at my companions like they're dinner. Their jaws click together as their emotions bombard me.

Hunger.

Aggression.

Eagerness.

They want to feed, and they've chosen my pack as their

next meal. Which means I'll have to work hard to change their minds.

I reach out with my still-groggy senses and soothe the edges of the aggression. When that doesn't immediately make them back off, I snarl low under my breath.

They scarper, unwilling to challenge me.

With them gone, and their feelings getting duller and less demanding with every step they take away from us, my mind is free to remember what happened.

Eve.

I shove at Silas's abdomen, and my foot connects with a different body as I struggle to free myself from the pile.

I can't scent her, so I know without looking that she's not here.

How the fuck did we end up like this? I was crawling towards the bottom of that tunnel. I saw Morwen get dragged away, and then... nothing.

My hand goes to the side of my head, looking for the earbud which isn't there any longer. Only, the second my palm gets too close, I grimace.

The scent of the sewer wall is imprinted into my palm.

I *really* need to wash my hands. Fuck, maybe I should've just walked in the sewage with the rest of them...

Shit. Samuel has Eve and we have no idea where we are, or how to contact our people to tell them.

"Get up," I growl, kicking out again. "We have to find her."

Silas is on his feet first, and together we manage to wake up Vane, who looks around groggily, scrubbing a hand down his face before coming to the same realisation we have.

"Evie."

He's on his feet, only to stumble and crash into a bin seconds later.

"What the hell did they drug us with?" He groans.

"I don't know, but Morwen's still out cold."

Silas rolls his eyes and scoops the vampire psycho into his arms and over his shoulder. Both Vane and I raise our brows at him in unison.

"What?" he demands. "Mia will kill us if we leave her knocked out in an alley."

Vane's shoulders slump, and he rolls his eyes. "Fine, but does anyone have any idea where we are?"

I walk out to the mouth of the alley, and stare at the ocean. We've been dumped on a street lined with restaurants on one side, and sun-drenched beach on the other.

"They must have known the salt water and the scent of food would cover their tracks," I grumble.

"Wait here," Silas mutters. "I'll see if there's a sign or something that tells us where we are."

"Fuck figuring out where we are," I reply. "We need to go after Eve."

"We can't do that if we don't know where she is. We need the rest of the pack. Finn must be able to track her. He'll have a better idea of where to look." Silas has a point, as much as I hate to admit it.

When did he become the reasonable brother?

Vane grunts and shoves past me. "You'll draw too much attention. I'll go."

I'm about to ask why the hulking lycan is going to draw less attention than I will, but he just shakes his head.

"Silas is hauling an unconscious woman, your fangs are out and your hair is covered in shit."

Great.

It turns out, Samuel—or his minions—have dumped us in a town over seventy miles away from the resort where we set up base.

Unfortunately, the unrelenting heat has another unwelcome side effect. As the day wears on, whatever gunk is in my hair is slowly baked until the stench of it becomes unbearable. I don't want to waste time dealing with it, but the others evidently think differently. In the end, the brothers take matters into their own hands, shoving me off the end of the pier and into the sea for an impromptu bath.

So when I burst into our rooms, I'm encrusted with salt and in a foul mood. Something which only gets worse as I take in our omega curled up on the sofa, clutching a cushion as Mia, Immy, and Gideon argue over the top of him.

A hush descends as the three of them realise we've returned. They turn and stare at us.

Mia descends on her brothers in a whirlwind of curses, prying her girlfriend from over Silas's shoulder and running her hands over the vampire's body, searching for injuries.

"Calm down," Vane mutters. "I already checked her over. She's fine. They must have just dosed her heavier than the rest of us."

I don't blame our captors for being unwilling to take the chance with an elder vampire. But it's annoying that Morwen slept like a baby while the rest of us were forced to run the entire distance home.

Mia grumbles more, curses, and hauls Morwen off, muttering about getting her cleaned up.

With her gone, I look directly at my co-alpha and announce, "We have a problem."

"Let me guess," Gideon retorts. "*She* caused it?"

"Will you just *stop*!?" Finn rubs his eyes, dislodging his glasses in the process. "For one second. Please. All this anger is—"

Whatever he might've said is drowned out by Immy.

"This boorish coward won't go after Evie. We have her last known co-ordinates, and I, for one, am not content to sit here and wait for her to turn up dead."

The redhead stalks from the room in a cloud of anger, and I glare at Gideon.

Silas gets between the two of us before either of us can say anything. "You want to argue, do it away from Finn. He's straining, and this bastard's probably made it worse."

The beta doesn't wait for either of us to reply before crossing to the sofa and hauling the omega into his arms. Watching Finn relax under the attention soothes something in Gideon, and his eyes soften. But a second later his jaw clenches and he spins to give the two of them his back.

Good to know he's still the king of mixed signals.

"What the fuck happened down there?" he asks, and I can tell he's struggling to keep his tone modulated so as not to upset our omega—not that Finn and Silas are paying the two of us much attention right now. "We lost your signal when you went too far underground and it never resurfaced."

"Got ambushed," I grunt. "I literally can't remember anything after I climbed down to the base of the cistern."

"Finn and Mia have sent drones to map the entire sewer. We can't retrace your path," Gideon grabs a tablet from the table and flicks a hologram into the centre of the room. The elaborate warren of tunnels is seemingly random and punctuated by red dots travelling through it.

"That is where you entered," Gideon continues, pointing at an orange point in the top. "And this is your path." He taps the dot, and a matching orange line traces its way through the sewers. "You left the sewers somewhere around here, but as you can see, the route no longer exists. The arrows you followed are gone, and according to this, you walked through solid rock at several points."

"There was a fake wall which blocked off the last tunnel," I recall. "Eve found a way to open it."

He rubs at his eyes in frustration. "Well the drones don't have that ability. The trackers stopped working when you jumped down to the cistern, meaning you were probably out of range, or the signal was jammed. Even with Finn's thrall bond to guide us, the sewers are a labyrinth. If we go down there, we could be lost for weeks."

"Does it matter?" Immy demands. "It's still our only plan."

The alpha glares at her. "We're not going to be any help to Evelyn if we're wandering around, lost in a tunnel."

"Any help to who?"

Both Gideon and I whirl, pinning the intruder in the doorway with a glare.

"Where the *fuck* have you been?" I growl.

"Tone!" Silas growls, reminding me that both he and Finn are here too.

"Why?" Draven's eyes travel over the group, pausing on Immy, and then on Finn curled up in Silas's lap. "I had a lead, I followed it, but it was a dead end. Then I was taking care of a few things, but the damned sun came up and took me out of commission. What's going on?"

"We found Samuel—" Vane begins.

"Or rather, he found Evie," Silas finishes.

The hybrid raises a single brow at his brother. "She was taken, and the rest of us were dumped in a town miles away."

Draven's expression sharpens, turning dark and terrifying in a blink. He holds up a hand for silence, and a heartbeat later, he frowns. "She feels fine."

The quiet, blade-like fury radiating from him doesn't cease, but he does turn it down a few notches before he looks to Finn for confirmation.

Wise move. Turning that kind of anger towards the omega wouldn't have ended well.

Finn chews at his lip and adjusts his glasses as he does the same thing. "Yeah, no signs of torture yet. It's more like she's asleep."

Just like Morwen. They must've used a bigger dose on the older vampires. Maybe they miscalculated, or perhaps she's being moved far enough they needed reassurance she wouldn't wake up.

Both scenarios aren't good.

"It's unlikely our brother would torture her," Immy interrupts, speaking for the first time. "But I don't get why he'd take her and leave Morwen... That makes no sense. If he's looking for hostages to use against Cain, it would make more sense to have multiple bargaining chips at his disposal."

"So he wants Evie for something else," Silas mutters. "But what?"

"Who cares?" I growl. "Can you two use your bonds to get us close to her?"

Finn and Draven share a look. "Yes," the latter finally answers.

"But if she's underground and the tunnels keep changing..." Finn trails off.

Doesn't matter to me. "I'll fucking dig."

I lost her once. I am *never* letting it happen again.

CHAPTER FIFTEEN

EVELYN

THIS HEADACHE IS REALLY TRYING TO KILL ME. THE POUNDING pain has settled right behind my eyes, and I dread opening them because I suspect that's only going to make it worse. I breathe slowly, forcing down the urge to vomit. My thoughts are unusually slow, like I'm battling the worst case of brain fog. It's familiar, and it takes me a few more long minutes to figure out why.

Silver.

Sure enough, when I open my eyes, the small six-by-six room I'm in is swathed in it. Thick bars are bolted to the tan stone, and the door has been reinforced as well. Even the bare light bulb above is caged in the metal, preventing me from breaking it and using the glass as a weapon. It's a cell built to hold an immortal, just like my coffin, but on a larger scale.

Goosebumps tickle my skin as I make the connection, and I force myself up onto my knees, moving just to prove that I can. My weapons are gone and so is the tiny earpiece I was wearing.

Not that I expected my kidnappers to make it easy for me, but it would've been nice of them to leave me with something.

My thrall bonds to Draven and Finn are roiling in concern, and I reach out, trying to reassure both of them. But the fog makes it harder than it should be, like trying to reach across a vast, fathomless void.

I must make a noise in my frustration, because the tiny hatch in the door slides open, and a pair of dark eyes peer through.

They say nothing, and neither do I. After a second, the hatch slides closed once more, and I let out the breath I wasn't aware I was holding. The loud, metallic clunk which follows echoes through the small space, and the door swings outward.

My captors haven't used restraints, and when I look into the well-lit passage beyond, I see why. I'm so outnumbered I'd be a fool to try anything. There are easily a dozen of them. All armed with silver. All vampires.

The man who opened my cell door says something, but he's using a language I don't recognise. My cluelessness must show on my face, because he grumbles something, and sweeps his arm out in a universal gesture for me to leave the cell.

Thank God.

I rise to my feet slowly, trying my best not to make any sudden moves. They've even taken my boots, I realise, as my bare feet come into contact with the cold, stone floor.

Where are the others? The passageway is large, well-lit, and lined with more heavy doors. There's no way to tell who's behind which one—or if anyone is. My thralls don't feel close by, and that worries me.

The vampires lead the way out of this hall and towards a set of stairs. I stumble a little on the uneven stone floor and take a deep breath to try to dispel the lingering fogginess from the silver.

The tunnels become larger and larger as we get farther away from what must have been the dungeon. This place—whatever it is—is military-neat. Somehow they've got electricity, and it's not much of a stretch to assume they have running water as well, given the pipes and wires on the smooth stone walls.

We've even passed a few vampires who were dressed like civilians. Most of them have the dark, rich skin I'd expect of this part of the world, but a few are pale like me. Just how far does Samuel's reach extend?

The implications are astounding. Somehow, Samuel has gone beyond siring just one or two other vampires. He's created an entire underground base beyond our sire's reach and filled it with vampires from more than one continent.

A vampire society that doesn't have Cain at its heart is inconceivable. He's always been the first of us, and his entire claim to ruling us is based on that fact. Younger vampires—especially those under a century old—need the guidance and discipline of an elder.

And that elder doesn't have to be Cain.

Multiple turns and another flight of stairs later, we reach an imposing door. The man before me—the one who opened my cell—says something else, and I curse inwardly. Of all the languages I've learned in my immortal lifetime, how have I not heard this one? It could almost be Greek or Hebrew, but it's not like any dialect I've heard before.

The vampire, evidently realising that I still can't understand him, smirks. Someone behind me says something, and he rolls his eyes, like it was a terrible suggestion, before turning and opening the doors.

I follow him inside, blinking at the sudden gloom. It's not dark per se, but the lighting is so low that it takes a second for my eyes to adjust. When they do, I take in the circular room with its subtly domed, raised floor with confusion. Around the edge, on low cushions, other vampires recline and watch with eagle eyes as I'm led in, but it's the man sitting cross-legged in the centre who commands my attention.

Samuel.

He really is alive.

His clothes are dark and plain, but tailored to his slim build and edged in gold stitching that sets off his chestnut skin perfectly. Around his neck is a long chain hung with a simple wooden cross, and in front of him, my sword and dagger are laid out like offerings, almost within my reach.

A hand on my shoulder forces me to my knees, and I hit the stone with a bone-jarring force. Samuel raises one palm in a restraining gesture, and the grip holding me down disappears.

"Evonnia. I wondered how long it would take you to seek me out." His voice is quiet, but the words echo off the walls of the chamber, lending more gravitas to them.

God, how long has it been since I heard my birth name? Centuries surely.

Cain renamed all five of his daughters once we'd proved ourselves. Even before that, we weren't allowed to use the names our mothers gave us. We were just 'daughter.' Our whole identities were stripped away overnight. A psychological trick to break us down so we could be remade as his creatures.

When we were young, I used to fall asleep to Morwen whispering her true name over and over again.

My eyes drop back to my weapons, silently calculating if I can make it to them before someone stops me. But there are still guards behind me. They've released me for now, but they're still tense. Waiting for me to try something.

My odds of reaching my things before they can react are slim-to-none.

Samuel notices where my focus has drifted to and arches a single pierced brow. "But, are you here because our sire ordered you to take my head or for some other reason?"

I shake my head. "I'm not answering any of your questions until you release my thralls and my sister."

"Already done," he replies, easily. "They were not invited. I returned them to the surface as soon as we captured them. You are here because of a promise I made and nothing more." He pauses, and one side of his lips quirks upward. "So which is it? My head? Or something else?"

The vampire who brought me here mumbles something harsh under his breath, but both of us ignore him.

"Maybe it's both," I hedge.

He looks taken aback by that answer, and the vampires behind me visibly bristle with hostility. "Don't play games here, sister. I went to a lot of trouble to fake my death, so tell me plainly; does Cain know I'm alive?"

I shake my head. "He thinks we're here to hunt down a vampire you sired."

Samuel's nostrils flare and he looks heavenward, as if praying for patience. "You've made him suspicious. I would've rather you'd found some other excuse to seek me out. One that didn't involve drawing his attention to this corner of the world."

"I'm here because there's a rumour you have a weapon which will kill him."

He smirks, and soon enough it's turned into a full-blown smile. His startled chuckle seems to drain a little of the tension away from the others, but I don't make the mistake of thinking they've relaxed.

Again, I calculate the odds of getting to my sword before anyone else can react, and once again I dismiss the idea. I thought I'd be relieved that the others were safe above ground, but in reality, I feel more cornered than I did before.

Samuel wants me here alone. Surrounded by other vampires who are clearly under his command.

He finally stops laughing long enough to ask, "Do you think I'd be hiding down here if I possessed such a weapon?"

The hope I've been quietly nursing since I found out about his survival at the gala vanishes. He has a good point. Clearly, he has the ability to stay out of Cain's radar, and enough vampires to organise an attack if he wanted to.

No. I *refuse* to believe he knows nothing when our sire was scared enough to send *three* of his daughters on this mission.

"You know something then," I challenge. "Whatever it is, I need that information."

That piercing glints as he raises his eyebrow again. "You'd only need such a thing if you were planning to try to kill him yourself..."

"I am."

His tone is mocking when he replies, "With what army?"

I don't remember him being this... infuriating before. Although, I'll admit it's been centuries since his 'death.'

Before I can respond, he sighs and gets to his feet, picking up my weapons as he does so, "What are you willing to do to see our sire dead?" he asks.

"Why does that matter to you?" I retort.

He shakes his head. "Because when I last saw you, you looked at him like he hung the moon and told the stars when to twinkle. And he... he doted on you in a way he'd never doted on *anybody*. I find it hard to believe you're here, seeking to end him, when you were so close."

It's my turn to snort. "You're out of touch, *brother*. I've spent the last two centuries in a silver coffin, being punished for daring to love someone other than him. Whatever favour I once held is gone. Right now, all I want is my freedom, and that can only happen if he's dead."

Samuel is silent for one heartbeat, staring into my eyes with an eerie intensity before flicking his questioning gaze to the men behind me. The vampire who spoke to me earlier says something—once again using that damned language—and Samuel clenches his jaw in answer.

No one is more surprised than I am when he holds my two blades out in offering. "Come with me."

I accept them, tucking them into their sheaths as he strides past me. Being armed makes me feel better—even if it can't fix how outnumbered I am. One of the vampires who brought me to him says something else, but Samuel holds up a hand to silence him, before replying in their language.

He leads me past the gathered group of soldiers, rolling his eyes when the one talkative guard insists on following behind us, but he says nothing to stop him. The three of us leave through the immense doors, but walk in the opposite direction to the way I came from. We turn into a larger corridor, and I make out another heavy door at the far end.

Other vampires pass us, heading into the various rooms and corridors which branch away from this one without giving our trio more than a sideways glance. Most of the rooms seem to be offices of a sort, crammed with tech I can't really understand.

Samuel has to drag a heavy bolt out of the way to open the door, letting in a burst of blinding sunlight. He doesn't stop to let his eyes adjust, and I don't have a chance to either, because the guard behind me shoves me forward after him.

When I followed him into the sewer it was the middle of the night.

Just how long was I asleep for? And where are we?

I stumble out onto a balcony and stare in wonder at the hidden city before me. We're standing at the bottom of a desert crevasse, riddled with caves which seem to have been fitted with yet more doors, and carved to have more balconies. High above us, sunlight and rivulets of sand stream downwards into the narrow canyon, and the floor at the base is littered with sharp rocks.

Now that we're outside, away from the protection of the deep, cool earth, the heat is almost unbearable.

It's probably the least hospitable place a vampire could imagine, and yet Samuel and his people must have been here for a long time.

"We have lived here for several hundred years," Samuel begins, echoing my thoughts. "Unlike with you, Cain chose warriors well into adulthood when he picked my brothers and I, so I recalled perfectly my childhood, growing up on the banks of the Aegean. But it was too populous to return, and I would've been too easily recognised, so when I chose to hide, I moved farther south, knowing that the sun would keep me safe."

"And you built a city…"

"No. They did that themselves." Samuel chuckles. "I was just a cave-dwelling hermit for the longest time. I used my speed to run across the dunes each night so I could feed from the people of the village on the other side of the desert. I thought it was the best way to keep my location secret. Still, word got out."

"Did you turn them?"

"Not by choice. I healed a street urchin in a moment of weakness. The next thing I knew, they'd started leaving their dying on their doorsteps after dark."

I raise my eyebrows. "I never took you to be so compassionate."

He shrugs. "I had a lot of sins to make up for."

"So you turned them to save them?"

Turning someone isn't always necessary. Most of the time, vampire blood can cure a human without turning them —as long as they're not too far gone. Mine just does it faster than others.

"I turned them when my wife asked me to."

His *what*?

"You're *married*?" Such a commitment is almost unheard of among vampires, especially since the thrall bond is so much more meaningful.

He rubs the back of his neck, almost ruefully. "It is a long story. I'll introduce you, if you turn out not to be a threat. Needless to say, I turned her first, and then her family requested the same, and she insisted..." He trails off in a shrug.

As if he hasn't just admitted to creating a whole canyon full of powerful second-generation vampires.

"So you turned them and built a place to hide."

"A place to *live*, free of our sire."

That sounds... like heaven.

"And I invite you to stay here, in safety, as family."

There's a sharp reprimand from behind me, and Samuel glares at the man behind us. "She is your aunt, Bakari. You will show her the respect that is owed and speak in a language she can understand."

I blink at him... *I have a nephew?* But biological offspring are a physical impossibility for vampires...

"This is reckless. She could bring danger here."

"We will speak on this later. She is our guest. If you can't use your manners, you may leave us."

Bakari glowers, taking several steps back, but doesn't leave. He leans against the wall, spewing venom at me with his eyes.

"You must forgive my eldest. He does not like strangers."

151

"How do you have a son?" I ask, unable to hold back my curiosity.

He shakes his head. "It is not what you think. I haven't found a magical way to overcome the imperfections of our species. He is my wife's child from her first husband, but my son just the same."

The disappointment hits me for a second before I can contain it, but I shrug it off with practised ease. I thought I'd gotten over my infertility centuries ago and learned to be content with life. But every now and again, it rears its ugly head to bite me once more and I grieve all over again for the babies I'll never hold.

It would be irresponsible to bring a child into my world, and that hasn't changed in all the years of my long life. I knew what I was getting into when I was turned. What I was giving up.

It didn't hit me until decades later, when I met Frost and realised I would never be able to bear him a child with his floppy hair. Yet some part of me has always wished that maybe somehow...

No. I cut off the thought before it can take root and fester.

"It would be good for him to get to know other vampires, outside of our community," Samuel muses. "The downside of living like we do, is that few among my family have ever had the chance to travel far. Regardless of what he says, my home is open to you. It is the least I can do."

We lapse into silence, and I stare out into the canyon with my mind whirring. The sand falls down over the top of the rocky cliffs with each gust of wind. It's relaxing to watch and gives me something to focus on as I consider his offer.

Would it be so wrong to take him up on his offer after all we've been through? Is it so bad to crave a little bit of peace?

"I'll understand if you say no," he adds. "Living this way

isn't an easy adjustment for anyone to make. It's not like at Court. Everyone here works hard to earn their keep…"

"That doesn't scare me," I retort. "But if there's a way to kill Cain—to return things to how they were—"

Samuel scoffs. "You are not so naive as to believe that is possible, surely? Cain has revealed our existence to mortals and chained them to the bottom of a hierarchy that always existed, but that they were never privy to. He has shifted things permanently.

"If our Sire dies, an older vampire must be prepared to take his place. Otherwise the newborns and the most sadistic of our kind will run rampant and turn the streets red with blood. The ghouls will get out of hand without us keeping their numbers in check, and the lycan packs…" He sighs. "They'll begin to clash with one another once more, but without the fear of discovery which kept their battles small pre-Triumph. Humans will be slaughtered."

Damn him, he's right.

"You could lead them," I suggest.

Samuel's grin becomes huge, and he mock-punches me in the arm. "Don't be obtuse. Who will follow a hermit from the desert whose one gift is being forgettable? No, if anyone is going to replace our sire, you'll need to look at your sisters— or yourself."

It's my turn to snort this time. "I'm not leadership material."

If any of us were suitable, it would be Bella. She's always been a leader and a problem solver. Our oldest sister already does a lot of the administrative work that would come with ruling—if Cain were the type to bother with such trivialities.

But would she change things, if given the chance? Or just continue to maintain the status quo? Morwen is probably the most revolutionary among us, but no one sane would leave her to rule anyone…

"Think on it," Samuel suggests. "Heaven knows, Cain's new world order isn't going anywhere in the next few days. Take a week or so, enjoy the feeling of being out from underneath our Sire's thumb."

"I'm no longer alone," I finally say. "Cain forced me to take six thralls, and two of my sisters are with me. I can't make any kind of decision without consulting them."

I made a promise on that plane, and I intend to keep it. My gut is telling me to accept Samuel's offer, but I won't make another choice that separates us.

"Six thralls." Samuel leans back on his heels, stunned. "So many…"

"He meant to destabilise me."

"And has it?"

I shake my head. "The bonds are solidifying at different rates. So far, I'm managing."

"Have you considered breaking them to ease the strain?"

I meet his eyes. "Have you ever felt a thrall bond break?" I know my tone is haunted, but I can't seem to keep the memory of the pain out of my voice. "It's like having your soul scoured from inside of you."

"But surely having six of Cain's minions following you around… what?"

I'm shaking my head, laughing. "You don't know the *half* of it."

He cocks his head to one side. "Then I'll have them brought here." He pauses. "You've changed, sister. I didn't think our sire's darling would ever be the type to consult others before she acted."

Me either.

CHAPTER SIXTEEN

EVELYN

I'D UNDERESTIMATED SAMUEL.

So had everyone. That's why he's still alive.

He told me a lot about his life since he faked his death. What he's built is incredible. A place where Cain has no influence, big enough to be the equivalent of a small town, but with the kind of close-knit community where everyone knows everyone else. I would never have expected something like this to work. Especially with vampires, who are normally loners.

But seeing the way they work here, I have to wonder: are we loners by nature, or because Cain only chose isolated people to join his ranks to ensure they would be less tempted to rally together against him?

But he won't answer the one question which matters most.

How can we kill Cain?

Samuel danced around the topic whenever I brought it up. That evasiveness will piss Gideon and Frost off. I just hope they don't push him so hard he decides to throw us out, because I accepted his offer to spend time here. I think we need a place like this right now. Some way to get our heads screwed on and our pack back together before we try to take out Cain.

I told Samuel about my suspicions regarding my sisters, and he even agreed to have them monitored for me.

For the first time in forever, I don't have to be planning the next step, or thinking about how to keep myself alive, or putting myself into Cain's headspace to anticipate the danger he'll throw my way next.

This is a gift, and I plan to take it.

I'd like to get to know Samuel's family, if he'll let me. And maybe, when the pack is here, and we've sorted out where we stand with one another, we can ask Samuel again, and he'll trust us enough to tell me how we can kill our sire.

Until then… Is it so wrong to just need a break?

Well, I suppose I'm about to find out.

I glance around the room again, smiling softly.

It's not quite what the pack is used to. In the cabin where we stayed before, and even at the crumbling resort we were based in, there was a room each for personal space. Here, spare rooms are a luxury, but the other vampires have done their best to make the space feel like home.

At least Morwen and Mia have their own room.

I'm happy for the two of them, but no one wants to be privy to a graphic live performance of their sibling's sex life. Poor Immy has to share with them, but there's a screen that should hopefully prevent her from catching an eyeful of them in the middle of the day.

All of the vampires here—relatives of Samuel's or not—address me as 'Aunty Evonnia,' a custom which is as endearing as it is strange. More than once, I've tried correcting them, or asking them to just call me Evie. It's not really working.

The younger ones slowly started calling me Aunty Evie as we chatted while making up the dorm room for the pack, but getting them to drop the family title is impossible.

Dare I say, I kind of like it?

There are three double beds, spaced evenly across the back wall. They're piled high with covers, because apparently the desert sun doesn't do much to heat the caves during the day. Textiles are everywhere for that reason. The walls are hung with woven tapestries, decorated with patterns that make up for the bare stone, and the floor is piled high with rugs until it squishes beneath my feet as I pace across it.

I've explored every inch of the room, and now there's nothing to do but wait.

The door opens, and I look up, eagerly only for my face to fall when I realise it's not them.

Instead, Samuel's son, Bakari, is framed in the doorway.

Before I can speak, he holds a hand up to silence me.

"You need to leave."

I grind my teeth, caught between the urge to tell him to fuck off—with my sword if necessary—and the knowledge that doing so will probably cut short my visit here. If I leave before I find out what Samuel is hiding, we may never be free of our sire.

"I plan to," I reply, deliberately keeping my tone even. "As soon as my pack has healed and your sire tells me how to kill Cain."

He spits on the ground. "You've brought us to his attention. It's only a matter of time until you lead him straight to our doorstep."

"Bakari! Your father said you'd be lurking, but I thought you'd have the decency to at least do it outside."

The soft voice makes him stiffen, and his expression turns

from suspicious and guarded to almost… *guilty*. A small hand taps lightly at his shoulder and he shoots me a warning glare before shifting to one side to admit the much smaller woman behind him.

The first thing I notice is her large, beaming smile. Her warm brown eyes are decorated with laugh lines, and her lip, nose, and ears are all pierced with golden rings. Unlike most vampires, who are turned young, she wears her experience like a cloak. Streaks of silver flash like lightning through her gorgeous mane of bushy black hair, and her struggles have written themselves into the lines across her brow.

Her dress is loose and flowing, but there's no tell-tale bulk of weapons hidden beneath the modest blue garment.

"Mother," Bakari mutters, "Does Father—"

"Of course he does." She dismisses his concern with a shake of her head, barely paying her son a glance as she reaches forward and takes both my hands in hers and squeezes them in greeting. "As if he would try to deny me the chance to meet my sister after all this time. I'm so glad you're here, Evonnia. I hope my son has made you comfortable?"

I meet his eyes over her head, and a satisfied smile tugs at my lips at the look of pure panic that covers his face. This soft-spoken woman clearly terrifies him. I like her already.

After giving him a *look* which reminds him exactly how nice I'm being, I say. "He's been really helpful, actually. And I go by Evie now."

"You're being too kind." She snorts. "I know what he's like —I'm his mother! Let me guess, he was probably lecturing you on security before I interrupted him?" She winks at me, before looking back at Bakari. "Go and help the others bring your uncles up from the garage."

"Mother…" He trails off again, then picks up in that other language.

"Don't be rude!" she snaps, cutting him off. "While your

aunt visits, we use her language. Now, go and be useful, and I'll make sure she's settled."

His fists clench, but he doesn't object again. He doesn't spare either of us a second glance as he spins on his heel and strides from the room.

"Lord save me from firstborns and their over-developed sense of responsibility." She sighs long and hard. "I'm Noha, Samuel's wife." She squeezes my hands a second time before dropping them. "It's good to finally meet you after so long. I want to let you know, whatever my husband or son have tried to convince you, you're welcome to stay here as long as you like. In fact, I hope you come to call this place home."

Taken aback by such a sudden and earnest sentiment from someone who is—for all intents and purposes—a complete stranger to me, I can't do much more than nod mutely.

"I know this is nothing like New York," Noha continues. "But if there's anything you need to make you more comfortable, let me know. We've never had lycans here before, so I didn't know what you'd need…" She trails off.

"I'm sure it will be fine, this room is more than enough, and the full moon is two weeks away, so…" I shrug, unsure of what else to say.

The silence which falls between us is awkward, but she doesn't let it linger.

"You'll have to tell me some stories of Samuel when you knew him. He barely ever talks about his past, or his family—though I know it's not a conventional one. I've been so curious."

I can see why he hasn't told her. Our family isn't exactly easy conversation. But still, it's a lot to keep from your spouse for…

"How long have you two been together?" I ask. "Obviously a few centuries, given you're awake in the daylight…"

"We just celebrated our six hundredth anniversary a few years ago." She smiles fondly.

Has it really been so long since our brothers were killed? I suppose it was longer... Cain set each of them the task of creating an empire of their own and maintaining it, but none of them managed it. One by one, they conquered, and then one by one they lost their grip on power. Failure was the excuse Cain needed to order them executed—or hunted to death if they tried to run.

The process took centuries.

Samuel lasted longer than the rest of our brothers. I was at least a thousand years old before he 'died.'

I can't remember why his toy empire failed, but I remember suspecting foul play. I felt that about all of our brothers' failures, come to think of it...

It was just a little too hard to believe that such old and powerful vampires were incapable of building and ruling a mortal empire for longer than a few decades. I remember wondering if the 'humans' responsible for their undoing were actually placed there by Cain.

But I *cannot* remember how Samuel's empire fell. His gift is so infuriating.

"Cain ordered him killed when he failed to defeat the Byzantines..." I muse, trying to focus on the specifics for a few seconds before I give up. "So that meant he was alone for four centuries before he met you?" That's a long time to be on the run, even for a vampire. And Samuel said he was hiding in a cave.

God. It's a miracle he didn't go insane.

"Yes. Our village thought he was a spirit. The number of elders who tried to exorcise him before they declared him benevolent was ridiculous," Noha babbles. "What was he like before then? Any less serious?"

I shake my head. "Sorry to disappoint you, he was always

the most cautious of our brothers. It's probably how he survived."

"Bakari takes after him," Noha agrees. "Too serious, both of them. And I get the feeling you're going to be the same, aren't you?"

Am I?

I bite my lip as I consider her question. "I've never thought about it—"

But I'm cut off by the shuffling of feet and the grumbling of some familiar voices.

They're finally here.

"When I get free…" That's definitely Vane's baritone threatening them.

"Shut up," Frost retorts. "I scent Eve. Is she here? What the fuck have you done with her?"

Bakari arrives first, pulling his mother to one side to allow the other vampires to wrestle my thralls and sisters in through the doorway. All of them are struggling, and there are bags over their heads to stop them from seeing anything. Their hands are bound behind them in silver cuffs, and their movements are sluggish. Samuel's men must have drugged them like they did me when they picked them up.

Draven is the worst of the lot. It's still daytime, and the effects are obviously wearing on him. His feet drag on the floor, and he wobbles as they release him.

"The cuffs aren't necessary," I insist, watching as everyone's attention snaps straight to me.

"If they become violent," Bakari begins, glaring at me as some other men arrive and start lining up our luggage and equipment against the wall.

"They won't."

Noha shakes her head in exasperation. "Did I teach you no respect for your elders?" she asks her son. "Listen to your aunt. She knows a lot more about them than you do. And two of these women are your family." She rubs at her temples. "Release them. Then we can leave them in peace for Evie to get them up to speed."

Because *that's* going to go well.

I've had plenty of time to think about how the others are going to take this. I'm pretty sure Finn and Silas will leap on the opportunity, but the others…

No. As far as they're concerned, we're here to kill Cain, not to take a holiday.

It's going to be tough to convince them not to hunt Samuel down and pummel him for the answers they want.

Not that it would work. He might have been in exile for over a thousand years, but he's still a son of Cain. Torture is the bread and butter of our sire.

"Come find me when you're done," Noha insists, as Bakari half-drags her from the room and his men start uncuffing their prisoners. "I can give you a proper tour."

The other vampires follow them as my men start ripping their blindfolds off. Finn wastes no time in rushing straight for me and hugging the life out of me, and Silas does the same. Draven gives me a once over, checking for injuries, before he follows the others in checking out the room.

"This is the oddest cell I've ever been in," Mia comments, lightly.

"Definitely among the cosiest," Immy agrees. "What's going on, Evie?"

I take a deep breath and launch into the tale of the past few hours.

CHAPTER SEVENTEEN

SILAS

SHE'S A GENIUS.

Evie is sitting on the edge of the bed, curled up against Finn's side as she waits for our judgement of her unbelievable story. Draven has collapsed against her other side, his eyes closed. He might be asleep, but I doubt it. Either way, he hasn't reacted to her story.

Frost and Gideon don't like it—that much is obvious from their stony expressions—and neither of her sisters look that fond of the idea. But a single shared glance with Vane and Mia confirms that we're on the same page.

"This is perfect," I say, as soon as she looks at me. "If Cain doesn't know about this place, then I say we stay here until we're at full strength. Turn it into our new base of operations —if Samuel will let us. How often does an opportunity like this come along? We'd be stupid not to use it."

My quick response stuns the others, giving them pause and hopefully stopping whatever rant Gideon was about to lay at her feet.

"Agreed." Vane gives Gideon a meaningful look. "It's a safe place for Finn and Mia. I say we stay."

"What about the secret that Samuel's hiding?" Gideon growls. "You want to just forget about that in exchange for him harbouring us? And what if we've drawn Cain here already? We've been careful, but you can never be too sure…"

"He's not going to tell you if you just barge in there and demand it of him." Mia sighs in exasperation. "This guy obviously has a good thing going here. You can't threaten him, because we'll never find him again. You can't bribe him because he's got everything he needs. The only way he's going to give up what he knows is if he trusts us and sees the need for it." She looks at Morwen and rolls her eyes. "Which means we're dependent on a bunch of emotionally stilted vampires rebuilding their sibling bonds to get the info we need."

Gideon looks ready to have an aneurysm at the thought. His face is slowly turning a terrifying shade of puce as his frustration works its way free.

"How long is that going to take?" Frost asks, and I blink as I realise for once, he's the more level-headed of the two of them. "A week? Two? We can't stay here for the full moon. I doubt they're equipped for it."

I see what he's doing, trying to give Gideon a time frame to focus on.

Unfortunately, it's not going to work.

The one with the best chance of convincing Gideon to calm down is Finn, and he… isn't moving closer or seeking to comfort his alpha at all.

What the fuck?

Omegas are drawn to raging alphas. The compulsion to soothe is in their blood.

So why is Finn keeping distance between them and holding Evie like she's a shield?

Yes, I know things have been strained between them recently, but never so much that Finn was reluctant to ground Gid when he was in a rage. We spent so many years building up that trust, reassuring him that whatever happened in his old pack, we would never, ever hurt him, or belittle him for following his instincts.

What did Gideon *do*? What stupid stunt has he pulled that our omega is fighting his own nature?

I frown and glance at Vane, wondering if he knows what's going on. My brother is glaring at Gideon with a vehemence that surprises me.

Okay, so it looks like he has some idea about what happened.

"Gid, cool off." Frost gives the order, and it works... slightly.

The other alpha shakes himself and looks around the room, though his hands remain clenched at his sides.

"We need to kill Cain," he says, voice surprisingly even given the colour still staining his cheeks. "This place won't remain safe forever, and we're only increasing the risk of Samuel's family getting hurt the longer we stay here."

"But he doesn't know where here *is*," Evie pushes. "We need a break, Gideon. After everything... Do you even know how many fingers Draven has regrown in the last month? How many toes? God knows what Frost suffered in the dungeon. And Finn..." She waves a hand at him. "Finn's been working so hard he's burned out. I thought omegas were the heart of the pack?"

"I'm fine," Finn mutters, quietly. "I don't want to be involved in this."

Evie stares at him, arching a single brow, and he actually blushes.

"Yeah, okay, maybe I am a bit tired," he concedes.

Gid flinches subtly at his words, and the motion is so small that I think I'm the only one who notices.

Finn doesn't, because he's still looking at Evie as he continues, "But I still don't want to get involved."

And that's the problem.

If Finn is so emotionally worn down he's no longer able to deal with pack quarrels, then he needs a break. We all do. A pack with a worn-down peace-keeper often ends up tearing itself to shreds.

I don't say it, but I catch Gideon's eye and hold his stare rather than dropping my eyes as expected, letting him see exactly how strongly I feel about this.

Immy sighs. "We're not getting any further without what's in our brother's head," she mumbles. "And I... I'd really like a break. I agree with Evie. Let's just breathe. Take some time to figure out who we all are without our sire watching every move we make."

"It would be nice to be together openly," Mia murmurs to Morwen, clearly tackling our other holdout. "We can ditch these losers and explore. I've always wanted to try sand kiting."

I grimace, but say nothing. Mia *is* immortal, as much as we tend to forget that. If she wants to try extreme sports, then there's not really much we can do to stop her.

Vane, however, has no such chill. "Have you got the protective equipment for that?"

Morwen hisses at him. "I'll keep her safe."

Mia rolls her eyes, glancing between the two of them with amusement. "The more you try to keep me safe, the more I'll misbehave," she promises.

Morwen arches one delicate eyebrow. "Try it and I'll spank your ass, brat."

Okay. That's *way* more information than I needed about my sister's sex life.

Vane growls, and I hurriedly put a hand on his chest. "Dude, not our business, remember?"

And like he can talk, anyway. I know exactly what kind of things he's into… spankings are practically *tame* by comparison.

He shrugs me off, but says nothing, earning him a smug grin from our sister, who doesn't even thank me for being the 'cool' brother.

Likely because she realises I just plan to be sneakier about ensuring her safety.

That leaves only Draven and Gideon.

The former is all but asleep against Evie, and I have to bite my lip to resist the urge to start messing with him just because I can. I hope someone brought my prank supplies with us during our kidnapping, but I can be resourceful if they didn't.

With this new development, there will be plenty of opportunities to taunt him.

"We stay," the vampire mutters.

Gideon's outvoted now, and he knows it. Running an exasperated hand through his hair, he gives Finn a long, indecipherable look, before turning and heading for the bed in the far corner.

"Fine. But I want us out of here by the full moon, *with* that information." He aims the last part at Evie, who shrugs. "I mean it. This is not a holiday. Just a…"

"Pause," I add, helpfully.

"A *brief* pause," he stresses. "Now it's been a hard few days. I'm getting some rest. So shut up or clear out."

Good, I think. *He needs it.*

"You guys have a separate room across the hall," Evie murmurs to her sisters and Mia. She extracts herself from Finn and Draven, then slides off the bed and heads for the door. "I'll show you where it is."

With her gone, Finn heads straight for the piles of our equipment, searching through it without paying the rest of us any further attention. Draven collapses into true sleep with a loud snore that makes me grin. I guess that leaves my brother and Frost to help me sort out what's happening within our pack.

Making eye contact with them, I jerk my head towards the door.

"What's going on with Gideon?" I ask, as soon as we're all outside, with the door muffling our words. "Finn…"

Vane sighs and leans back against the wall of the corridor. "That would be my fault."

I tilt my head to one side. "How?"

"Gid was hyper-fixating. I took him to Finn to see if he could snap him out of it… I'm not sure what happened in there, but when Finn came and got me, the room reeked of sex, and he was stressing." Vane glowers at the door. "It's Gideon's mess, but I'm pretty sure the idiot has no idea how to fix it."

Frost groans. "Just what we need, an alpha with hyper-fixation who's pissed off the only omega who could do something about it."

That just about sums it up. "Hopefully, some time with Evie will clear Finn's head and the enforced R and R will bring Gideon's intensity down a few notches." At least, I hope it will.

If not, there's a chance Evie might be able to distract him, but Gid has his thrall bond locked down tight.

"Do either of you feel like this is just…"

"Too good to be true?" I ask.

Vane grunts. "Yeah. How often does a Cain-free paradise pop up and open its doors to us?"

"Never." Frost tugs at the scruffy stubble at the side of his face. "Keep an eye on them, though. I want this to be genuine, but there's something… iffy about this place. And no one can remain hidden forever. I don't want to be taken off guard if Cain somehow follows us here."

Wise words. Vane nods once. "I'll have a quiet look around," he mutters. "Listen in on what people are saying." He pauses, looking back at the door. "Silas, you need to keep an eye on Finn and Gideon. Try to keep them out of each other's way until it looks like they're ready to work on their issues constructively."

I will not call my big brother bossy. I will not call my big brother—"Yes, sir." My mock salute is the crowning finish which earns me a pointed glare from both him and Frost.

Tough. Someone needs to keep them humble.

It's a good call, though. Finn isn't combative by nature, but the omega has always had ways of making his displeasure clear when the pack has a falling out. Last time I pissed him off, he 'accidentally' used salt rather than sugar in the batch of biscuits he was baking. The time before that, a 'laundry machine malfunction' meant that all of my clothes shrank three sizes.

And, being the one in charge of shopping for the whole pack, he didn't feel in the least bit guilty. If anything, he probably secretly relished the chance to go out and buy me a whole new wardrobe.

If Gid is on edge, our omega's quiet displays of displeasure won't help—no matter how justified they may be.

"I'm going to keep an eye on Immy and Morwen," Frost mumbles, staring at the two doors opposite us. "I trust Mia, but those two… If one of them is a spy, they could ruin everything."

"Cain hasn't caught up to us yet," I argue. "He's not the kind of person to let Evie's defection stand. If he knew where to find us, we'd be six feet under."

Frost shakes his head. "Maybe."

"If I were him, I'd use us to find Samuel and take care of the threat all at once," Vane mutters. "Makes more sense."

"But with multiple targets, there's more chance of someone slipping through the net," I say. "Besides, Samuel might have told other people. I would've done so in his position."

Frost shakes his head. "If a whole group of people had a way to kill Cain, why haven't they done it? I thought I understood it when we thought Samuel was alone and on the run. Now... have you seen this place? They probably have enough resources to pull off an assassination. Cain would never see it coming. He has no idea they even exist."

That worrying thought leaves a grim silence in its wake. For the first time since Samuel's survival was confirmed, I start to question whether this trip will actually prove fruitful.

It has to, right? Surely, we can't have come this far for nothing.

No. I won't believe it.

CHAPTER EIGHTEEN

FROST

FOR THE FIRST DAY, ALL WE DO IS SLEEP. I'M PRETTY SURE THE entire team is fucking exhausted, both mentally and physically. No one is able to summon the energy for more than a quiet day where nothing gets done beyond moving the last of our stuff in and poking around the immediate area. Samuel's people delivered food and blood to our room, and Silas and Eve sneaked off halfway through the night, only to return stinking of sex and blood.

Any jealousy I had disappeared with the relaxed, happy feelings that floated from amongst the static consuming her end of our bond.

I knew I'd have to share her once I got her back, but it's only now that I've seen her with the others that I'm beginning to accept it. Welcome it, even.

Watching her come apart on Vane's lap was beautiful. Before, I worried endlessly that I'd never be enough for her. I was a mortal, and she was an ancient creature of legend. No matter how many times she assured me otherwise, I knew there would always be some parts of her that I could never satisfy.

I could never make her relax like Silas does, or draw out the softer parts of her like Finn. Heck, I definitely can't give her *whatever* it is Draven brings to their relationship.

But I don't have to.

All I have to do is be me, and hope that she can fall in love with me again.

So this evening, I've got it all planned out. All I need is for sleeping beauty to wake up. I glance over at where she's entangled with Draven, having been dragged into bed with him the second the sun came up. The two of them look so cosy that I'm loath to wake them, but if I wait for the rest of the pack to wake up, I'll never get her to myself.

With that thought firmly in mind, I creep over to them and stroke a lock of her hair out of her face.

She comes awake instantly, without moving or making a sound. Almost like she was never truly asleep in the first place. I have the sudden urge to make sure that she never has to wake like that again. I want to see her bleary-eyed with the perfect comfort of a woman who knows she's safe in her own bed. I want her to yawn and snuggle back into the covers and mumble about five more minutes.

But our world doesn't allow for those kinds of tiny luxuries, so I press my finger to my lips and jerk my head at the pile of clothes I've prepared for her.

She frowns, her ice-blue eyes narrowing as she tries, and fails, to figure out what I'm up to. She still does as I ask without complaint, twisting out of Draven's arms like a snake.

When she emerges from the bathroom in the shorts I found in her luggage and turns around to grab something she's forgotten, I almost come in my boxers.

Fuck, Finn never said he was buying her clothes that would fucking paint themselves onto her body.

I can't decide if I love or hate him right now, but what a *view.*

Picking my jaw up from the floor, I usher her quickly out of the door and into the tunnel.

"Where are we going?" she asks as soon as the door closes on the rest of our sleeping pack mates.

Hesitating—because there's a very real risk she'll just turn around and leave—I do my best to buy myself time by running a hand through my hair and looking around. Shit, I didn't realise how nervous I'd be until we got here.

"Frost?"

"It's a date," I blurt, then curse. "I mean, if you want it to be, that is."

Smooth, Frost, real fucking smooth.

"A date?" A shadow flashes through her gaze, and I just know she's thinking of the corny shit I did when we first started seeing one another. Thoughts of the tiny smirks she used to give me back then—even painful as they were—were the only thing that kept me going while she was locked away.

Those memories are now tainted by the knowledge that our relationship started as a ruse to get closer to her. So I'm reclaiming them for us. Starting tonight, if she'll let me.

"A date," I confirm, grateful that my voice is stronger the second time. "That ravine is begging for a moron like me to climb it, and I thought you'd like to watch me fall and break my neck."

She snorts, and a flicker of hope sparks behind my sternum.

Say yes, Eve. Come on. Say yes.

"I'll beat you to the top and watch you fall from above," she retorts, using her best haughty tone. "It'll be far more entertaining."

There she is. I wondered if the old Eve was completely broken, but she's still there.

The sun is just setting as I open the door that leads us out to the bottom of the ravine where Samuel's built his hideaway village. I scouted the area earlier, and picked the most challenging section because I *knew* Eve would've killed me if I'd tried to go easy on her.

She's so quiet. Why hasn't she said something? Is she waiting for me to say something?

I'm so paranoid that this is going badly, that when she does speak, I miss it completely.

"Sorry?" I say, with a grimace.

Eve has never been one for blushing, but there's the slightest hint of colour to her cheeks as she replies.

"I just asked what brought all this on," she mumbles.

"Your orgasm," I say, then I realise what I said and press the heel of my hand into the middle of my forehead, groaning. "Not like *that*. I mean, it was a significant factor but not the main—it's not as pervy as it sounds—"

Eve's tinkling laugh rockets through me, stopping me before I can dig myself further into the hole I'm creating. "You haven't changed."

Her smile falls too quickly, and I hasten to continue. "I thought I'd feel jealous, watching you get off with the others," I explain. "But I didn't. I loved it. I just… I want that for us again, and I don't want to be left behind."

"You're taking me climbing to get me to sleep with you?"

Did I say it like that? I guess I did. *Shit.* "No! That's not what I meant." I run another hand through my hair and stride ahead, grumbling as I try to figure out how to phrase it so it *doesn't* sound like I'm a pervert who wants to fuck her until we both can't walk. "I just meant…"

A delicate hand covers my mouth, stopping me mid-sentence. "I missed you too."

The wound up coil of tension inside of me loosens, and I breathe for the first time in what feels like years. "I want to earn you back, Eve."

The smile falls. "I…"

"Don't say it," I beg. "I know I fucked up. Badly. Saying I'm sorry and taking you on poor excuses for dates doesn't cut it. But I have to make sure you know I'm not going to let this go… unless you want me to, but you didn't say that…" Please don't say that. "I want to make this our new beginning. New me, new you… old love."

Fuck, that sounded corny. I should've thought this through better. Come up with good, suave answers. Talking from the heart just *isn't* romantic. Or going well.

Her quiet chuckle distracts me from my own self-directed internal rant. "I forgot how awkward you were when we first met," she admits. "I found it cute then."

And now? Wait, is cute good? Vampires don't generally want cute thralls, do they? Otherwise everyone would just have pets and never shackle themselves to a person.

Before I can think of something better to say, we reach the spot I picked out.

I wave my hand at the sheer, vertical ascent and grin. There are a few points where the cliff forms overhangs where we can rest, but they're few and far between.

"Ladies first," I say, once again vacillating between wanting to praise Finn for the view of her ass in those shorts and wanting to kill him for the boner I'll have to endure.

I swear, if I make it to the top without coming in my boxers, I deserve a sainthood.

She gives me a knowing look before turning to regard the rock. In the daylight, the stone is a warm, ruddy tan colour, but the slim crescent moon shines brightly over the desert, turning the sand and stone silver wherever it touches, and creating dark shadows everywhere else.

The darkness is no problem for either of us now. Eve's always been quick, and I watch as her pupils dart across the cliff, figuring out her preferred route. She never goes for the easy way, or even the way I expect, and I watch, fascinated anew by her process. That tiny frown line appears between her brows, and I barely resist the urge to smooth it away.

Once I would've done it without hesitation. Now I'm fighting to reclaim that privilege.

When she springs upward, catching a barely visible crevice with one hand and holding herself to the rock with that grip alone, I grin.

We're off.

The two of us stick to human pace and use as little of our enhanced speed as possible to keep the climb more challenging. It doesn't take long for sweat to slick down my spine, and I take a deep breath as the scent inevitably starts to draw a far-off ghoul pack into responding.

I'll have to deal with them later, but for now, I'll leave them be. It can't be a bad thing to have backup all the way out here if we're planning to stay a while.

"You're awfully quiet," Eve teases, drawing my attention back to her. "I thought you'd be talking my ear off trying to convince me of all the reasons for us to get back together."

It's a quiet reference to the time when I first asked her if I could court her. Back then, I'd listed all of the reasons and had them written down, ready to whip out when she inevitably shot me down.

Only she never did, and when she found the list later on, she never let me live it down.

"Number one," I begin, glancing upwards and suppressing a groan. "I've been fully reformed since we were last bonded. I no longer leave my dirty clothes everywhere, and I've even been schooled into putting the seat down by Finn."

She snorts, and I keep going.

"Reason number two, I come with minions."

"What good is a group of ghoul minions going to do me?" she asks.

"Oh, I was talking about the pack," I retort. "Gid loves it when I call him my minion. Didn't you know? But I suppose the ghouls are all right." I pause, running my fingers over the stone, searching for a new handhold. "Three, I'm convinced being turned gave me another two inches."

She's silent for a while, scrabbling for her next hold, until she figures it out and looks down at me with wide eyes. "That is *not* a known side effect of vampirism."

"Four," I continue as if she hasn't spoken. "I've got us a house. A few, actually, but there's this one place, back in the Old Country…"

This time, she nearly falls from the cliff in surprise.

"That's a little presumptuous—"

"I had it designed so it was perfect for you." I obsessed over every tiny detail, dragging up every memory of our time together when she expressed a preference on *anything*. "It kept me sane." And tortured me at the same time.

All I could think about was her, anyway. At least when I was working on the house, I could remember the good moments.

And not the way she looked when she was forced to break our bond and locked into that coffin.

"Five?" she whispers, and I give myself a shake, forcing myself to move upwards and cross the gap between us.

"Five," I say, swallowing the hoarseness that threatens to choke me. "I'm still in love with you."

The air around us goes still the moment I say it, and her silence bands around my chest until I have to keep talking or just stop breathing.

"I'll always love you. No matter how long we're apart, or whether we're immortal or mortal. I'd love you if you were a ghoul. I just can't stop. Believe me, I tried. After the thrall bond broke, I wanted to stop. I would've given anything to be able to stop—"

"Well, you must've succeeded," she retorts. "Because you didn't rush to my rescue for almost two hundred years."

I nod, pressing my head against the stone. "I'll grant you that one. I didn't."

"Why?" Her voice is strong, but the word holds a wealth of uncertainty. "You could've come for me earlier. Enacted your plan at any point. Why leave me there for so long if you claim you've always loved me?"

"At first... I was too broken," I admit, hating myself. "It took a decade for Draven's team to get me out of there, and I was just a shell. People hid me, made me eat, but I couldn't do anything."

"Obviously that passed."

"Yes, in time, and thanks to the dedication of a few people who knew me from before and didn't want me dead because I was an abomination..."

"What?"

"I was part of a resistance that hated vampires, Eve. When they found out I *was* one, there were a lot of people who wanted to put me down."

Her outraged hiss is a good sign, right?

"There was a lot of debate about whether I should be allowed to live. Then Cain did me a favour and decided to wipe out a whole load of the resistance at once. After that, everything was about survival. I could barely breathe without vampires breaking down the door of my safe house..."

"But you had Gideon and the others..."

I snort, because I *wish* I'd had the pack back then. "Not for almost sixty years. I was alone, and I had no connections. No way to find you." I take a deep breath, not sure if I should admit the next part. "I left the resistance behind for a while, traipsed all over Europe, searching for you, and then the Americas when Cain moved his Court there. Almost died or got recaptured a hundred times... Then I went back to the resistance, hoping that with the right resources I might be able to get somewhere, but..."

"The Triumph happened," she breathes, filling in the gap.

"I tried," I insist, shifting my weight and propelling my body up to grab a handhold beside her. "I... failed." God, it hurts to admit that. "I'm sorry."

She's stopped moving, but she still won't meet my eyes.

"I'll do anything, even though I know that will never be enough," I continue, when I can't take the silence anymore.

Eve gives me a look I can't quite decipher. "You're not at all who you were before, are you?"

Scoffing, because she's probably right, I meet her eyes and mutter. "A lot of shit changed when I lost you. I was a cocky idiot before, and look where it got me."

Without replying, she shifts her grip and starts climbing once more.

I'm almost certain I've just fucked up when she calls down, "What's number six?"

Relief washes over me, and I glance up only to get side-tracked again by her gorgeous ass as she claws at the rock with her foot. I'd gone soft during my confession, but my cock rears up again like a damned Eve-seeking-missile.

"Six." I pause, pretending to think while I attempt to subtly adjust myself while clinging to the cliff face. "I'm a walking buffet."

I'd give anything to have her fangs sink into me again. Her venom must be addictive, because there's no other explanation for the way that the memory of her bite haunts my dreams.

"True," she muses, heaving herself up the ledge. "But what if I've gone off your blood?"

"You think my blood is delicious," I retort. "Unless somehow becoming a ghoul has soured my taste…"

I know it hasn't. She didn't complain when she drank from me back at the safe house.

"Maybe I was too addled by silver last time to notice," she murmurs speculatively. "I suppose I'll have to drink from you again to make certain. After all, you dragged me out of the base before I could grab breakfast."

If not for immortal reflexes, I would've fallen off the damned cliff.

She wants to drink from me.

Suddenly, the urge to just use my immortal speed to climb this cliff is overwhelming. My focus narrows down to the finish line, and I push myself harder, silently willing her to do the same.

But Eve wants to play with my emotions, because she keeps herself to the same deliberate and painfully slow mortal pace, and I—still leery of going ahead in case she falls —am forced to match it.

We finally haul ourselves over the edge, and a sharp wind immediately hits me, laced with biting granules of sand that sting my flesh. The desert around us is empty and peaceful— beautiful in its own, alien way—but I can't pay it any attention while Eve's standing next to me. She consumes all of my attention without trying, or noticing.

Always has.

"Breakfast?" I ask.

The breathlessness of my own voice sabotages my chipper attempt to hide the hopefulness in my voice, and she chuckles in response.

"You seem a little winded," she teases. "Do you need a second to catch your breath?"

Fuck. No.

In two strides I'm in front of her, and she doesn't fight me as I haul her against my chest until her face is inches away from the vein at my throat.

The move backfires. Spectacularly.

Because now *my* face is also inches away from *her* throat. Shit.

I can smell her blood, racing beneath her fragile skin with every harried beat of her heart.

That scent… haunts me.

The first and last time I tasted Eve, was when her sire forced her to break our thrall bond. A huge part of me is terrified to ever drink from her again because she could say those words again.

A smaller part of me doesn't care about the risk. It just wants Eve.

And all of this worrying is cut off the second she strikes.

"Fuck, Eve." I groan, supporting her with one arm beneath her ass as my other hand winds into her hair and holds her in place. "Drink from me, baby. That's it. Fuck."

Pleasure sears me from the inside out, spreading further around my body with every second. I'm so hard it's *painful,* and my hips rock against her, seeking whatever relief I can get. She's not holding back on her venom, and she's old enough that it's powerful stuff. All my instincts scream at me to lay her out on the nearest sand dune and fuck her until we're both spent.

My sanity is holding on by a thread. Only the knowledge that she hasn't fully forgiven me, and that I definitely don't deserve to lose myself in her body keep me from driving into her. I'm this close to coming in my boxers, but I will not let myself take those kinds of liberties with her.

My mouth doesn't get the memo.

"You know what you're doing to me," I accuse. "Use as

much venom as you want, Eve. I'm going to remember this, and when you decide to let me loose on your body again, I'm going to wreck you in revenge."

Her smile whispers across my skin a second before Eve proves just how much of a brat she can be by pumping another huge surge of venom into my neck.

"Fuck." I erupt into my pants with a strangled curse. My orgasm lights up every single nerve ending, damn near blinding me with its ferocity, and my knees shake as she slowly slips her fangs free of my vein and gives my neck a long, slow provocative lick to seal the wounds.

"Oh dear, I guess your stamina hasn't improved with age?" she teases, tugging her way out of my arms and striding back to the edge of the ravine before flashing a smile over her shoulder at me. "Such a pity, but I hear they have lubricant to help with that."

I'll show her stamina. "Just wait, baby. Eventually, I'm going to earn you. When that day comes, clear your calendar for a full week because you won't be able to walk anywhere." I suck in a breath and take a step, grimacing at the wetness trapped against my skin. "And you won't need any lubricant, because I'm going to make sure you're dripping for me before I take you."

Her blue eyes heat, and I shoot her a cocky grin in response. Deep inside, I feel the click as the thrall bond winds itself a little tighter, inching closer to completion—no matter that we're still a long way from feeling the full bond—but Eve doesn't say anything. Turning her back on me, she steps over the edge and free falls back down to the base of the ravine. I hesitate a second before following after her.

CHAPTER NINETEEN

EVELYN

THE SOUND OF MIA AND MORWEN LEAVING FROM ACROSS THE hall wakes me up. I haven't seen them since I returned to the base after Frost's date yesterday, but I know the two of them have been holed up in their room, exploring and preparing excitedly for their sand kiting trip. I can't say I understand the urge to surf over dunes, using a giant parachute to ride the powerful desert winds while getting pelted by sand. The amount I inhaled while scaling the ravine was enough for me.

But it seems Morwen has finally found someone who can match her unique brand of crazy.

Most of my thralls are still asleep when I hear their door slam shut. Only Gideon is awake. He's sitting at the desk that Finn set up on our arrival, swiping through things on the holo display too fast for me to follow.

Workaholic. Doesn't he know he's supposed to be resting?

He was doing the same thing yesterday when Frost and I

got back from our date… His dedication to the cause—and his pack—softens me a little, and I watch him through my lashes for a few moments as he clenches his jaw in frustration, glances over his shoulder at the sleeping bodies of his pack, and then sighs and gets back to work.

Gideon might be a bossy, commanding, controlling ass, but I'm beginning to think he is that way because he doesn't know any other way to show he cares. It doesn't mean he couldn't work on his people skills, though.

When I finally manage to untangle myself from Finn and Silas and sit up, he doesn't acknowledge me.

The alpha is so grumpy I can practically feel the force of it pulsing at my skin, so I don't linger. Pushing out of bed, I head for the bathroom and dress, using a baggy bomber jacket to hide the knives strapped along my forearms— because as much as I like Samuel and Noha, I don't trust anywhere enough to walk around unarmed. When I emerge, I head straight for the hallway without stopping.

If Morwen and Mia are gone, then that means Immy has been left alone in their room.

Which means no one is there to keep an eye on her.

Knocking quietly at her door yields no response, so I enter quietly and sneak around the screen that separates her bed from the one Morwen and Mia share. My youngest sister is wrapped in the covers with her arm flopped across her face.

"Go away," she grunts. "It's too early."

"The moon's out." Crossing to her bed I perch on the corner of it, trying to smother my grin.

"I can *feel* how satisfied you are to be waking me up, you bitch," Immy complains, rolling over until she's nothing more than a mass of ginger curls against the white pillowcase. "Gimme fifteen minutes and I'll be ready for whatever schemes you've cooked up."

"I wanted to explore this place. It's huge."

"Can't we explore when the sun is fully set?" she complains, her voice so muffled by the pillow that it's hard to tell what she's saying.

"No way," I retort, slyly grabbing a pillow from the other bed in the room and raising it above my head. "When did you get so boring?"

"Don't you dare pillow fight me," she grumbles, pushing to her elbows on the mattress, and I roll my eyes. "I can feel your sneaky feelings, remember?"

Shrugging, because pretending that I'd forgotten can only give me the advantage, I chuck the pillow back onto the other bed and bounce to my feet. "Come on, I bet there's plenty of stuff here and we've barely wandered farther than the end of this corridor. I—for one—want to know what that language is they all speak. I've never heard it."

"Coptic," Immy grumbles as she swings her legs out of bed. "Fayyumic dialect, I think. It went extinct a long time ago, so I don't remember much of it."

I'll take her word for it. She was always much better at languages than I was.

"I'll meet you in the hallway in ten minutes," I say, levelling my best playful warning glare at her. "Don't be late, or the pillow fight is happening."

Leaving her alone to dress, I close the door and run straight into Noha.

"You never came to find me," she explains, at seeing my startled expression. "I figured you were probably tired, but I wanted to invite you on my trip to the town later tonight."

"Sure," I reply, easily. "I didn't realise you left here so often."

Noha chuckles. "My husband *wishes* he could keep me locked away for my own safety, and I think Bakari would sell his soul for any excuse. But we can't live in total isolation.

Our vampires make regular trips into the cities to collect blood for the rest of us, and other things. If you come with me, we can get whatever you need to be more comfortable here. Even if that's ear-plugs."

I stare at her blankly, and she giggles. "Come on, six men and you're telling me *none* of them snore? Samuel sounds like a freight train most days."

Snorting, because she's not wrong, I reply. "A few of them do, but I don't mind it so much."

In my younger years, I spent a lot of time living amongst Cain's soldiers, on trips to hunt ghouls or defend our lands from lycan threats. I grew used to sleeping wherever and whenever I could, no matter how noisy it was.

"You'll have to tell me your secrets," Noha winks, just as Immy leaves her room, already dressed. "Are you two off somewhere?"

"Evie dragged me out of bed to explore," Immy yawns, rubbing sleep from her eyes. "But if you want to rescue me..."

Noha shakes her head. "Come on, I'll give you the tour. You can grab breakfast in the dining hall with the rest of us."

I'm about to refuse—because just the thought of feeding from anyone other than my thralls has become nauseating—when Finn pops his head through the door.

He looks adorably sleep mussed with his glasses askew and his eyes still blurry as he stumbles towards us. "I'm coming too," he grumbles. "Too much testosterone in that room for me to handle."

Raising a brow—because Finn never seemed to have a problem with the pack's testosterone before—I shrug. "The more the merrier."

Noha leads the three of us through the tunnels, pointing out the different rooms with their different coloured door frames as she goes.

"Yellow are private rooms," she explains. "Blue are for our security force, so best not to wander into those either, and white are public spaces."

"What do you all do down here all night?" Immy asks, peering into one of the public rooms curiously.

"A lot of us work in technology or investments." Noha grins. "We can't make too much money or it would draw Cain's attention, but we keep ourselves comfortable. Outside of that, there are plenty of recreational spaces, and the occasional trip to town—provided those who go keep a low profile when they're there."

"Sounds pretty idyllic," I mumble. "I still can't believe you've kept all of this a secret all of this time."

Noha shrugs. "Samuel believes Cain knows we exist, but not who we really are. A small vampire enclave keeping to themselves and not actively increasing their numbers doesn't cause him any harm, so he leaves us alone. The moment we see signs of him encroaching on our territory, or trying to infiltrate our ranks, we'll leave." She sighs. "Though I don't want to go. This is my home."

That makes no sense. The existence of any enclave not under his rule is an obvious threat to Cain. Our sire's power comes from the fact that *all* vampires are unified solely under his rule. If other vampires heard of this place...

Schisms would form in Cain's Court. The old and powerful would undoubtedly seek to create their own kingdoms. Cain would be forced to spend too much of his time and resources putting all of them down, which would inevitably give the packs and humans the free reign to cause their own brands of chaos.

No. Cain can't know about this place.

He would never have let them live this long if he did.

"For what it's worth," Immy says, comfortingly. "I've

never heard him mention this place, or any vampires who weren't under his control. Though Bella would know best."

"You have to tell me more about your other sisters," Noha instructs, as we come to a set of white-framed double doors and pass through them into a huge hall.

Instead of the buffet tables I'd expect of a human establishment, there are taps along the wall, above tables full of glasses. Each tap is misted with condensation and labelled with the blood type and species. Around the room, vampires sip from glasses, or from each other, all while talking.

The conversation doesn't stop when we walk in, although we do get a few looks, most people simply give us nods and move on.

"Not much to tell," Immy mutters. "Callie is shallow, and Bella is a workaholic."

Noha glances at me, as if wondering if I'll elaborate. I don't. No part of me wants to think about our other sisters right now. Perhaps she senses our reluctance because she changes the subject swiftly.

"We don't get any of the fancy synth blood they have in the big cities," she laments, gesturing at the taps along the wall. "It doesn't keep as long. But we do have pretty much every species you could want."

Immy lets out an appreciative sigh and drifts over to the vampire A positive, which has always been her favourite. It's nice to see some things haven't changed.

I go to follow, only for a hand on my arm to stop me. "You thirsty?" Finn asks.

My stomach rumbles, as if it's determined to answer for me. "A little," I mumble.

I haven't fed since I drank from Frost yesterday, and the dry feeling at the back of my throat is beginning to gnaw at me. The scents in the air aren't helping.

Thank God, I'm better at controlling my bloodlust than I was, but I shouldn't go too long without feeding.

"Then you drink from one of us," Finn growls, in an uncharacteristic display of possessiveness. "Not from strangers or donated blood. We made a promise when we pledged to you, remember?"

I nod mutely as I try to hide the way my fangs have lengthened in my mouth. I'm not ashamed to admit I'm more than a little turned on by his statement, but I don't want it to be obvious to everyone here.

Noha smiles and fans herself with her hand. "If that's what it's like to be bonded, maybe I should've let Samuel talk me into it," she says. "There's regular food for your men who require it in that fridge over there."

She points to a small station in one corner which I hadn't noticed until now. There's a small laser oven-grill combination cooker and a fridge directly below it.

"Thanks," Finn says, but he still isn't looking at her.

In fact, I'm pretty sure his attention doesn't leave my lips as Noha leads us to a table. I try to sit on a chair, but I'm quickly swept into his lap. On any other man, my face would be easily level with his neck, but Finn is tall. I have to put my hands on his shoulders and pull myself up until I'm at his vein.

I take my time with the bite, running my fangs up the side of his neck until he shudders before lapping the place I want to drink from.

When I finally pierce his skin, he's rock hard beneath me.

I hold most of my venom back because I have no idea how comfortable Finn is with public feedings. Some thralls are happy to be drunk and fucked in front of the entire Court—and it's not unusual for feeding frenzy to overtake everyone in Cain's throne room on occasion—but I don't want to push his boundaries, or our hosts'.

189

Still, there's enough of the intoxicant in my bite to have his hands clenching on my hips. A tiny gasp escapes his lips as I take my first pull on his vein, and the unique sweet flavour of his blood bursts on my tongue.

He shifts beneath me. To any onlooker, the movement would seem completely innocent, but it has the unexpected consequence of driving the line of his cock right up against my core.

It takes all of my self-control not to claw open the flimsy barrier of our jeans and drive myself onto his length. I've never felt as empty as I do now. My pussy clenches on nothing.

Another thrust like that, and I won't hold back.

"Behave," I warn, not removing my fangs from his neck.

A fine shudder runs through him, and I grin.

The omega loves it when his lovers get bossy with him in bed. So do I.

Don't get me wrong, I enjoy surrendering control to a demanding lover as much as the next woman. But there's something unexpectedly addictive about being in control of a strong, smart, sexy man.

Especially when he's tied up.

My mind flashes back to the memory of when we consummated our bond for the first time. When Silas tied him up for me to feed on...

Nope. I've got to stop thinking about that. Noha is right there...

I draw back with a lick and a kiss to my puncture marks, and let myself slide back down his chest until I'm curled up on his lap.

He hasn't eaten yet, and I frown.

"I'll be back," I murmur, slipping from his arms. "Do you want anything specific for breakfast?"

Finn shrugs. "Whatever's got plenty of protein, and iced coffee, if they've got it."

Nodding, I head over to the fridge. It takes an embarrassingly long time to identify what half of the food is—in my defence, I've been on a diet of blood for centuries—but I eventually return with the promised coffee and a pre-made bacon and potato omelette that heats up quickly in the small oven.

"Thanks," Finn smiles, pressing a kiss to my cheeks as I sit back down with his prize.

Immy has returned in my absence, sipping her blood carefully from a mug.

"So you're not bonded to Samuel?" she asks Noha curiously.

The other woman shakes her head. "I didn't want it. To me, marriage before God is a deeper commitment, and I value my independence too much to have my husband sitting in on my thoughts." She laughs. "What if he annoyed me? I wouldn't even be able to call him names in my head without him knowing!"

Finn leans down to me. "It's not so bad… but then again, Evie's never called me bad names in her head."

"You don't hear thoughts so much as feel each other's emotions," I murmur. "And most of the time they're background noise—something you can ignore unless they're particularly strong. But it's not for everyone."

If I'm honest, without Cain forcing my six current bonds on me, I likely never would've bonded anyone again. Especially after feeling the bond to Frost break.

So yes, I understand her hesitation more than I want to admit.

I'm just glad that—although my sire definitely didn't intend it to be this way—my thralls are decent men.

I glance at Finn, who's raising his eyebrow at me, no doubt reading my feelings on the situation.

Okay, maybe he's more than decent.

"You two are so sweet together it's rotting my teeth," Immy complains. "I can feel how much you care. It's adorable."

Noha looks up from the organiser she was studying. "Is that your gift?" she asks. "Samuel said all the first-generations have extra powers, but I always thought he was joking with me."

"Yeah, we have gifts." Immy grimaces. "Mine is more of a headache, though. I feel what other people feel. Evie has supercharged healing blood. Morwen can track anyone— which is how we found you guys."

"That's so interesting." Noha's eyes glimmer with unasked questions, but she doesn't press us, which I appreciate.

I'm still not used to my gift being talked about so openly.

"I was going to make a run into the city after this," Noha repeats for Finn and Immy's benefit. "It's mostly to pick up blood, but I wanted to check out one of the new bars which opened recently. Would you all like to come with me? Your other friends are invited too, of course."

"Girls and omegas only," Finn protests. "The others are all buzz kills."

"You should bring them all," Noha insists. "It will be good for them to see the city and leave the base for a while."

I understand that she's being nice, but too big a group could draw the wrong kind of attention. I don't say it, but I have a feeling the others are thinking the same thing, because Immy quickly agrees with Finn.

"I think we'll have more fun with just us four. No offence, Evie, but some of your men are total buzz-kills."

"Especially Gideon," Finn grumbles, startling me.

Biting my lip, I resist the urge to ask what's happened

there. Sure, Gideon has been a bit more overbearing than usual since we got on the plane, but I put that down to how long it took us to find Samuel. Surely he should return to normal now that we're at least on the right track.

Noha looks between us all, seeming just as confused as I feel. "It must be difficult balancing so many men," she finally says.

That's a very diplomatic way of putting it.

The rest of breakfast passes pretty uneventfully as Noha and I wait for Immy and Finn to finish. Immy takes the longest, even with the amount of food that I brought Finn. It could be because the two of us are grilling Noha on life outside of the Court. The community she and Samuel have built seems to be almost completely self-sufficient.

In turn, we answer her questions about our family, telling her a little bit about Callie and Bella, and what details we can remember of our brothers. Samuel's wife brings up asking the rest of my thralls to come twice more, and both times, the other two shut her down gently.

We're just leaving the dining hall when the rest of the pack catch up with us, but Finn shrugs them off when Silas suggests we sit with them. The thrall bond pulses with a deep, emotional exhaustion as he stoically regards his alpha.

Gideon says nothing. He doesn't even look at his omega.

Now I *know* something's wrong, but I'm definitely not going to bring it up in front of Immy and Noha—even if Immy probably knows more about what's going on in their heads than I do.

Not for the first time, I wish I had her gift. It's a thousand times more useful than mine.

No one mentions where we're going to the others, and I bite my lip as we walk away, wondering if we should've. Ordinarily, I would have mentioned something, but the way

193

Finn feels right now… the others would've insisted on accompanying us, and I think he needs a break.

"Do you spar, Noha?" Immy asks, as she climbs into a sleek black hover car in the underground garage.

Across the lot, I see our van, parked and empty. It's the most battered-looking vehicle here, and I wonder just how much money Samuel's vampires are bringing in without calling Cain's attention to it.

But asking would probably be rude, so I hold my tongue and climb in beside my sister and my thrall.

Noha rolls her eyes. "I should," she admits, taking the driver's seat. "Samuel insists on me practising every now and again as a precaution, but I'm more of a movies girl myself."

"Ugh. What is everyone in this age's obsession with movies?" I bemoan. "All the films are so…"

"Propagandised?" Noha nods. "I know. But some of the older movies aren't so bad. The human ones. They're not as fancy, but at least they don't all start with a declaration of Cain's glory." She makes a gagging face, which Immy duplicates.

"I don't know why they insist on doing that," she agrees.

"It keeps his presence fresh in people's minds," I murmur. "They're trying to relax, but he can't let them truly forget who rules them. People become numb to an abstract threat pretty quickly. Reminders of who he is and what he's done prevents that."

Immy sighs and rolls her eyes. "It never gets less creepy when you do that," she says, good-naturedly, before turning back to Noha. "Don't mind Evie, she's just a direct line to our Sire's brain. She really can't help it."

Noha laughs. "Samuel warned me," she says. "Don't worry. I think it's amazing. Not to mention, it's a pretty common coping mechanism."

"What do you mean?" I ask, before I can help myself.

The other woman shrugs. "I studied human psychology back in the nineties to fill the time. It's fairly normal for abused children to be hyper-aware of their abuser's moods and reactions. Learning how to read and predict their behaviour is a survival mechanism."

I… never thought about it like that before.

Finn must realise I've been struck dumb because his hand comes to rest comfortingly on my thigh and squeezes.

Was I abused? The old Evie would never have said so. Sure, Cain wasn't exactly… careful when raising us, but why would you be when you knew your blood could heal any injury? He was just a vampire who treated us as he would any other vampire troops. Right?

Why have I never thought about this before?

"So is trying to appease them," Immy whispers, looking out of the window.

With a jolt, I realise that all of my sisters—except Morwen and I—fall into that category. Callie, who sleeps with Cain to try to earn his protection. Bella works herself to the bone to prove her worthiness, and Immy…

Immy betrayed me, believing it would make her deserving of his love.

"I'm sorry," Noha says, breaking the heavy silence as she starts the car and pulls out of the garage. "I shouldn't have said anything."

"No… it's okay," Immy says before I can. "I figured it out a while ago, when I was doing some… re-evaluating of my life choices."

When she realised that nothing she did would appease Cain and started to regret betraying me.

I stare at the poorly lit tunnel beyond the window as I think it over.

CHAPTER TWENTY

FINLEY

IS IT WRONG THAT I FEEL BETTER THE FARTHER I GET AWAY from the pack?

Of course it is.

I'm an omega. We don't do alone time. It's not something we need. We thrive on being around our pack, on caring for others and soothing the frayed emotions that inevitably arise between the more dominant lycans.

But God, I *needed* this. It feels like the farther I get from the rest of them, the clearer my thoughts become. Without the alpha around, my instincts are free to relax and stop focusing on the undercurrent of negative emotions surrounding him. Of course, logically, I know what's going on in Gid's mind. But it's weirdly easier to empathise with distance.

Perhaps because my own shit isn't fucking with me at the same time.

I'm no idiot. I know I struggle with emotional rejection. I also know that Gideon is only shutting me out because he's shutting *himself* out. Throwing himself into his work to avoid dealing with his mistakes has always been his MO.

Most of the time I can deal with his baggage, but I'd been pretty vulnerable during sex—open in a way I knew would help him to shake the urges he was resisting—and his rejection afterwards just hit me.

"We're here," Noha announces, and I think I hear relief in her voice.

I don't blame her. She's been stuck in a car with three people who were all mired in their own thoughts for the entire trip.

She pushes open her door, and the scents of the city rush into the car. Street food and the fumes from the older vehicles they use in this part of the world assault my nose.

"My contact who delivers our blood supplies won't be here until later," Noha says. "But the bar is still open."

"Sounds good," Immy says, her face lighting up with a smile I'm not quite sure is genuine.

But hell, it looks more convincing than Evie's.

None of us are really dressed for going out, but neither is Noha, but she doesn't let it bother her as she leads us out of the underground garage we've parked in and up to the street level. Immediately, our small group is engulfed by the crowds. Wherever we are, the late hour doesn't seem to have put off the inebriated humans. There are a few lycans here and there, and—more worryingly—a few vampires as well, but the majority of the crowds are humans.

Noha ignores them all, heading straight to the line that winds around the edge of the building across the street. When she goes to join the end of the queue, Immy surprises us all by dragging her away and towards the door instead.

The bouncer says something, but Immy just smiles at him and pulls out a black metal card from her pocket. I barely have time to recognise Cain's mark on the front before she puts it away and the bouncer—now pale as a ghost—unclips the barrier to let us all through.

"Are you mad?" Evie hisses.

"He's not going to hear about it," Immy protests. "Come on, plenty of Cain's favoured generals have similar passes. That guy is probably used to seeing them, given this is clearly an immortal establishment."

Shit. She's right.

Everywhere I look there are vampires and lycans, mingling... feeding. The few humans in here are clearly wealthy, or beautiful, or both.

I turn to stare suspiciously at Noha, who shrugs. "You don't have to worry about being recognised," she insists. "We're a long way away from the Court here."

Don't have to worry about being recognised?! She does realise that Evie and Immy's faces have been all over the media since their return a month ago, right?

This was such a bad idea.

I can see Evie agrees with me, but I can also feel her unease down the thrall bond. The closer I listen to our link, the clearer her feelings become. She doesn't want to offend Noha, or draw more attention to us by insisting we leave, but at the same time, she knows that this is just about the most reckless thing we could've done.

A night out at a human bar, without Immy flashing that card, might've gone unnoticed. But the odds of one of these vampires *not* recognising the two of them are slim to none.

"What do you want to do?" I ask her, quietly.

She bites her lip, and I can feel the force of her indecision against the inside of my skin.

"We should go," she murmurs. "Slip out of the back exit before anyone notices."

Noha visibly deflates, but nods. "If you're uncomfortable," she acquiesces. "I'm not sure if there *is* a back exit, though."

Looking around, I realise a second problem. If there is an exit, it's undoubtedly across the large—and packed—dance floor, which takes up most of the room.

I thought she said this was a bar? It looks more like a club to me.

Immy leads our small group around the edge, but we're already attracting attention.

So much for 'before anyone notices.'

"If we leave now," Evie mutters, realising the same thing I have. "They'll know something is wrong."

"So what?" Immy says. "We stay and dance and hope Cain's forces don't show up?"

The decision is made for us when a suave giant of a vampire sashays towards our group. His long black hair is razor straight and tied out of his almost feminine face in a half-up style that leaves it free to hang around his shoulders. If the way the crowd parted for him wasn't an indicator of how important he was, the sleek cut of his clothes and the ouroboros pin on his lapel would be.

"Lady Imogen"—he bows low—"and Lady Evelyn. How wonderful of you to grace my establishment. We weren't aware that Lord Cain was sending his envoys to this part of the world."

Evie flounders. She doesn't know this man who's greeted us by name, and it's caught her off guard.

Immy surprises us all by taking the lead. "Armin." She smiles, and it's a sultry expression. One that almost looks out of place, given how awkward and quiet she normally is. "How lovely to see one of our Sire's newest generals so very far from home."

Shit.

What are the odds?

"Please." He sweeps out an arm. "Join me. The VIP area in the basement is a little more... discerning of the clientele. I'm sure you'll enjoy your evening far better from there." He glances over their heads at Noha and I, then dismisses us immediately. "Of course, your companions are welcome to wait for you up here."

"We're on business, Armin," Evie counters, adopting a considerably more aloof air than I've ever seen. "We'd rather not be interrupted."

Immy casts her sister a *look*. It's so fast I barely catch it, but Evie must know what she means, because she backtracks.

"Unless our companions are happy to wait?"

Because I'm still paying attention to our bond, I grasp her real meaning straight away.

She wants me to get out of here. Find help.

"Of course we are," Noha says, and I bite my lip as I realise she's shaking.

"Excellent." Armin dismisses the two of us without waiting for my input. "Please, ladies, follow me. I'm excited to hear what business has brought you so very far from home."

"Oh, you know we can't tell you about our Sire's personal affairs," Immy says, smiling coyly at him. "But I'll never say no to your company."

Looking at her now, I'm forced to wonder which is the act. The shy sister? Or the smiling seductress?

The three of them move away, back across the dance floor. Like an idiot, I stand there staring at Evie's retreating back until it disappears.

"We should get out of here," Noha says, pulling me towards the front entrance. "I'm so sorry, I had no *idea* this would happen."

I can't hold back my growl, but luckily, it's swallowed by the heavy bass which echoes through the club. It's difficult *not* to be pissed at her right now. Sure, I get that she's clos-eted and doesn't get out much, but you'd think living an underground life free of Cain would instil *some* sense of, I don't know, secrecy,

"We can't leave them behind," I argue.

"Let's go to the bar," she suggests. "We can see more of the room from up there. Maybe they won't be long."

I follow her outstretched arm to see that the bar she's talking about is actually on a gallery overlooking the dance floor. It's a good idea, but Evie specifically wanted us to leave…

Screw that. I'm not leaving her here. There must be something I can do to help.

Think, Finn!

Tech. If I can get into the systems of this place—and this bar is far too upscale not to have at least a climate control system—then maybe I can trip a fire alarm, cause some chaos to get them both out of here.

"Can you see a console?" I demand. "Any kind of tech panel?"

In answer, she tugs me towards the bar, where holographic displays allow the customers to order their drinks.

"Distract anyone who looks too curious." I take a seat on the stool beside the bar, pull my folding glass tablet from my pocket, and begin the process of hacking into their systems.

This isn't the most ideal entry point, but as long as it's connected to the network somewhere, I should be able to use it.

I'm halfway through bypassing their security when a hand clenches on my shoulder. I don't even need to look up to know who it is because my entire body relaxes, leaning into the safety he represents like a lifeline.

What is *he* doing here? And how did he follow us?

"Finley," Gideon growls. "Want to explain what you're doing?"

"And where Eve is?" Frost is just as pissed.

The ghoul is wearing a beanie and a pair of fake glasses to disguise himself, but he still shouldn't have taken the risk of coming here. Behind the two of them, Draven, Vane, and Silas complete the group, hemming us against the bar, forming a living barrier between us and the rest of the clientele.

"She's downstairs," Draven growls, starting to head after her, knife in hand, only to be stopped by Vane.

"You rush in there, you could make things worse," the older beta cautions.

"Finn?" Gideon is still waiting for an answer from me.

The alpha's voice demands my attention, and I turn away from Vane and Draven's argument and back to him with a sigh.

"No time," I hiss. "I'm trying to set off the fire alarm, but the security in this place is insane."

"That's probably because it's a sham front for Armin's base of operations." *Oh, perfect, Mia's here too?*

I can't grouch when she shoves her way between her brothers and joins me at the terminal, snatching out her own tablet to join me. Morwen follows her girlfriend's path and joins the scowling circle of protective idiots surrounding me.

"Have you—?" Mia begins.

I brush her off, predicting her question with ease. "You think I haven't thought of that?"

"There's probably a blackwire somewhere."

I grimace, knowing she's definitely right. Blackwires are pieces of code that act like a failsafe, locking down the system if an intruder is detected. Pure dumb luck means I haven't triggered one yet—I would've been more cautious if I'd known this wasn't 'just' a club.

"Where. Is. Eve?" Frost demands through gritted teeth.

"In the basement," Noha answers for me, her voice thin. "With Immy. I didn't realise, I swear."

"Armin found them as soon as they got through the doorway," I growl.

Frost runs an agitated hand through his hair and curses.

"You think they're going to let them go because you set off the alarm?"

"Oh yes, that's exactly what I thought. I've got four degrees, but you're right, I really am *that* dumb. Give me some credit—"

"Finley." Gideon's bark is so strong that it shuts me up straight away. "Tell us the plan."

Fucking Alpha commands. Using my instinct to please against me like that? Who does he think he is?

Your alpha. The one who wants to get his whole pack out of here in one piece and who needs all the available information to do that.

Ugh, I really hate my inner voice of reason sometimes.

"Set the alarm off, use the distraction to hack the door codes, and get her a free pass out. The rest was going to be up to her and Immy."

"Get the doors open," Draven growls. "We can get her after that."

"No." Gideon counters. "We don't need to declare open war on Cain in the middle of this city. If Evelyn and Imogen slip out in the midst of an evacuation, no one will be any the wiser about our presence here. They're *supposed* to be together."

"I'll find them," Morwen agrees. "Cain won't have to know for certain that we teamed up with your pack…"

"I'm already scrubbing the camera feeds," Mia adds, leaning back to give her girlfriend a kiss. "We were never here. But I can't do the same for the ones on the street."

"Good thing I never liked Armin," Morwen mutters, peeling away.

I have the oddest urge to ask Mia if that's Morwen's way

of saying she's about to kill him, but I shrug it off and go back to my work.

"Bingo," I hiss.

The music cuts off, replaced with the squealing of the universal alarm sound. Beyond my wall of protectors, the other patrons groan and reluctantly start heading towards the doors, shepherded by bored bouncers and staff.

The bartender—a curvy woman with one arm covered in scars, and a rusty old locket around her neck—shoots me a suspicious look, then sighs and winks once before ushering the group of women on the other side of our group away.

"You did good," Silas murmurs, patting me on the shoulder.

"Get to the van," Gideon orders. "They're going to need a quick getaway, and I want the pack out of here."

Sensible words, but I sense what he isn't saying. There's nothing else we can do, and he's just as pissed about that as I am. Or maybe he's still annoyed that we're here in the first place.

Me too.

I shove my tablet into my pocket just as the curtain of betas surrounding us opens, and we hurry into the crowd. Silas grabs my hand as soon as I pass him, giving it a reassuring squeeze which I return automatically, despite the tension buzzing in my body.

CHAPTER TWENTY-ONE

EVELYN

THE BASEMENT FLOOR IS NOTHING LIKE THE ONE ABOVE AND much more typical of a vampire court. The music is similar, but quieter with a deeper bass that's less offensive to sensitive hearing, and in the centre is a stage where mortals are twirling seductively around metal poles. Along the edge of the room are private leather-cushioned booths.

The servers are scantily clad humans who—by the look of the bite marks decorating their wrists and necks—are serving themselves alongside the drinks on their trays.

"Quite the little place you've set up for yourself," Immy murmurs.

She's draped herself over Armin's arm, but I haven't done the same. I don't know this new general, but I'm not going to play the simpering fool to get on his good side.

My acting skills have never been that good, anyway. He'd probably see right through me.

A bolt of tension hits me from Finn's thrall bond, and I

have to work hard to keep my face straight. What's happening to my omega? Is he safe?

Armin claims the largest booth at the very back of the room and farthest from the exits. I try to perch on the edge, but a burly vampire joins us, forcing me to move up.

I don't make the mistake of thinking he's here to join the conversation. His only purpose is to block our escape. This isn't a friendly chat. It's an interrogation.

The bronze-skinned general grins at me, as if he can read my thoughts.

"Lady Evelyn, I can't believe we've never had the pleasure of being introduced," Armin says, focusing on me with a sly grin. "We've heard whispers of your legend, of course, and I've always been curious—naturally. Now you've walked straight into my headquarters. How fortunate."

"Evelyn's not much of one for conversation," Immy interrupts. "She's more of a warrior than a diplomat."

She shoots me a look, so quick I wouldn't have caught it if I hadn't seen it a dozen times before.

Trust me. It means.

I have no choice, so I leave her to charm the general and turn my attention to the obvious threats in the room.

"What a shame," Armin purrs. "Then I suppose you'll have to tell me what business it is that requires three of Cain's treasured daughters to disappear from the face of the earth for days on end."

"That's our Sire's business." Immy's pleasant tone doesn't falter. "If he hasn't seen fit to share his reasoning with you, you shouldn't ask."

I lean back in the booth, sinking into the leather as I drum my fingers against the table. Three then five.

Fifteen guards in this room.

She taps one nail against her arm in answer.

The signal to wait.

God, how long has it been since we played this game? Used these gestures?

When we were younger, Immy used her gifts to try to manipulate the target Cain gave us, and I acted as her backup. Returning to the routine is like slipping into a well-worn pair of shoes. Comfortable.

"Interesting then, that our Lord has told all of his generals to report any sightings of you and Morwenna." Armin is either immune to Immy's charms, or he's just suspicious by nature, because he hasn't relaxed.

And Finn is still stressed and tense down the bond.

The only reason I haven't rushed back upstairs is because Immy told me to wait. She better be right about this because if Finn gets hurt, there'll be hell to pay…

Most of the guards have guns and swords—an interesting combination. A month in Cain's court proved that my sire hasn't revised his opinions about the crude modern weapons, so they must be using them without his approval.

I've stopped paying attention to Immy almost completely, so that's why I notice the second Morwen strides into the room.

I relax at once, because there's no way she would've come alone. Finn must be with the rest of the pack.

Armin is distracted by Immy, but he'd have to be blind not to notice Morwen striding towards us in all her leather and combat gear. Our middle sister is many things, but subtle isn't one of them.

"If it isn't my favourite sister of them all." He beams, moving out from the booth as if to greet her.

Morwen just hisses in his face. "Why the hell are you fucking with our mission, Armin?"

Immy's hand clenches on her lap, her little finger rises once and unfurls until it's straight. The signal for arousal. I raise my eyebrows at Morwen.

She's somehow made the general horny.

"*Your* mission?" he asks.

"We're hunting, and we could've caught them if you hadn't dragged them down here." Her tone is dismissive, but there's no disguising the animosity in her tone.

Whoever this Armin is, my sister hates him and he... apparently gets off on that?

"Evie, Immy, let's go." She turns on her heel, only to reel back and hiss as the general grabs her arm.

"Stay." Armin growls. "I must insist."

But he's cut off by a siren filling the air. Morwen curses loudly, before rounding on him.

"If we lose this mark, maybe Cain will finally let me stake you," she growls, jerking her chin at Immy and me to follow her. "We're leaving. If you don't believe us, check your camera feeds. I bet they got wiped as soon as *you* drew attention to us. It'll take *weeks* for us to get this close again."

Immy slips around Armin, and I follow her lead. He stands there, unmoving, as those dark eyes scan over us, as if he thinks we'll slip up and give ourselves away.

"I'll report this to your sire," he says, as I brush past him.

"You do that," I retort, as my stomach clenches in fear. "And make sure to tell him about how you fucked up our mission while you're at it."

The guards start to follow us, but Armin throws his hand out, stopping them. Whatever his reasons, I don't trust them, and I find myself double checking behind us as we follow Morwen up the stairs and away from the building.

"Keep walking," she hisses, as we pass the crowd of evacuated humans grumbling about the fire alarm.

As if I haven't already noticed the men tailing us.

The three of us stride along the busy street, and I'm thankful that it's still busy despite the late hour. More scents around us means it will be easier to lose whoever's following us.

We don't make it far before the low hum of a hover drive assaults my ears. I turn, just in time to see Vane and Draven jump out of a van and drag Immy and Morwen into it. I go to follow, but a pair of hands lands on my shoulders before I can take more than a single step. My hand falls to my weapon and I whirl, expecting it to be the vampires following us. Before I can turn more than half-way, I'm yanked backwards into a different car. A glance is all it takes for me to recognise it as the one we drove here in.

"Drive," the alpha orders.

Oh fuck. I can tell from that one snapped-out word that Gideon is *pissed*.

I try not to pay too much attention to him; instead, I seek out Finn. Our bond is still practically vibrating with his tension, and it doesn't feel like it's related to what's happening.

Frost is in the driver's seat, careening our car through traffic like he's trying to kill us—but I'm beginning to suspect that's just his natural driving style. Silas is in the passenger seat beside him, holding his phone to his ear as he shoots frantic glances in the mirror, and Gideon is beside me, in the middle of the back seat, having been the one to drag me off the street.

On the other side of the alpha, trying to crush himself into the door in order to avoid so much as touching him, is our omega.

"Vane confirmed. They've got Morwen and Immy in the van," Silas mutters, putting his phone down and dumping it on the dash. "Noha is taking them a different route back to evade anyone else who might be following them."

"Good," Frost mutters, and I grimace as he takes yet

another corner too fast, and I end up half-falling onto Gideon's lap.

"Good?!" the other alpha spits. "What about this situation can be described as 'good?' She went out to collect blood and decided to go dancing in the HQ of one of Cain's most ambitious upstart generals!"

"It wasn't her fault, okay? So don't give her shit about it." I'm not used to Finn snapping back, and neither is anyone else if the silence that fills the vehicle is any indication.

Down the thrall bond, his emotions are engaged in a chaotic war against the force of his instincts. Finn the omega wants to cuddle the shit out of the grumpy alpha until he calms down. But Finn the man is so pissed with Gideon that he'd rather hug a cactus.

Gideon, to his credit, says nothing back. If anything, he withdraws into himself slightly.

Silas finally breaks the silence. "It sounds like this was an innocent mistake—"

Whatever kept Gideon from arguing with Finn evidently doesn't apply to Silas, because the alpha cuts him off without waiting for him to finish. "That 'innocent mistake' practically waved a red fucking flag in Cain's face, telling him where we are!"

"This discussion can wait until we have all the details and everyone is calmer." Frost's tone leaves no room for argument.

Gideon's jaw clenches. "You—"

"Don't make me turn on the radio to drown out your shit." Frost meets his eyes in the mirror, daring the other alpha to call his bluff.

I don't have to be lycan to feel the silent battle taking place. It's a bit like watching two giant predators circle one another, both knowing that once they start the fight, there's no going back. I'm willing to bet that, if they ever did go against each other, neither would win. The only thing they would accomplish is tearing the pack apart.

Some part of Gideon must realise that too, because he shuts his mouth and settles for glaring moodily out of the windshield.

With nothing else to do, and no desire to speak and ignite the powder keg of discontent that's brewing in the backseat, I rest my head against the window and close my eyes. It doesn't block out the tension, but I do manage to drift off. When I wake, it's to the sound of Silas speaking to someone on the phone. I've missed most of the conversation, so I tune him out and focus on the world beyond the window.

I expected to return to Samuel's hideout, but we pull into a hotel after what can't be more than an hour of driving.

"Why have we stopped?" I ask, confused.

"It's their protocol," Silas mutters, putting down his phone. "Samuel's people don't want to risk anything coming back to them. We've been given orders to find a place to crash and wait until tomorrow evening. The others are doing the same thing in a different town."

"Sensible," I mutter, but at the same time, I hate the idea of splitting up. I can practically feel Vane and Draven's absence.

Gideon scoffs, but keeps his thoughts to himself.

Finn gets out of the car the second we stop, as if he can't wait to escape the toxic atmosphere. Gideon sighs, rubbing his eyes before following him. The rest of us sit in the car as the door slams behind the alpha.

"What's going on between them?" I whisper.

Silas rolls his eyes. "If we knew, we could fix it."

"Finn is so *angry*," I mutter.

It wouldn't disturb me so much if I couldn't feel how unlike him it was down our bond.

Frost shakes his head in exasperation. "Ninety percent of

the time, when something like this happens, it's because Gid is fighting his instincts and Finn has him sorted out by the next morning."

"What about when it's Finn fighting *his* instincts?" I ask.

Silas turns to face me, his stormy blue eyes flicking over me. "That hasn't happened before. Usually, Finn is a bit more understanding of Gid's... baggage. Omegas are naturally forgiving."

Scoffing, because to me that sounds an awful lot like something made up to give alphas the right to be dicks to omegas guilt free, I run my hand through my hair.

The only reason I haven't pounced on Gideon for how Finn is reacting is because he doesn't seem like he expects Finn to just get over himself.

If anything, the alpha is giving his omega a kind of apologetic space.

"I'm not sure waiting for Finn is going to work this time," Frost mutters, shoving open the door. "Until we figure it out, the plan is the same: give them space and listen if they ask for it, but otherwise let them work it out for themselves."

Reluctantly, I follow him out into the cold, grimacing at the state of the place we've pulled into. It's a fairly bland, large chain hotel, but it's definitely seen better days. Part of the sign isn't illuminated, and beyond the glass doors, the paint on the front desk is peeling. Thanks to the late hour, the receptionist is asleep, snoring with her mouth wide open.

Gideon is already approaching her, and I grimace at how much barely leashed tension is contained in the aggressive tilt of his shoulders as he pushes inside.

Poor woman.

Silas heads inside after him, probably to smooth things over with the rudely awoken receptionist, and Frosts stands by the door, keeping an eye on them without going inside.

Abandoning the mortal to deal with the pissed off alpha, I

turn instead to Finn, who's leaning against the wall a little way away.

"You okay?" I whisper, tugging him into my arms.

All the stiffness in his body seems to evaporate at the contact, and he makes a tiny strangled sound of exasperation in the back of his throat.

"I'm okay," he lies.

I know it's a lie because the bond is screaming his hurt and anger at me.

"What happened?"

God, it's hard to keep my voice level and soft rather than demand it from him. But I get the feeling that Finn has had enough of people demanding and ordering him around.

Finn sighs, leaning back against the wall and hugging me against his chest.

"The same bullshit that always happens. I just don't have the energy to pretend it *didn't* this time."

"Finn," I begin, but he sighs, cutting me off.

"Betas protect the pack. Omegas keep the pack together, and alphas…"

"Lead the pack?" I suggest.

"Yes," he acknowledges. "It's why they can be so… controlling. But they also have one major flaw: hyper-fixation. When a threat to the pack becomes so significant, and they're on high alert for so long that they stop eating and sleeping and start running purely on instinct. Sometimes it can go on for months. Their biology allows it—encourages it —because they need to function to lead the pack out of danger."

"And Gideon…"

"He's prone to it," Finn admits. "In general, the stronger the alpha, the worse it is; and Gid is strong."

There's a hint of pride in the last part of his sentence. It's magnified down the thrall bond as—for a second—his anger clears, replaced by softer, sweeter emotions.

Thank God. Whatever issues they're going through, Finn still clearly loves Gideon.

But the fond moment breaks as Finn continues, "Hyper-fixation usually happens when their pack feels threatened for a prolonged period of time. Or when the alpha feels like the situation is out of their control. It's evolution's way of ensuring the pack survives by making sure our leader is alert and ready for anything."

I bet that goes down well. Gideon is the dictionary definition of control-freak. Having his own biology wrench that away from him must piss him off to no end.

Finn must be paying attention to our bond, because he nods. "But the pack knows, and we help him manage it." He sighs again. "Usually, I can break him out of it. And I did—"

"Wait... break him out of it, how?"

The omega takes off his glasses and starts twirling them around his hand as he thinks. "Sex, Evie. The best way for them to feel in control is for them to have it. Omegas submit completely in the bedroom so that their alphas can feel in control, and then their instincts are satisfied and the hyper-fixation retreats."

Oh, I see where this is going.

They had sex, and something went wrong.

"Normal alphas rut their omegas regularly to give them that peace... that way it's not too much. But Gid has a lot of history with his old pack. He doesn't like using me, even though I've told him over and over—" He cuts off with a curse. "It's his story to tell. But it doesn't help that *my* old pack were a bunch of assholes either. He doesn't want me to feel like I'm only good for sex, so he puts all these schedules and plans and contingencies in place to make sure he doesn't fall into hyper-fixation."

"But he spends so much time on those that the only time you ever spend that kind of time together is when he loses control," I guess.

Finn doesn't answer, but the pulse of sadness down the thrall bond tells me I'm right.

"I'd be okay with that—some great rough sex with no emotional strings can be great, and Silas makes sure I get romance and the cuddly stuff—but the way Gid hates himself after every fuck isn't great for my self-esteem."

God. That's got to be the understatement of the century. To have sex knowing that the person you're with will regret it afterwards is the kind of thing that would ruin any relationship.

"Bastard."

"It's not—"

"He's an asshole." I can't believe anyone would do that to someone they profess to love. "I don't care how much he hates himself, if he's putting that on you straight after you've been intimate with each other... No relationship can be all about one person meeting the needs of the other, Finn. That's not healthy."

Even *I* understand that, and I grew up around some of the most messed up relationships in history.

"It wouldn't be so bad if he'd just fuck me more than once every few years and during the full moon." Finn's head drops back against the wall. "If he'd just listen to his instincts, he'd be less at their mercy. I'm convinced that would make him less rough during, which would make him less angry at himself afterwards. I don't really want him to change and give me soft sex all the time, but if that's what will make him happy..."

So the answer is making sure Gideon gets laid in the hopes that it will miraculously turn him into a gentle lover? I bite my lip, sceptical.

Finn might believe that will fix this, but I don't think it will. Having sex isn't the way to fix any relationship, not really. Even if it did somehow change Gideon's entire personality, that would only lead to Finn being dissatisfied.

The two of them being together more regularly in a healthy way would be great, but they have to deal with their issues first.

I can feel Finn's anger. Even if he goes in there and Gideon does miraculously agree listen to his instincts and the two of them fuck like bunnies, I don't think anything will change. The same thing will happen. Gid will continue to disbelieve everything Finn says and nothing will be solved.

It's clear the omega doesn't really want his alpha anywhere near him. The way Finn was trying to merge with the car door to avoid touching Gideon made that much very clear.

The alpha would have to be blind not to have seen it, and it's likely added fuel to his beliefs.

If Gideon's self-hatred and refusal to listen to Finn is the real problem, perhaps the answer is different too.

Maybe he needs to have sex with someone who isn't an omega, someone he'll listen to.

Silas? No. I dismiss the thought as soon as it comes. The relationship between the two of them is practically familial. I don't imagine either of them have ever thought of one another in that way. Vane is much the same—not to mention I'm pretty sure he's only interested in women, just like Frost and Draven.

Which leaves... me.

"So what Gideon needs is someone who can take rough sex regularly, that he doesn't care about hurting," I surmise, slowly. "Someone who he would have no choice but to believe if they said they enjoyed themselves. A third party.

Would that work? Would it give you space to rebuild your relationship?"

Finn freezes, and the bond between us pulses with stunned shock.

"Evie…"

"Answer the hypothetical." I'm not offering anything. Not yet. This idea might not work, and the last thing I want is to make things messier by sticking myself in the middle of things.

His chin drops down to rest on my head, making it difficult to read his expression. "It would. But that hypothetical person would have to be able to submit completely to Gid. No arguments. No taunting."

"But only in the bedroom," I argue. "And he'd stop if they asked him to."

"I've told him no before," Finn confesses. "And, yes, he did stop. He was really good about it and careful with me afterwards. He likes to make out like he's a beast in rut, but he's not. Not really." He pauses. "You're not an omega."

I draw back, meeting his eyes. "As long as it's sex where he's in control, will that matter?"

He shakes his head, putting his glasses back on.

"And would you… would you be okay with that?" I continue, hesitantly. "It wouldn't make things messier if I were with both of you."

He laughs. Actually laughs. "Evie, I was expecting it to happen from the moment I first met you. You fit with the pack—and not in a platonic way." His smile slips as he waits for my answer. "No. No, I wouldn't mind. In fact… It would be a relief. I know it's not going to magically fix our problems, but maybe the two of us can work things out from there. I still… I still love him." He whispers the admission, as if he's scared of it. "I love the sex too—no matter how rough it gets. But I need a break, and then I want to build things back up slowly. I can't just be the person he uses to justify hating himself anymore. I need more. Romance. Affection. Hell, I'd give my left nut for him to just hold my hand or open a door for me. I want to feel…"

"Cherished," I whisper. "You need to trust him again before you let him back into your bed."

Not so different from how I feel about Frost.

He gives a sharp nod that dislodges his glasses and busies himself pushing them back up his nose before he continues. "Right now, I feel like a crutch that he hates but can't live without. I'm just a tool he uses to break himself of hyper-fixation and then punish himself for who he is."

So the mission is simple. Give Gideon an outlet for his sexual needs so he can work on winning back Finn. Because it's obvious to me that the omega does want the alpha. He wouldn't be standing here, considering this if he didn't.

Anyone who wasn't already in love with the alpha would've called it quits and cut their losses by now. I care for Finn. I can feel him, pure and perfect and gentle along our thrall bond. He deserves whatever he wants. So if this is what it takes, I'll do it.

I can't even pretend my motives are entirely altruistic. I've been curious about the alpha since I first met him, and now that he's decided to remain as one of my thralls, I want to know him better.

"Gideon has to agree first," I mutter.

I'm still half certain he'll say no. He's not the sort of man that enjoys feeling manipulated into anything.

"I have to agree to *what?*"

Both of us stiffen, turning around with guilty looks to face the alpha brooding behind us. We've been so caught up in our own little bubble that we didn't notice the rest of our group approaching.

"Evie can explain," Finn grunts, his cheeks darkening as

he strides away from his alpha and back towards the hotel. "Which rooms are we in?"

"They only had three," Silas says, keeping his tone light. "I figured I'd share with—"

"You're sharing with me." Finn grabs his arm and turns him around. "Evie is sharing with Gid. I guess that means Frost gets his privacy for once."

The two of them disappear through the sliding glass door without another word. Frost looks at me, a question in his eyes, only following the two of them when I give him a small nod.

Leaving Gideon and me alone.

CHAPTER TWENTY-TWO

EVELYN

"Evelyn..." Gideon says, eyes narrowing. "What were you two talking about?"

There's a rough demand in his words, one I choose to ignore.

I sigh, shake out my hair, and head after the others. "Before I tell you, I want you to know that if I'd known Noha was taking us somewhere with a lot of other vampires, I would've stopped her. I didn't mean for all of this to happen, and I'm sorry for my part in it."

Better to get our argument over with before I broach the bigger one.

Thankfully, Gideon doesn't drag it out. "Apology accepted," he grunts, as we enter the hotel and pass the sleepy-looking receptionist. "But Noha has some questions to answer."

"I don't think it was purposeful," I mutter. "I could be wrong, but she seemed genuinely confused and upset when we wanted to leave."

He grunts, pulling me to a stop in front of a door and swiping the key card in the lock.

The moment we're inside the darkened room, he shuts the door and rounds on me.

"Now, what were you and Finley plotting?"

I sigh, crossing over to the window as I consider how to broach the subject. It's a clean room, if a little dated, and I can't help glancing at the bed as I pass it. At least there's an en suite.

"Finn says the reason you're struggling with your control is that you won't have sex with him."

"That's a vast oversimplification of the situation," he retorts, already on the defensive. "Did Finn also tell you how his old pack used him like a fuck-toy, ignored his needs, and almost destroyed him?"

No, but I file that information away for later. "I'm not here to tell you to fuck Finn."

He leans back against the door, crossing his arms. "Then where are you going with this?"

I take a deep breath. "I have no problems with rough sex. I prefer it, actually. I have no triggers, no history, and to be frank, I'm perfectly capable of getting myself off after you finish if I need to." I did that with more than a few old bedmates who weren't what they promised to be.

He rolls his eyes, then freezes as my words sink in. "You're not saying…"

"I'm saying, I'll submit to you." The look of shock on his face would've been funny if I wasn't so serious. "But *only* in the bedroom. *Only* for this. In return, you'll go back to normal—well, hopefully, better than normal. Once you no longer have to worry about becoming fixated, you can put your efforts into making sure Finn knows you love him."

He scoffs. "He knows I love him. Just like *I* know I don't deserve him."

"No. You don't deserve him," I retort. "But he loves you, and he deserves to feel like more than a tool you use to regulate your emotions and punish yourself with."

"Every part of my life is planned so I don't *have* to use him like that," Gideon objects. "He should only be a last resort—"

"Which is not how *anyone* wants to be viewed by their lover," I point out. "I'm offering you someone to fuck who doesn't care how rough it gets, and in return, you use the time you would've wasted planning your life down to the second to make him feel treasured and adored. Like he deserves. And *not* like a last resort."

He's staring at me like he's trying to find some ulterior motive. The silence between us is unnerving, but I'm prepared to wait it out until a different thought occurs to me.

"Unless you don't *want* a romantic relationship with him. In which case, man up, apologise and *tell him* that." Better Finn's heart be broken with honesty, and cleanly, than he be strung along by a coward who can't vocalise his feelings. "Either way, my offer still stands."

Gideon shakes his head, finally pushing away from the door and stalking over to me.

"Do you even know what you're asking for?" he demands. "There will be days when I'm so out of control, there won't be time for foreplay. You'll be lucky if I can find the will to hold off long enough to finger you. And when I fuck you, there's no sass. No room for arguing. I tell you to kneel, you kneel. I tell you to suck, you do it. If I tell you to take your clothes off, bend over the dresser, and spread your legs, you don't hesitate."

I nod, my mouth going dry. He doesn't realise it, but his words and the images they've conjured are turning me on. The alpha keeps going, moving closer and closer until he's within reach.

"I'll give you a safe word," he mutters, reaching out to

stroke my hair out of my face. "You use it and this whole experiment is over. I go back to what I know works— routine, careful planning, and a strict schedule." He shakes his head, as if to clear it. "Why am I even considering this?"

I snort. "For the same reason I am. For Finn."

"This changes nothing," he adds. "I'm not going to magically start approving of every—"

"Did I ask for that?" I retort.

He pinches the bridge of his nose. "Pick a word."

God, we're doing this. My mind blanks, and suddenly I forget every word in the dictionary.

"Silver," I eventually say.

He nods once.

"Take off your clothes and get on the bed," he orders.

I know what he's waiting for—some kind of hesitation. Anything that will prove to him that I'm not capable of this.

He won't get it.

My fingers drop to the button of my jeans flicking it open. I drag my clothes off and dump them, uncaring of where they land, then head for the pastel floral sheets with my head high but not making eye contact.

I can't do anything to challenge him.

Gideon hisses out a breath when my legs part and he sees the evidence of my arousal.

That's right, Alpha, I want this. I might have suggested this to help Finn, but that doesn't mean I'm unaffected.

The second I lie back on the cool sheets, he snaps out, "Hands above your head."

I do it.

"Arch your back. I want to see your breasts."

Once again, I comply, my nipples pebbling in the air.

"Legs wider." His voice is rougher now. The command hoarse.

My core clenches as I follow the command, and his nostrils flare.

"Last chance, Evelyn." His whole body is strung tight, like an elastic band about to snap.

I open my mouth to speak, then snap it closed as I remember not to sass him.

So I do the one thing I know means submission across all species.

I tilt my head and bare my neck.

Gideon is on me before I can blink.

A rough hand palms my breast, squeezing to the point of almost-pain, and a moan tears out of me. His other hand scrabbles at his belt, ripping open his trousers and freeing his already leaking cock.

God. I've never seen one so thick. Gideon isn't as long as Finn and Silas, but the alpha makes up for it in girth. My mouth goes dry as I start to wonder if that will even *fit*.

His hand releases my breast only to spank it, and I gasp as the sharp sting sends a bolt straight to my core and my body clenches on nothing. When his mouth descends to brush against my throat, I forget all about my concern over his size.

Gideon runs his teeth along my neck, testing me as he runs the mushroom head of his fat cock along my slit.

Teasing me with what I could have. Giving me the barest taste of what our joining will be like.

He releases himself, and his cock falls away. A finger dips into my damp folds a second later, and he hisses as he realises just how wet I am.

I should be embarrassed, but I'm not. Getting horny is going to be a useful survival skill if he hopes to get that *thing* inside me on a regular basis.

Two fingers force their way past my entrance in the next heartbeat, stretching me open as his thumb comes to rest over my clit.

He doesn't tease. Doesn't deliver light, testing strokes. No. Gideon presses down on the little bud and rotates his thumb. Hard. At the same time, those two fingers hook deep inside and scrape against my g-spot, drawing a shocked little scream from me.

He works me furiously, building me up to one of the most frantic orgasms of my life. Forcing my body to take the pleasure he offers with his characteristic bossiness. I topple over the edge as my orgasm is ripped from me, leaving me a shaking mess spread out on the bed.

But the alpha isn't finished with me yet. There's no time to recover as his hand disappears, replaced by his cock. Gideon shoves into me without stopping. My body protests his invasion even as I cry out with delight.

Oh. My. God.

Even with how drenched I am, he has to go slow. Inch by torturous inch, he forges forward. Stretching me. Claiming me. I pant through the sensations, writhing and whimpering in his hold.

The low growl that echoes from his chest is approving, yet he says nothing.

I dare a glance up at his face, only to catch myself and stop before I meet his eyes. Gideon's neck and shoulders are so tense that I can see the tendons beneath his skin. Ripples of fur explode and disappear in micro-shifts he can't seem to control. He lowers his head and opens his mouth, stretching his jaw and using his teeth to pin me in place as my body yields to his.

That's when I realise he's not speaking because he *can't* right now. He's caught between beast and man, and I think… I think the beast might be winning.

I want to touch. To hold on to him as he ploughs into me.

Gideon must sense what I want. His free hand reaches up to capture my wrists above my head. He squeezes them, keeping them in place as his hips finally come to rest against mine.

For a brief second after he bottoms out, he doesn't move. The sound of his harsh breaths fill my ears, and the heat of him scorches me as he waits for some silent signal. Eventually, I can't take it anymore. My hips buck against his, begging wordlessly for friction. For more.

Then he draws back and slams home.

Rough, raw, and more than a little bit furious, Gideon pistons into my body like he's possessed. Every thrust is so deep that it causes my breath to hitch and my voice to catch. He's so wide that my pussy is stretched to what feels like breaking point, and he just seems to get bigger as he fucks me brutally into the mattress.

And I love it.

The headboard bangs loudly against the wall, but neither of us pay it any attention. No. My world has narrowed to the two of us. To the place where our bodies are connected. The only thing my ears can focus on are the lewd, wet sounds coming from my body, the gasps and moans he drags from my throat, or the heavy grunts and snarls of pleasure that rip from him as I clench around his length.

My orgasm takes me by surprise, and I bow off the bed, my mouth open on a silent scream as my channel grips him. His free hand works its way into my hair, fisting the strands and holding my throat immobile as my body trembles beneath his.

Against my neck, Gideon growls in satisfaction, and his teeth dig into my jugular, just the slightest fraction.

As if my orgasm was permission, he drives into me faster. Harder. Without mercy. Chasing his own release until he comes with a roar that almost deafens me. His cock jerks inside me, and I feel the telltale spurt of warmth as he ejaculates into my still quivering cunt.

Then the pressure starts.

At first, I can't identify it beyond a subtle stretch. Gideon shudders and snarls as his cock expands within me, hitting spots I didn't know I *had*. Demanding I make room for him.

If he gets much bigger, I'll break.

The thought should scare me, but I'm too caught up in my own pleasure.

"God," I cry out as the unusual sensation tips me over the edge. *Again.*

My pussy wants to clamp down on him, but I'm stretched so wide that all my internal walls can do is flutter in surrender. I come so hard I black out for a second, and when I come to, he's still there. Locked inside me. Filling me with more lashings of his cum.

Everything after that happens slowly. Gideon's fingers release my hair, and then my wrists as he moves to brace himself over the top of me. His teeth leave my neck, but he doesn't move his head until he's laved the spot with his tongue. He must have caught my skin without my noticing, because it stings slightly.

Slowly, ever so slowly, the bulge at the base of his cock starts to go down, and I groan as my pussy clenches like it's begging for it to return.

When Gideon finally draws back and settles onto his knees with the tip of his cock still inside of me, he blinks like he's coming out of a trance.

I know he's back to his normal self when he flings himself across the bed in his haste to get away from me.

So *this* is how he hurt Finn. Not with the sex, but with the rejection afterwards.

I get it now.

The alpha's eyes rove over my body, cataloguing the bruises, so I make sure to keep my face disinterested as I sit up and stare at him expectantly.

"A towel would be nice," I say, my voice surprisingly calm, even after the spine-breaking orgasms he just put me through.

The words jolt him into action and he heads into the bathroom, returning a second later with a damp towel. He chucks it at me, and I busy myself with wiping the traces of our combined cum from between my legs.

His eyes track the swipes of the cloth, burning with something that almost looks like possessiveness before he blinks it away.

"You didn't… you never used your safe word." He sounds a little broken by the fact.

I shrug. "I told you I liked rough sex. Sure, I can see that you're going to be a bit of a mess afterwards, but I enjoyed myself more than I thought I would. Could've warned me about whatever *that* was, though…"

I wave at his cock, which has returned to its normal—still mildly terrifying—size. I almost wonder if I imagined the whole thing, but the ache in my lower body isn't fictional.

I keep my words cold and clinical because I can tell he's expecting an emotional outburst. He's braced for it, so I can only assume that Finn—

Oh my God, Finn.

I reach for his bond, expecting to feel his anger, or even sadness. I know he gave me his blessing for this, but still, he must have *felt* how much I loved that.

Yet, instead of the resentment or anger I'm expecting, there's only a sense of relief. I dig deeper as I clean myself, searching for any hint of discomfort.

If I find it, then no matter what I promised Gideon, this is over.

I won't be the cause of any more drama between them.

Thankfully, Finn is *happy* with the situation. I can't even find a hint of jealousy lingering in the back of his psyche. I allow myself one tiny internal sigh of relief before I release the bond and turn my focus back to the lycan in the room with me.

He's still tense, but I try not to let that bother me as I finish cleaning up. As soon as I'm clean, I chuck the towel at the bathroom door and pull the covers over myself.

"It's a knot," Gideon says, abruptly. "Alphas have them, but if you don't like it, I'll pull out next time."

I snort. "Don't you dare."

The poor man's eyes will bulge out of his head if he stares at me any harder.

"You can get in bed now, you know. I'll only bite if you ask me to."

He hesitates, and I roll over to give him my back, cracking a small smile once I'm certain he won't see it.

"If you don't believe that I'm fine, drop the damned wall and check the thrall bond."

Given his reticence about the entire situation, I'm almost certain he won't do it. But I should know better than to assume I know what the alpha is thinking.

Having the wall drop between us is like a dam breaking. It's not a full bond—we're not even close to that yet—but his emotions are so loud that they cross the distance, anyway. His own self-loathing hits me first, followed by his complete disbelief and certainty that I must be lying.

Then, after a few seconds of processing all of that, he notes how calm and unbothered I am by the entire experience.

"I hurt you."

I shrug, not turning over. "I actually enjoyed my orgasms, thank you very much. I can see how you fucked things up with Finn, though. Being treated like a leper right afterwards definitely kills the mood."

The bed dips, and I wait patiently for him to slam his wall back up.

It doesn't. I turn back to face him, my question written across my face.

"It makes it easier to keep an eye on you," he says dismissively. "I quite like the idea of knowing when you're lying to me."

I roll my eyes and turn back. "Typical."

The mattress jiggles as he gets comfortable, and I expect that to be it.

"Finn told me the same thing," he whispers. "I didn't believe him."

Yet he has no choice but to believe me because of the bond.

"And can you see how you not trusting him to tell you the truth might be a bit of a problem? Given that he puts all of his trust in you when you go into that state?" I try my best to keep my words light and prompting, rather than accusatory, but I don't fully succeed.

"I owe him an apology," Gideon says, like it's a curse. "I assumed because he was an omega he was just trying to placate me... I should've known he wasn't like that."

I hum an affirmative.

"Are you..." The alpha hesitates again, and I resist the urge to snort. "Are you still sure about this arrangement?"

I check on Finn one more time just to make certain he's still calm and happy before I nod into the pillow and let out an embarrassingly loud yawn.

"Yup." I pause, checking the bond to make sure he's mellowed enough to withstand a little teasing before I add, "I'll sacrifice myself on the altar of good sex until you and Finn make it back to a place where you're both comfortable again."

A flash of irritation tumbles down the bond between us.

"I was just teasing," I say, before his grumpiness can return in full force. "You know I want a true thrall bond with you. Even if you and Finn sort things out, and our relationship becomes strictly platonic, you're still pack."

More quiet grumbles down our bond. I frown, sleepily. I thought Gideon would've been glad for the out I presented him.

"I expect it will take a while." I sigh. "You have plenty of grovelling to do, after all."

CHAPTER TWENTY-THREE

GIDEON

Bang. Bang. Bang.

I wrench myself free of the arms banded around my chest and drop to a crouch, facing the door with a snarl. Every instinct in me rears, ready to protect the omega in my bed.

"Gideon? Eve?"

The tension leaves me as I realise it's just Frost, then reappears as I realise Evelyn is on *my* side of the bed, looking adorably sleep mussed. My mind works backwards in steps, remembering the way we'd been *cuddling.*

I thought of her as an omega.

I was half-asleep at the time, but that doesn't change the fact that she's not a lycan. That shouldn't have happened. Neither should my fucking knot.

But the instinct is there, bristling beneath my skin. Insisting this is one of my most vulnerable and precious pack members. Memories of the night before, where she calmly and methodically shattered every single preconception I had about myself and called into question everything I've ever believed about myself, about alphas and omegas, about fucking…

Without pausing to think too deeply into the ramifications of my actions, I reach inside myself to the nascent thrall bond that—in a fit of madness—I laid wide open in my search for the truth. I have no doubt that this is what's fooling my instincts into thinking Evelyn is an omega.

What have I done?

Ignoring the fist still banging on the door, I try my best to shove that bond back into the box at the back of my mind.

It doesn't work.

No amount of resistance or wall building seems to have any effect. The bond is just there, impervious to it all. Evelyn is inside of me now. Cain's vampire daughter has a line straight to my emotional core. A direct road map to my every vulnerability.

Right now, that connection is fuzzy. Limited. I can sense things from her if they're strong enough and I try hard. But it's only basic things, like thirst, tiredness, and pain. Last night, when our emotions were high, I could tell that she wasn't lying to me. Her honesty and loyalty were absolute. But right now, I can't feel a single thing beyond that. No emotions.

If this bond solidifies—if the connection strengthens to the point where we can feel each other at all times—then there will be no more secrets. Nowhere to hide.

I'm not ready for that yet.

"Gideon! Get your pants on, I'm coming in."

Without any further warning, Frost breaks the flimsy handle and shoves his way into the room.

"Ugh, I *said* put some pants on," he groans, then looks behind me at Evelyn.

Slowly, ever so slowly, his nostrils flare. That sensitive ghoul nose picking up every lingering trace of what I did to her last night. His fists clench, and he forces his gaze away.

This is why I didn't want a thrall bond between the two of us. Frost could understand and accept Silas and Finn being with her because of their relationship and their softer personalities. They're good for Evelyn. Healthy. They'll help her heal from her trauma in a way that dominant, forceful personalities like his and mine can't.

Even Vane—for all his kinks—is a beta at his core. A protector.

Accepting me in her bed will be a lot harder.

Perhaps, if he'd formed his bond to her and I was the last member of the pack to jump into bed with her, he would've taken it better. That was what we were all expecting. I was certain, going into this, that Evelyn would bond with Finn and Silas first, then maybe Vane or Frost, and me or Draven last, if at all.

None of us expected this to happen. Least of all me.

Frost knows that. It doesn't make it any easier for him to bear, though.

He takes a second deep breath through his mouth and grunts, "Meeting. By the car. Ten minutes. Urgent."

Then he shoves out of the room like he can't stand to be in our presence any longer.

Something hits me in the back and I whirl, only to find my clothes on the floor by my feet and Evie already dragging her own back on in a flurry of vampire speed.

I reach over and stop her with one leg in her jeans. "Shower first."

She looks at me like I've gone insane.

Hell, my instinct thinks I am. It wants her covered in my scent—my claim—always. A declaration to other packs that she belongs to me and mine.

"You're washing my scent off you before you go out there," I insist.

Instead of just doing as I tell her, like I wish she would, she raises a single brow in question. Almost like she's saying 'make me.'

All of that beautiful submissiveness from earlier is gone, and a large part of me wants to order her onto her knees and remind her not to question her alpha.

But I agreed to this, so I can't.

"You want to rub what we just did in Finn's face?" I demand. "Or perhaps Frost didn't get a good enough whiff the first time."

I'm coming to expect that Evelyn will never do what I expect her to, so when she yanks her arm out of my grip and continues pulling on her clothes, I shouldn't be as surprised as I am.

"You don't know your omega very well at all," she retorts. "Finn is *ecstatic* about this. I don't understand it any more than you do, but he's been fucking Silas all night to celebrate —or maybe that was because I set him off…" She shrugs, as if she couldn't care less. "And Frost hasn't earned the right to dictate who's in my bed. We're still a long way from him being back in the running."

She pulls her top over her head, covering her tits, and I have to look away or face how disappointed I am that she's no longer bare to my gaze.

I'm so busy *not* looking at her that I almost miss her striding out of the door.

The instant she's gone, I want to go after her. Damn it. *This* was why I blocked my end of the bond. Women just have ways of getting under your skin and making you panic about them—just like omegas. Evelyn is even more distracting now.

I sigh as I start the search for my jeans and some

semblance of my missing control. The shower washes *her* scent off *me*—because no matter what she says, I don't want to broadcast the fact that I fucked another person to my omega—and as soon as I'm clean, I rush out of the door after her.

I expect it to be just our small group waiting by our car. It's not quite dusk, but the darkness is settling in slowly, lengthening the shadows around the gathered bunch. My eyes run over all of them, checking for injuries, making sure that my pack is okay in a way that's second nature to me now. Once I'm certain that they're all healthy and whole, I allow my irritation to come forward.

"You're supposed to be at the other location," I growl at Vane.

Mia, Morwenna, Imogen, and Noha are all with him, and Draven is sitting in the van with the side door wide open, hiding from the last rays of the dying sun while remaining part of the heated conversation that's happening.

Evelyn is curled under Finn's arm, her arms wrapped around his torso like a vine, as he stands back from the middle where Vane is arguing with... Noha?

"We haven't heard anything. Going there now could put you in danger."

"They told us they were under *attack*." Noha's hair is a mess, and her eyes are wild and sunken in her face. If I had to guess, I'd say she was woken up just as suddenly as the rest of us. "My *son* is in danger. My husband—"

"Specifically told you to stay away." Vane is just as calm as always. There's very little that can faze the elder beta.

"What's going on?" I demand, the role of alpha sliding over me like a welcome cloak.

Responsibility shoves my personal problems aside, and for the first time in days, my head feels clear and able to focus.

Or maybe that's just the result of having my hyper-fixation fucked out of me by a vampire.

Evie took my knot like she was born to do it.

That should not make me as smug as it does.

I should've fucking warned her, but I never thought my body would react that way to someone who wasn't a fucking omega. Guilt hits me hard, but a large part of me is happy that it did, because the thrall bond made it clear she liked—no, *loved*—it.

I shove that unwelcome thought away and watch as all eyes turn to me.

"Noha got a call from Samuel," Imogen answers, surprising all of us. The red-haired vampire looks almost as heartbroken as Noha does. "He said the base was under attack and warned her—and the rest of us—not to return until he or Bakari gave the all clear."

"He hasn't phoned since." Noha is trembling as she points to where Mia is still tapping away at her tablet, frowning. "Now your beta has found satellite images of *smoke*."

"When was this?" My voice is level, but my mind has gone into disaster management mode.

"They called Noha less than an hour ago," Mia grumbles, accepting a takeout cup of steaming coffee from Morwen as she continues to type, one handed. "Finn, do you have a back door into the base's cameras yet? Getting in from the outside is taking too long."

Finn grabs his own tablet from his bag and starts typing furiously. "My computer is hooked up to their internal network, I should be able to…"

Drowning the two of them and their tech speak out, I look around at the group of us.

This is not good, and they all know it.

"We're not going back there," Vane growls. "Not if there's even the slightest possibility that Cain is there."

"We have no choice," Evie retorts. "We might be able to help, and besides, we *need* whatever Samuel knows. If Cain kills him before we get there—"

Noha laughs hysterically. "We should never have gone to that club..."

"It's unlikely they followed us back—"

"They already *knew* where we were." All of us freeze at her confession. "Cain has known for *decades* that we had our enclave in the desert, but he left us alone until *you* showed up. We were no threat to him, and now because I failed to hand you over, he's gone after my family."

My shoulders are rigid, and I can barely breathe as the implications wind through my brain.

"Noha," Evelyn whispers. "What are you saying?"

The other vampire is coming apart at the seams. She wraps her arms around herself and squeezes so tightly that for one irrational second, I fear she might burst.

"You don't think I *accidentally* walked us into Armin's club, do you?" A single tear drips down from her eyes. "I made a deal almost a century ago to protect my husband and my son. I kept Armin apprised of what goes on in our little community, and in exchange, he left us alone. When you arrived, I had to tell him. I had no choice. He demanded you." She glares directly at Frost. "But your omega refused to bring the rest of you. I knew if I took Evie to the club, you would all follow—thralls don't leave each other's sides—but then Armin fucked up by letting you escape, and now my family is going to pay the price."

"Did he know about Samuel?" Evie demands. "Did he tell Cain?"

Noha shakes her head. "No. He knew we were independent. I think he assumed we were runaways."

"But our presence here taught him otherwise." Morwen

stands up. "If we want that information, we have to go back now and pray we get to Samuel before Cain does."

"Cain won't be there himself," Immy mutters. "Even if he jumped on a jet within seconds of us landing in that club, he hasn't had the time to get here."

"But Armin will." Morwen doesn't look upset about that. "Along with plenty of others."

"Please," Noha begs. "You have to help them. He'll kill my boy. My husband!"

I thought perhaps her entreaty might've elicited some sympathy from Evelyn, but a glance at her proves me wrong. Pure, unbridled fury is etched into her face, and Finn's hold on her has switched from comforting to restraining. I don't even mean to check the thrall bond, but I find myself reaching for it anyway. And her emotions are so strong they're blasting across the space between us loud and clear.

Betrayal.

Self-blame.

Shock.

Panic.

Rage.

The potent cocktail is so strong that I have to let go or risk losing my own cool. It makes sense that Evelyn would have such a strong reaction to betrayal, but I have to keep a level head. Finn has no such urge. He tugs our vampire even further into his embrace until her smaller frame is completely surrounded by his.

Without meaning to, I subtly angle my body so I'm between the two of them and the threat.

At Noha's back, Draven has withdrawn one of his silver-bladed knives, and he twirls it lightly around his fingers, ignoring the burn against his flesh as he waits for the chance to strike. It's clear he doesn't like how Evelyn's feeling right now either, and his solution is simple: kill Noha.

I give him a warning look, then turn my gaze back to my co-alpha.

"Gid…" Frost looks at me, indecision warring on his features as he glances towards Finn, and then Evelyn.

I want to sigh.

He wants to return to the base. If it was just him, he wouldn't have hesitated. But it's not just him, and he won't risk our omega, or Evelyn, without my agreement. So he's asking me to make a decision that will either send us into a heated situation with little to no preparation or put the lot of us on a plane out of here.

It really comes down to this: is the chance to kill Cain worth more or less than the safety of our pack?

Are the two things even separate? How can my pack ever be truly safe while Cain still lives?

I shock them all by turning to Imogen. "Has she lied?"

The redhead jerks her head from side to side. "She's in shock. Everything she's feeling is real, and it's painful." She gnaws at her own lip, her large guileless eyes shining and haunted.

"Did Samuel know?" Evelyn asks, her voice hoarse. "Did my brother know any of this?" Her eyes gleam. "He didn't, did he? That's why you didn't want a thrall bond. It would've exposed you."

Noha weeps harder as she shakes her. "I didn't tell him. I couldn't. He would've left me."

She's a sorry sight, but all of my pity dried up the second she tried to hand over my pack.

"Is Armin going to set a trap for us?" I demand. "Does he know where we are?"

"I don't know!" she wails. "Please…"

"Bullshit," Morwenna grumbles. "You must know *something*."

Her anger is understandable, but if Noha is to be believed, she's merely the victim of blackmail. Hardly the sort of person Cain or his generals would ever trust with anything of importance. I glance back at Imogen, seeking her opinion.

"Truth," she whispers. "I think… there's so much desperation it's hard to tell."

"We can assume he thinks we're there already," Mia mutters. "There are a *lot* of vehicles on the satellite images. Enough troops that he must be anticipating three elder vampires at the very least."

"There are other ways into the base," Noha insists. "Secret ways. They'll be using them to evacuate. We could get in that way. Find my son." Her breath catches on the last word, and she dissolves into quiet sobs that fill the quiet.

Draven gives me another look, flicking his blade into the air and catching it in a silent request to kill her. I shake my head, reluctantly. The urge to shut her up is overwhelming. I want to see her staked for what she tried to do to my pack, but she might be our last chance to find Samuel and get him out of this.

Once he's given us what we need to know—no excuses— then the decision about what to do with her belongs to him. Providing we all make it out alive, of course.

"We'll go back through the tunnels," I decide. "But the second you try *anything*," I spit the word at her. "I will stake you *and* your family. Do you understand?"

Yes, it makes me a bastard, but she's already put my pack in danger once. She won't get a chance to do it a second time.

"Good thing we brought weapons," Silas grunts, heading for the van.

"We're going to need them," Morwen says, sharing a grin with Mia.

Unfortunately, Vane notices. "Mia, Finn, you're on

241

support." Mia glares at him, opening her mouth to object, but her eldest brother growls. "No arguments."

"I agree," I add, backing Vane because I'm not going to deal with infighting right now on top of everything else. "We need you two to get us in and out. Our priority is Samuel and getting our stuff. If Cain gets his hands on our tech, he might be able to hack into the resistance's servers."

We're not here to rescue everyone. Evelyn gives me a dark look, but she's been a general before. She knows what the tough decisions look like.

"Into the van," I mutter. "We leave the other car here. Finn, I want a plane on standby to get us out of this country the second we have Samuel."

"Done," he says.

Good boy.

I glance at Frost, who nods. "There are a few ghouls in the vicinity—but not many, and the sun's an issue. I'll have them follow us when they can."

I look at the rest of the team and nod. "You have five minutes to get everything together," I announce. "After that, we move."

They disappear immediately, except for Finn, who makes to get in the van, likely to take inventory of what he's got to work with. I grab his arm before he can move past me.

It's probably not the right time, but there's a good chance I might die in the near future, and before that happens, I have to apologise. Emotional rejection is akin to torture for an omega, and I haven't been seeing to his needs properly. Even before our relationship sank this far, I ignored him when he told me what he liked, convinced I knew better.

The extent of my own arrogant egocentricity only became clear in the middle of the night after Evelyn pointed out what I was doing. I shouldn't have needed *her* to tell me that pushing Finn away after sex was worse in his mind than all the rough sex in the world. I should've known my omega needed cuddling and cosseting. Providing that for him should've been instinctive. But I was too caught up in self-loathing.

In trying to be my father's opposite, I somehow became his clone.

After I've grovelled, I have to make certain Finn's really okay with what Evelyn and I did. No matter what happened, he's still my omega. I don't want him to think I'm getting rid of him. Or worse, replacing him with her.

"We need to talk." I keep my voice soft.

"No," he whispers. "*You* need to talk because you think it will fix things. We're past that, Gid. I tried to get you to talk for years and you refused. I… I'm taking a break, and I'm damned thankful that Evie offered herself up so it's possible."

I rub the back of my neck and stare at him. "A break?"

Is that…? What does that mean? Is that just something to soften the blow of the breakup that's round the corner? Is it no sex? No touching? No talking?

Is he… kicking me from the pack?

The floor falls away beneath my feet, and it's a miracle I manage to stay standing.

I never wanted a pack—I swore I'd never have one after seeing what my father did to his—but now that I have them, I can't imagine life without them. They're my purpose. My reason for living.

Finn gave me that, but I never thought he'd take it away.

If he kicks me out… I have nothing.

Finn shakes his head. "Space. You need it too—whether you realise it or not. We… Do you ever think about how we started?"

I nod, unable to speak past the lump in my throat. "You were too young."

I knew that even then. He was barely twenty-four and

recovering from the shit-show that was his birth-pack. It took him weeks to stop flinching every time I spoke, and once he settled in, he claimed everyone. Even *Draven*.

The first time he found me in the grip of hyper-fixation, he didn't even talk. Just bent over, expecting to be used like the animals of his old pack no doubt used him. When I wouldn't touch him, he started sobbing until Silas managed to calm him down.

After that, I waited years to accept his advances because I wanted to make sure he wasn't doing it out of some misplaced sense of duty. Because his old pack had taught him all he was good for was servicing alphas.

And despite growing up with my father as an example, I knew that omegas were far more than that.

If my hyper-fixation hadn't gotten so bad I was physically starving and the rest of the pack hadn't intervened, my resolve might not have broken. I might never have fucked him, and we might not have gotten into this mess in the first place.

"You didn't *want* a pack," Finn says. "I'm still not certain you do. My arrival forced it on you. You had to step up and be alpha because I would've shattered if you rejected me." He pauses, then gently tugs his arm from my numb grip. "I was grateful—I still am. But we're not those people anymore. That's why our relationship can't keep going like it was. I think… we need to figure out if we're really compatible or if…"

He doesn't finish the sentence.

I can't believe… *Of course* I want the pack. Have I really been so distant that he thinks I don't? Do the rest of them think that?

"I'll…" I clear my throat, embarrassed by how rough that one word was. "If you let me, I'll do better. I can listen."

It's not enough, or what he wants to hear. But I don't know what else to say. I've never been more out of my depth in my life than I am with this gorgeous man.

I'm not surprised when Finn only replies with a small, sad half smile before he turns away and clambers into the van.

CHAPTER TWENTY-FOUR

EVELYN

WE SEE THE SMOKE BEFORE WE REACH THE BASE, FLOATING over the desert like a foreboding cloud. The black, armoured vehicles around the entrance to the garage are visible a mile off. With a curse, Gideon disengages the hover drive and takes us left, down a sand dune and out of sight.

I take the offered earpiece from Silas and slide it into place,

"Which way to the tunnels?" he barks, glancing over his shoulder to where Noha is sitting, isolated at the very back of the van.

Her hands are clenched on the sides of her chair with a white-knuckled grip as she stares out of the windscreen in red-eyed shock.

"They're in the north," she whispers, her voice thin. "About a mile out from the base."

Finn passes her a tablet, and she taps diligently at a spot hidden amongst the holographic blue dunes. Automatically, the screen on the dashboard adjusts, and a red line appears, directing Gideon towards the hidden entrance.

Sure enough, as we approach, I catch sight of a dozen or more figures streaking away across the dunes.

Fleeing.

"Noha, you'll remain here with Mia and Finn," Gideon growls. "The van is cloaked, and they have permission to stake you if you try anything."

She blinks, then her face transforms into a mask of outrage as she processes his order. "I'm going to find my son! My husband!"

In my chest, I feel Draven's irritation, though he's keeping his distance from the distraught woman. My vampire thrall doesn't understand why we're keeping her alive. In his icy black and white world, Noha became an enemy the second she betrayed us.

I think Gideon must know that. That's why he's keeping such a close eye on both of them.

"We'll find both of them," Morwen growls, strapping her sword to her waist. "But you've done enough damage."

Noha hasn't given up, but before she can argue her case, Vane turns to her and growls. "If you want to live to see them again, sit there, shut up, and don't move."

Maybe it's just because he's the most intimidating-looking of my thralls, but his threat seems to work.

The van skids to a stop, and Finn passes me my sword. "Stay safe," he whispers as my hand clasps the leather scabbard.

I don't reply. Not because I'm being deliberately cold. I'm just unused to anyone saying something like that before a battle. Fortunately, the thrall bond pulses with under-standing between us, letting me know that he gets it.

"No time for dilly-dallying," Gideon snaps, slamming the door behind him as he strides out into the desert.

I'm the last one in the van, and I give Noha one more look before glancing at Finn again, and then Mia.

"If she breathes wrong…"

Mia winks one heavily kohled eye at me, and that's all it takes for me to feel fully reassured. With a grin, I disappear out of the vehicle and down the dune behind the others.

Morwen would never have fallen for someone who couldn't defend themselves. I can trust that Mia will keep Finn safe—as much as Silas and Vane want to believe she's delicate.

The tunnel Noha told us about is little more than a thin crevice among some rocks, concealed beneath a stone over-hang in the desert. It's barely big enough for one of us to pass through at a time. Frost goes first, followed by Silas, then Morwen. Draven ushers me through after my sister, but he's right behind me, with Gideon and Immy bringing up the rear.

Beyond the initial entryway, the tunnel quickly widens out into the hand-carved, familiar style of the rest of the base. The air is clear here, but the farther we go, the more the smoke and sounds of fighting become evident.

Gideon and Frost take point, with Silas and Vane sticking close to my sides. All of us have our weapons drawn, and the tension is so thick that the appearance of the first tactically armoured vampire is almost a relief.

Frost takes him out without blinking and steals the vampire's gun as he lowers him to the floor.

"I'll head back to our rooms and destroy any evidence," Morwen mutters as soon as we reach a fork in the tunnels.

"Silas, go with her," Gideon growls, and I get a hint of irritation from his end of the thrall bond. "Pack up what you can."

Because it's clear, no matter what happens, we won't be coming back here.

Draven moves up to take Silas's position at my side as the two of them disappear.

"I've got footage from the command centre," Finn says, his voice echoing from the earpiece. *"They're barricaded inside. It looks like Bakari is wounded..."* I hear a small groan of pain from the background, and Vane curses.

"What was that?" he demands.

"Noha tried to leave the van as soon as you left," Finn admits. *"Mia's got her staked to the seat for now."*

Savage, but effective. I knew Mia would keep them both safe.

"What numbers are we up against?" Gideon asks.

"It's bad," Finn replies, instead of answering directly. *"Armin is there. The barricade is breaking. It looks like Samuel and his remaining men are preparing for a final stand."*

"Shit," I whisper. "We have to get there before they open those doors."

Our steps take on a new sense of urgency, only to stall at the sound of gunfire.

"Armin," Immy mutters, her voice cold. "Cain humours his love for modern weapons, but it's a point of contention between them."

"I hate bullets," Vane grumbles.

"Aww, are you still sore about that tiny little shotgun incident?" Morwen retorts.

"Fuck. You."

I'm coming to realise that, even though the hybrid doesn't speak often, his voice is a pure invitation to sin, and I'm not immune. Those two words, in that dark but controlled tone...

It's far too easy to imagine him using a similar voice in bed.

Damn it. Now is not the time.

"Wait," Mia says. *"What shotgun incident?"*

The silence from Morwen and Vane is telling.

"When you two get back, we're having a family meeting. Babe, we said no family shootings."

"Don't be too hard on her, Mia. To us, torture is the basic family bonding method." Immy laughs.

It wouldn't be so funny if it weren't true, but I keep that thought to myself.

The next vampires we come across aren't alone. Frost takes out one with a light crossbow strapped across the back of his wrist, delivering a bolt straight to the vampire's heart. I step over the rapidly shrivelling corpse, intent on taking out the second.

Vane gets in the way, ripping away the vampire's gun before tearing his throat out with his claws.

He's the only one of us without a weapon, and it's clear why.

The hybrid's strength and claws are just as deadly as silver.

It soon becomes apparent that my thralls are intent on keeping me from doing any of the fighting. Every time we come across an enemy, they take out the threat before I can. At first, I find it amusing, but it quickly gets old.

"I *can* fight, you know," I grumble under my breath as we pause amidst the carnage, flattening ourselves against the wall to allow a handful of fleeing civilians to pass us.

"You're still recovering," Gideon growls.

"Save your strength for the real fight," Frost adds.

Vane isn't so tactful. "I would've preferred if you'd stayed behind with Mia."

Immy catches my eye and we share a *look*.

"You realise Morwen and I trained hard until I was back to full strength, right?" I check.

They shrug as one. "Still recovering," Gideon insists.

"How many years were you in that coffin? A month is nothing."

The woman in me wants to call them out on it, but the general knows now isn't the time.

"We'll be discussing this when we're out of here," I inform them curtly, pushing off the wall and heading towards the command room.

We must be close now.

"Armin's main force has broken through Samuel's barricade," Finn announces.

My blood chills. All of us speed up, heading for the command centre with a single-minded focus. We turn the corner and come face to face with the splintered, scorched, heavy doors. Beyond them, vampires and shifted lycans are fighting at speeds too fast for the mortal eye to follow.

This time, my men have no hope of shielding me from the brawling. The gunfire is deafening, and I duck out of the way before anyone has a chance to warn me.

Vane roars, shifting as a bullet catches him in the thigh. For a second, I just stare. I've never seen any of them shifted before, and Vane is *huge*. Perhaps it's a perk of being a hybrid, but he towers over the other lycans. His toughened grey skin, wiry fur, and lupine face are similar to the rest of them, but his fangs seem longer. Now they're practically sabres slicing down from his upper jaw. His muzzle is slightly shorter, more human, and his eyes seem to hold more wildness than the others.

"Remember, the aim is to get Samuel and Bakari out," Gideon hisses, and his voice echoes through the earpiece. "We get them, then we get the fuck out of here. No heroics."

His plan makes sense, because we can't possibly win against these numbers. Our group carves a steady path through the doors and into the room beyond. The carefully organised room beyond has been laid to waste. In the centre,

Armin is wielding a grenade launcher, of all things, and each blast makes the cave shake.

The maniac is laughing like the idea of collapsing the tunnels on top of us is somehow *funny*.

I can't see Samuel.

Beside me, Draven is practically vibrating with eagerness. It funnels down our bond, but his expression never changes as he beheads a lycan with a cruel smirk on his face. But a vampire uses the opening to sneak past him. I'm forced to abandon my search for Samuel and I strike back, slicing his hand off with a clean sweep of my sword.

I try to dodge out of the way of his outraged counter strike, but everyone is too close. I back into Immy and can't go any further. My attacker's blade rakes a line across my thigh.

The pack's protective bubble is literally going to get me killed.

With a huff of frustration, I duck down and strike up, forcing my sword through the underside of his jaw and kicking him back to create my exit.

Finally free of the stifling circle of thralls, I weave and duck into the room, killing and striking at random.

And it feels *good*.

This is what I was made for. Not running. Not games of cloak and dagger.

Bloodshed. War.

Death.

I have always been a warrior. This is where I belong.

"Evie," Finn whispers, sounding more than a little awestruck.

I must have gotten farther from the pack than I thought, because Frost's voice echoes from my earpiece as well. *"Where the fuck is she?"* he demands. *"We can't protect—"*

Finn whistles low and soft in my ear. *"She doesn't need it. Believe me."*

Out of the corner of my eye, I spy a familiar face.

Bakari stands over his father, brandishing a silver spear which he uses to keep everyone back. His mouth is stained with blood, and it's not hard to assume that he's been draining the corpses around him to enable him to keep fighting.

"Found them. East corner," I mutter, stabbing my claws into a lycan's face and ripping the bottom of her jaw off without looking away from my nephew.

I manage to make eye-contact with Bakari, and he stops twirling the spear just long enough for me to slip past. I check his injuries with a critical eye and determine that he's healed enough to keep fighting, before turning my attention to Samuel.

His chest is wide open and unrecognisable. A mess of flesh, bone and burns. He must've taken a grenade to the chest—given how bad the damage is. His eyes are swivelling in their sockets, not focusing on anything, and his pupils have shrunk until they're two pinpricks in the centre of his eyes. At least his heart is still beating—even though the rhythm is slow and stuttering.

He's not dead yet.

"You need to cover me," I say, dragging back my sleeve to expose my wrist. "I'll give him my blood. It will give him enough mobility to get out of here."

The alternative is carrying him, and given the ferocity of the battle around us, that will never work. Samuel needs to be able to walk.

My fangs sink into my own wrist, and I let the blood drip into his open mouth freely. He gulps it down straight away, and soon his burned arms come up to hold my wrist.

Thankfully, everyone around us is too busy fighting for

their lives to notice one man's chest knit itself back together. I tug my wrist away before I start to get dizzy. Samuel still has a wound, but it's surface level.

Survivable. With his age, it'll be healed by tomorrow.

"Evonnia," he gasps, eyes finally focusing on me. "You must leave."

"Working on it," I retort, tugging him up. "We're leaving together."

"Where is Noha?"

"Back at the van," I reply, not willing to get into it just now. "Get your son. We're leaving."

"My men—"

I pin him with a level stare. "You know the mission is you and you alone. Don't make me fight you on this. Be thankful we're taking Bakari with us."

"Head for the door," Frost orders. *"We'll cover you."*

"Bakari," I snap, dragging his attention from the lycans surrounding him. "To the door. Go."

"We're running away?" he hisses, outraged.

"Do as she says," Samuel snaps, though he makes no secret of his own resentment.

I slap a blade into my brother's hand, and together, we join Bakari in the fight to get back to the rest of my thralls. We take three steps in the direction of the door when Armin finds us.

"So the great Evelyn has turned traitor, as I suspected," he booms. "Once a backstabbing bitch… always a backstabbing bitch."

"Ignore him," I hiss at Bakari, who's stopped to listen to the drivel.

"And to side with a bunch of cave dwelling rats… my, how you've fallen. Cain would've made you a queen."

But Samuel's son is too proud to take such an insult lying down. Combined with the adrenaline rushing through his veins from what I'm assuming is his first immortal battle, it's no wonder he stops moving to listen.

"Bakari!" Samuel barks.

But the press of bodies is too strong for either of us to reach out and grab him.

I turn to block an incoming blow just as Bakari yells, "Put down your fucking gun and face me!" He pauses. "Or are you too cowardly to fight a cave dwelling rat?"

CHAPTER TWENTY-FIVE

EVELYN

"Idiot boy," Samuel hisses, his words tinged with pain. "Bakari, come. Now."

But his son isn't listening.

Oh well, fuck him. We came here to get him out, if he wants to stay and get killed, he made that choice.

"Eve, get Samuel out." Frost's voice rings in my ear.

But the press of fighting is too close. A lycan barrels past us, forcing us to dive even closer to the centre. I take out his Achilles tendon as he passes us, then duck under Samuel's arm to take out another in front of us.

"We're not going anywhere," I growl.

"Stay there, Princess." Vane's voice has been morphed by his lycan form, replacing his normally smooth words with a guttural, snarling speech that's hard to understand.

"Kinda hard to do anything else," I retort.

It's stupid, given that we're in the middle of a battle, but I can't help but look back at where Bakari went.

Things are worse than I feared. Armin is playing with the

younger vampire, slicing him open in a thousand controlled cuts while Bakari tries futilely to land a single mark. Armin must have been trained by Bella. He uses her favourite tricks far too often for it to be coincidence.

Bakari goes down as Armin takes out a tendon in the back of his knee with lethal precision. A second blow renders his dominant arm useless.

He's going to die. Samuel's pained groan confirms he knows it too.

"Sister," Samuel growls. "I beg you, save my idiot son."

I roll my eyes. "He chose this. He's more than old enough to know what a stupid move—"

Samuel cuts me off. "I'll tell you what you want to know if he lives. If he dies, my lips are sealed forever."

The litany of curses that spill from my mouth actually make some of our attackers back up for a second.

"Evelyn," Gideon begins in my ear. *"Don't even—"*

But I know what he's thinking. I've already had the same idea and discarded it because it won't work.

Samuel is Cain's son. Nothing we can say or do will get him to spill his secrets if he decides he's keeping them.

Which means the only way out of this is to save the ungrateful son of a bitch.

"Someone get Samuel out of here," I growl, directing my anger into my next strike, which takes the head of a snarling vampire. "It appears the plans have changed."

I sink my fangs into the throat of my next attacker, gulping a mouthful of potent—but bland—lycan blood before using the hold to rip out their throat. My chin is dripping scarlet, but I don't pay any attention to that as I take a breath and catalogue Armin's weaknesses.

Which are really just Bella's weaknesses.

Lazy footwork. Weak on parries aimed below the waist.

One. Two…

I slide between his legs and kick his knee with all the strength I possess.

His bones shatter, and he falls backwards, but he's old enough to anticipate the blow to his upper body, which he parries. No matter. I've managed to put myself between him and Bakari.

I shove Samuel's idiot son farther out of the way as Armin is forced to sink his fangs indiscriminately into the vampires battling in the crowd, drinking until he can put even a fraction of his weight on his knee.

"Ah, the traitorous prodigy has come to save the Neanderthal. How sweet."

"You know you're outmatched," I say, keeping my tone even as I block his next blow and the one after that. "So let us leave."

"Outmatched by a weakling woman who spent the last two centuries locked away in silver?" Armin scoffs, putting a little more weight on his leg. "That's right, Evelyn. Your sire told me exactly what's waiting for you when I deliver you back to him. He wanted to put you back in the same hole, but I suggested the bottom of an ocean trench instead. I can't wait to see what's left of you after a few centuries of drowning."

From my earpiece, six matching growls echo in response to his words, but I'm not listening. I'm not some young blood, to be easily distracted by words.

He gets in a blow to my shoulder, but it's only shallow. Still, the scent of my blood, potent and strong, seems to affect him, and his pupils dilate. Smiling, because the distraction will only make him sloppy, I feint another strike before catching my ankle behind his supporting leg.

Armin slams back onto the ground. Hard.

His head hits the floor with an audible and satisfying crack.

One more blow to sever his spine, and he's done. I move towards him, only to freeze.

In his hand is something I recognise from my research. A grenade. The modern ones are a far cry from what humanity was using when I went into the coffin. These new explosives can blast through metal.

Armin smirks as he hooks his finger through the key, and my gut sinks.

No. He's bluffing. He won't do it. He'll bring the entire place down.

"By the time we crawl out of here, Cain's reinforcements will have arrived." He grins maniacally, exposing bloody teeth. "That's right." He taps his own earpiece. "Your daddy knows you're here. He's seen all of this, and he's going to pull me from the rubble and raise me up above every other general. Above all of the traitorous scheming bitches he calls daughters."

In slow motion, I watch as he yanks out the pin and releases the strike lever. My first step towards him is too late, but I keep going.

I'm old enough I might survive if I can just put my body between it and the rest of the—

A hand grabs my waist and shoves me out of the way, just as a second pair of fur-covered arms band around my waist, keeping me immobile. I watch, frozen with horror, as Bakari lands on top of Armin and the two wrestle.

Bakari is still on top when an explosion rocks the room. His body jerks, absorbing most of the impact, but he can't mute the grenade's effects entirely. Shrapnel and dust fly out, making it impossible to see, and the cave—already damaged by Armin's antics earlier—shudders.

Groans.

Trembles start beneath my feet, and I realise what's coming as a broken scream rings in my ears. It takes me a second to realise that it's Noha's scream, echoing through my ear piece.

The hands around my waist drag me backwards just as the back of the room starts to crumble. Vane tosses me over his shoulder and moves at immortal speed, but there are so many people in the way still fighting, oblivious—or uncaring —about the danger they're in.

We make it past the broken door with seconds to spare. Rock crashes down in a deadly cascade that tumbles out into the tunnel. The crumbling avalanche of stone chases us without slowing.

God. It's not going to stop.

We're going to be buried down here in the dark.

I watch over Vane's furred shoulder as the wave reaches for us. Gaining. Gaining.

Until, with one last, angry rumble, it stops.

A final rush of dust and grit stings my eyes, but Vane doesn't stop.

The lights around us flicker. Then die, leaving us in a gloomy blackness that makes it impossible to see—even with immortal eyesight. The tunnel rumbles menacingly in the dark, and panic grips me at the thought of being sealed down here forever by a cave in. I fight against Vane's hold, needing to run, to move.

His grip is too strong. I can't do anything except allow the hybrid to carry me towards our exit.

"What the fuck just happened?" Morwen demands.

"Sound off." Gideon coughs. *"Frost's with me. Who else is still alive?"*

"I've got Evie," Vane growls, without giving me a chance to respond. "Silas?"

He slows down while we wait for his brother's response, and for a second, I think he's debating going back and digging through the rock for him.

"Still here." The younger beta chirps, and both of us relax. *"Draven took a boulder to the skull, but he's drinking. Looks like he'll be fine."*

"I'm here too," Immy mutters.

"Did anyone get Samuel?" Silas asks.

"He's with us." Frost's tone is grim.

That's when it sinks in.

Bakari is dead. Even if—by some miracle—he's still alive, he's buried under so much rock…

No, my pragmatic mind whispers. *He's gone.*

Even *I* likely wouldn't have survived such a thing. And with him dies any hope of getting the truth out of my brother.

The crushing weight of that realisation saps the fight from my bones, and I collapse fully against Vane. The hybrid doesn't react beyond bundling me up more securely in his arms, but I can sense his anger. It's strong enough to cross the partial bond we share.

Only it doesn't linger. He takes a deep breath, then another, and that anger diminishes so rapidly that soon our bond is silent again. His lycan form starts to retreat, until he's just a man once more.

That level of self-control is unbelievable, especially for a hybrid at the mercy of two wildly different natures.

"I won't lecture you," he begins, continuing to walk. "Gideon will want that honour. But if you put yourself in danger like that again, princess, I will tan your ass red every day for a week."

I stiffen in shock. "Excuse you?" I choke.

"You heard me, and I'm not in the habit of repeating myself. It's not up for debate, so save your arguing for Gid."

He picks up the pace, shifting back to speed things up. The rest of the tunnels pass in a blur as I scramble to think of

261

a response. Unfortunately, by the time I've thought of one, the moment has passed.

It's a good distance back to the exit, but Vane runs tirelessly until we reach the end of the tunnel, where he drops his lycan form for good and carefully places me on my own two feet. He must not trust me, because his hand envelops mine, holding tightly as he pulls the two of us through the crevice.

We're the last to arrive. Everyone else is already there, helping to silently load our gear onto the van. Morwen is sitting in the front passenger seat with Mia on her lap, drinking heavily from her neck as a wicked looking wound on her chest seals itself before our eyes. Vane notices, and he grumbles something unintelligible under his breath as he pulls me along with him.

Even when we stop, he doesn't let go. He keeps me pressed against him and wraps his arms around my waist as he turns away to give our sisters their privacy.

Draven's eyes meet mine, and the thrall bond pulses with possessiveness at the grip the hybrid has on me. The wound on his temple is no longer bleeding, and the puncture wounds on Silas's neck explain why.

I scan the area, making sure none of my thralls have serious wounds before checking on Immy—who miraculously seems unharmed—and finally searching for the two people I know I'll have to face now.

But there's no sign of Noha. Or Samuel.

Silas reads my questioning glance. He shakes his head and finishes shoving his trunk into the van before pressing a quick finger to his lips and jerking his head at the dunes beyond.

I guess they've gone over there to talk.

"She's okay," Vane grumbles, and I whirl to find out who

he's speaking to, only to discover Gideon's furious face just inches from my own.

While I've been giving everyone a once over, it seems the alpha has been doing the same to me.

"You ignored my orders," he growls.

"Because they were going to get me killed!" I retort.

"Then you should've said something, rather than disappearing off on your own."

"I'm not your subordinate," I snarl back. "I spent decades of my life training and earning my place as a general in Cain's army. Just because I submitted to you in the bedroom does *not* mean I'll do the same outside of it. I told you that when I suggested the idea."

Vane stiffens, and I'm momentarily distracted by the sensation of his dick hardening against my ass.

My head spins reflexively to stare at him in shock.

Of all my thralls, he's definitely the most reserved. Aside from the wicked orgasm he gave me, he's barely interacted with me at all. Most of the time, he's just *there*. A silent, glowering presence.

"That has no bearing on this!" Gideon hisses. "Frost and I are in charge of this pack. If you want to be a part of it, you respect that hierarchy."

"I didn't see you coming up with a plan!" I growl. "What would you have had me do?"

"That doesn't matter."

"You had no better plan—"

"And your plan got a lot of people killed!"

"Enough." Vane says the single word so harshly that it silences both of us.

Glancing back, I stiffen at the darkness in his eyes.

At times like this, it's hard to remember that he's a beta—a protector. Sometimes I swear he's as alpha as Gideon and Frost.

"You," he begins, and his voice has become calm once more as he addresses Gideon. "Should not blame her for the actions of one of Cain's unhinged generals." I relax for a second before he turns to look at me. "And *you* agreed to work as a team. You broke that promise."

Swallowing down my argument—because, like it or not, he is right about that—I shake my head. "I'm sorry, but no one else had a plan, either."

"Doesn't matter. You could've asked for orders. Or suggested a better strategy. You shouldn't have broken formation like you did."

"You were keeping me from helping."

"We were keeping you safe," Vane says. "You are an outstanding warrior"—I try my hardest not to preen—"but that means nothing if you get injured early in the fight. Put your pride aside and think about it. You were always our best shot at killing Armin. Why waste your energy on the small fries?"

I raise a sceptical eyebrow. "You expect me to believe he intended to send me against Armin all along? I'm not an idiot."

"It was one eventuality," Gideon admits. "Not the one I was hoping for, I'll admit. The plan was to keep you in reserve in case we needed you, and then you went off on your own and endangered everyone." He's shouting by the end, but I refuse to back down.

"If not for that grenade, I would've saved Bakari *and* Samuel." I retort, wrenching myself free of Vane's hold and striding up to the alpha until we're toe to toe. "If I'd waited for you to get your ass in gear, both of them might've been dead by the time we reached them.

"Evie…" Vane cautions.

"How many times do I have to drum it into your head

that we're a *team*?" Unlike his perpetually calm beta, Gideon is so angry he looks like he might actually explode.

The vein at his temple dances in fury, and his eyes have narrowed until they're completely overshadowed by his bold brows. Both of us are breathing deeply, the two of us still riding a high from a battle that hasn't quite worn off yet.

For a second, I can't decide if I want to hit him or fuck him. From his thunderous expression, I'm pretty sure he's feeling the exact same way about me.

Then Finn steps in between us, somehow finding a space to insert himself into, despite how close Gideon and I have become. He faces down his alpha, bringing his palms up to rest on Gideon's chest.

"Hey," he murmurs. "Why don't you take a step back? Frost has gone to get Noha and Samuel, and there's some stuff on the monitor I think you really need to see."

The effect is instant. The fight drains out of Gideon like a balloon deflating, and his body visibly starts to shrink. I didn't even notice his clothes stretching, but now they're visibly looser on his frame.

He must have been close to shifting.

The alpha and omega take one step away from me, and then another. Gideon has a wary look in his eyes, but it's directed at Finn, not me. The omega shoots me a look I can't quite decipher as he leads his pack leader away and over to the van.

Everyone is staring, but they duck their heads as I turn my attention to them.

"That was childish," Vane censures.

Somehow, without Gideon there, pushing my buttons, I too have lost my fight. "God, it was, wasn't it?" Mortification burns at my cheeks, but the elder beta doesn't level any judgement at me.

He nods once and looks over at the dunes where Noha

and Samuel are apparently still arguing it out. "Tensions are high. It was expected. You are still finding your place among relationships that have existed for decades."

"If he thinks I'm going to bow down and ask permission to piss—"

Vane's unimpressed look shuts me up, and I sink to my ass on the sand with a huff of frustration.

"I've gotten between Gideon and Finn when all I wanted to do was help them," I mutter. "I've fucked up any chance of ever getting Samuel to tell us how to kill Cain. I'm not even certain I trust everyone I've brought into this…"

"The road to Hell is paved with good intentions…" he mutters.

I scoff. "Then I should have a marble road with a red freaking carpet rolled over it."

"Get up." He doesn't seem interested in letting me wallow in my self pity. "We've got to get out of here, and preferably far away from Egypt. Finn said Frost is going to get Samuel and… Noha. Once they're back, we're going."

But only two silhouettes reappear over the top of the sand dune minutes later.

"Where is she?" Draven grumbles.

A wave of his disappointment hits me and it takes me a second to realise it's because he was hoping to be the one to kill her.

"Gone," Frost mutters, clearly just as displeased as the vampire.

"My wife and I have decided to separate." Samuel looks absolutely wrecked, for all that his tone remains even. "She blames me for the loss of our son, and I… can no longer bear to look at her."

"Are you coming with us?" Morwen asks, hanging her head out of the passenger window. "Or will you try to rebuild with your people?"

Samuel shakes his head. "They had their instructions. Should our home be taken, they were under orders to leave and never try to contact one another again. I made the decision for their own safety. They will be better able to blend in with society as individuals. There can be no rebuilding now. Cain will be looking for them, and we have no idea how much Noha let slip."

He turns to regard me with sad eyes. "You know what I said."

"I tried," I whisper, grateful when someone—Silas—comes up behind me and wraps an arm around my waist in a silent show of support. "If he hadn't—"

My brother holds up a hand to silence me. "I am a man of my word."

"You can't do that!" Immy argues. "Cain is the reason Bakari is dead. He's the reason your wife betrayed you. We're the only family you have left, and we're all going to die if you don't—"

Samuel shakes his head. "I cannot tell you how to kill Cain, because I do not know."

CHAPTER TWENTY-SIX

EVELYN

His words fall over us in a wave of disappointment that
steals my breath from my lungs.

"So you just led us on?" I ask, too tired to even summon
the energy to be angry. "Let us stay and believe there was
hope for no reason?"

Samuel gives me a dark look. "I do not know for certain.
But I do know how Cain was made."

I frown. "Made?"

"You do not think he just sprang out of the ground, fully
formed, do you?" Samuel snorts, shaking his head. "What is
the one thing Cain hates above all others? The thing he has
burned entire villages to eradicate?"

Morwen answers before I can. "Witchcraft."

"That's not real," Silas protests. "No one has ever seen any
evidence of witches, they're a true myth."

I shake my head. "If they weren't real, he wouldn't be so
scared of them."

"Exactly." Samuel takes a deep breath. "I believe our sire

made a bargain with one, who granted him his cursed form of immortality. I suspect the same witch may have created the other two immortal races as well, hence why hybrids are possible. But by the time I figured it out, Cain had killed almost every living witch. Since then, he has eradicated them entirely."

"No." Gideon argues, his anger at me forgotten as he leans against the side of the van, holding Finn's hand. "That's not possible. Lycans aren't the product of witchcraft."

"If they created him, they must have had some defence against him," Finn says, ignoring his alpha's angry outburst. "Who would be so stupid as to create a monster they couldn't control?"

"It's doubtful the witch who created him intended for him to take over the world," Samuel says. "You know our sire can be charming when he wants to be. Perhaps he convinced her into it."

"So he tricked the witch into making him, then decided to kill an entire species, just in case there was a way to undo the spell?" Immy breathes. "That would make so much sense."

Samuel nods slowly, sighing. "I believe it's also why the vampires become weaker with every generation of separation between them and Cain. The magic in their blood grows weaker."

"That doesn't explain lycans," Gideon insists. "We're not getting—"

"Lycans are born," Finn reminds him. "That's different from being fed blood and dying."

"And ghouls?" he grumbles. "What's their excuse? Pretty sure all of us would love it if *they* got weaker with each generation."

"Their venom is incredibly potent," Samuel mutters.

Finn nods. "A thousand times more potent than most

other toxins, and the most recent studies have shown that it continuously evolves, making it resistant to antivenom."

"Whatever spell the original witch used," Samuel concludes, "it can't have been the same in all instances. Perhaps she was experimenting, trying to perfect her work… Cain is the only one who could know for certain."

"And you're certain there are no more witches?" Vane asks. "None?"

"None living who remember their craft." Samuel looks out over the dunes. "The last family I know of was descended from an ancient bloodline from the very north of Europe, and moved to the Old Country, hoping to lose him. I found them and watched them for a day or so, just long enough to confirm that they were what I thought they were, and devise a strategy to approach them. But I took too long. Cain set their house ablaze with them in it." He pauses and looks me straight in the eye. "Your parents' screams will haunt me until the day I die."

Shock roots me to the spot. "What?"

"You were born to a witch in hiding. I wanted to warn your parents of what was coming for them, but my hesitation cost them their lives."

"That's not possible." I haven't got even the slightest inkling of magic. Nothing. No special powers beyond what I gained when Cain turned me.

I look around our group, only to find everyone is staring at me with differing looks of awe, confusion, and even… resentment.

Immy banishes the expression before I can blink, but I see it.

She can't seriously…

Samuel ignores me. "When I couldn't find your body in the wreckage, I searched the entire village until I found you at the house of your father's sister. She wasn't of the bloodline, but she was sheltering you—which might've gotten her killed had Cain found out. I took you from her and brought you to my sire's palace as a means of assuring your safety. I believed you'd be safest hidden right under his nose where I could keep an eye on you. I had no idea…"

"The Night of Five Knives," I whisper. "You brought me to him."

"Along with a dozen other children whose deaths will stain my soul for the rest of my life." He bows his head.

"Wait," Finn grumbles. "What's the Night of Five…" He trails off as Morwen, Immy, and I all look away.

Thankfully, Samuel answers for us. "My brothers and I were not the first sons of Cain. He used to turn men who showed promise on the battlefield. Or offer his curse to those he considered cunning enough to be worthy. All of them were adults. All male."

"Until Evie and her sisters," Frost mutters.

"Precisely," Samuel nodded. "He made us go out into the world and pick the girls we thought held a spark of something special. The only requirement was that they couldn't be too old for him to mould into his perfect children. Of course, most of my brothers went for the promise of beauty. That didn't help them." He sighs, running a hand over his bald head as he recounts a day I do my best to forget. "I thought he'd interview them. Pick them by testing them somehow. Instead, he put five knives in the middle of the room and commanded the girls to kill each other until only five remained."

The vampire looks up at all of us, tormented. "I never knew. I swear. If I had, I *never* would've gone along with it."

"Get on with it," Morwen growls. "We don't need a rehash of the past."

Samuel swallows and nods, turning back to me. "Once you survived that trial, you were safe. I watched you grow, hoping you'd show some sign of the power... I was ready to get you out of there at a moment's notice because if Cain even suspected I'd hidden a witch under his roof..."

"But I haven't got any powers," I insist.

"I know. It became apparent quickly that without anyone to train you, it was unlikely you would ever learn to use the power," Samuel concludes. "It's not just an innate gift. It's a craft which must be practised. From what little I saw, there were chants, ingredients, herbs, crystals, and other things you'd never think to combine unless you knew what you were doing. That is why there is no way to kill Cain. Even if vampirism hasn't stripped you of the ability to use magic, there is no way for you to learn, and no guarantee that you'd be as powerful as you'd need to be to end him."

Silas's hold on my waist feels like the only thing holding me up. My legs have turned to jelly.

"So there's no hope then," I whisper. "He will find us, and we'll all die."

Finn tuts at me, and a pulse of disapproval echoes down our bond. "No. Now we research. You're telling me an entire race was erased without a trace? I call bullshit. *Something* must have survived." He pins Samuel with a look. "I'm going to need every location you know of where the witches were before Cain killed them. They might have left something behind, or there may be survivors or records or anything..."

Samuel shakes his head. "You won't find anything. Cain was meticulous." He sighs. "But I will ride with you to the airstrip and tell you what I know on the way. Then I'm leaving."

"Where will you go?" Immy asks, her eyes wide and watery. "We just found you again—"

"I'll go wherever the wind takes me. My gift will ensure everyone forgets about me in a few weeks, and I'll return to living in hiding." He pauses. "I suggest you all do the same."

"You could—" I begin, but Gideon cuts me off.

"We don't have time to argue about this. Cain's troops are canvassing the desert."

Finn nods. "He's right. It's only a matter of time until they start searching out and killing survivors. We need to get in the air."

And go where? I think to myself as we file into the van.

I'm still feeling numb as I take a seat between Silas and Vane, and I think the betas can tell because they both press their bodies against me, like their touch alone might help me maintain my grip on my sanity.

My mother was a witch.

I could be a witch.

All this time, Cain's favoured daughter has been the key to his undoing.

Only I'm not, because there's no one to teach me.

In the seat ahead, Finn and Samuel sit with their heads pressed together, the former tapping away at his tablet as Samuel rushes through every piece of information he remembers. Frost is in the driver's seat, and he starts the van with a rumble and drives like a maniac.

Through it all, I can only stare at the back of my brother's head, wondering how any of this can be real. Everyone else seems to be taking it in their stride and I just… can't.

Then I catch onto the thread of Samuel's conversation. "And this is the village where Evonnia was born…"

Finn frowns, and I feel his confusion. "But that's where…"

Samuel nods. "He moved his Court there as a declaration of victory. The manor was built directly over the ashes of Evonnia's home."

"Asshole," Frost grouches.

"Did the villagers know?" Vane asks, leaning forward. "Because when we went to collect Evie…"

"That old woman bowed to the coffin," Frost finishes.

Glancing back at me from his position beside them. "But when I lived there, no one ever breathed a whisper about witches. Just blood-sucking demons in the house on the hill."

"It must have been nothing," Samuel dismisses the theory with a wave of his hand. "Evonnia was so young... barely eight..."

Gideon frowns. "That was old enough to remember something of this, surely."

He turns to me with a suspicious glare that I just don't have it in me to return. "I don't... I..."

I should have childhood memories, but...

"Cain did everything he could to beat talk of anything *before* out of them," Samuel explains. "He took away their names, their clothes, shaved their heads. Basically erased their identities until they earned the new ones he gave them. The older girls might have some memories, but Evonnia and Alice were the youngest and most impressionable."

"Don't use that name," Immy hisses from behind me.

Samuel inclines his head in apology. "You must have seen Cain's brainwashing techniques on educated immortals. Imagine how effective they'd be on illiterate human children."

An uncomfortable silence falls over all of us, and I catch all of them sneaking glances at me. Finn senses my discomfort and sends a silent hug down our bond before coaxing Samuel back into conversation until the van loses the eerie silence it held before.

Thank God for the omega.

CHAPTER TWENTY-SEVEN

CALLISTA

"Sire, Armin is dead," Bella announces quietly.

For a second, Cain remains still as a statue with his head resting on my lap. The parlour we're in is the smallest, most intimate room in his island mansion. He hasn't left his Triumph Island home in days, instead choosing to delegate the hunt for Evie and her band of merry freaks to Bella. A lot of the human and lycan staff have been banished—apart from Ivan, who hasn't dared to complain about the work of running the whole household by himself.

If I didn't know better, I'd say Cain was hiding.

But I will never dare to say that to his face.

The tension in these dark halls has only gotten worse once Armin reported back to Bella saying that our idiot sisters were in league with Frost. Cain raged for hours once his own men confirmed it. CCTV footage showed Evie was once again playing around with her ghoul. Since then, the entire island has been locked down and the city put under a strict curfew.

Cain has kept me holed up with him, but thankfully, his demands of me have been few. I'm not stupid. I know silence and obedience are the two things keeping me alive right now. So I keep my mouth shut as I rub his temples, letting my fingers play in the silver-streaked strands of hair at his forehead.

"And Samuel's progeny?" His words are silky smooth. Dangerous.

Bella hesitates. "Dead. But sire... there are reports that Samuel himself was present. Those of my men who survived say he fled with our sisters and Frost's pack."

Our sire erupts from the chaise, ripping his head from my grasp with a roar that shakes the building.

I can't help it. I flinch back into the velvet seat, hugging my chest reflexively. Even Bella—normally so unflappable and cold—takes an involuntary step towards the door.

"And your team let them escape *together*?" Cain hisses.

"We're doing our best to locate them," Bella promises, her tone clipped and professional, but her fingers are white as she grips her tablet like a shield. "Already, we've picked up several rogues who lived under Samuel's rule and brought them in for interrogation—"

She chokes off as Cain's hand wraps around her throat and slams her up against the wall.

Oh, this is good. If I weren't so terrified, the sight of miss-goody-two-shoes finally getting an earful from our Sire would be amusing.

I'm not stupid, though. He'll scare her a little, but he won't risk putting her out of action. He needs Bella to run his empire. Once he's sent her off, it's me who'll have to bear the brunt of his anger. I'll be the one left aching and bleeding on his bed.

"Interrogating runts is going to get us *nowhere*. By now, Evelyn and her thralls almost certainly know what Samuel does. If your men—your wretched progeny, Armin, who you were so fond of—were worth a damn, they'd have killed your sisters and your wretched, traitorous brother. Instead, they're incompetent, just like you."

Bella chokes as she blabbers and claws at his hand. "But, Sire, there's no rush. You said yourself, Samuel's claims are ludicr—"

Cain's other hand goes to Bella's jaw and—in a movement so fast I barely see it—he digs his claws in and rips her head straight from her body.

My throat burns with vomit. Bella's old enough to over-come beheading, but it still hurts like a—

I don't see the stake until it's too late. One second Bella's corpse is lying on the rug, bleeding into the plush blue fabric, staining it an awful shade of black-brown. The next, a splinter of silver is sticking out of her chest and she's shrivel-ling away into nothing. Soon, all that remains of my eldest sister is a husk. When Cain drops her withered head to the carpet, it disintegrates entirely.

He killed…

Oh God.

He *killed* her.

A scream lodges in my throat as he turns his cold grey eyes on me. Only self preservation freezes the sound before it can emerge. My lungs burn, but I can't seem to physically force myself to breathe past the crushing terror in my chest.

I sit in silence, staring with wide eyes at the grey, cold corpse wearing my sister's clothes and jewels.

"If I'd known all it took to shut you up was killing Bella-trix, I would've done it a lot sooner," Cain mutters, striding the length of the room. "Clean that up. I'm taking command of our troops. Be in my chamber at sunrise. I'll need to feed."

The door slams behind him, but I barely notice him leaving. I can't rip my eyes away from Bella. Instead of a scream, my lungs clench, forcing free a ragged sob.

The second I manage to draw in a shaky breath, I collapse.

"Bella," I whisper, sliding from the sofa and landing hard on my knees.

I reach out, but stop with my perfect French manicure just inches from her crumbling form. If I touch her, she'll disintegrate entirely.

Not that it matters. She's unrecognisable now. Only her prim tailored suit and favourite bangles give any clue that the corpse before me is even her.

She was the perfect daughter. Cain's shadow who took care of *everything*. She worked loyally for centuries without a hint of hesitation. I didn't *like* her, but she was always there when I called. Never turned me away. Never complained about my spending, or my partying. Reliable to a fault. The perfect eldest sibling.

And he killed her. My sister.

Worse, I said nothing. *Did* nothing.

I'm next.

I feel it with a cold certainty that slithers into my bones and wraps around my heart. Grief, shock, and disbelief war inside me until my finger crosses that final distance and touches her hand.

It turns to ash at the contact, collapsing under the lightest contact. Her bangles roll across the blood-soaked rug, and the diamonds in them are quickly coated in scarlet. By the time they come to a stop, they could be mistaken for rubies.

Some primal part of my mind recognises that her blood still smells good. First generation. Powerful.

I seal my lips and force myself to swallow down my rising bile.

"Oh my God, Bella."

I'm falling apart, but I don't have that luxury.

Deep breath in, I pick my jacket off the arm of the chaise and slide it on. Twiddle the rings on my fingers, stroking the stones in a rhythmic pattern.

I've seen death before. This is no different.

Except it is.

Because for Cain to be so terrified of Evie finding Samuel, means that our brother knows something. Something that could harm our sire.

Perhaps even a way to kill him.

My jaw sets as I turn my attention to the door he left through, then glance back down at Bella's corpse.

If anyone has a chance of killing our sire, it's Evie. All I have to do is keep myself alive until then. With my mouth shut and my ears to the ground, I might even hear something that will convince her to spare me when she's done.

I'm nothing if not a survivor.

Ivan steps through the door as I go to leave, and I toss my hair back in a familiar motion I know will draw his eyes to my cleavage and away from my face. "Clean that up," I snap. "And send her jewellery up to my room after it's been cleaned. No use letting good diamonds go to waste."

At least I can keep some remnant of my sister. In Cain's current mood, I wouldn't put it past him to erase her completely.

My Louboutins feel like they're made of lead as they click across the black marble of the foyer and up the stairs to my room. I pointedly ignore Bella's door on the other side of the hall, but it's difficult. Vampire servants are already going in and out. Removing her things. Destroying any trace of her.

I close my own door with shaking hands, blocking out the sight. My mind is still replaying her death. Over and over, I see her panicked eyes. Her clawing hands.

The hour it takes me to get ready goes slowly. Every

minute is haunted by Bella's final moments—made worse by the knowledge that if I displease my sire, I'll share her fate.

Normally, when Cain summons me, I focus on pretending that the lingerie in my wardrobe is armour. Today, that trick isn't working. I spend every second resisting the urge to lock myself in my bathroom and hide from my sire.

But I want to live. So I stride down the corridor with my head held high and arrange myself on his covers in a pose I know he's partial to.

I'm not religious, but when the door swings open, I pray to God or whoever is listening to let me see another sunset.

CHAPTER TWENTY-EIGHT

SILAS

EVIE HASN'T SPOKEN A WORD SINCE SAMUEL LEFT US HALF AN hour ago. She's been sitting in the back of the van with her eyes closed, and I wonder if she's even noticed that we're ready to leave. The jet is loaded and fuelled, and the van is sitting on the tarmac.

Gid will set the vehicle on auto-drive to a remote location and rig it to explode somewhere in the desert. No loose ends.

Right now, the alpha is doing the final checks on our aircraft, making sure that nothing is amiss. His obsession with safety is understandable, given Evie's recent admission.

Our silly vampire has no idea what she agreed to when she made that deal with the alpha. Despite what Gideon might've promised her, I'm betting his instinct won't make *any* distinction between omega in the bedroom and omega in daily life.

The second he fucked her and she submitted, our alpha was lost, and I can't wait to see the fireworks when the two of them realise that. Whether her not being a lycan will let him curb the worst of those instincts is yet to be seen. But for now, a pack with two omegas means he's being twice as paranoid.

I take a step back towards the van, only to stop.

Draven is already there, tugging Evie out and into his arms.

Shit. If he takes her to the bedroom…

I spent fifteen minutes removing the bed slats and balancing the mattress over the frame to mess with him. If he puts Evie on the bed…

Disaster control time…

I head for the two of them, only to careen to a stop as Vane steps in front of me.

"I need you to back me up," he growls. "Morwen and Mia are trying to convince the alphas to split up so they can investigate a different site. No way is our sister…"

I blank him out, staring at Draven as he carries our girl into the jet like a princess. "That sounds fine," I mutter. "Gotta go."

"Silas!" Vane steps in front of me *again*. "You can't be serious…"

"I've really got to go…" I weave around him, ignoring his growl of frustration as I trail our girl into the plane.

Evie needs me to be her white knight, and that trumps whatever he's going on about.

Of course, she wouldn't need a white knight if I hadn't set the prank in the first place… Eh. Semantics.

I snatch her out of Draven's arms with a grin. "You don't get to run off with her and trap her in your lair until sunrise," I call over my shoulder as I carry her over to the sofa. "Sharing is caring, D."

The vampire narrows his eyes at me, and I wink down at Evie, who doesn't react.

"I'm much cuddlier than he is," I promise. "It's the lack of knives poking out everywhere."

An unforgiving hand traps my shoulder. "What have you done this time, wolf-boy?" Draven demands.

"Moi?" I turn my best innocent smile on him. "What makes you think I've done—"

A loud thump cuts me off, followed by an irate: "Fuck! *SILAS!!*"

Oh shit. I guess Frost found the trap first.

Draven's lips curl upwards in a cold, calculating smirk as the fuming ghoul storms from the bedroom.

"Care to explain why you rigged the mattress to collapse beneath me?" he says, arms crossed over his chest.

I offer him my best guilty expression. "In my defence, I rescued Evie."

Yes, I'm aware I'm holding her between us like a shield, so I suppose it's no surprise when Frost slips his arms around her and steals her away.

"Fix the damned bed."

"Yes, Alpha. Whatever you say, Alpha."

Offering him a grinning salute—because his purple-faced glower is *almost* as hilarious as Draven's colourful death threats—I hasten back down the aisle to undo my mischief, only to snort as I see the destruction Frost's ass has caused.

The puff of air against my neck makes me jump out of my skin.

"Try to fuck with my sleep one more time, lycan." Draven's voice is soft like silk, but I don't want to turn around and see the cold, dead look in his eyes. "And I'll turn your pelt into a nice fur coat for Evie's Christmas present."

I whirl, but he's already gone.

Creepy bastard.

By the time I fix the bed, the jet is taxiing onto the

runway. I enter the cabin and take my seat, frowning in confusion when I note Morwen and Mia's absence.

"Wait… where's…?"

Vane pins me with a glower. "Without anyone else to object, our sister is accompanying Morwen to Alexandria, where they'll take a boat to Greece so they can investigate the Greek witches."

Greek witches? That's a new one. No doubt Mia is enjoying the chance to get out from under Vane's constant supervision. The poor girl has been grumbling about being under his watch since we left New York.

At least Vane gave up on trying to mother-hen me pretty early on in our lives. Good thing too. If he'd worried about me like he always has over her, he'd probably have suffered an aneurism by now. As a kid, I found every single piece of trouble a young boy could, and then some.

Mia, on the other hand, spent her teenage years in the shadow of what happened with Isla and our mother. When other girls were going out and enjoying themselves, she was mourning a parent and a sister and dealing with suddenly finding herself packless.

All of which made Vane more overprotective than ever.

The last few centuries apart have probably given her some much needed space from our older brother.

"We're headed for the Old Country," he continues. "To chase up Evie's ancestors."

I look at our girl, to see how she reacts to that statement. Evie's sitting quietly on Draven's lap in the arm chair in the corner, letting him play with her hair. She's not taking this latest revelation well. Perhaps she's in shock, or maybe she's just desperately trying to remember something of her childhood to disprove Samuel's story, but I don't think it's sunk in for her yet.

Cold Draven isn't really the right person to help her

handle this, but Finn is too worked up with whatever is going on between him and Gideon to help.

I know I'm risking life and limb, but I switch seats until I'm closer to her.

"Hey, beautiful. What's going on in that head of yours?" I whisper.

She startles, eyes finally focusing on mine. "I don't know," she admits. "I thought maybe if I really tried, I'd remember something, but I can't. If Samuel's lying, I don't know. And if he's telling the truth, then I'm the reason we can't kill Cain. Because I can't remember the first thing about being a witch. Not even what my mother looked like."

"You were only a child," I reassure her, gently. "I..." I glance at my brother, and then back to her. "I can't really remember what my mother looked like, and I was twenty-three when she died."

I feel Vane stiffen, and I grimace in response. Our mother has been an elephant in the room for what remains of our family for too long. By some unspoken agreement, we never speak of her. Or Isla.

Perhaps in part because of the pain it will cause Gideon. But he's up front right now, so I don't see the harm in bringing her up. Besides, the curiosity Evie's feeling seems to have banished a little of the confusion and shock that's been weighing on her.

"Ma was a beta too," I continue. "Apparently, I'm a bit like her. She loved people, so our house was always full of visitors. Vane got all of our father's bossiness."

Evie swallows, then asks the inevitable question. "How did she...?" She trails off. "Never mind. It's rude to ask."

"Our old alpha—Gid's dad—killed my older sister." After all this time, it's finally less painful to say the words. It took decades to think of Isla without remembering the way her blood ran in rivulets down our front door. "Our mother was never the same. She became a shell of herself, and eventually, she chose to take her own life rather than live with the pain."

I know my voice is bitter, but I can't help it. For the longest time, I considered her actions selfish—cruel, even. Mia was barely fifteen. Too young to survive without a mother.

It took me a long time to understand how she must have felt. She'd already lost our father, and then to lose her omega daughter on top of that…

I'm pretty sure Vane and I kept going out of sheer spite. If Gid hadn't stepped in and killed his own father in an official challenge, the two of us would've given it our best shot. Then Mia would've been completely alone in the world, because there was no way two betas could put down an alpha. Our instincts would've been fighting us every step of the way— not to mention the rest of the pack.

It was unheard of for an alpha as young as Gid to win a challenge.

Him dissolving the pack afterwards was just as incredible. Everyone thought he was insane, but he knew exactly how rotten the pack had become.

It didn't take long for similar corruption to appear in other packs. Decades later, it turned out to be Cain's doing all along. Weakening us from within so that lycans were in no state to interfere with the Triumph. Only a rare few—like the Echo Lake Pack—managed to avoid such a fate.

"I'm sorry," Evie whispers. "That must have been awful."

"It was a long time ago," I whisper. "And they were both avenged."

For that alone, Gideon won the loyalty of what remained of our family.

I dare a glance up at Vane, only to find he's staring at me with a look that flickers between sadness and regret. Then he looks at Evie and those tender feelings disappear, replaced with determination.

Evie follows my gaze, and her eyes meet his. My thrall bond surges to the forefront of my mind, overflowing with her guilt and remorse. Her emotions hit me all at once, giving me a taste of what a true bond would be like.

"I'm sorry," she says, a second time.

But I don't think she's talking about Isla and our mother this time. Evie has finally realised what it did to Vane when he discovered her trying to stake herself on her first night of freedom. I never saw our mother hang herself. It was my brother who walked into our house to find her dangling from the bannister. He stopped me and Mia from coming inside and dealt with everything by himself.

Afterwards, he got blind drunk—and it was the only time I've ever seen him do so.

Evie's suicide attempt hit him in a raw spot, and now she understands why.

"Forget it," Vane grunts, turning away.

Like a switch has been flicked, the burst of clarity between the vampire and me shutters, and my bond to Evie closes itself off.

Damn, I want a full bond with her. Just the thought of Finn and Draven already being at that point is making me green with envy. How can a man whose heart is made of ice have earned the right to call himself her thrall in all ways, yet I can't seem to bridge that gap, no matter how hard I try?

"So what's your earliest memory?" I ask, trying to get the two of us back on topic.

Evie shrugs. "Other than the Night of Five Knives? Training, maybe?… I keep trying to recall…"

"Could her mother have cast a spell to make her forget? Is that a witch power?" Immy asks, peering at her sister like you would a science experiment.

Yeah, that's not going to help anyone. At least it's better than the pure jealousy that flashed across her face when Samuel told Evie about her heritage.

"Let me just consult my copy of witches for dummies," Finn snarks as he steps out of the cockpit. "Or we could ring up our local coven…"

"Finn, cut it out." Vane isn't in the mood for our omega's brand of defensive sarcasm, and I have to admit, I'm not either. "Helpful suggestions only."

Evie shoves out of Draven's arms and leaves without another word. I let out a sigh.

"Guys, she needed reassurance, not more fighting."

Finn groans, collapsing into a chair beside Vane, and leaning against my brother. "Sorry, Gideon's doing my head in."

Vane cracks his knuckles. "Is he pressuring you?"

We've all heard about the 'break' the two of them have agreed on, and—while I'll admit, I understand why Finn has done it—I don't think it's going to end well.

"Nothing like that," Finn says, eyes fluttering closed. "He's trying to be considerate…"

I snort, rising from my crouched position and moving to sit on his other side. "You wanted a break, remember?"

"I don't know what I want," Finn admits.

"That's relatable," Immy mutters, then yawns. "I'm going to head after Evie and see if she's okay, then I'm going to sleep."

EVELYN

Whatever Silas did to the bed before, it's perfectly made when I retreat to the small cabin at the back of the jet. Still, I give it a wary prod before I sit on it.

This plane is smaller than the one we took across the

Atlantic. Still comfortable and obviously designed with luxury in mind, but there are only two private sleeping areas. So my stint of isolation won't last long.

Still, I need alone time.

Nothing has seemed real since Samuel dropped the witch bombshell on me. I've been trapped in my head, trying to remember something—anything—that might disprove his story.

Yet I can't remember anything before that night. For so long, I've prided myself on that. Cain used to tell us that our lives began when we got our hands on those blades.

I pull mine out from its sheath and stare at it. The silver edge has nicks and scratches, but it still gleams like it did back then. Parts of the pattern along the hilt have worn smooth over time, but I can still remember how it looked.

"It's a waste of time," Immy mumbles, slipping into the room and closing the door. "I don't remember anything from that day... Cain forbade us from speaking about our lives before, remember? He whipped Morwen when she dared to speak her mother's name."

"At least Morwen remembered it..." I hiss. "I don't want this, Immy. Of all the things Samuel could've said, I thought we'd have a weapon. A spring of holy water, an ancient white oak, or *something*. This is so useless, he may as well have told us nothing."

"Well, I'm sorry that the great Evelyn just became even more special. I really am." Bitterness drips from her words. "But you should really be used to it by now. You were always the chosen one. What's changed?"

I blink at her, confused. "You think I *wanted* this?"

"I know you didn't," she counters. "But you got it just the same, didn't you? Now all you have to do to save the world is learn whatever magic spell will kill our sire, and poof, everyone will love you again, just like they always have."

"Immy." I don't know what to say. "I… do you want this? Because I'd give it to you if I could!"

She scoffs and paces away from me. "That's the worst part. You've never had to try for anything. I've scraped and begged and suffered for centuries, and I'll never match up to you. Even if you could give me whatever magic runs in your veins, it would never be enough."

"Enough for who? Cain? Because you've always been enough for me," I object. "You're my sister—"

"A sister you've treated with nothing but suspicion ever since you returned," she retorts.

"And whose fault is that?" I growl in frustration. "I can't do this right now, Imogen. I just… I don't have the energy to fight you after the day we've had. So either shut up or leave. Don't expect me to deal with your self-loathing on top of everything else." Her green eyes gleam with anger, and I drop my head into my hands. "I'm sorry. I didn't mean it like that. Your feelings matter to me. *You* matter to me. I just… I'm so tired. Can we talk about this after I've slept?"

The way she shrugs it off makes me feel like I've failed some kind of silent test, but I'm so drained that I can't find it in me to care.

"Sure. Sweet dreams."

The door closes behind her with a snap.

CHAPTER TWENTY-NINE

EVELYN

I FALL INTO A DAY OF DISTURBING DREAMS WHERE FROST AND Gideon take turns forcing pointed hats and broomsticks on me while Cain watches on, laughing in the distance. When I wake, it's with Draven and Vane wrapped around me, keeping me so warm despite the fact that I've kicked the covers away at some point in my sleep.

Ugh, I feel like shit, and a shower doesn't make much difference. When I re-enter the room wrapped in a towel, Draven is gone, and Vane is pulling my clothes out of a case.

"We landed a few hours ago," he admits. "But I told Gideon to let you sleep. You thirsty, princess?"

"Not really, but I *should* drink," I mumble, rubbing at my hair with the towel.

"Yes, you should." He abandons the twisted mass of fabric —Morwen evidently still doesn't believe in folding—and moves closer to me. "But before you do, there are some things we need to discuss."

There... are? I blink at him, confused.

"Not about feeding," he clarifies. "You're always welcome to my blood, princess. It's everything else that comes with it."

"Sex," I reply, smirking.

"Among other things… I don't need details, but I need to know if you were okay with what Gid did to you in his rut."

Things low in my body clench at the memory. "It was great." I shrug. "Afterwards…" I make a face that causes him to chuckle.

"I can guess."

"So why are you asking?"

He reaches up to rub the shell of his ear, playing with the hoops there as he thinks. "Because I need to know before I start playing with you. I have… preferences that not everyone is compatible with."

I swallow, suddenly nervous. I've seen a lot of different kinks in my time—everything from the obscure to the malicious—and I'm not stupid enough to rush into something with a man who comes with a warning label.

Cain once gave Callie to a vampire who liked to drown her lovers in different—often colourful or stinking—liquids in front of an audience while they fucked. Immortals have a tendency to get bored easily. Especially when it comes to basic bodily needs like food or sex.

I can't see anyone in Finn's pack being into that kind of thing, but I'm also not going to make any assumptions.

"What preferences?" I ask.

There's a glint in his eyes that seems a lot like approval. "I like being in charge," he admits. "And pain." He hesitates. "But you've experienced enough pain to last several lifetimes. It would be selfish of me to ask you to endure more, which is why I'm happy to keep things platonic between us."

"I thought you were a beta," I whisper, confused. "I thought that meant you were a protector."

Alphas are supposed to be the ones in need of control.

"You can protect people and still admire how beautiful their skin looks painted by a flogger." He offers me a soft grin, and something in me switches.

It takes me a second to realise it's the thrall bond between us waking up… starting to grow. It's so cautious that I barely notice it, and Vane obviously hasn't because he continues talking.

"I don't *need* control like Gideon does. I don't want you to lie back and take everything I give you without a fight. I like earning it. One of my biggest fantasies is letting you run loose into the forest, tracking you down, and taking you on the floor while you fight me."

"That still makes no sense."

His lopsided grin makes him look a little younger than he should. "It does. Trust me. I have two degrees in psychology, princess. I'm fully aware of the reasons for my preferences. In fact, I doubt anyone has done quite as much thinking about it as I have. All you have to know is that I'll never do anything to you without your consent."

"Care to be more specific?" I waver. "Because drowning and scat is a no go…"

He snorts. "Here I was worried you'd run from the room."

"The Marquis de Sade was a failed experiment of Cain and Callie's," I inform him. "One *I* was sent to clean up. I doubt there's much that you can shock me with after seeing what Donatien created at Lacoste." I brush my hands over my towel, using the sensation to ground myself. "Besides, I'm old. I've seen a lot and tried just as much. I'd rather know, in exact terms, what it is you want of me. That way I can make a well-informed choice, and there won't be any misunderstandings later."

Vane waits for a second, pinning me with those soulful, hazel eyes of his until I start to squirm and reach for the bag of clothes just for something to do.

"Why don't you describe to me what you want in your lovers?" he suggests at last.

I laugh. "Haven't you figured it out yet? I like different things on different days. There are times when I want Finn's softness and love, and there will be times when I want Draven's savagery or Gideon's dominance. Even times when..." I trail off, not wanting to bring up Silas's dirty talk to his brother, or think too much into how much I miss Frost's talented tongue. "My point is, I'm glad I have you all, because I don't think one man could ever hope to fulfil all those different wants." It would be too much to ask of any one person, and unfair.

I couldn't ask Finn to tie me up when I know it would make him uncomfortable. Nor could I ask Draven to give me the soft, emotional sex I know my omega excels at. It's not anyone's duty to change their sexual preferences to suit someone else.

Vane twists the loop in his ear one last time before releasing it.

He's quiet for so long that I think he's not going to tell me about whatever shameful secrets he's holding back on.

"I want to punish you," he admits. "For that stunt you pulled, going off on your own in the middle of a battle..." His eyes darken. "I know I have no right to ask this of you, given how much you've survived already, but if you let me, I'll use your body until you weep from pleasure and swear that you won't do anything like it again as long as I let you come."

My breath hitches, and I blink in disbelief. I'm not... getting turned on by this?

But Vane isn't finished. "Then I'll tie you down, strap a vibrator to your clit and leave you for hours, until you can't physically come anymore, just to make sure the lesson has sunk in."

My pelvic floor clenches, and I become acutely aware of

the moisture slowly creeping down my inner thighs. Apparently, Vane's brand of sexual sadism is something my body didn't know it craved. I swallow and lick my lips, trying to combat the dryness that's taken over my mouth.

It's no use. Every drop of moisture in my body seems to have been dispatched between my legs to try to extinguish the ache that's steadily growing there. And given the way his nostrils flare and his eyebrows arch in surprise, he knows it too.

"Safe words?" I ask, my fangs sinking into my lower lip.

"Mine is Mango," he admits. "Yours."

I hadn't thought about him having one, but I suppose it makes sense. For all that Vane likes to cause pain, there are lines that can be crossed that might make even him feel uncomfortable. He should have a way to stop things if that happens.

"Silver," I whisper.

The thrall bond takes another inch.

He takes another deep breath through his nose, and I wonder if he's noticed it. Should I bring it up?

"If you want me," he says, cutting off my train of thought. "Then I'm going to need you to say it. I won't have any miscommunications between us. Something doesn't work, you safe word. You have second thoughts afterwards, you come and talk to me. Understood?"

His stare pins me in place, and the seriousness in his tone makes me shiver.

I nod, but he doesn't relent until I open my mouth and reply, "I understand."

"And it won't stop when you leave the bedroom like it does with Gid," he pushes. "I have no interest in taking your decisions away from you, or making you bow to my every whim, but I do have rules. If you put yourself in unnecessary danger, or disparage yourself in any way, I'll have one of the others restrain you, then I'll spank you until you get the point. If we're out in public, I'll drag you just out of sight and fuck you raw, and leave you hanging with my cum dripping down your thighs as a reminder."

My breathing is so shallow that I'm getting dizzy. I'm interested in what he's saying, despite everything in my sensible brain telling me to say no. Aside from Gideon, I've never really given up control to a lover completely before. And Vane has always felt... safe. No matter what he says about wanting my pain, I don't think he genuinely wants to hurt me.

And with an immortal body, anything that goes wrong won't be permanent. If something did go wrong, I'd trust him to fix it.

With that realisation, something snaps between us. The thrall bond crackles, binding us closer, and this time I *know* he can feel it too because he frowns at me.

"Did our bond just—?"

I nod. "It's getting stronger. Does that bother you?"

He snorts. "Princess, you wouldn't even ask that question if you knew how jealous I am of Finn and Draven."

He's jealous?

"It comes with trust," I whisper. "On both sides."

"Oh, I figured that out a while ago," he admits. "That's why I want it so much. There's nothing on this planet as precious to a beta as someone who trusts us to keep them safe."

That makes me smile and gives me the boldness necessary for me to make my next confession.

"I want to explore this, but I might... I might not like it. I'll tell you if it becomes a problem." Right now, I'm turned on just from his words, but I'm not stupid enough to assume I'll stay that way. "If I try this, and I never want to do it again, then we won't."

Vane nods, then quirks one eyebrow. "Naturally. We won't do anything if you dislike it. But if you're willing to give me a chance, take off the towel and get on your knees."

I can tell from his tone that this is a test, so I slowly unhook the fabric from around my chest and allow it to fall away. My knees hit the cold wood floor with a quiet thud, and I look up at him through my lashes, wondering what comes next.

"I'm not like Gid," he repeats. "You can brat as hard as you want. I look forward to it. Just know, I'll be keeping count."

I nod, and he tuts, taking a step forward. His fingers trace along my hairline before weaving into my wet locks and tugging sharply. This time, when he talks, his voice has dropped several octaves, and I can see the erection tenting the soft fabric of his sweatpants. It's like being with a different man, and a shiver runs down my spine as I wonder just how much of himself he's been holding back.

"When I give an order, you say 'yes, Vane'. I'd have you call me sir, but you've got so many thralls that I'd rather know you remember which one you're talking to."

"Yes, Vane," I reply.

"And you look at the floor when I tell you to kneel. Hold your breasts up, offer them to me."

I do, gasping involuntarily as my hands accidentally graze my pebbled nipples on their quest to obey.

"Spread your legs. I want to see the needy little pussy I can smell creaming for me."

I follow his instructions, but it isn't enough.

"Wider," he chastens. "Feet together, knees apart."

Once he has me how he wants me, he releases my hair and smiles darkly. "Stay."

With that single, barked out command, he turns around and goes back to the bag.

"Because this is your first time, I'll give you something to make it better," he says, drawing out a 'v' shaped silicone device with a bulbous ridged end and a circular nub on the other.

It's unmistakably a sex toy, but not one I've ever seen before. I frown at it. Obviously the ridged part must go inside of me, but that would leave the tiny circular piece... directly over my clit.

I swallow, suddenly nervous.

Then he pulls out a riding crop. *Where the hell did he get that from?*

When he turns around, he's holding the promise of plea-sure in one hand and pain in the other. My own hands dig into my breasts a little harder.

"Thank me," he prompts.

"Thank you... Vane." I tack his name on the end as an afterthought, and he shakes his head.

"Gotta learn faster than that, princess." He presses the ridged end of the silicone toy to my lips. "Suck."

I part my lips, allowing him to slide it into my mouth inch by inch.

"Don't think I'm ignoring how slowly you're obeying," he notes. "I'll allow it for now, since you're new to this, but hesi-tating without good reason will get you more punishments if you keep it up in the future."

I don't answer him. I can't. My mouth is stuffed full of silicone and he rotates it inside, so that I can trace the ridges on the inside with my tongue. It's heavier than I thought it would be, and when he lets go, I have to work hard to keep it in my mouth without taking my hands off my aching breasts.

"Get it wet," Vane orders, taking a step around me. He lets the crop sing through the air, testing it, before tracing the tip down the length of my spine.

Anticipation—headier than any drug—buzzes through me at that simple touch.

"Pinch your nipples."

I do.

"Harder."

The sting zings through my blood.

"Harder."

God, it's starting to hurt, but he hasn't told me to release them.

"Harder, princess."

The crop traces a new line along one ass cheek and I moan helplessly around the toy.

"Good girl. Release them."

I cry out, the sound muffled, as the blood flows back to my breasts at the same time Vane gives me my first experimental swat. I don't feel the sting at first, but then it's there, battling with the sensation of blood rushing back to my nipples to consume me.

He pauses, waiting for me to spit out the toy and safe word.

I don't. My body is confused, but my mind is filled with a pleasant, lust-filled fog. For the first time in hours, my mind is blessedly still. All I can think about is what he'll do next and pray for someone to deal with the wetness that's now trailing down my thighs like water.

And between us, the bond winds tighter and tighter.

"It's only going to get harder," Vane warns. "You put yourself in serious danger yesterday."

True to his word, the next thwack of the crop on my opposite cheek stings even more fiercely than the first. He follows it up with a third, and then a fourth, pausing and increasing the force each time.

"I think you can handle it," he mutters, almost to himself.

He returns to my front and tugs the toy from my mouth, crouching before me. It pops free, coated in an embarrassing amount of drool, and he wastes no time in sliding it between my legs, rubbing it over my clit once. Twice.

But not a third time.

My shaky breaths must have warned him that once more was all I would need to come. Then the pressure at my entrance starts.

"You can't come until I tell you to," Vane orders.

"Yes, Vane," I whisper, automatically.

I don't bother telling him the situation might be out of my hands. He pumps the toy into my pussy slowly, drawing it out, and my body stretches delightfully as the ridges scrape over that hidden spot inside of me. It seems to take forever to go in, but when he nestles it securely against my lower lips, I whimper.

Then he turns it on.

As soon as the tiny ring latches onto my clit and sucks, I lose the ability to think. The toy starts to slip away, and Vane shakes his head admonishingly before pressing it back into place.

"Hold it there," he growls. "If you let your treat fall out, I'll have to punish you even harder."

I can hear him, but I can barely process his words, let alone respond. I clench my pelvic floor, trying as hard as I can to keep the toy inside of me as he releases it and moves back around until he's facing my side.

The ridges on the bulbous end give me some traction, but the sucker conspires against me, making my inner walls spasm.

Then the crop comes down for real.

I scream as the pain travels right from my ass to my clit. Pleasure and pain fuse and I can't tell which is coming from where. I'm so close to an orgasm, but my own arousal works against me. My sopping wet cunt clamps down, but fails to stop the toy sliding down an inch, taking away the suction. I moan in disappointment.

Vane notices—of course he does. The flat, leather tip of the crop snakes around my body and gently taps the toy, sending shock waves through me.

"Please," I gasp.

Instead of putting it back where I so desperately need it, he draws back and delivers a stinging blow to my inner thigh. My whole body arches, and the toy slides farther.

But he wants me to disobey, my mind whispers. *He admitted it...*

"Why should I reward someone who can't even follow orders?" he demands. "I told you to keep it there." Another lick of the crop, another inch of fullness lost.

My hands are digging into my breasts as I try desperately to hold the toy in place.

It's a losing battle. He must've known it was when he set me the task.

Vane's sadistic smile confirms it. The next licks of pain pepper my ass, and in a spurious moment of rebellion, I meet his eyes.

And let go with a smirk.

The toy pops free and I anticipate a thud as it lands on the floor, but Vane uses his immortal speed to catch it before it hits the ground.

"Oh dear," he murmurs, bringing it up to his triumphant face. "You've made a mess of this, haven't you?"

I know I'm supposed to be staring at the floor, but I can't help but watch as he brings it to his mouth and laps at it like a lollipop.

"You taste delicious," he growls, and for a second, the cold, dispassionate facade flickers, revealing the slightest hint of the animal that lurks beneath his skin before he shutters it away and takes a second lick. "Fucking addictive, but…" His eyes snap to mine before I can look away and pretend I wasn't breaking the rules. "You earned yourself two more punishments. Get up."

"Two!" I splutter.

"I told you to keep this in, and you were warned to keep your eyes down unless told otherwise." Vane smirks, and the expression almost makes him seem more dangerous than Draven for a second. "You disobeyed on purpose, princess. No use pretending otherwise. Now. Get. Up."

I wobble up on shaky legs, releasing the death grip I've been keeping on my breasts and gasping as I realise just how badly I've been mishandling them.

Vane tuts again, reminding me of a disappointed school teacher. "I didn't say you could hurt yourself. That's a third punishment. Bend over the bed."

I glance at the bed, and then back at him, only to rear back as he slaps my ass with the open palm of his hand.

"Remember what I said about speed? Next time, I expect you to do things when I tell you to do them."

But I want to play this game now. I take one step away from the bed, then another. Grinning.

The spark in his eyes at my defiance is more exciting than I care to admit.

I turn, heading for the door, but his free hand wraps around my hair and tugs me back. This time, I have no choice but to follow as he guides my body until I'm bent over the bed with my ass in the air. The moment I'm in place, he lets go and pulls over a pillow, shoving it under my hips until I'm properly supported.

"Fold your arms behind your back," he orders.

I do it faster this time because I can feel the toy prodding back at my entrance once more.

I want it back. Need it.

It slips into place and I grab my own forearms to hold

myself in place as Vane expertly lines up the tiny tormenting sucker with my clit again. Apparently, the toy was at its lowest setting before. I almost leap off the bed as he clicks a button and the intensity of the suction ramps up. Too much. Too intense.

Then he flicks on the secondary function I didn't know existed. A low level vibration starts inside of me, and I squirm so much that he encompasses both of my wrists in one large hand and uses his grip to pin me down.

"God," I moan, but my face is pressed into the quilt, so the word is unintelligible.

The crop comes down again, harder. I cry out with each blow, squirming against Vane's hold even though I think I might die if he stops what he's doing. Oddly, I start to crave the darting bite of pain it brings. It makes the intense sensations running riot in my pussy manageable.

"Don't come," he growls. "Don't you dare fucking come, princess."

But I'm so close. The edge is right *there*.

I reach for it in another moment of rebellion—

And then the crop is gone. A second later, the vibrator follows, leaving me empty and clenching on nothing. I feel his stubble at the top of my thigh a second before an entirely different type of pain flashes through me.

His bite.

I wail into the pillow as his venom lashes at me, trying to tip me over the edge. But it doesn't. He won't let me.

I twist my head to one side so he can hear me. "Please," I beg. "I need to come. Please, Vane."

My pleas turn nonsensical as he continues to feed, dragging out the pleasure until tears are streaking my face. Every muscle in my body has turned to jelly, and even though I can't physically take any more, I don't have the strength to wrestle myself away, either.

Then, in a stroke of mercy, he withdraws his fangs and licks the wound. I barely have time to take in the sound of the zipper being drawn down before the warm head of him presses insistently at my opening.

I'm soaked and stretched from the toy, but he's still a big man, so I'm surprised when he manages to shove all the way home in one savage thrust. There's no pain as my body adjusts to his girth, but he doesn't move. Even when I deliberately clench my muscles around him, trying to spur him to take me with the roughness I desperately need from him.

"Fuck me," I order, forgetting everything in the venom-induced frenzy still roaring through my veins.

Vane delivers a sharp smack to my ass, but his hips don't move. He won't give me the friction I need. I thrust back against him, but he's caged me in place. I'm speared on his cock, unable to get the one thing that will send me over the edge.

"You don't give the orders," he reminds me, slapping me a second time before groaning. "Fuck. Every time I do that, you strangle my dick."

He does it again and—true to his words—my whole body tenses around him. If I can just find some way to get any kind of friction against my clit...

Vane must sense my mutinous inner thoughts because he leans down to whisper in my ear.

"You're going to be a good girl, aren't you? You've racked up four punishments in the last hour. If you keep going, I'll take them all at once by pulling out and making you suck me off instead. Then you won't get that orgasm you want so badly."

His hot breath whispers over my throat and across my cheek, making me shiver, and I moan, trembling beneath him.

"I'll be good," I breathe.

Because after seeing this new side of him, I have no doubt he'll follow through on that threat.

"Then don't move."

He leans back and I gasp as he slowly drags his hips back until barely the tip of him is still inside me, then slowly forges back in at the same insanely slow pace. I swear I can feel every ridge and vein of him. My eyes roll back in my head as his hips meet my still-sensitive ass and I pant through the intense sensation.

"Please, Vane," I whimper, two thrusts later. "Please."

"Use the words, princess," he chides. "How can I give you what you want if you don't ask for it?"

"Please fuck me harder." Any inhibitions I have about how crude the words sound leaving my mouth are long gone.

And with the confession, our bond twists. Anchoring deeper. So close to completion that I feel his joy as he notices the change.

"You just had to ask," he says. "Now, come for me."

And then the gloves come off.

He powers into my body with unrestrained abandon, his breathing harsh and interspersed with growls and snarls. Savage. Hard. And so fucking glorious that I see stars. With my thighs parted and pinned beneath his, my clit is exposed, and his balls slap into it over and over and over.

My orgasm has been waiting patiently, but there's no holding it back. I scream out my pleasure to the tiny cabin room as one peak rolls into another, then another. My whole body shakes and squirms, but there's no letup. Nothing I can do except writhe on his cock and come while my soul leaves my body and I shoot for the stars.

He erupts inside of me with a savage roar, filling me in waves of scalding hot cum. There's too much for my body to hold, and I feel it trickle out of me as his thrusts lose their intensity and slowly patter to a stop.

We're both panting like we've run a marathon and my muscles are still trembling as he releases my wrists and sits beside me on the bed. He wastes a few seconds righting his clothing and then pulls me against him, holding me against his chest.

I just had one of the most out-of-this-world sexual experiences of my life, and he didn't even get undressed.

"Shhh, princess, I got you." His voice—so domineering and low earlier—has gentled into a softer, comforting tone, and he brings his hands up to cup my face, using his thumbs to brush away my tears. "C'mere."

He draws my face closer to his neck, and reaches up using a claw to slice a line along the muscular line of his jugular. "Drink up, then we can talk about how that went."

I sink my fangs into him without hesitation and I sigh against him a little more as the taste of him hits me. His massive arms surround me completely, protecting me from the outside world as I suck in greedy pulls. My venom sneaks into his veins, but I don't push too much his way. Just enough to keep the bite from hurting.

Even that still draws a stir of interest from beneath me, but we both ignore his renewed erection.

This time... doesn't feel sexual. All of the intense desire I felt from Vane before has dissipated, replaced by care, comfort and... concern.

That's when it happens. The bond solidifies, becoming ironclad. Just like Draven and Finn, except Vane's bond is unique to him. Protective, watchful, and with a hint of wildness.

When I pull away, lazily licking the wounds shut, I expect him to let me go. He doesn't. Instead, he drops his head to kiss the top of mine.

"You okay?" he whispers.

I nod, then remember his earlier edict. "Yes... it was... more than I expected."

"Look at me." This command is soft, but I can feel the edge to it, so I tilt my head back until our eyes meet.

For a second, I can't breathe. His hazel eyes bore into mine, searching out every invisible piece of my soul that I've never dared show anyone else and acknowledging them. It's such a quiet, intimate moment that when he speaks again, I almost jump out of my skin.

"More in a good way, or was it too much?"

"It was too much," I agree, only to regret the words as he tenses beneath me. "In the best way. I liked it a *lot*. More than I should've."

I was a general once. A commander of men. I don't understand why I liked being ordered around so much, but the lingering hum of pleasure still radiating from me doesn't lie.

He shakes his head. "There's no shame in liking it. Plenty of strong women need somewhere safe to let go."

"And being beaten with a riding crop is safe?" I can't wrap my head around it.

Vane runs a hand through my hair. "You spend all day making decisions, giving orders, using that sexy mind of yours to lead others. Letting go and finding a place with defined limits, roles, and punishments, where you're under no pressure to do anything or make any decisions, is a kind of relief. You know I'd never really hurt you, and we both know there's an instant out when it comes to our safe words." He smiles. "Is that your only objection to what we just did?"

"What other objections can I possibly have to multiple orgasms?" I grumble. "I'm not too sure about it continuing outside the bedroom, though."

He shrugs. "Then don't put yourself in danger or talk

badly about yourself. Those are my only rules for outside of playtime."

"The bond is complete…" I trail off, wondering what to say.

His happiness winds through my blood—bright and more than a little smug.

"I'll treasure it—and you—forever, princess." Without warning, he lifts me up and carries me back into the bathroom. "Now, let's clean you up."

CHAPTER THIRTY

EVELYN

I HAVE NO IDEA WHAT I EXPECTED WHEN WE DECIDED TO return to the site of Cain's old court, but it wasn't this.

We landed on the outskirts of the Old Country, then drove into the mountains. Vane, Frost and Gideon are all sandwiched on the front bench, and currently arguing quietly between themselves about where we'll stay. Draven is asleep with his head pressed against the heavily tinted glass, and Silas is doing the same, even though he's not compelled to by the sun. Finn is busy scanning the web for any news of Cain's reaction to what happened in Egypt.

Which leaves me with Immy, who chose to sit beside me in the back after mumbling a half-arsed apology for her earlier behaviour. My few attempts to get her to talk to me haven't really amounted to anything, leaving me with nothing to do beyond gazing out at the forests that seem so alien.

The trees have aged, and they're not the only things.

After how different New York became in my absence, I

expected my childhood home to have been turned into a shrine to vampirism. A modern glass and steel monument in place of the sleepy little village from before. Hell, given how people are forced to worship Cain, I wouldn't have been surprised to find it a city for pilgrims with a statue of him rising a hundred feet into the air in the centre.

But as we drive along the single track road that forms the entire settlement, past run-down houses and hungry gazes, I realise I couldn't have been more wrong. If anything, it has shrunk, becoming more of a run-down hamlet than a village.

What houses and shops remain are fortified to within an inch of their lives. The few people still lingering around are busy rolling down thick metal shutters, glancing furtively at the dimming light of the setting sun in the sky beyond.

"I don't understand," I whisper, looking over at Immy. "This is the place he built his empire from. Surely…"

I don't expect much of a reply. The awkwardness caused by her angry outburst on the plane hasn't disappeared, despite hours on the road together. She apologised, but there was no taking back what she said. Neither of us knows what to do now that she's exposed her true thoughts.

So I'm surprised when she shrugs, shrinking in on herself. "I haven't been back here since…"

Her sudden shift from bitter, silent anger to shameful awkwardness makes no sense. "Since what?" I prod. "Since you were released?"

Immy's hands fist around the ends of her coat sleeves. "Since Cain let me loose on the villagers after he released me. I slaughtered a lot of them."

My frown deepens as I mull over her explanation. "Why?"

She shrugs. "I don't know. I woke up, and I was set loose. When I'd done enough damage, I was contained and unleashed on the next village. He said he was trying to find a use for me."

But what purpose does destroying this place and keeping it so impoverished serve? Why would Cain try to erase this place when his narcissism normally drives him to aggrandise his personal history?

"It's because *you* betrayed him here," Immy growls, answering my unvoiced confusion. "I thought you were supposed to be able to figure out his every move. You were apparently born here, and you betrayed him here. *You* are the one thing that makes him hate this place, and the reason why these people have been abandoned by every-one. They're not on any map. No government will claim them, no centralised services will help them. They're fair game for the lycans, ghouls, and vampires in the area to terrorise. In fact, every few years, Cain orders a purge, where the humans who live here are hunted and their homes looted. He gifts participation to the vampires who've pleased him and treats it like a tournament. There are *leader boards.*"

She scowls in disgust.

My lips purse together, and I stare out of the window silently as guilt overtakes me. "But the humans had nothing to do with any of that…"

Not that it would matter to Cain, who has always viewed mortals as little more than animals.

"There's one hotel, and surprisingly enough, they don't allow immortals," Finn mutters, shattering the conversation. "I wonder why." His sarcasm is sharp enough to cut, but thanks to the thrall bond, I can feel the shame and sadness beneath it all.

None of us like the picture Immy has painted.

"We can make camp in the ruins of the old manor," Gideon grumbles, without looking back at me. "It's far enough away that we shouldn't cause the humans any distress."

"They won't even know we're here." Frost rubs the back of his neck.

"Until we come sniffing around and politely start asking them all if they're witches in hiding," Finn mutters and then turns to me. "Before I forget, I need a sample of your blood to test."

"What? Why?"

He shrugs. "If we can isolate your DNA, we might be able to discover what markers indicate someone is a witch. It's a long shot, because vampirism alters a person at a genetic level, but if you've become a hybrid, those markers will still be there. All humans nowadays are indexed and catalogued. With that knowledge, we might be able to locate any remaining witches who are in hiding."

"And they might be able to kill Cain." Alleviating the pressure on me to learn magic and do so. "You're a genius, and I love you."

I don't mean for it to slip out, but his easy grin undoes me. "I know, and I love you too." He says it so effortlessly, but it still makes butterflies dance in my belly. I'm so distracted by his confession that I almost miss his next words. "Now, blood, please."

He passes me a science beaker, and I shake my head, wondering where he got such a thing.

I'm beginning to learn the resistance can get anything they need, despite Cain's influence. My sire rules through fear, and that creates a perfect breeding ground for rebellion.

I score my wrist with my fangs and Draven tenses in his sleep as my blood rushes forth, dripping into the beaker. Immy stares at the dripping wound with a kind of quiet pensiveness that makes me feel uncomfortable. When did she last feed? Is she struggling to find blood now that we've left Egypt? I never even thought about it, and I grimace as I realise what a bad sister I've been.

When it's about halfway full, I seal the wound with my tongue and pass the beaker to Finn, who carefully divides it into three smaller vials, before capping each one.

"Perfect. I'll send one off to the labs for testing when we get back to civilisation, and we can keep the other two for emergencies." He opens the door to the mini fridge which the resistance supplied with the van, revealing a dozen blood bags stashed safely within, and tucks my little vials on the top shelf.

I expect Immy to speak up and ask for a bag, given her blatant hunger, but she says nothing. I frown, but don't bring it up. She's an adult vampire, I remind myself. She knows how to ask for blood or find her own.

We finally leave behind the winding main street and head up the mountain, deeper into the forested hills. I used to ride along this path all the time. I patrolled these woods endlessly. Yet, I recognise almost nothing. As much as I want to tell myself it's just the daylight making the scenery look odd, I know I'm just kidding myself. Unlike me, this place has moved on. Aged.

I glance over at Frost, only to see his face is carefully blank. Like he also doesn't know how to feel about returning to the place where we first met.

There's a strange, sad wistfulness in returning to a place you once considered your home, and finding it's moved on without you. But dwelling on those thoughts won't help me now. I push them from my mind and force myself to turn to the task at hand.

"What are we looking for?" I ask, directing the question at Finn, who's been buried in research for most of the trip.

He chews at his lip before he replies. "Honestly, I don't know."

"I thought you were researching?" Gideon growls.

Thankfully, Vane elbows his alpha, saving me the trouble of doing it myself.

Gideon sighs and shakes his head as if to dispel his own bad mood. "I'm sorry. I just hoped there would be more to go on."

Finn rubs a hand over his short hair and straightens his round glasses. "Unfortunately, the only thing most of my research *does* agree on is that witches passed their traditions down through their families. There's very little just lying around for the general public to find. That's why I wanted to test the DNA theory."

That makes sense.

"There's *nothing* else?" Gideon is barely holding his exasperation in check, and I wonder idly if a quickie against a tree would fix his mood. I dismiss the idea just as quickly when I see Finn's face and feel his anxiety down the bond.

The omega in him doesn't like disappointing his alpha.

And I already decided that I want to discuss what happened with Finn to make absolutely *certain* that he's still okay with our agreement before we do anything else.

Gideon drags his head out of his ass after a second elbow to the ribs from Vane. Finn misses the motion only because he's so close to his monitor his glasses are almost touching it.

"You did great," the alpha grunts. "The DNA idea was a good one."

Finn visibly brightens, then grimaces. Feeling him down the thrall bond is the weirdest thing. The lycan side of him instantly relaxes, yet the human in him understands what just happened and feels conflicted over it.

Just being a bystander to all of his confusion is giving me a headache. I don't envy lycans one bit.

"I can feel a lot of ghouls nearby," Frost mutters. "Too many."

"Cain lets them terrorise the villagers, remember?" Silas

glares out of the windows. "Think you can do anything about that?"

Frost nods. "Someone cover up D for a second."

Silas dutifully throws a coat over Draven's sleeping form. Frost waits until the vampire is completely covered before he presses the button to roll down the window a crack, and sticks a hand out, letting it float in the breeze.

"I can gather them around the manor and keep them away from the village," he begins, thoughtfully. "But there are a lot of them. Maybe even more than there were in New York."

"Makes sense," Vane mutters. "If these people have no protection from other immortals at all, then the ghouls must think this is an all-you-can-eat buffet."

Even before Cain took over the world, vampires and lycans played their part in keeping ghoul populations small. Mostly to protect themselves or their food supplies, but it had the indirect effect of keeping the humans safe and helping all three species avoid detection.

For Cain to just leave such a large nest unculled... It shows just how much he hates this place. After a second, Frost pulls his hand back in, shuts the window, and Silas takes the coat off Draven once more.

"Why doesn't everyone just leave?" I whisper. "It makes no sense."

No one seems to have an answer for me, and we sit in silence until we reach the manor.

The grand old house is little more than a husk of its former self. The once colourful windows are broken, the bricks are covered in moss, black mould, and lichen, and the wrought iron weather vanes which once crowned the roofs are missing—likely stolen and sold for scrap.

Even the lawns, once immaculately trimmed in the latest style, are yellowed and overgrown. The forest around has begun to encroach on the grounds, and in the distance I can see a small building which I don't remember being there before.

"The mausoleum," Immy whispers, following my gaze. "That's where he…"

She doesn't say it, but her jaw locks and her eyes turn watery with regret.

So that's where he buried us. In the back garden, like we were pets.

I'm not going back there. Someone else can search that place… if it comes to it.

"I doubt looking in there will be necessary." Draven's cool voice gives no indication that he was just asleep, and I wonder if he was faking it just to get out of talking to the rest of the pack. It's dusk, but he's begun waking earlier and earlier recently—normally a sign that a vampire is ageing to the point where sunlight ceases to affect them.

Eventually, he'll become a daywalker, but until then, he's reliant on the special coating on the glass of the van to keep him protected.

"There's no reason to," Finn agrees, and I realise they've both picked up on my hesitance along their bonds.

"Agreed," Gideon mutters, pulling up the weed-strewn drive to the front of the mansion. "The mausoleum was sealed off from everyone. We should focus our search on the village and the manor."

The engine cuts off, and Frost is out of the van before I can even blink. "Stay here. I'll clear the place out."

Without even explaining what he means by that, he strides away from us and towards the splintered great front door.

After a minute of silence, the first ghoul appears.

It lopes into the sun, burning and hissing with each step as it streaks towards the trees. It must be old enough to withstand the worst of the weak evening rays, because it makes it to the forest. Some of the others who follow it aren't so lucky. They collapse halfway across the ruined gardens, turning to ash where they stand.

When Frost walks out again, he glances at the sun once more. "Fuck, I'm glad I'm a hybrid," he mutters.

"Good for you," Draven retorts, and I feel his annoyance, accompanied by a rare bout of self-loathing which disappears before I can look at it further, encased in ice. "Fuck, I hate this place. Inside is dark?"

"Dark enough," Frost nods. "You guys get set up. I won't be long. I'm just going to make sure the other ghouls are definitely dormant. When there are so many of them, they can get distracted from my commands."

Without waiting for an answer, he follows the trail of ashes towards the trees.

Then, in a move they must have practised, Silas flings open the van door and Draven sprints for the mansion at vampire speed. He stops just inside the entryway, protected by the shade, and I breathe a sigh of relief I didn't know I was holding.

"Home sweet home," he announces, wafting the smoke from his shoulders like it's a pesky inconvenience and not a sign of the lethal solar gauntlet he just ran.

Silas follows him, then reaches back and offers me a hand. "You okay?" he checks.

His concern is touching, and I offer him a small smile. I'm not sure how I feel right now, but I've battled far worse in my life than a few bad memories.

"I'll be fine," I promise, letting him pull me out until I'm standing on the gravel. "It feels weird to be back… though I suppose I didn't really leave…"

The words fall awkwardly into the space, but thankfully Silas doesn't let me dwell on them. He wraps an arm around my shoulder and drags me into his body, leading me over to the door where Draven is still waiting.

"Come on. Let's leave the losers to unpack. You can give me the tour."

"*Us* the tour," Draven corrects, hooking his arm around my waist the second we reach the shadow. "After all, I only got to see the dungeons when I stayed here, and I doubt I'd be much help with all of that." He waves a hand at where Finn and Vane are already getting started on unloading the tech that seems to follow them everywhere.

Oh right. This was where Draven was held prisoner after he helped Frost escape, which must mean it's also where he was turned and forced to kill his friends. No wonder he doesn't like it here.

Over my head, Silas gives Draven a suspicious look, but the vampire just returns one of his signature impassive stares.

"I'm going to check out the mausoleum," Immy whispers, lingering in the door. "I have a feeling..."

"I'll go with you," Vane offers, putting down his own box.

"Go. We'll set up camp in the foyer," Gideon says, striding past the rest of us with a giant box under each arm. "It has the most avenues for escape if we're discovered. Our main focus is the village, but a preliminary search of the manor is a good idea. Stay cautious. We don't know if Cain left any traps."

With permission granted, Silas grins and leads our trio over to the grand marble staircase, which is still standing— even if it's cracked and chipped beyond recognition.

"Come on then," he says, "Where should we start looking?"

"For traps?" Draven shrugs. "I'd have put one at the front door."

"The ghouls probably triggered most of them—if they existed at all," I point out.

"That doesn't mean there aren't more," Silas argues. "Or we might stumble on some clues about witches if we're lucky."

"It's unlikely that he'd have kept anything," I mumble. "Honestly, searching here is a waste of time. Cain would've burned almost anything he found that had even a hint of witchcraft about it."

It's not like they're going to find my sire's long-lost diary floating around. He's not the sentimental type. If he was, maybe he'd have bothered taking the art that is still hanging on the walls, rotting.

"That doesn't mean there's nothing here. He might've left some records of his hunts for other witches. And I still have questions about how he was 'made' in the first place," Draven says, clearly on Silas's side.

"We should at least search his rooms to try to confirm Samuel's hunch," Silas agrees. "Let me guess, he took the biggest suite in the place on the top floor?"

I shake my head and tug the two of them along the hallway, our footsteps echoing on the broken tiles. "No. He was very keen on emphasising that we were 'family.' His rooms were beside ours."

"Creepy," Silas growls. "Especially considering how he treats Callista."

I shrug, glancing at an old portrait that still hangs drunkenly on the wall. "Callie isn't his daughter in truth, and given that all vampires are descended from him, it wasn't like any other woman would've been much better. I don't know, it just… never seemed weird until recently. It just *was*."

"Challenging the status quo is a luxury," Draven mutters. "Every second you spent living under Cain's thumb was focused on survival. Believe me, Callista does not regard

Cain as a father figure. She's too self-centred to see other people as anything beyond a plaything or a means to an end."

"Which were you?" I ask, quietly.

If I thought Draven was cold before, he turns arctic at the question.

"Both." He hisses, but doesn't remove his grip from my waist. "She knew I hated her, and she got a twisted sense of pleasure out of it."

Grimacing, because I'm fully aware of how sadistic Callie can be. "You want revenge?"

He meets my eyes levelly. "Planning on pleading for your sister's life, doll?"

My fangs sink into my lip as I consider my answer. "I should," I whisper. "We were all children, forced into a hell-hole together, and I think she's still that same scared girl even now. But... fear has warped her. She could've tried to help me, or warn me before Cain punished me." I would've done so for her, even if it meant disobeying our sire. "Instead, she smirked as they forced me into that coffin."

Draven's curt nod reveals nothing, so I'm surprised when he speaks. "She smiled when she forced my wife into my cage and let me drink her to death on my first night as a vampire. Then she laughed as she fed me the rest of my family."

His family? Oh God.

He'd told me something similar before, but I never knew he was married. Did they...? Oh, please, tell me they didn't have children. I wouldn't put that kind of evil past my sire, or Callie, unfortunately.

How is Draven still alive? How on earth did he stand there and let Callie speak to him—touch him—without screaming or attacking her? The more I think about it, the more that wall of ice he has begins to make a horrible kind of sense.

It's his survival mechanism.

"Shit." Silas grunts and both of us startle as we remember we're not alone. "That fucking bitch."

Draven eyes us both coldly, but there's no mistaking the pulse of pain burning away beneath his ice. "I spent seventy years as her pet. Believe me, a quick death at my hands was a mercy to them."

Seventy years doing Callie's bidding during a time when she—a vampire who thrives on attention—was forbidden from taking other pets or lovers… It's not hard to figure out what such a life would've been like, and I won't make him relive it.

I never meant to make him confess to his family's deaths either.

It wasn't his fault. Newborn vampires have no control. Turning requires energy. Energy requires blood. In those initial days, they'll drain anyone they come into contact with —family, friend, lover. It doesn't matter to the primal instincts which drive them. Callie knew that. Which makes her responsible, not Draven.

I want to reach out and comfort him, but it's like wanting to touch an enraged tiger. I'm not sure if he'll accept the gesture or snap my hand off. So I settle for pushing all of my comforting feelings down the bond towards the ice. I'm not sure it makes much difference, but he doesn't reprimand me for it.

"And after you get your revenge?" I continue, trying to change the subject subtly as we reach the first of our family rooms. "What will you do then?"

Draven freezes, and his ice disappears for a second.

I've thrown him with my question, and a glance down the bond reveals why. "You never planned on surviving it."

He intended to either die in the attempt, or walk into the sun soon after.

God. *No.*

He doesn't meet my eyes, which is as good as confirmation.

"Circumstances have changed," he mutters, releasing me and striding ahead to the door at the end of the hall, effectively ending our conversation.

I go to follow him—to rage at him for even thinking that way—pulling Silas along behind me. My angry march peters to a halt as I pause automatically at my own bedroom.

"This you?" Silas asks, eyeing the monogrammed door handle.

I nod jerkily. "Let's leave it for now…"

But he's already turned the knob and swung the heavy wooden door open, unleashing an unholy squeak as the hinges protest the sudden movement.

CHAPTER THIRTY-ONE

FINLEY

The instant Evie leaves with Silas and Draven, things become tense. Gideon's presence seems to be everywhere now that there's only him.

Even when Frost returns, barely ten minutes after going to check on the ghouls, his presence does little to alleviate my nerves.

I start setting up my tech in silence, grumbling over the state of the wires. The generator is up and running—thank God, because the manor's crude wiring was ancient and was never going to be able to support modern tech—but I can't run my computer if I can't find the right cables. *Gah.*

"Did Morwenna just chuck everything in here?" I mutter, staring in dismay at the box of tangled cables. "Has she not heard of cable-ties?"

Logically, I know that she was in a hurry, trying to escape a battleground when she packed away my things, but my nerves are urging me to fill the silence in any way I can. I'm a nervous talker. I know it.

Worse, they know it.

"Frost, can we get a moment alone?" Gid says, cutting off my muttered tirade with a handful of quiet words.

Alone? Why does he want to be alone? And why am I so nervous about that? This is Gid. The alpha who'd rather cut off his own paw than let me get so much as a paper cut.

There's a deep silence, and I don't dare look up to see what silent communication is passing between the two of them. A minute later, Frost's footsteps retreat, heading up the stairs.

The hairs on the back of my neck rise as he moves closer, triggering that prickling awareness of my alpha's nearness that's impossible to shut off.

"I've been thinking about what you said," he begins when he's within touching distance. "And you were right."

I blink into the box of wires, wondering if I heard him correctly. When I finally gather the courage to look up, he's crouched right beside me.

"And you're surprised?" I'm almost proud of how steady my voice is. "Honestly, you should be used to it by now."

He rubs the back of his neck, ignoring my sarcasm. "I wasn't listening to you." I breathe a small sigh of relief, but he's not finished. "But we can't have the break you want."

My eyes snap to his, only to glance away again. "What? How does that even make sense? You admit you're not listening to me, and then you decide—"

His finger presses over my lips. "A sex break, yes. I agree. An emotional one? No."

I straighten, but being taller than him doesn't give me any advantage in this situation. "You do realise the sex isn't the issue, right? It's the emotions."

"You need me, just as much as I need you. I still—" He breaks off, clears his throat, then looks away. "I still love you. I can't shut that off."

My heart does a little flutter. He *never* says it first. Ever.

Damn it, I've got to stay strong. Even if emotionally vulnerable alpha is my kryptonite.

I demanded a break because I thought it would give me a reset. Allow us to start completely from scratch.

"I'll always love you, even if sex is taken off the table completely." He meets my gaze boldly. "I can live with that. If anything, I'd trust myself more…"

"I don't want that," I interrupt, then grimace. "I *want* sex, Gid. You've given me some of the best fucks of my life. I just can't take the shit that comes after. I want to wait until you've sorted your shit. You're not your father. I'm not your mother or Isla—thank fuck. That baggage shouldn't be in the bed with us, and I deserve better than that."

Should it feel so terrifying to say that? Am I being too mean? I've wondered the same thing over and over again. But it all comes down to this.

Gideon has been using me to perpetuate his own self-destructive tendencies since we first got together. As long as we continue to have sex, he'll continue to see himself as the bad guy afterwards, and he'll continue to put me into the box of poor, helpless omega at the mercy of my own urges.

Ugh! This is a mess. I thought this break would make things easier. That he'd go away, do the work to fix himself, then come back and we could just start again. Like we were strangers.

Maybe that was short-sighted.

We have decades of history. It was stupid to assume we could just gloss over it.

"I need help," he admits, rather than snapping at me for mentioning Isla like I half-expect him to. "I need to work on being a better alpha. A stronger one. I need to show you and the pack how much I care. And I will. But I'm never going to manage it without you. This distance is driving me insane, and my instinct is insisting you're about to kick me from the pack—"

"Never!" I stare at him, horrified. "I wouldn't!"

Has he been worried about *that,* of all things?

"Logically I know that, but you know how it is…"

I do.

Lycans tend to see the world through the lens of instinct rather than logic—especially when it comes to the people we care about.

"I need you. Evelyn… isn't you. Whatever is between her and me is different. I barely know her—though I hope maybe that will change. She's buying us time to work things out, but she can't fix our relationship for us."

That… wasn't why I accepted her offer, was it?

Okay, so maybe I felt relieved when she offered, but that was because she was my out. Not because I expected her to…

"I'll fix it," he vows. "But I can't do that if you avoid me. I can barely focus as it is… and I'll probably pounce on her when she returns, and even then I'll be overthinking it, wondering if that will only drive us further apart."

I stumble to my feet and press my hand over his lips.

"I want her with you. She belongs with all of us." Why am I fixated on the way his flat, hard lips feel against my palm? "I've thought that since the beginning. *Never* think I don't want you two to be together. I didn't realise I was making you doubt your place in the pack… I just thought maybe after a break, everything would be clearer. I was wrong. I've only been more confused."

He frowns at me and I grimace as I realise I'm probably giving him a bunch of mixed signals.

"I still want the plan," I backtrack. "No sex. But waiting for a month and then pretending everything never happened was never going to work—I get that now."

He moves my hand gently. "Spell it out for me, omega." He keeps his tone low, not using any of that alpha bark that could so easily force me into compliance. "Exactly what you want. Your terms. Whatever it is, I'll do it."

I take a deep, shuddering breath. "A non-sexual, romantic relationship where we enjoy one another's company. When I feel okay with that, we can move forward, if you still want to."

Gideon nods sharply. "I'll want to. But I want to ask Evelyn to be there, as a moderating force, to help stop any misunderstandings. Our thrall bonds will give her an advantage."

It's a good idea, and I grin, because sharing him with Evie sounds like it will be just as much fun as sharing her with Silas.

"Yes. But only when we're both comfortable. And... I think you should talk to someone. There are professionals in the resistance, and some of them specialise in dealing with lycans, and they work long distance—"

"Done."

Did he just... agree to therapy? I blink in disbelief as my heart thuds to a stop in my chest before restarting.

Gideon Lancaster just agreed to talk about his feelings with a professional.

Maybe... maybe there is hope for us after all.

"Is that everything?" he checks.

I nod jerkily just as a silhouette fills the doorway.

"I don't want to interrupt," Vane grumbles. "But we've found something in the mausoleum."

"What?" Gideon asks, finally turning away from me.

The beta wipes a hand down his face in exasperation. "Prisoners. Lots of them. Mostly lycan, but there are a few vampires."

The alpha's mouth hangs open for a second before snapping shut.

"Release them," he rasps. "But be cautious about the vampires. We don't want anyone getting drained or them preying on the locals. How long…?"

"Not as long as Evie," Vane mutters. "But long enough."

CHAPTER THIRTY-TWO

EVELYN

My old room is a mess.

More so than everywhere else in the manor. The furniture is smashed to splinters and every piece of fabric in the room seems to have been torn up. Shards of my dressing-table mirror litter the ground, glinting like jewels among the carnage.

"Seems like someone ripped this place up in a temper," Silas notes, stepping inside.

He tries to pull me forwards, but I'm rooted to the spot in shock.

"This…" Isn't Cain's doing.

I don't know how I know… but I do.

"Who did this?"

Silas clicks his tongue. "I'd say it's pretty obvious."

"No. It wasn't Cain." I take a step forward, toward the bed. "He would never lower himself to destroying mere things like this. People, yes. They can be hurt. But objects? He'd see breaking chairs as a waste of time…"

"It was me." Frost's voice is ragged, his expression gaunt as he stands in the doorway.

When did he get here? I thought he was checking on the ghouls...

"What?" I stare at him, confused.

"After what happened... Cain wanted to torture me, but nothing worked." The ghoul moves into the room and I notice his hands are shaking before he curls them into fists to hide it. "The thrall bond breaking was... indescribable. I couldn't feel *anything* beyond the hole in my chest where you used to be." My own heart throbs in sympathy, and I blink away the burning in my eyes. "Once the urge to punish me receded, he switched to trying to gain my co-operation in making more hybrids. But the only thing that got a reaction from me was you. So to torture me, he put me in this room where all I could smell was you, hoping it would make me co-operate."

"Did it work?"

Frost snorts and glances around at the wrecked room. "Does it look like it worked?"

Not in the slightest.

"Cain has a lot to answer for," Silas mutters. "And he—"

"If you've all finished reminiscing," Draven's calls from somewhere beyond the hall. "I think I found something."

I don't believe it.

Frost turns first, and Silas and I abandon my broken room in favour of hunting down Draven. The scent of blood coming from the end of the hallway only pushes us to move faster. He's inside Cain's personal chambers—a room few people ever saw. Buried in the wall behind him is a silver stake, and another is sticking out of his thigh, which explains the blood.

He yanks the stake free, and I wordlessly offer him my wrist, but he ignores me. "This painting is protected."

The picture in question is a dark, desolate landscape depicting a large boulder and a spindly tree. It's old and faded, but otherwise unremarkable.

There's no reason for Cain to protect it.

Silas reaches for the frame, taking a step forward, only to jerk backwards as the tile gives way beneath him. A hissing sound fills the air a second before another stake comes zooming out.

Silas drops like a sack of potatoes, hitting the ground just as the weapon soars through the space where his chest was moments ago.

"You could've warned me!" he growls, as Draven chuckles. "How many stakes are loaded into that thing, anyway?"

I take a step forward, only for Frost to hold me back. "I'll go first," he mutters.

Avoiding the pressure plate that Silas set off, he cautiously runs his hand along the edge of the frame.

"Don't press the button on the base," Draven calls. "That's how I got the one in my leg."

"Oh sure, warn *him*," Silas says, glaring at the vampire. "Don't worry about me, though."

"Payback for the damned pranks." Draven finally takes my offered wrist, latching on slowly and meeting my eyes as he does so.

His venom is a languid pulse in my veins this time. A promise of what he'd do to me if we were alone. Enough to leave a trickle of arousal threading through my veins, but not so much that I can't think past the urge to jump his bones.

When he withdraws, his leg as good as new, I can't help but sigh. His tongue darts across my skin, chasing the last drops of ruby red and sealing the wound in one sweep.

I turn around just as Frost steps away from the painting, and it swings sideways to reveal a secret nook...

With a ladder disappearing down into the darkness beyond.

"So," Silas whistles. "Who wants to be the first one to go down the creepy old ladder that's probably also covered in traps?"

"Scared?" Draven mocks, stepping forward. "Don't worry, wolfie, I'll protect you."

But the second he places his hand on the ladder, he hisses and withdraws it.

"Who's scared now?" Silas taunts.

"It's silver," Draven retorts. "Looks like Cain *really* didn't want anyone coming down here."

"We can go back and get gloves," Frost mutters.

"I'll go," Silas mutters, heading for the door.

Curiosity tugs me forward, and I carefully avoid the pressure plate on the floor as I lean over the ladder, trying to see down to the bottom.

It's too dark for me to make out much.

"It might just be an escape tunnel," I suggest. "It would make sense for there to be several around the mansion, just in case. Cain couldn't be killed, but he was always paranoid."

"That makes no sense," Draven replies. "If you're immortal, why be afraid of anything..."

I grimace. "He's been imprisoned before. Betrayed by one of his sons, who used lycans to outnumber him and force him into a silver cage. It was years before my time, but he told me about it once."

"Why tell you that?" Frost asks.

"Probably his fucked up idea of a bedtime story," Draven mutters.

"It served two purposes." I stroke a lock of hair behind my ear as I think about it. "One, it taught us the futility of betrayal. The silver didn't hold Cain. He waited until his captors were asleep and then snapped the bars to walk free.

And two… it illustrated the punishment that we'd face. The lycans were forced to drink silver and suffer an agonising death that took hours. And that son? The one who betrayed him? Cain told us he weighed him down with silver shackles and dropped him into an undersea volcano."

As a child, I'd wondered if he drowned first, or been boiled alive.

As an adult, with a better understanding of vampirism, I know he burned in the acidic waters. Drowning wouldn't have killed him. At best, he might've been unconscious for it.

"What a way to go." Frost echoes my thoughts.

"Got them," Silas says, bursting back into the room. "God, I couldn't get out of there fast enough."

I frown. "What do you mean?"

"Well, Immy and Vane have gone to investigate the mausoleum, so it's just Finn and Gideon down there." All four of us exchange grimaces as we accept the thick gloves from him. "It's so awkward, it's uncomfortable."

"I shouldn't have gotten involved," I whisper, watching as Draven heads for the ladder once more. "I never meant to make things this messy."

"Nah." Silas shrugs. "You can't see it, but you're actually helping. Finn and Gideon need a break. The two of them kinda got forced together and it never really worked. Once Finn feels comfortable enough to voice what he wants, and Gid gets over his…" Silas waves a hand in the air, searching for the word.

"Self-loathing?" I suggest.

All three of them stare at me curiously.

"I was going to say his preconceptions about how an alpha-omega relationship should be," Silas continues, frowning as he follows Draven towards the ladder. "What do you mean, self-loathing?"

Can he not see it? I suppose it only became obvious to me

after the thrall bond, but I'm not sure if I should share that with the rest of his pack.

"Nevermind," I whisper, following the other two down into the gloom.

No one says anything for a while, and we continue our descent into the darkness in quiet thought. But the subject hasn't been forgotten.

"Is it the sex?" Silas asks. "Is Gideon punishing himself for needing Finn?"

My silence is as good as confirmation, and he swears. "For fuck's sake. He's going to work himself into his own grave trying not to become his father." I can't see him below me, but I hear his exasperated sigh. "I'll get Vane to talk to him about it. He could've fucking said something—"

"Gideon doesn't like asking for help," Frost says, cutting Silas off. "You know that. Don't get mad at him for something that's not his fault."

"I think it would help if we all stopped gossiping and started focusing on staying alive," Draven comments dryly. "Now watch your grip, because I'm pretty sure I've just been poisoned."

"Fuck this," Frost growls. "Let go of the ladder. We're dropping the rest of the way."

"Is that wise—"

Draven doesn't listen to my objection. The heavy thump below confirms he's already followed Frost's order—or fallen to his death thanks to the poison. A second thump says Silas has done the same.

Ugh, men. I let go of the rails and drop to the stone floor below, landing in the lycan's arms with a small grunt. He carries me out of the way a second before Frost lands.

The room we're in is dark, and all I can smell is Draven's blood. There's a spitting noise, followed by a wet smack, and I realise he's draining whatever's in his blood by himself.

"Think I got it all," he grumbles a second later. "Don't feel so worried, doll. Poisoning is my idea of a fun Friday night."

"Where are we?" Frost demands, switching on a flashlight I didn't know he had and slicing through the gloom with a beam of bright white light down the narrow, sloping passageway.

"Tunnel," I announce, rolling my eyes. "I told you as much. Cain wouldn't have left anything important behind."

"Let's see where it leads before we make any assumptions," Frost grumbles, but I get a flash of his resignation along our thrall bond. He knows I'm probably right.

"There are probably more traps." And Draven has suffered the effects of enough of them already.

"Better that than poisoning ourselves trying to climb back up," he argues, taking the lead. "Come on, I'll go first this time."

Fortunately, the next few traps are obviously more aimed at mortals than immortals. Trip wires and pressure plates that are easy enough to dodge. The reason why becomes apparent half an hour later when we emerge into the darkness.

"We're outside the village," Frost remarks, and I don't ask how he knows.

"Well, we may as well explore," Silas shrugs, pulling out the slim phone from his pocket. "I'll message Gideon."

I'm not sure that the villagers are going to welcome us with open arms, but he has a point. We're here now.

My suspicions come true when we stride out of the forest and everyone on the street just… disappears. Like rabbits scurrying back to their burrows at the scent of a fox. They hasten into houses, shops… anywhere in their quest to get away from us.

The sounds of locks engaging is deafening in the night.

"Friendly place," Draven mutters.

Can we blame them? Cain has been using these people for sport for centuries.

"Should we go?" I ask, hesitantly.

"No." Frost steps in front of me and leads the way along the pavement. "We act natural, and let them see we're not a threat."

"I'm not sure that will work," Draven retorts. "How many immortals have tried to befriend them for an easy meal?"

"They won't trust us." My heart sinks. "If they do know anything, they won't tell us."

"Then we prove our good intentions," Frost argues. "We protect them until they're willing to open up. I've already gotten rid of the ghouls. We turn back any other immortal— kill them if they don't comply. They're Cain's cronies, anyway…"

"And tell him exactly where we are?" I grimace, glancing into the general store only to have the blinds drop closed.

Frost's plan requires the one thing we don't have: time. At any moment, Cain could figure out where we are and launch an attack a thousand times more deadly than what happened to Samuel's people. These humans would be wiped out before they could blink, and no amount of hiding would save them.

"Then we just kill any immortal who breaches the perimeter." Draven cracks his knuckles, smiling. "They won't be missed for a while, at least."

All of the men nod, as if this is the perfect plan, and I bite back my scepticism. It's not like I have a better plan, and it's no more of a long shot than searching the manor was.

"We walk along the street, and then head back to the manor," Silas announces, hooking an arm through mine. "Then we do the same tomorrow night. They'll put our presence and the lack of attacks together quickly enough."

"And when they get curious enough, we what? Ask if they happen to have any hand-me-down witch-related paraphernalia hanging around?"

My cynicism isn't enough to dampen Silas's spirits. "Exactly. Luck's been on our side so far. We got you, didn't we?"

"You turning out to be Cain's downfall is pretty fortunate," Draven admits, although he's clearly less enthusiastic about it than Silas is.

"Fate," Silas insists. "Must be."

"If you say so," I murmur, leaning into him as if I can absorb some of his optimism just by being close to him.

Unfortunately, our stroll through the village doesn't seem to accomplish more than making the villagers jumpy. The four of us trudge back to the manor in silence, only to find the foyer transformed into a camp, complete with separate tents and a portable stove—atop which a pot sits, merrily bubbling away. Gideon and Finn have dragged an old sofa into the space, and the two of them are actually reclining against one another.

Is that a sign that whatever went on between them, they've fixed it? Or is that too premature?

It seems strange, but the dilapidated manor seems to hold more life like this than it ever did when it was polished to a sheen.

"Finn." Silas shakes his head. "Guarantee, he got nervous and started nesting."

"I'm not complaining," Frost mutters. "God, that food smells good."

I take a deep breath through my nose, inhaling the scent of herby stew with interest. I can't eat it, but I appreciate the skill that goes into making food just the same.

"You're back?" The omega in question jumps up from his

seat and rushes towards us, tugging both Silas and me in for a hug. "Gid and I set up, but we couldn't find you, then I got your message."

"Turns out Cain had a secret escape tunnel." I shrug. "We didn't find anything else." Not that we'd searched very hard.

Silas uses that as his cue to launch into the plan, aiming most of his words at Gideon, who takes it all in in silence. Draven melts into the shadows, muttering about going to check out more of the upstairs rooms, and I look around for Immy and Vane, only to find they're still missing.

Finn releases his beta and drags me towards the sofa, situating me between him and Gideon. Not as a shield—like I was before—but more like a pillow. He curls into me, and Gideon wraps an arm around my shoulders, until I wonder if I'm actually dreaming.

We were gone a handful of hours at most. What changed?

"It's a good plan," Gideon mutters. "We'll strip the ID of anyone we kill, and Finn can lay some false trails, make it look like they've gone on an unplanned holiday or something. If we play our cards right, we could eek out a few weeks here."

"Where's my sister?" I ask, cutting into the conversation. "And Vane? I thought they'd be back by now?"

"There were other immortals trapped in the mausoleum," Gideon grumbles. "Prisoners who pissed off Cain for one reason or another. None of them were locked up for nearly as long as you, and they're mostly lycan. Vane and Imogen are releasing them and making sure they don't cause trouble."

"We'll go and lend them a hand," Frost says, grabbing Silas by the arm and leading him back towards the door. "It smells like you three have something to talk about."

What does he mean by that? I take a deep inhale, but all I can smell is stew. Damn his ghoul nose. It makes a vampire sense of smell seem almost mortal by comparison.

Finn and Gideon both stare at me, and I blink back at them.

The alpha breaks the silence, and I sit quietly as he explains what they've been discussing in my absence. Through it all, I keep an eye on my thrall bond to Finn. In my absence, the cautious anxiety that's been plaguing him since his issues with Gideon came to a head has disappeared. He's flooded with cautious optimism, and it's sweet to watch him interact with his alpha now that he's settled.

"So, let me get this straight," I say, when Gideon finishes. I take a breath to give myself time to think it through. "You don't want a sexual relationship yet…"

"But when we get to that stage, we want you there," Finn confirms.

I glance at Gideon, and then back to the omega. "And you're sure you're fine with this," I clarify, searching the bond for any hint of discomfort.

Finn nods. "More than fine. Gid?"

"I'd invite a goddamn alpaca into the bedroom if it made you more comfortable," Gideon grumbles. "Having someone with a link to both of our emotions there to keep us both communicating seems like a good idea."

"Ewww, I didn't realise you were into fancy sheep," Finn jibes, breaking the solemn mood.

"You're the one with the stuffed wolf collection," Gid retorts.

"They were gifts from you!" Finn objects. "Where else was I going to put them but in my room?"

Gideon's face cracks into a rare smile that holds more than a hint of mischief. "Do you know how much they freaked Silas out when you two first started dating? I had to listen to him telling Vane how Van Howlsing stared him down while he was—"

Finn puts his hands over my ears, blocking out the rest of what must have been an embarrassing story. When he removes them again, Gideon is grinning like a cat that got the cream.

"But are you okay with that?" Finn presses.

I frown. "You know I enjoy being shared." Being caught between him and Silas ranked as one of the hottest moments of my life. "Why would I have any issue with that?" I pause. "I understand that it might get... messy. But we're adults. We can talk it out when things go wrong."

"We might have to pin Gideon down and gag him to get him to listen," Finn jokes.

Gideon—still smiling—nods. "I'm sure between the two of you, you'd manage it."

"Shut up and eat," Finn mutters, getting up and ladling out a bowl full of stew.

The next hour or so is weirdly relaxed. Slowly, the rest of the pack trickles back in, bringing with them the news that the prisoners Cain was keeping have been freed, supplied as best they can manage, and dispersed in the opposite direction to the village. Silas and Vane volunteer to run a first perimeter—although there's not much need with Frost's ghoul sentries stationed in the forest—and the rest of us start to relax for the first time since our encounter with Armin.

I'm restless, and it must show, because Gideon pulls me out of the pile of male bodies which has taken over the sofa and towards the stairs. I might've resisted, if not for the scorching heat in his gaze. I do glance back at Finn, only to receive a saucy wink for my troubles. Just before we move out of sight, I catch the omega turning to Silas and whispering something in the beta's ear.

Looks like he plans to make use of the lust we're putting off for his own benefit.

Now Gideon has planted the seed of an idea in my head, and I can't help but wonder: what would it be like to have all three of them in bed with me? Silas's dirty talk, Finn's eager submission, and Gideon, commanding us all.

Just the thought is enough to make me pant.

CHAPTER THIRTY-THREE

EVELYN

So begins a week of relative peace.

One which quietly turns into two while I'm not paying attention. My days quietly start to fall into a routine. At dusk, I join either Vane or Draven on a walk through the village—though the villagers still flee at the sight of us—and occasionally Frost or Gideon will join us. The pack takes turns patrolling the mountainside in pairs, looking for any indication that Cain has found us while Finn monitors the media constantly.

Nothing.

It's almost like Cain has given up—not that I believe that for a second.

Still, I'm happy to pretend that's the case. While at the manor, I spend most of my time with Silas and Finn, working on filling the remaining gaps in my education and trying to find small ways to be useful to the resistance. There's not much I can do with my limited grasp of technology, but I'm learning.

Mostly, I end up distracting the two of them. We often wind up spending hours in bed when we should have been working—not that I'm complaining. If it's not them fucking me raw, it's Draven or Gideon pushing me up against a tree whenever we're out on patrol together.

Overall, I barely manage to go a day without sex, and I love every second of it.

Immy is the one dark point in all of this. Despite both of us being on speaking terms once more, she's begun to drift away from the rest of the pack. I'm doing my best to give her space, since she so clearly wants it, but her absence is grating on me.

I'd be suspicious if not for the fact that one of my men has an eye on her at all times. If she was working for Cain, surely he would've ordered her to plaster herself to my side?

Finn has every piece of tech in the manor under constant surveillance, and Immy has made no outward attempts to contact our sire.

So I suspect she's just sulking.

Because somehow she thinks being a witch who can't do magic makes me special, even though it might just have doomed us all.

Her pettiness annoys me more than I care to admit. Since I no longer bother to hide my emotions, I'm probably driving her further away, but I refuse to live my life as a robot because it makes her more comfortable.

The longer we stay here without anything to show for it, the more despondent I become. We've combed the manor from dungeon to attic and we've found *nothing*. Not even a note that mentions witches.

Perhaps it says more about me than it does her, but Immy erecting this silent wall between us feels like she's punishing me for being a failure.

Sibling fights are nothing new, but she's beginning to

343

seriously piss me off. More than that, the situation is messing with my head and my sleep. Which is why I'm awake hours before dusk while everyone else is still asleep.

I slip out from underneath Silas, who snuck into my bed in the late hours of the morning, and dress silently in the tactical trousers and dark turtleneck sweater which has become my go-to outfit in the misty, rainy mountains. We've been here so long that we could've claimed individual rooms, but the foyer of the manor has become our camp site instead. Tents and furniture have been rearranged to apportion each of us our own space and it's better this way. Like a new home rather than a haunted one.

But it does make it harder to sneak outside without being seen.

Frost grabs my elbow the second I cross the threshold. "Going somewhere, Eve?"

He's smirking, probably enjoying having caught me in the act, and I arch one eyebrow at him before dragging him out of earshot of the rest of the pack.

"You'll wake them all up," I hiss. "And isn't Vane supposed to be on this watch?"

"He was tired. Woke me early." Frost shrugs, releasing my arm. "Now, stop dodging the question. What's up?"

"Can't sleep," I reply, glancing across the courtyard.

Of course, the first thing I see is the damned mausoleum. I swear I can't move without being confronted by it. The white marble gleams in the afternoon sun, and I grimace before turning away from it.

"Do you want to take the walk down to the village early?" I ask him, itching to do something—anything—that might wear off the antsy energy buzzing beneath my skin.

He chews his lip, considering his answer.

"I'll wake Gid," he mutters at last. "Wait for me."

The ghoul disappears into the manor for a second,

returning wearing a leather jacket and with my coat slung over his arm. He passes me mine wordlessly and I accept it with a small smile.

"It's going to get cold tonight," he warns.

"In August?" I snort, beginning the walk.

He lifts one shoulder, as if daring me to disbelieve him. "The ghouls never lie."

And because I used to hunt them, I understand. Ghouls can't go out in the sun, but they also hate cold weather, so they typically seek out warm, dark, sheltered spaces.

"Does that make it harder to control them?" I ask curiously.

He nods. "Sometimes. I've got most of them in a dormant state for now, so it doesn't matter so much."

I bite my lip, because centuries of experience with the venomous creatures still makes me uneasy. My dislike of being surrounded by a small army of ghouls is not going to go away just because Frost is one. Especially when he openly admits his hold on them is tenuous.

He must sense my apprehension, because he loops an arm around my shoulders and offers me a wink. "Don't worry, Eve. I'll keep the monsters away."

There's a long pause. "Do you... do you remember this place?"

Do you hate it? Is what I really want to ask, but I'm not sure I'm brave enough.

"This random part of the forest in particular?" He raises a single thick brow. "No. Should I?"

A smirk plays at the edge of his mouth, and I mock punch him when I realise he's being deliberately obtuse. "Stop teasing."

Those grey eyes go deadly serious. "I remember every second we spent together. I spent decades reliving those memories to stay sane."

Even though I asked, his answer leaves me lost for words. "Do you regret it? If we hadn't... you'd still be human."

"I'd be dead." he shrugs.

"You wanted that once," I remind him. "You told me death was preferable to immortality."

He sighs. "This is too deep a conversation for this time in the evening," he complains, but continues. "I'd only ever seen immortals like Cain and the ghouls. Gideon and his pack changed my perspective."

"I suppose I wasn't the greatest ambassador for immortality," I mutter.

He gives me a wry smile. "You did follow your sire's every order," he admits. "An eternity of *that* would've driven me insane. Then the bond broke, and I realised I should've taken it."

That makes me snort. "I don't know what I was thinking. You wouldn't have lasted five seconds before Cain staked you out for the sun to fry."

"You're probably right." He rubs the back of his neck sheepishly. "After all, he found out about my part in the resistance easily enough, if you could even call what we were doing a resistance back then. It was more of a bunch of grieving peasants than an actual resistance..."

"But look what it became," I protest. "It must have grown significantly if you can just call in a van full of tech to any airstrip."

"Cain has a lot of enemies. Some of them have money." He shrugs like it's no big deal. "There are even a few vampires happy to help us out—fuck knows why."

"Boredom," I explain. "After a while, purposeless days meld together. The old ones will do anything to feel a hint of risk, or shake up the system, just to break the monotony of immortality."

"I like to think that most of them have nobler motives," Frost hedges, "But you might be right about the rest."

The conversation dries up as the forest drops away, revealing the main street and the humans still scurrying up and down it.

Heads snap up as soon as we take another step. The people here seem to have developed the same constant sense of alertness that you'd find in prey animals. Not surprising given how they've been treated.

I expect them to do the same thing they do every single day: scurry into their homes and bolt the doors.

But this time they don't.

They still cower in fear, pressing their backs against walls in their haste to keep us in view at all times. But as Frost and I slowly meander down the street, they don't rush inside.

"Is this progress?" I murmur to him.

"I think so," he agrees. "Should we try talking to them?"

"No. Silas and Finn said we should let them make the first move." I was only too happy to listen to the two most personable members on the pack on this one.

After all, befriending humans isn't my strength.

Frost grimaces. "I'd almost feel less awkward if we said something."

He's not the only one. Having the entire village line the streets and stare at us is more than a little creepy. I have no idea what we can do to seem less threatening, but I settle for hooking my arm in Frost's and doing my best to seem like I'm doing nothing more or less than enjoying a stroll with him.

That illusion fades as we reach the end of the street, and I look behind us.

"They're following us," I hiss, instantly on the defensive.

Have the mortals decided we're a threat, after all?

Frost turns back, following my gaze.

A human I don't recognise pushes to the front of the pack. He's short and dressed in worn clothing, like all the others, but he has an air of authority they seem to lack.

"What trick is this?" he demands. "What sick game is Cain playing with us now?"

I have to swallow to get rid of the dryness in my throat before I can answer.

"No game," I promise. "We're not with him."

Frost grimaces. "You're all too young to remember, but we were—"

"We know who you are." That same man looks annoyed. "Evelyn and her mortal. The two of you brought Cain's wrath down on our village in the first place."

"That was an accident—" I protest, but Frost cuts me off.

"We both paid for that, so if you're here to inflict some kind of mob justice on us, you're a few decades too late."

The man ignores Frost's comment. "Why are you here?"

It's clear from his expression that he expects an answer, and I also get the feeling that, should we decline to give one, this mob might try to force one out of us. The wrong words might incite their anger, and lying might not go down well if our relationship turns collaborative like the pack hopes it will.

They're not a threat to us—they're just humans, after all—but even defending ourselves might put us on the wrong foot.

Frost glances at me, then back at their spokesman. "We're with the resistance," he admits. "We came here in search of knowledge we think will allow us to kill Cain."

The silence that falls over them is immediate. Both Frost and I are so tense that we might as well be made of stone. At any second, they could attack, and I have no idea what the right course of action would be.

But the villagers don't attack. Instead, they turn around and… flee.

In seconds, all of them have disappeared. The street is deserted and the two of us are standing alone, rooted to the spot in shock.

"What the hell was that?" Frost asks.

"I think…" I whisper. "That was confirmation that there *is* something here."

He swallows, and when he glances down at me again I see my own wary optimism reflected back to me in his eyes. "I hope you're right."

CHAPTER THIRTY-FOUR

VANE

THE THRALL BOND HAS BEEN VIBRATING WITH EVIE'S EMOTIONS since she left. First it was a kind of sadness-tinged nostalgia, which isn't unusual for her to feel around Frost, so I did nothing. But after that shock and apprehension took over.

The only reason I didn't charge down the mountain was because she wasn't wounded or unsafe, and I knew Frost was with her. Now, as I watch Frost and Evie return to the manor just after darkness has fallen, her emotions are murkier than ever, as though she doesn't know how to feel.

Over the past two weeks, the two of them have lost most of what remained of the awkwardness between them, though I'm not sure Evie is aware of the change.

Watching them now, both frowning and huddled together as they walk, I get the horrible gut feeling that our fortnight of relative harmony is about to come to a crashing end. Damn, I hope I'm wrong. It's been nice to stop running for our lives and just be a pack for a while.

Evie has slowly worked her way into the centre of our

group. Sure, she's spent a lot of time with Silas and Finn, but we've all noticed the way Gideon has been sneaking her away into dark corners. She's even dragging Draven further into the fold. He's her ever-present brooding shadow whenever he's not out on patrol.

Whatever plan the alpha and his omega came up with, it's working. Finn is happier than I've ever seen him, and without the discord at the heart of the pack, the rest of us have been able to function.

But Evie's biggest miracle has to be Gideon. Our alpha has been more relaxed than I've ever seen him—fuck, he actually *smiled* today. Whatever grip hyper-fixation had on him is gone. He's begun to take my advice on board again, and a few days ago, he even let slip a rare few words of praise that left Silas glowing.

But there's no sign of his good mood as he comes up beside me and follows the direction of my gaze. He takes in Evie and Frost quietly, then comes to the same conclusion I have.

"Trouble," he mutters, and I nod once.

"I'll get the others together," I murmur, stomping away from the doorway and back into the shadows of the manor.

My absence will give Gideon and Frost a chance to decide what they want to do before they have to talk about it with the pack, and I have a feeling they're going to need it.

Finn is at his desk—or rather, under it—grunting as he fiddles with the wires coming out of his computer.

"Pack meeting," I grumble.

"In a minute," he says, though his voice is muffled. "Something's going on with our signal. It cut out midway through my call with the lab. I need to fix it."

"The lab?" I frown. "Is this about Evie's—"

"Oww! Fuck!" Finn's head hits the underside of his desk with a dull thump. "Stupid, fucking…"

The omega shuffles out from the space, still cursing, and I roll my eyes at him, offering my hand to help him up. He takes it and leans into me in a casual half-embrace.

"The lab?" I prompt, staring at the blank sheet of glass.

"Evie's blood results came back. Completely normal." Finn shrugs, but I sense a kind of defeat. "Well, as normal as any first generation vampire's blood can be, I guess. If we're going to identify any remaining witches..."

"It won't be by DNA testing." Shit.

"At least that means Cain can't find them that way either," Silas says, dropping a grinning kiss on Finn's lips as he saunters by, not even bothering to pretend he wasn't eavesdropping. "Did I hear someone say pack meeting?"

"SILAS!" Draven's furious roar echoes seconds later, and I raise a brow.

"What did you do this time?" Finn asks, exasperated, as the three of us trail behind my brother towards the door.

"Nothing!" He holds his hands up in mock innocence. "Honestly, I've been a saint since we got here. I'm practically reformed."

"Then how did my tent mysteriously get filled with portraits of Cain?" Draven demands, his voice silky with danger as he appears behind Silas, flicking a knife between his fingers.

My idiot brother—who clearly has no regard for his own life—shrugs. "We've all got our kinks, D. I'm not going to judge yours. But... I do have to wonder what Evie thinks of you yelling 'Grandsire' every time you come."

Draven lunges, only my incremental shift to the left trips him, giving Silas just enough time to dodge.

"Your ass is mine," the vampire hisses at my unrepentant sibling, who's currently skipping away towards the door. I groan as he turns his eyes on me. "Next time, don't intervene."

I shake my head. "Unfortunately, if I let you kill him, Mia might kill *me.* And don't forget, Evie likes him."

Draven's frown only deepens, like he's trying to calculate whether Evie would eventually forgive him for killing my baby brother.

"He doesn't have a full bond with her yet," he murmurs.

True.

Neither does Frost or Gideon.

Frost is understandable, given how much history the two of them have to overcome. And Gideon can be such an asshole at times, so I'm not surprised it's taking him so long to connect with her. But my brother? They're almost joined at the hip. He can read her moods almost as well as Finn, and the three of them are so comfortable together.

By comparison, my relationship with Evie is quiet, and it seems like we barely know one another. Yet that one night together on the plane was enough to snap the bond together. Since then, I've stayed back, and she's obeyed my rules so well that I haven't had any excuse to drag her back to my bed and punish her.

If not for the subtle hint of defiance she showed me, I'd almost think she was a perfect good girl. No. There's a brat in there, and I can't wait until she feels safe enough to let herself act out.

At least my absence has given her time to spend with Silas. I want my brother to have the full bond. He's so obviously head over heels for her that it's amusing to watch, but the thrall bond will cement that in a way he can't even understand.

For betas like us, just to experience the utter comfort of *knowing* she's okay without ever having to check or second-guess ourselves, is the most wonderful thing in the world.

I want that for him. For the whole pack—but especially for Silas.

I haven't said anything, but I suspect he's the one holding them back. Surface level friendships are easy for him, but getting deeper takes time. Losing our mother, our sister, and then our entire pack, at a relatively young age for an immortal, shaped him, made him guarded. But Evie is good for him.

And my brother is perfect for Evie too. I get the impression that she didn't laugh much in her old life, but he brings the sound out of her more than any of us. She hasn't said anything, but we can all feel her amusement at his pranks. It's part of the reason why—despite his threats—Draven hasn't actually retaliated against him as he once would've.

There have been no lost fingernails, not even a sneaky nut-shot.

It must be a record.

Or maybe he's just taking out all of his anger on the vampires and lycans that Cain is 'rewarding' by sending them to the village.

The three of us reach the doorway just as Frost and Gideon look up. Gid is rubbing his eyes in the way he always does when he's exasperated or trying to think of what to do next, and Frost doesn't look much better.

Evie still looks as bad as she did before. Her apprehension and anxiety has returned in full force, but it dissipates slightly as Finn pushes past both alphas to draw her into a hug.

"What happened?" he demands.

"The villagers know something," Frost surmises. "They approached us, and when we told them why we were here, they ran."

"That's not exactly encouraging." Draven scowls.

"They thought we were just playing with them on Cain's orders," Evie murmurs. "I think they need more time."

"We might not have it." All of us turn to look at Finn, who pulls back from Evie with an uncertain look on his face. "My signal went down right after the lab got back to me about Evie's results. That shouldn't have happened unless…"

Unless someone unfriendly knew to target it.

"Shit," I curse.

"What did the lab say?" Frost demands.

"Nothing," I reply. "There's no way to track down witches using DNA."

Evie's eyes widen, and her already pale face goes ashen. "If Cain was keeping tabs on us, that's the kind of information he'd wait for." She turns to Finn. "How certain are you that he can't have hacked your system?"

"Completely," Finn argues, scrubbing at his short hair in frustration, only to growl as the action dislodges his glasses, forcing him to adjust them before he can continue. "He'd have to have found a way to interfere with the hardware directly."

I meet Gideon's eyes. "Where is Imogen?" I ask, trying my best to keep my tone level.

Silas swallows and glances back towards the tent in the far corner of the room. "I—she was asleep. I swear—"

Evie's shock hits, punching down the thrall bond so powerfully that if it were a physical blow, it would've stolen my breath. "She's not—" She cuts off. "She can't have. We've had eyes on her at all times."

I hate the hurt that's wafting from her in waves, but I can't help it. Evie's blind spot where Immy is concerned was how Cain bested her last time. While she's been more cautious this time around, I think she was slowly starting to trust that her sister was telling her the truth.

Striding away from the pack, I pick my way between the tents and equipment and rip open the front of Imogen's.

Empty. And the fabric on the far side has been torn.

Fuck. I should've seen this coming, but we've had two weeks of peace. I got complacent. We all did.

"I want us ready to go," Gideon snarls, before turning back to Evie. "And you need to go back to that village. Whatever they know, we're running out of time to find out." He looks at me. "Find. Her."

"I'll help," Frost mutters. "Gideon, you go with Evie and Draven."

"Finn, stick close to Silas," I order, noticing that the omega looks like he's about to follow Evie.

Gideon, Draven, and our girl disappear through the door without waiting, and Frost reaches me seconds later.

"Too many scents in here," he grumbles, taking a deep breath at the entrance to her tent. "But the freshest trail leads this way... I think."

Without waiting for us, he leads us away from the tent, pausing every few seconds to take a breath, ensuring we're still following the trail.

"The fridge?" Silas mutters, echoing my confusion.

Surely if she knew her cover was about to be blown, she'd have headed for the door.

"That's where the trail leads," Frost retorts. "Now shut up so I can think. I'm not a damned bloodhound and this isn't as easy as it looks." He pauses, pressing his face towards the door of the small portable fridge we've been using to store blood and food.

Finn's face pales, and he darts past the ghoul, wrenching the door open and pushing blood bags aside. To withdraw a single test tube of blood from a rack at the back.

"She's taken one of Evie's blood samples," he whispers, staring at the red liquid in the tube.

"What? Why would she bother?" Silas asks.

"She must have intercepted the communication that said DNA testing was useless." So why take the blood? "Unless..."

"Eve's blood has healing properties," Frost mutters. "Maybe she's anticipating needing those."

That's not a good sign, and the four of us share a grim look before Frost goes back on the hunt for the trail.

When he leads us back into the centre of the main room, I almost think he's going to go for the door. But he doesn't. Instead, he leads us straight to the stairs. We end up back-tracking several times, going down different hallways.

"She knew we'd try this," I realise, after the third 'wrong turn.' She's been laying false trails to buy herself more time."

That's not good news. It speaks of planning.

How long has Immy been working against us? Logic says from the start, but I hope for Evie's sake that's not true.

Finally, her trail leads down a corridor. "Shit." Frost speeds up, tossing open the door at the end. "She's used the tunnel to escape. She could be anywhere in the woods right now."

"What about your sentries?" I ask, grabbing one of the stakes that is buried in the wall from the traps and ignoring the burn of silver in my palm.

"They haven't sensed anything." Frost runs a hand through his hair. "We need to pack. This is bad. Get the stuff together. I'll message Gideon. Hopefully, they've reached the village by now."

CHAPTER THIRTY-FIVE

EVELYN

THE RUN TO THE VILLAGE IS FASTER THIS TIME. GIDEON IS furious. The emotion is so strong that I can feel it chasing me down our partially formed bond.

He's ahead, with Draven and me hot on his heels, so when he starts muttering under his breath, both of us can hear him. "We should never have brought her with us."

"Well, I'm sorry," I retort, angrily. "She seemed genuine, and it wasn't like I could ditch her without arousing suspicion, anyway. Cain insisted on Immy going, remember? The only reason I'm not still stuck in New York is because she fought for me to come!"

She'd had the perfect in from the beginning, and I arrogantly thought I could outplay her. Fuck.

He doesn't have an answer for that beyond a growl which makes my hair stand on end. I find myself wishing I was with Silas or Finn. Hell, even Vane or Frost would be able to give me some kind of comfort right now. But they're distracted. The quiet sense of purpose that Vane and Finn are radiating forces me to remember that this isn't the time to dwell on Immy's second betrayal, or my anger at my own naivety.

That will come later.

Still, I wish I could reach out to them for support.

All I have to lean on is Draven, who remains as impassive down the thrall bond as ever. His calculating calmness is nothing like the hugs that Finn can send me when he chooses, but it's comforting in its own way.

Then he mutters the words I don't want to hear: "Doll, you realise we have to kill her, right?"

My heart stops. All of the rage that's been building flickers for a second as I think about what that could mean. "She's my sister."

For as long as I can remember, it's been the just five of us surviving.

"She's betrayed you twice," Gideon growls.

"Forgive me for having an emotional attachment to someone I've known for centuries!"

But he doesn't let up. "The first time, you were tortured for decades. If Cain catches up with you now…"

I'm dead.

He doesn't have to say it.

Immy knows I'm a witch—even if I'm harmless. Cain has never. Ever. Allowed anyone accused of witchcraft to live. There's no way she hasn't told him, which means my sire will do anything to see me dead.

"I wish…" Things had been different. That all five of us had been born and raised apart, by human families, living human lives.

What would we have been like if Cain had never touched us?

Those kinds of wishes are foolish and pointless. Wishing won't help me survive, and it won't end Cain's life. It won't change Immy's fate, either. So I shove the fanciful thoughts aside and focus on the buildings which are just becoming visible beyond the trees.

We burst onto the main street at full speed, only to find it just as deserted as it was when Frost and I left.

"Where are they all?" Gideon demands.

"Frost told you," I grouch. "They all disappeared as soon as we said why we were here. Unless you want to start knocking on doors…"

I trail off as Gideon's phone buzzes. The alpha flicks it open and then curses. "Imogen escaped via the tunnel," he announces. "With a tube of your blood. It looks like she's been planning this for a while."

My stomach drops. "We need to hurry. If she's removed herself from the danger zone… it means something big is on its way."

"Cain?" Draven asks.

I swallow, then nod. "This… he wouldn't leave this to his generals. Not now that he knows we've killed Armin, and Samuel betrayed him."

God, my brother is in danger now. Immy won't have forgotten everything about him—although the precise details of our encounter are already starting to fade from my memory. She will have relayed every last detail of his betrayal to Cain.

Which means that my sire might already be here, and when he finds us, he'll be furious.

"Tell Morwen and Mia to go to ground," I say. "They'll be on his hit list now."

"Already doing it," Draven grunts, tucking the slim device back into his pocket. "Focus on finding the damned humans. If they want to live, they need to leave. Now."

I wish he was being overly cautious, but he's not.

Cain will kill everyone here. Probably anyone within a ten-mile radius just to make certain.

Fucking Immy. She must have known this would happen.

"Knocking on doors it is, then," Draven grumbles, marching up to the first home and slamming his hand against it.

No answer.

He waits a second, then bashes the wood again before shrugging and kicking the door down.

I expect screams—or at the very least, some kind of objection.

Nothing.

"No one's home," Draven confirms after disappearing inside for a second.

The same is true for the next house we try. Then the next. A slow drizzle starts as we waste time searching for the villagers, and I glance up at the heavy clouds in grim panic.

"Damn it, did they all leave already?" Gideon asks.

A scratching sound breaks the silence, and I tilt my head, trying to get a fix on it. "Quiet," I hiss.

It's coming from farther up the street. From the ramshackle stone church just off the main road. I follow it until I'm at the main door of the small building where a mongrel is whining and pawing at the wood, asking to be let in.

"It's just a dog," Draven sighs.

"So where's his master?" I reply, tugging at the iron handle.

It gives way easily enough beneath my strength, though the snapping of metal tells me it was locked. The second I step inside, I realise why.

The entire town must be here, sitting in the pews. Atop the pulpit is the man I spoke with earlier. Is he a priest? He doesn't look like the type.

"You need to leave," I announce, cutting through whatever's being said as I stride down the aisle with Draven and

Gideon close behind me. "Cain is coming, and he's going to wipe this place off the map. If you want to live, then you need to get out and go. Now."

A heartbeat passes. Two. Then the first people process what I've said. One man stands and leaves, then another, dragging his spouse and child by their hands. But about half of them remain stubbornly in place.

"How do we know you're not lying?" the man in the pulpit demands. "We have survived Cain's purges before. Where is your proof that this will be different?"

I let out an aggravated groan. "I don't have any proof. But we know about the witches. We know that this is the last place they existed before he wiped them out, and we know that he's coming."

At my words, more people leave. So when an old woman with long grey hair at the front stands, I expect her to do the same. Instead, she pins me with a set of ice blue eyes that look eerily familiar.

"And you, Evonnia? What will you do?" she asks, but she's speaking Romanian, not English.

And she used my old name.

I swallow and respond in the same language, cursing myself for not thinking about the language difference before my original outburst. "I'm going to try to save as many people as I can, and then I'm going to protect my pack."

And maybe hunt down and kill my traitorous sister.

Not going to think about that right now.

Immy is probably miles away. Gloating. My fists clench, but I can't let my anger show and risk scaring the humans.

The older woman nods. "Andrei, get the book."

"Grandmother..." The man in the pulpit looks taken aback.

"Quickly, boy, and then we'll leave. I will speak with your cousin."

Cousin?

My shock resonates down my bonds, and beside me, Draven and Gideon straighten, frowning. Andrei trudges from his pulpit and into a small room behind the altar, but the older woman takes no notice of him.

She addresses the few remaining villagers. "What are you waiting for? The girl told you to flee. So, *flee.*"

The mass exodus I expected happens as soon as she finishes. Humans push and shove in their haste to leave but give the three of us a wide berth as the old lady approaches us.

"I am Ioana," she says. "Andrei is my son."

"And my cousin?" I still need that explained to me.

"We are related," she confirms. "Our family is descended from your father's sister. I don't know if you were told, but she was looking after you…"

"When Cain killed my mother," I finish for her.

"I had a sister, too." Ioana's eyes go soft with sadness. "She was killed by Cain when he took you from that place."

From the mausoleum, I realise. The old woman my thralls mentioned, the one who bowed to my coffin, must have been her sister.

I knew, in theory, that it was possible I had a human family somewhere. But I never bothered trying to track them down before my imprisonment. Why would I? I was Cain's perfect puppet, convinced humans were barely better than animals.

To be confronted with them now, with so little warning… I don't know what to do. How am I supposed to react?

For Ioana's part, she doesn't seem to expect me to hug her or participate in any kind of emotional reunion. No. The old lady just stands there, subdued yet dignified, as she examines me.

Andrei reappears, holding a charred and battered book

363

which is so old the binding has broken and the pages are yellowed. The volume is thick and held together by two belts, which are buckled securely around it, concealing whatever faded writing remains on the cover.

"Yes." Ioana nods. "He burned your house, and everything in it. But my ancestors managed to recover this from the ashes. Your mother's grimoire. Our family doesn't have the gift, but we have kept it safe for the day you, or someone else with the power came for it."

"And it can tell me how to kill Cain?"

Ioana shrugs. "We are not witches. We can't even read it. The pages appear blank to us."

So without a witch, the book is useless. Yet… I can see the ink on the pages from here.

Relief slams into me and I hold my hands out for it. "May I take it?"

At the same time, the buzzing of blades reaches my ears.

A helicopter. No. More than one.

Gideon and Draven both stare pointedly at me, and I can tell they want to grab the book and run.

Thankfully, Andrei must be thinking the same thing, because he shoves the book into my hands. "We're leaving," he tells his mother. "Good luck… cousin. I hope that book is worth all our lives."

"Wait," Draven says, drawing out a small card from his pocket. "This is the address of a safe house in Bucharest. You should be able to lie low there until this blows over."

Andrei nods, accepting the card, and ushers his mother from the church without another word.

Too late, I realise I should've asked for some way to contact them, but they're already gone. It's for the best, I tell myself. Disappearing is safest for them.

Draven gave them the address of that safe house. Maybe when this is over, I can go there and get to know them…

I long to open the book, but I know with certainty what I have to do. So I turn to the two men, biting my lip.

"The book and I have to be kept separate," I begin, holding it out to Draven.

"But the book is useless without you," he protests.

I stare at the alpha, who understands. "No. She's right. Keeping the two most important things together right now is foolish. Cain knows about Evie, but not about the book, but if something goes wrong, and he finds her with it, he'll destroy it."

"You have to take it," I insist, pressing it into the vampire's hands. "And you have to run."

A rare burst of anger hits me from his bond, cracking the ice. "I won't abandon you."

"You're not," I insist. "But we don't have time for this."

"Stay off the roads. We'll meet at the rendezvous point. If we're not there by tomorrow, find a safe house and get in touch using the old method," Gideon orders. "I'll keep her safe, Draven."

The vampire meets the lycan's eyes, and they seem to communicate silently for a second before Draven wrenches me into his arms and takes my mouth in a furious kiss. Along the thrall bond, his frustration and reticence echoes loud and clear.

"You get your ass to safety, doll," he growls before turning to Gideon. "Nothing touches her."

"She's the most precious weapon we have," Gideon replies evenly. "I'm not going to jeopardise that. We'll go back and get the others to safety and meet up with you."

Not exactly flowery poetry or a romantic declaration of his feelings, but the thrall bond says what the alpha cannot verbalise. For the briefest moment, it flies wide open, and his concern and protectiveness surrounds me like a cloak. Then it's gone, and I'm left feeling oddly bereft.

Draven releases me, nods once, and then heads for the door, clutching the grimoire to his chest.

Gideon gives me a single look, then sighs. "Stay close. We go fast and stealthy."

"Agreed." I draw my sword, because the choppers are drawing closer, and follow his lead out of the church and back into the rain.

Then a boom shakes the mountainside. Smoke rises from above us, and both of us glance at one another.

"Finn," Gideon gasps, eyes flying wide as his whole body freezes in place.

It's the first time I've ever seen the alpha look... afraid.

I reach for him down the bond. Urgency, nerves, focus. He's not calm by any means, but he's still there, and unhurt.

"He's alive," I promise. "But still at the manor."

Gideon shakes his head, reaches for his phone, and then curses as the screen blinks on.

"They're jamming the whole area."

I still don't have much of a clue about how technology works, but I understand his meaning.

Cain has brought out all of his toys for this confrontation.

"Fast and stealthy," I repeat. "We get Finn and the others, and we get out together."

He offers me a nod and takes off at a run. I follow, keeping to a crouch as we skirt the buildings, heading for the trees in tense silence. All around the village, people are flee-ing. Rusted cars are pulling out, creating chaos as the humans do their best to escape what's coming.

There's no sign of Draven, and I silently pray to any power that will listen that he makes it out safely.

I hear them before I see them.

Above us, through the branches, I can see the lights of what must be dozens of military aircraft. The sound of them fills the air, mixing with the sounds of my own frantic breathing as I run as fast as my legs will carry me.

The ghouls start to shriek in warning. Cain's troops must be landing. All around us, the vegetation starts to rustle as Frost's troops spring to alertness.

Then the first vampire, in full tactical gear, crosses our path.

Gideon rips his throat out with his claws before he can scream, but he's not alone.

I barely parry the blade that's aimed at my neck, but my attacker doesn't get the chance to strike again because Gideon is on him.

I stare, and stare, and stare some more.

I've never seen him shifted before. In fact, I'm beginning to think I've never seen an alpha lycan shifted, because Gideon is larger than any I've ever seen.

He's huge, towering over me with the remnants of his clothes hanging from his frame in shreds that just about cover his modesty. Like most lycans, he stands on two feet, with a lupine muzzle, large ears, wiry black fur and gleaming eyes.

He dispatches my attacker and whirls to take out the next, and I'm forced to break my perusal of him to duck and smash my fist into the face of the next one.

In seconds, we're surrounded by withering bodies. Gideon snarls out something which might've been 'get moving' but which is distorted by his lupine jaw, and the two of us streak up higher into the mountain.

This high up, the cloud surrounds us, forming a thick, cold mist that shrouds everything. It works wonders for keeping us hidden, but does the same for our enemies.

By the time we burst out into the gardens of the manor, we've taken out three squads between us and are breathing heavily.

"The van is gone," I realise, as I take in the scorched and burning front entrance of the manor.

I check the bond to Finn, only to find that he's moving away from us, and fast.

"They've left without us. Why would they do that?"

Gideon snarls, losing his hold on his lycan form and shrinking back to human. "Frost must have made the call to protect Finn," he mutters. "We had no way to communicate and when shit gets dangerous, we have an understanding that we'll split up and meet at the rendezvous... either that, or they've already been taken."

I shake my head. "No. He's not struggling. He's stressed, but not in pain."

That calms the alpha a little. His shoulders lose some of their rigidity, and he casts a glance my way. "Then we need to leave."

I suck in a breath and turn on my heel. Only to forget my exhaustion as the move brings the mausoleum into my field of vision and I catch sight of a blazing streak of red hair at the entrance.

CHAPTER THIRTY-SIX

EVELYN

"Immy," I snarl, automatically taking a step forward.

Gideon's hand on my arm stops me. "We don't have time for this," he says.

He's right. We don't. But Immy makes the decision for us. She stops cowering and steps out of the mausoleum, striding across the space between us.

She's not alone.

Behind her, a pack of ghouls is stumbling and shambling out of the marble building, forming an entourage that just keeps growing.

None of them make a move to attack her.

"I thought Frost was commanding the ghouls," I murmur. "Why are they not attacking her?"

Gideon's hand tightens on my arm. "We're getting out of here. Now."

I don't fight him as he starts to tug me away. In fact, I run with him for the first few steps, glancing over my shoulder as we go.

She's closer now, and the lack of distance allows me to see that there's something *wrong* with my sister. She's not walking as gracefully as she normally does, and for a second, I think she's injured herself. Then I realise her mouth is half-open, and held that way by teeth that are just a little too… long.

It's the claws still pushing through her fingertips that make everything click.

"She took my blood and used it to turn herself into a hybrid," I growl, fury rising up once more.

She must've used venom from the ghouls which were hiding in the mausoleum, and now she's transforming.

A slow clap answers my revelation, and both Gideon and I freeze in place as Cain strides out of the forest before us. Behind him, a small legion of his men files out in an unbroken line. They're armed with crossbows which are all pointing directly at us, and there are silver swords at their waists.

My heart stops in my chest, and I back up a step automatically. The alpha places himself at my back, putting the two of us firmly on the defensive.

"If I make an opening, you run," he growls. "Your survival is the most important here. Promise me, Evie."

But I know it's a fool's notion. Cain has us surrounded, and with him—the most powerful vampire—right here, winning a physical fight, or outrunning him, is impossible.

"Wait," I whisper. "We might be able to get out of this…"

Or at the very least, I might be able to get Gideon to safety.

"Promise," the alpha demands, meeting my eyes and imbuing the command with the force of his stare. "No matter what happens, stay alive and protect Finn."

In answer, I rise up and claim his lips with my own. I

don't know why I do it—maybe it's simple desperation—but the effect is instantaneous.

The second our tongues meet, the thrall bond snaps into being. Neither of us can acknowledge the tiny miracle without putting ourselves in more danger. Gideon's presence hums through me, a bossy, commanding thing that holds hints of the same wildness that lingers in Vane and Finn but is tempered by so much responsibility that it makes it hard to breathe. I can feel his determination, his unshakeable faith, and then his shock as he realises what's happened.

"How sweet," my sire croons, a hint of anger in his voice as we jerk apart. "One last kiss? Pathetic. I raised you better, Evelyn, but lately all you seem to do is disappoint me."

Cain is dressed in his usual style, having forgone the tactical wear of the vampires behind him in favour of a sleek dark suit. Unlike normal, however, there's something dangerously unhinged in the way he stares at me. Something terrifying.

The view behind me isn't much better. We're surrounded, with vampires ahead of us and Immy and her ghouls behind us. Nowhere to run.

"Poor little Imogen," he says, but his tone is anything but sympathetic as he finally stops a few feet away from me. "Imagine my surprise when she contacted me out of the blue in tears because she'd been led astray by her elder sister yet *again.*"

He pauses, then looks past me at my sister, frowning. "Did you really think I was so stupid as to fall for such a lie?"

Immy falls over herself to defend her actions, but her teeth make her words lispy and hard to understand. "It wasn't, Sire. I kept an eye on Evelyn, just like you said—"

"You went along with her plan because you thought she could win and you resented me for not taking you as my favourite in her absence." Cain dismisses her with a wave of his hand. "And then, when you learned how special Evelyn truly is, your jealousy got the better of you. Hence this little unauthorised stunt where you polluted the purity of *my* bloodline."

His words have turned harsher and colder, but I don't make the mistake of thinking he's forgotten about us.

No, he's just making a point. He has always loved drama, and this must be catnip to him.

"But, Sire, you always wanted a way to create more half-ghouls," Immy protests. "I saw the opportunity and—"

"And you weakened yourself," Cain snaps back, drawing a small torch from his pocket. "What's the problem with hybrids, Imogen?"

Her eyes widen.

"Half of them have the strengths of both races…" she whispers.

He flicks the torch on, and a powerful beam of violet light cuts the space between us, hitting my sister squarely on the chest.

"… and the other half have all of their weaknesses combined," he finishes for her.

Immy squeals, collapsing in on herself as her chest burns and the sound of crackling flesh fills the air. She's an elder, like me. Sunlight shouldn't have that effect on her.

Except by becoming half-ghoul, she's brought it on herself. Pity stabs at me as I realise Immy has become one of the unlucky fifty percent. That explains why her appearance is so much more ghoulish than Frost's.

It's not until his nails dig bitingly into my other arm that I realise my mistake. I've allowed Immy's punishment to distract me from the threat at my back. Cain wrenches me away from Gideon and drags me to the vampire side of the circle, ignoring my futile struggles.

I reach for my dagger, only to have it wrenched away and tossed carelessly into the group of ghouls. Cain's aim is impeccable, striking one's head from its shoulders. A second later, he rips my belt away and tosses that aside too, confiscating my sword and the other dagger.

It leaves me weaponless, and my alpha alone, surrounded by enemies. Cain jerks his head at one of his vampires, who steps forward, holding a pair of silver manacles. My sire forces my wrists out, one at a time, to allow them to cuff me.

I struggle—of course I do—but he doesn't react to my jabbing limbs or my snapping fangs. He might as well be made of stone. His grip is unyielding, and I've never been a match for him. My breathing picks up and panic starts to fog my mind as the second cuff clicks shut with a deafening *snick*.

Shit.

I search for a gap in the ranks. An escape. A distraction. Anything. But I might as well be back in the manor, all those years ago, watching Frost prepare to die.

Only this time it's Gideon who's in danger.

Thankfully, the bulk of Cain's attention is still on Immy… who's becoming more unstable by the second. Her eyes have started to glaze over from pain, and the wound he created isn't healing as it should. Instead, the skin around it is starting to rot away.

He disliked her before, but now she's an embarrassment, so I know what's coming.

And I think, given the pleading look in her watering eyes, she does too.

Something in my chest breaks at the sight. Despite her second betrayal, I can't help but wonder if I caused this. Should I have tried harder to love her the way I did before? Focused more on her and less on my thralls? Would any amount of love or attention have ever been enough? Or would she always have returned to Cain's side in the end?

"I can be useful," she promises. "Sire, please. I'll do better!"

And then she does the one thing we don't expect.

Lunges at Gideon.

The alpha dodges, but Immy's stumbling steps make her movements difficult to predict, she sways, almost falling, and reaches out.

Her venomous claws rake across his chest, and thanks to our new bond, I feel his pain like it's my own. Fire streaks across his breastbone, and the hurt is so real that it steals my breath. But Gideon isn't down. He roars, striking out with his own claws.

But Immy is now a lethal combination of fast and unpredictable. Her stagger draws her just out of his reach, only to lurch back in time to sink those needle-like fangs into Gideon's neck. With one savage yank, she clamps her teeth into the space above his jugular and rips out his throat.

Fire consumes us both. His pain bleeds into me until it might as well be my own. I feel it when his muscles give out and the two of them sink to their knees. My alpha is still fighting, ripping into her, but his movements are slowing. The pain he's feeling is almost enough to make me lean on my sire for support.

No.

No. No. *No.*

I want to scream, but I can't. My body has locked up in shock.

My sire has no such problem.

"Foolish girl," Cain hisses as Imogen tears further into my alpha, snarling like a beast.

Keeping my arm in one hand, he switches the powerful beam of light on once more, this time directing it at her head.

She's so distracted that he doesn't even have to try hard to burn a hole right between her eyes. The beam of light is powerful, and she is so weakened by her new nature that it cuts through her head, leaving a hole through which I can see the yellow grass.

The effect is immediate. She slumps to the ground beside a still-twitching Gideon, her fangs still biting at empty air as her body tries to continue feeding. An unholy noise tears from her throat, but it stops when Cain traces the beam of light across her neck, severing her head in a slow burst of fire.

My sister withers. Her once creamy skin darkens to ash and shrinks in on itself until she's gone.

Oh, Immy.

Despite my earlier anger, tears prick at my eyes. Not just for her, for Gideon too.

My alpha is still twitching on the ground, but his eyes have fallen shut. In my chest, the thrall bond is dimming, and what little of him I can feel is pure agony. A tear slips free, and Cain makes a tiny noise of disgust.

Fortunately, he doesn't have a chance to reprimand me for my emotional outburst. The ghouls around us are starting to bristle. Now free of whatever control Immy had on them, there's nothing to stop them turning on Cain and his men.

"Finish them," Cain orders his soldiers. "Then spread out. I want the rest of the rebels and whatever humans remain found and killed. Leave none of them alive."

The hail of bolts tears through the gathered ghouls with practised precision, as the vampires fire the crossbows into them. Disabling their prey. Cain's men draw their blades without hesitation and begin the process of hacking their heads from their bodies. It's a brutal and efficient mass execution, one that this squad is obviously trained for.

"Sir, what about the lycan?" one of them asks, his expression bland. "Do you still want it?"

Cain rolls his eyes. "It's not going to survive a ghoul bite, so it can no longer serve as leverage." His hand clenches on my arm. "Leave it."

Without another glance, he starts to drag me away. "Come, daughter."

Again, I struggle, trying to return to Gideon. Maybe if I can get him my blood, I might be able to save him.

He's still writhing. Still fighting. His wide, panicked eyes meet mine in the second before he's obscured by the forest.

Then he's gone. Stolen from my sight by the trees. Only the echoes of his pain along the thrall bond tell me he still lives, and even those are growing weaker.

His final order rings in my ears.

Stay alive and protect Finn.

Oh God. *Finn.* Losing Gid will destroy him. Not to mention the rest of the pack.

"Just kill me," I say, but my voice is hoarse and whispery, with nowhere near the force I wish it had.

"Kill you?" Cain sounds mildly amused. "Why would I do that when your blood is the key to harnessing the ghouls?"

I stare up at him in horror. "But I'm a witch," I hiss. "You would never—"

Cain's laugh startles me into silence. "Oh, yes, I've heard all about Samuel's little plot, and how useless you are. A hybrid witch with no idea how to do magic and no one to teach you? You're harmless. Barely worthy of the label. And the others are dead. I made certain of it."

His lethal smile turns into a frown. "Have no fear, daughter. Nothing and no one will be allowed to end my immortality. With the ghouls under my command, my empire will be eternal."

* * *

To be continued in
Crowned by Blood

ACKNOWLEDGMENTS

Thank you so much for reading! If you enjoyed Claimed by Blood (or even if you just want to rage at me for the cliffhanger!) make sure to leave a review. They're the lifeblood of small authors like me. I read each and every one and I'm so grateful for all of them. Make sure you follow me so you don't miss the finale of Evie's story.

We should all be thanking TS Snow, who answered "To knot? Or not to knot?" with "To knot, obviously." Along with the rest of my sprinting author buddies! Love you guys!

The betas put in a mammoth effort to make this one what it is, so they deserve a standing ovation for their hard work. You guys are the best.

Katie, as ever, you're my saviour. I'm sorry that, eleven books on, I still don't know what I'm doing when it comes to commas.

Finally, a big hug to the four men in my life who keep the house running while I type. Readers, don't get excited on my behalf. I'm related to two of them and one is a dog.

BOOKS BY MARIE MISTRY

DAUGHTER OF CAIN

Entombed by Blood

Claimed by Blood

Crowned by Blood

THE DEADWOOD

Traitor Witch

Liar Witch

Pirate Witch

DRESSED TO KILL (STANDALONE)

Darcy

THE FIFTH NICNEVIN

Beyond the Faerie Gate

Across an Endless Sea

Amidst the Insidious Courts

VICE COLLEGE FOR YOUNG DEMONS

A Demon's Horns

A Demon's Gifts

A Demon's Wings

A Demon's Heart

The Complete Collection

ABOUT THE AUTHOR

Marie Mistry lives in rainy Britain but spends most of her time escaping into imaginary worlds, whether that is in books or video games. She writes paranormal romance but has written books in other genres in the past. She has a mild obsession with happily ever after and true love which she blames on a childhood full of Disney goodness. She loves interacting with fans in her reader group, and feel free to stalk her on any of her social media or via her newsletter.